**Matt glance**
**he followed he**
**and she knew he was eager to**
**head back over to the park.**

But when they made their way down the stairs and into the empty living room, he frowned.

"Where did the babysitter go?"

"I sent her home." She hoped she sounded more confident than she felt, because now that they were really alone, her stomach was in such a mess of knots she didn't think they'd ever untangle.

"I thought we were going back to the park to see the fireworks."

"I changed my mind."

"Don't I get a vote?"

She shook her head. "No, but you have a choice."

"What choice is that?" Matt asked her.

She lifted her arms to link them around his neck. "You can go back to the park for the fireworks—" her fingers cupped the back of his head, drew it down toward hers "—or we can make some of our own right here."

And then she kissed him.

# FROM
# NEIGHBOURS...
# TO NEWLYWEDS?

BY
BRENDA HARLEN

MILLS &
BOON

First published in Great Britain 2013
by Mills & Boon, an imprint of Harlequin (UK) Limited,
Eton House, 18-24 Paradise Road, Richmond, Surrey TW9 1SR

© Brenda Harlen 2013

ISBN: 978 0 263 90117 7
ebook ISBN: 978 1 472 00491 8

23-0613

Harlequin (UK) policy is to use papers that are natural, renewable and recyclable products and made from wood grown in sustainable forests. The logging and manufacturing processes conform to the legal environmental regulations of the country of origin.

Printed and bound in Spain
by Blackprint CPI, Barcelona

**Brenda Harlen** grew up in a small town, surrounded by books and imaginary friends. Although she always dreamed of being a writer, she chose to follow a more traditional career path first. After two years of practicing as an attorney (including an appearance in front of the Supreme Court of Canada), she gave up her "real" job to be a mum and to try her hand at writing books. Three years, five manuscripts and another baby later, she sold her first book—an RWA Golden Heart winner.

Brenda lives in southern Ontario with her real-life husband/hero, two heroes-in-training and two neurotic dogs. She is still surrounded by books (too many books, according to her children) and imaginary friends, but she also enjoys communicating with real people. Readers can contact Brenda by email at brendaharlen@yahoo.com.

Because this series is about brothers, this book
is dedicated to Brett (AKA "BIL").

You became my brother when you married my sister,
and through all the years that you've been part of our
family you've proven yourself to be a terrific husband
and a wonderful father—a true romantic hero.

(PS You're a pretty good brother-in-law, too.)

## Chapter One

The house was finally, blissfully quiet.

Georgia Reed mentally crossed her fingers as she sat down at the antique dining room table, hoping for one hour. If she could have a full sixty minutes to focus on the manuscript pages spread out in front of her, she might actually catch up on her work. Unfortunately, the thought of catching a nap was much more tempting than the book she was currently reading.

Though she was officially on maternity leave from her job as an associate editor at Tandem Publishing, she had agreed to accept work on a contract basis to help out the senior editor and keep some money coming in. It had seemed like a good idea at the time, but Georgia hadn't been nearly as productive as she'd hoped to be, especially since she'd uprooted her kids and moved to Pinehurst only six weeks earlier.

She sipped from the cup of herbal tea she'd reheated for a third time and skimmed through the previous chapter to refresh her memory. But just as her mind began to focus on the story, it occurred to her that it was *too* quiet.

The realization kicked her protective instincts into overdrive. She pushed her chair away from the table and raced across the hall to the living room, where she'd left four-year-old Quinn and Shane with a pile of building blocks. The carpet was littered with the chunky pieces but her boys were both gone—no doubt through the wide-open patio door.

The door had been closed when she settled the boys down to play—closed *and* locked. But the lock was tricky, and sometimes just tugging on the handle would allow the latch to slip and the lock to slide free. She'd talked to her mother about getting it fixed, but apparently that detail had slipped Charlotte's mind.

And now her children were gone.

She hurried back to the dining room to grab the baby monitor before racing out the back door.

"Quinn! Shane!" She ran across the deck, cursing when she stepped on a red block. They couldn't have gone far. She'd only left them in the room a few minutes earlier. If anything had happened—

No, she couldn't even complete the thought.

"Quinn! Shane!"

A flash of movement caught the corner of her eye, and she spun around, her heart sinking when she didn't see the boys' familiar faces but the shadowed jaw of a grown man standing on the grass.

"Are you looking for two little guys about yay—" he held a hand about three and a half feet off the ground "—high?"

"Did you see where they went?" she asked hopefully, desperately.

"They wandered into my backyard." He gestured toward the adjoining property.

Georgia closed her eyes so he wouldn't see that they'd filled with tears. "Oh, thank you, God."

"Actually, my name's Matt—Matt Garrett."

She opened her eyes again and saw that he was smiling at her.

"And your kids are fine," he promised her.

"Only until I get my hands on them," she muttered.

His smile widened.

Now that the panic had subsided and her heart was beating more normally again, she took a moment to look at her new neighbor—and felt a little tug low in her belly.

Matt Garrett had thick dark hair that was sexily tousled, as if he'd been running his fingers through it, a slightly crooked nose and a strong unshaven jaw. His shoulders were broad, his long, lean body well-muscled. And as his deep blue gaze connected with her own, she felt a subtle buzz in her veins that made her feel hot and tingly in a way that she hadn't experienced in a very long time.

"One of the puppies escaped into your yard and caught their attention," he explained.

"Puppies?"

"Come and check them out," he invited.

She hooked the monitor on her belt and followed him, surreptitiously checking out his spectacular backside as she did so.

He'd moved in a few days earlier. She'd noticed the moving truck when she'd gone out to the porch to check the mail Wednesday afternoon—and then she'd noticed the tall, broad-shouldered man supervising the unloading of it.

He was in faded denim with an even more faded Orioles T-shirt stretched across his broad chest. Definitely a man's man, she decided, and felt a flutter of something low in her belly. He lifted an arm in casual greeting and flashed a quick smile that actually made Georgia's heart skip a beat before it began hammering against her ribs.

She raised her hand in response, waving her mail at him, then felt the flood of heat in her cheeks as she realized what she'd done. She wasn't sure if it was sexual deprivation or sleep deprivation that was responsible for her distraction, but thankfully, he was too far away to note either her instinctive physical response or her embarrassment. But wow—the man obviously had some potent sex appeal if he could affect her from such a distance.

An appeal that, she knew now, was further magnified up close.

"This is Luke—and Jack," Matt told her, gesturing to the two other men on his porch in turn. "My brothers."

The former was even taller than her six-foot-tall neighbor, with the same brown hair but blue-green eyes; the latter was of similar height but with broader shoulders and slightly darker hair. All three were sinfully handsome.

"I'm Georgia," she finally said, her heart rate mostly back to normal now that the twins were in her line of sight again. "And these pint-sized Houdinis are Quinn and Shane."

"What's a Houdini?" Quinn tore his attention away from the blanket-lined laundry basket for the first time since she'd stepped onto her neighbor's porch.

"A little boy who is in very serious trouble for leaving the house without his mommy," she admonished.

Her son's gaze dropped to his feet, a telltale sign of guilt. "We just wanted to see the puppies."

"Puppies," Shane echoed, and looked up at her with the heartbreakingly sweet smile that never failed to remind her of his father.

She took a few steps closer, as inexorably drawn to the basket as her children had been. But still, she had to make sure they understood that leaving the house for any reason wasn't acceptable.

"If you wanted to see the puppies, you should have told Mommy that you wanted to see the puppies," she said.

"But you told us not to bug you 'cuz you had work to do," Quinn reminded her.

And it was exactly what she'd said when she set them up with their blocks.

"I also told you to never go anywhere—even outside into the backyard—without telling me first."

But how could she blame them for being drawn away when even her heart had sighed at the first glimpse of those white, brown and black bodies wriggling around in the basket?

She looked at her neighbor again. "You have *four* puppies?"

"No." Matt shook his head emphatically. "*I* don't have *any* puppies—they're all Luke's."

"Only until I can find good homes for them," his brother said.

"How did you end up with them?" she wondered.

"I'm a vet," he told her. "And when someone finds an abandoned animal on the side of the road, it usually ends up at my clinic. In this case, the abandoned animal was a very pregnant beagle that, two days later, gave birth to eight puppies."

"Eight?" She cringed at the thought. As if carrying and birthing twins hadn't been difficult enough.

"My receptionist is taking care of the other four."

"They look kind of young to be away from their mother," she noted.

"They are," he agreed.

It was all he said, but it was enough for her to understand that the mother hadn't survived the delivery—and to be grateful that his response in front of the twins wasn't any more explicit than that.

"Nice puppy," Shane said, gently patting the top of a tiny head.

"Can we keep one?" Quinn, always the more talkative and articulate twin, asked her.

She shook her head. As much as she hated to refuse her kids anything, she'd learned that there were times she had to say no. This was definitely one of those times. "I'm sorry, boys. A puppy is too much responsibility for us to take on right now."

But she didn't object when Matt lifted one of them out of the box and handed it to her. And she couldn't resist bringing it closer to nuzzle the soft, warm body. And when the little pink tongue swiped her chin, her heart absolutely melted.

"He likes you, Mom," Quinn told her.

"She," Matt corrected. "That one's a girl."

Her son wrinkled his nose. "We don't want a girl puppy."

"We don't want *any* puppy," Georgia said again, trying to sound firm.

"We *do* want a puppy," Shane insisted.

"'Cept Dr. Luke says they can't go anywhere for two more weeks," Quinn informed her. "'Cuz they're too little to eat and hafta be fed by a bottle."

Shane pouted for another minute, but the mention of eating prompted him to announce, "I'm hungry."

"So why don't we go home and I'll make some little pizzas for lunch?" she suggested.

"With pepperonis?"

"With lots of pepperoni," she promised.

But Quinn shook his head. "We don't wanna go home. We wanna stay with the daddies."

Georgia felt her cheeks burning as her gaze shifted from one man to the next.

Matt's smile slipped, just a little; Luke kept his attention firmly focused on the animals; and Jack actually took a step backward.

"They're at that age," she felt compelled to explain, "where they think every adult male is a daddy. Especially since they lost their own father."

"He's not lost, he's dead," Quinn said matter-of-factly.

The announcement made Shane's eyes fill with tears and his lower lip quiver. "I miss Daddy."

Georgia slipped her arm around his shoulders.

Matt's brows lifted. "You're a widow?"

She nodded, because her throat had tightened and she wanted to ensure she was in control of her emotions before she spoke. "My husband passed away eleven months ago." And although she'd accepted that Phillip was gone, she still missed him, and there were times—too many times—when she felt completely overwhelmed by the responsibilities of being a single parent. "That's one of the reasons I moved in here with my mom."

"Charlotte's your mother?"

"You know her?"

"I met her the first time I came to look at the house," he said. "But I haven't seen her since I moved in."

"She's on her annual trip to Vegas with some friends," Georgia told him.

"Leaving you on your own with two young boys," he remarked sympathetically.

"And a baby," she said, just as a soft coo sounded through the baby monitor she'd clipped on her belt.

"Pippa's waking up." Quinn jumped up, his desire to stay with the "daddies" not nearly as strong as his affection for his baby sister.

"Pippa," Shane echoed.

Matt looked at Georgia, seeking clarification. "You have three kids?"

She nodded. "Four-year-old twins and a four-month-old daughter."

Well, that explained the shadows under her gorgeous eyes, Matt decided. A pair of active preschoolers and a baby would wear any young mother out—especially one without a husband to help ease the burden. But even exhausted, she was one of the most beautiful women he'd ever met.

She had a heart-shaped face with creamy skin, elegantly shaped lips, a delicate nose dusted with freckles, and the bluest eyes he'd ever seen. He'd caught his first glimpse of her on moving day. She'd been casually dressed in a sleeveless yellow blouse and a pair of faded denim jeans with her honey-blond hair in a ponytail, but even from a distance, he'd felt the tug of attraction.

Standing within two feet of her now, that tug was even stronger—much stronger than any self-preservation instincts that warned him against getting involved with a woman with three children who could take hold of his heart.

"You do have your hands full," he said.

"Every day is a challenge," she agreed. And then, to the boys, "Come on—we've got to go get your sister."

"Can we bring Pippa back to see the puppies?" Quinn asked hopefully.

His mother shook her head. "In fact, you're going to apologize to Mr. Garrett for intruding—"

"Matt," he interjected, because it was friendlier than "Mister" and less daunting than "Doctor," and because he definitely wanted to be on a first-name basis with his lovely neighbor. "And it wasn't at all an intrusion. In fact, it was a pleasure to meet all of you."

"Does that mean we can come back again?" Quinn asked.

"Anytime," he said.

"And within two weeks, you'll be calling someone to put up a fence between our properties," Georgia warned.

He shook his head. "If I did that, they wouldn't be able to come over to play in the tree house."

"Mommy says we can't go in the tree house," Quinn admitted. "'Cuz it's not ours."

"But a tree house is made for little boys, and since I don't have a little boy of my own—" Matt ignored the pang of loss and longing in his heart, deliberately keeping his tone light "—it's going to need someone to visit it every once in a while, so it doesn't get lonely."

"We could visit," Quinn immediately piped up, as Shane nodded his head with enthusiasm and Georgia rolled her eyes.

"That's a great idea—so long as you check to make sure it's okay with your mom first," Matt told them.

"Can we, Mommy?"

"Pleeeease?"

He held his breath, almost as anxious for her response as the twins were. It shouldn't matter. He didn't even know this woman—but he knew that he wanted to know her, and he knew that it wouldn't be a hardship to hang out with her kids, either.

"We'll talk about it another time," she said.

Quinn let out an exaggerated sigh. "That's what she says when she means no."

"It means 'we'll talk about it another time,'" Georgia reiterated firmly.

"I'm hungry," Shane said again.

She tousled his hair. "Then we should go home to make those pizzas."

"I'm *not* hungry," Quinn said. "I wanna stay here."

"If you're not hungry, then Shane will get all the little pizzas."

Georgia's casual response earned a scowl from her son.

"And you can help us paint the deck," Matt told Quinn.

The furrow in his brow deepened. "I guess I could eat some pizza."

"I'd take the pizza over painting, too," Luke told him.

"Unfortunately, we weren't given that choice," Jack said in a conspiratorial whisper.

"And since you weren't," Matt noted, "you can go get the painting supplies."

Jack headed into the house while Luke picked up the basket full of puppies and moved it under the shade of a nearby tree so the curious canines couldn't get in the way of their work.

Shane and Quinn stayed by Georgia's side, but their eyes—

filled with an almost desperate yearning—tracked the path of the puppies. And as he looked at the twins' mother, Matt thought he understood just a little bit of what they were feeling.

In the more than three years that had passed since his divorce, Matt had wondered if he would ever feel anything more than a basic stirring of attraction for another woman. Ten minutes after meeting Georgia Reed, he could answer that question with a definitive yes.

"Thank you," she said to him now.

"For what?"

"Being so patient and tolerant with the boys."

"I like kids," he said easily.

"Then you'll like this neighborhood," she told him.

He held her gaze as his lips curved. "I already do."

Matt watched as Georgia walked away, with one of the boys' hands clasped firmly in each of hers. Obviously she wasn't willing to take any chances that they might disappear again—even on the short trek next door.

The first time he'd seen her, it hadn't occurred to him that his gorgeous young neighbor might be a mother. Finding out that she had kids—and not just the adorable twin boys but a baby girl, too—had scrambled his mind further.

Now that he knew about those children, it seemed wrong to admire the sweet curve of her buttocks in snug-fitting denim. And it was definitely depraved to let his gaze linger on the sway of those feminine hips—or to think about the fullness of breasts hugged by the soft blue knit cardigan she wore.

She might have been a mother, but that reality did nothing to alter the fact that she was also an incredibly attractive woman. Something about the sexy single mother next door stirred feelings inside of him that hadn't been stirred in a very long time. And while he was intrigued enough to want to explore those feelings, the kids were a definite complication.

Matt had dated a lot of women without letting them into his heart, but he had no defenses against the genuine friendliness and easy acceptance of children. Especially not when the loss of his son had left a gaping hole in his heart that ached to be filled.

"I know what you're thinking," Luke said, climbing back up onto the porch.

"You think so?"

His youngest brother nodded. "Yeah, she's a pleasure to look at. But she's got *complication* written all over her."

"I was only thinking that it was nice to finally meet my neighbor."

"You were thinking about asking her out," Luke accused.

"Maybe I was," he acknowledged.

Jack dropped an armload of painting tools at his feet. "Don't do it."

"Why not?" he asked, unwilling to be dissuaded.

"Slippery slope."

"You mean like an invitation to dinner might lead to a second date?" Matt didn't bother to disguise his sarcasm.

"And the next thing you know, you're walking down the aisle," Luke agreed.

"You went out with Becky McKenzie last week." He felt compelled to point this out. "But I don't see a ring on your finger."

"That's because when our little brother invites a woman to dinner, it's just an invitation to dinner," Jack explained.

"And maybe breakfast," Luke interjected with a grin.

"But when you ask a woman out on a first date…" Jack paused, his brow furrowing. "Well, we don't actually know what it means, because you haven't been out on a real date with anyone since Lindsay walked out on you."

"I've been out with plenty of women."

Luke shook his head. "You've hooked up with plenty of

women—but you haven't actually been in a relationship with any of them."

Now it was Matt's turn to frown, because he realized that what his brother had said was true.

"And this one comes with quite a bit of baggage," Jack noted.

"A three-piece set," Luke elaborated.

"You're reading way too much into this," Matt told them.

"I'm glad you're thinking about jumping back into the dating pool," Jack said. "But I don't get why you'd want to leap directly into the deep end when there are plenty of unencumbered beautiful women hanging out by the water."

Matt didn't know how to respond. He wasn't sure he could explain—even to himself—what it was about Georgia Reed that appealed to him. Or maybe he was afraid to admit that he'd fallen for the two little boys who had snuck over to look at the puppies even before he'd realized that his pretty blonde neighbor was their mother.

Since the breakup of his marriage, he'd been cautious about getting involved again. Having his heart trampled by his ex-wife was bad enough, he wasn't going to risk having it trampled by anyone else's children.

Not again.

Or so he'd thought—until Quinn and Shane raced into his backyard.

"I'm not looking for anything more than a chance to get to know my neighbor a little better," Matt insisted.

"So get to know her," Luke agreed. "But don't get involved with her. A relationship with someone who lives next door might seem convenient at first, but it can be a nightmare if things don't work out."

"Almost as bad as falling into bed with a woman who was supposed to be a friend," Jack said.

The statement was made with such conviction Matt was sure there must be a story behind it. But since he didn't want to discuss his personal life—or current lack thereof—he certainly wasn't going to grill his brothers about their respective situations.

"If you're lonely, you should think about getting a pet," Luke suggested.

"Like a puppy?" Matt asked dryly.

His brother grinned. "Man's best friend."

"A dog is too much of a commitment."

"Less than a woman and her three kids," Jack pointed out.

Which was a valid consideration, so Matt only said, "Are we going to spend all day sitting around and talking like a bunch of old women or are we going to paint this damn deck?"

"Since you put it that way," Luke said. "I guess we're going to paint the damn deck."

## Chapter Two

After Pippa was changed and fed and the boys had helped make little pizzas for their lunch—using up all of the cheese and pepperoni and emptying the last jug of milk—Georgia knew a trip to the grocery store was in order. Since it was a nice day and Quinn and Shane seemed to have energy to burn, she decided they would walk rather than take the minivan.

The twins refused to ride in the double stroller anymore, insisting that they were too big to be pushed around like babies. Unfortunately, Georgia knew their determination and energy would last only so long as it took to reach their destination and not bring them home again, so she strapped Pippa into her carrier and dragged the wagon along beside her.

As she started down the driveway, she caught another glimpse of her hunky neighbor and his equally hunky brothers, and her pulse tripped again. The automatic physiological response surprised her. Since Phillip had died, all she'd felt was grief and exhaustion, so the tingles that skated through her veins whenever she set eyes on Matt Garrett weren't just unexpected but unwelcome.

She did *not* want to be attracted to any man, much less one she might cross paths with any time she stepped outside. But while her brain was firm in its conviction, her body wasn't nearly as certain.

Matt caught her eye and lifted a hand in greeting. She waved back, then quickly averted her gaze and continued on her way. It was bad enough that she'd caught herself staring— she didn't need her neighbor to be aware of it, too.

Of course, he was probably accustomed to women gawking in his direction. A man like that would be.

Not that she had a lot of experience with men like the Garrett brothers, but she knew their type. In high school, they would have been the most popular boys: the star athletes who had dated only the prettiest girls, the boys that other boys wanted to be and that all of the girls wanted to be with.

But not Georgia. She'd been too smart to fall into the trap of thinking that those boys would even look twice in her direction. And they never had. Not until Aiden Grainger sat down beside her in senior English and asked if she'd help out with the yearbook. Even then, she'd been certain he was only interested in her ability to correctly place a comma, and no one was more surprised than she when he walked her home after school one day and kissed her.

And with the first touch of his lips, she'd fallen for him, wholly and completely. They'd dated through the rest of senior year and talked about backpacking around Europe after graduation. Aiden wanted to see the world and Georgia wanted to do whatever he wanted to do so long as she got to be with him.

This willingness to sacrifice her own hopes and dreams in favor of his terrified her. It reminded her of all the times her life had been upended because her mother decided that she had to follow her heart to another city or another state— usually in pursuit of another man.

When Georgia was thirteen and starting her third new school in three years, she'd promised herself that she would never do the same thing. And now, barely five years later, she was preparing to throw away a scholarship to Wellesley College in order to follow some guy around Europe? No, she couldn't do it.

Aiden claimed that he was disappointed in her decision, but it turned out he wasn't disappointed enough to change his plans. He'd said he wanted to travel with her, but in the end, he wanted Europe more than he wanted her. And maybe Georgia wanted Wellesley more than she wanted him, because she went off to college and didn't look back.

But it had taken her a long time to get over Aiden, and a lot longer than that before she'd been willing to open up her heart again. And when she finally did, she'd lucked out with Phillip Reed.

Maybe theirs hadn't been a grand passion, but for almost ten years, he'd made her feel loved and comfortable and secure. It was all she'd ever wanted or needed.

So how was it that, after less than ten minutes, Matt Garrett had made her wonder if there might be something more? How was it that he'd stirred a passion inside of her that she'd never even known existed? And what was she supposed to do with these feelings?

Unable to answer any of these unnerving questions, she pushed them aside and led the kids into the grocery store.

When Matt decided to move, his real estate agent had repeated the same mantra: location, location, location. And Tina Stilwell had promised that this neighborhood scored top marks in that regard. There were parks, recreation facilities, a grocery store and schools in the immediate vicinity, with more shopping, restaurants and the hospital—where he worked as an orthopedic surgeon—just a short drive away. She hadn't mentioned the beautiful blonde next door, and

Matt wasn't sure how that information might have factored into his equation.

He hadn't necessarily been looking for a house—and he certainly wasn't looking for a new relationship. But he believed that real estate was a good investment and this house, in particular, had everything he wanted, not just with respect to location but amenities.

Jack had, logically, questioned why a single man needed four bedrooms and three bathrooms, forcing Matt to acknowledge that it was more space than he needed. He didn't admit—even to himself—that he had any residual hope of utilizing those extra bedrooms someday. Because he had a new life now—a new home and a new beginning, and he wasn't going to waste another minute on regrets or recriminations about the past. From this point on, he was going to look to the future.

But first, he had to cut the grass.

As he pushed the lawn mower across his yard, he kept casting surreptitious glances toward his neighbor's house, eager for any sign of Georgia Reed. He hadn't seen much of her in the past few days, and he knew she wasn't home now because the minivan was missing from her driveway, but that didn't stop him from checking every few minutes.

Thinking about what his brothers had said, he had to admit, albeit reluctantly, that it might not be a good idea to make a move on the woman next door. At least, not until he'd finished unpacking. If he moved too fast, she might think he was desperate. And he wasn't—but he was lonely.

Since his divorce, he'd had a few brief affairs but nothing more meaningful than that. He missed being in a relationship. He missed the camaraderie, the companionship and the intimacy. Not just sex—but intimacy. After a few unsatisfactory one-night stands, he'd recognized that there was a distinct difference.

He missed falling asleep beside someone he genuinely wanted to wake up with the next morning. He missed long conversations across the dinner table, quiet nights on the couch with a bowl of popcorn and a movie, and rainy Sunday mornings snuggled up in bed. He missed being with some-one, being part of a couple, having a partner by his side to celebrate not just all of the national holidays but all of the ordinary days in between.

But even more than he missed being a husband, he missed being a father. For almost three years, his little boy had been the center of his life. But Liam had been gone for more than three years now, and it was past time that Matt accepted that and moved on.

With a sigh, he considered that maybe he should let Luke talk him into taking one of those puppies. At least then he wouldn't come home to an empty house at the end of a long day.

Glancing toward Georgia's house again, he was willing to bet that his neighbor didn't know what it meant to be lonely. With three kids making constant demands on her time, she probably didn't have five minutes to herself in a day.

No doubt the twins alone could keep her hopping, and she had the needs of an infant to contend with as well. Although he had yet to meet the baby girl, he found himself wondering what she looked like, if she had the same dark hair and dark eyes as her brothers (which he assumed they'd inherited from their father) or blond hair and blue eyes like her mother.

It had to be difficult for Georgia, being widowed at such a young age. Not that he actually knew how old she was, but if she'd passed her thirtieth birthday, he didn't think she'd done so very long ago. Which meant that she'd likely mar-ried when she was young and idealistic and head over heels in love—and that she was probably still grieving the loss of her husband. But even if she wasn't, Matt didn't imagine that she had any interest in—or energy for—a romance with her new neighbor.

*A relationship with someone who lives next door might*

*seem convenient...but it can be a nightmare if things don't work out.*

Luke was probably right. So Matt was going to take his brother's advice and step back. Which didn't mean he and Georgia couldn't be friends. Surely his brothers wouldn't have any objection to Matt being friends with the woman next door.

And it seemed obvious that the first step toward becoming friends was to be a good neighbor. He finished the last strip of his grass and pushed the mower over to Georgia's lawn.

Having never owned anything with a yard before, he wasn't sure how he would feel about the required maintenance and upkeep, but so far, he was enjoying the physical work. And mowing the lawn, being unable to hear anything but the rumble of the motor, was almost relaxing. Or it would have been if the hum and the vibration of the machine in his hands hadn't started him thinking about different hums and vibrations that he hadn't experienced in a very long time.

Yeah, it had definitely been too long since he'd been with a woman. Which brought him back to thinking about Georgia again. The neighbor who was, he reminded himself, strictly off-limits with respect to any kind of romance.

But while his mind might be willing to heed the warnings of his brothers, his hormones weren't entirely convinced. Especially when Georgia's van pulled into the driveway and his pulse actually skipped a beat.

As Georgia turned onto Larkspur Drive, she mentally reviewed her plans for the rest of the day. First and foremost was the long-neglected manuscript still on the dining room table. And when she finally got that manuscript finished, she would set Pippa up in her playpen on the deck while Georgia cut the grass. She still had mixed feelings about letting the boys play in the neighbor's yard, but she thought she might indulge them today, trusting they would keep safely out of the way in the tree house.

She hadn't seen much of Matt Garrett over the past few days, which made her realize how little she knew about him aside from his name. She didn't know where he worked or what he did, whether he was married or engaged or otherwise involved. Not that she was interested, just...curious.

And when she turned into her driveway and saw him pushing a lawn mower over the last uncut strip of grass in front of her house, her curiosity was piqued even further.

She parked her minivan, then opened the back door to let the twins scamper out before she unlatched Pippa's car seat. By the time she'd taken the baby into the house, he'd finished the lawn and was making his way toward her.

"Need a hand?" He gestured to the grocery bags in the back.

Georgia turned to respond, but the words dried up inside her mouth. His hair was tousled, his bronzed skin bore a light sheen of perspiration, and the gray T-shirt that molded to his broad shoulders and strong arms was damp with sweat. She'd always appreciated men who were more *GQ* than *Outdoorsman,* but she couldn't deny that there was something very appealing about *this* man.

She swallowed. "No, I've—"

Ignoring her protest, he reached into the vehicle for the remaining two bags.

She blew out a breath. "Okay. Thanks."

He grinned at her, and her knees actually went weak.

Something *very* appealing, indeed.

The first time she'd seen him up close, she'd been struck by his stunning good looks—and unnerved by her body's instinctive response to his blatant masculinity. But she'd managed to convince herself that she'd overestimated his appeal, that he couldn't possibly be as handsome or as sexy as she'd thought. Face-to-face with him now, she was forced to admit that, if anything, she'd *under*estimated his impact.

Those deep blue eyes were both warm and seductive, and

his exquisitely shaped mouth seemed to promise all sorts of wicked pleasure. Not that she was interested in seduction or pleasure; she didn't even have the energy for an innocent flirtation. But the pulsing of the blood in her veins proved that her body was only exhausted, not dead.

Matt followed her into the house and set the grocery bags on the counter.

"Can we come over to see the puppies?" Quinn asked.

Shane looked up at their neighbor, too, the plea in his gaze as earnest as his brother's question.

"The puppies aren't at my house today," Matt told them.

Their hopeful smiles dimmed.

"Where are they?"

"With my brother, Luke, at his clinic."

"He's the doggy doctor," Quinn reminded Shane.

"He's a doctor for all kinds of animals," Matt clarified.

"Maybe we could visit the puppies at the clinic," Quinn suggested.

"Not today," Georgia told him.

Shane pouted. "I want a puppy."

"Well, you got a baby sister instead."

"I'd rather have a puppy," Quinn grumbled.

Matt turned to hide his smile as he washed his hands at the sink. "Those puppies were kind of cute," he agreed. "But your sister is even cuter."

"Do you think so?" Quinn's tone was skeptical.

"Absolutely." He smiled at the baby still securely strapped into her car seat but directed his next words to Georgia. "Can I take her out of there?"

She hesitated. "If you want, but she doesn't have a lot of experience with strangers so she might…"

Her explanation trailed off when she saw that he already had Pippa out of her carrier.

Matt looked up. "She might what?"

"I was going to say 'fuss,'" she admitted. "But obviously she is doing anything but."

Instead, the little girl's big blue eyes were intently focused on Matt's face and her mouth was stretched into a wide, gummy grin that filled his heart so completely, his chest ached.

"She's a charmer," he said, tucking her carefully into the crook of his arm so that her head and neck were supported.

"She has her moments," her mother agreed.

"Mostly she cries," Quinn said.

"'Specially at night," Shane added.

Georgia's sigh confirmed it was true. "Colic."

He'd had his own experience with a colicky baby, and he winced sympathetically. "Are you getting any sleep?" he asked.

"A lot less since my mom went away," she admitted. "But I'm managing—if you disregard the fact that I'm falling behind on my work, housework and yard work."

Shane tugged on the hem of her shirt. "I'm hungry."

"I know, honey. I'll get your lunch as soon as I get the groceries put away."

"Gill cheez?"

She smiled. "You bet."

"I want twisty pasta," Quinn announced.

"You had pasta yesterday," she reminded him. "We're having grilled cheese today. But you can go put cartoons on TV while you're waiting for your lunch, if you want."

Apparently that was an acceptable compromise, as the boys both scampered off to the living room.

"But you're not falling behind with your kids," he said. "And that's what really matters."

The smile that curved her lips was both genuine and weary. "And thanks to you, I'm no longer as far behind with the yard work as I used to be."

He shrugged. "I was cutting my grass anyway."

She took a jug of 2% and a tub of yogurt out of the bag, found room for them in the fridge.

"You should try soy milk," he told her.

She lifted a brow. "Because you have futures in soybeans?"

He grinned. "Because colic can be caused—or aggravated—by an intolerance to the proteins in the cows' milk consumed by a nursing mother."

She crossed her arms over her chest. "How did you know I'm nursing?"

To his credit, he managed to keep his gaze on her face without his eyes even flickering in the direction of her very lush breasts. "No baby bottles in the drying rack or the fridge."

"Very observant," she noted. "And how do you know about the soy milk?"

"I read a lot."

She'd finished putting away her groceries and reached into the drawer under the oven for a frying pan. "I used to read," she told him. "Sometimes even for pleasure."

He smiled. "You will again—someday."

"I'll take your word for it." She retrieved the butter from the fridge. "But for now, we're getting through one day at a time."

"I'd say you're doing better than that. You've got three great kids, Georgia."

She started buttering slices of bread. "I wish you could be here to tell me that at 3:00 a.m." Then she realized how her words might be misconstrued, and her cheeks filled with color.

He knew she wasn't issuing an invitation, but he found himself wishing that he could find some way to help her out, to be the man she turned to when she needed someone, to be the one who could ease some of the fatigue from around her eyes and put a smile on her face. But those were very dangerous wishes. She wasn't his wife, her kids weren't his kids, and he had to stop wanting things that couldn't be.

"I only meant that it would be nice to have *someone* around to reassure me in the early hours of morning when I feel like crying right along with Pippa," she hastened to clarify.

"Sharing a burden makes it lighter," he agreed easily, and scribbled his phone number down on the notepad on the counter. "And if you ever do need a hand—with anything and at any time—give me a call."

"You've already done me a huge favor by cutting the grass." Butter sizzled as she dropped the first sandwich into the hot pan.

"I didn't know there was a limit on good deeds."

She smiled again, and though he could see the fatigue in her eyes, the curving of her lips seemed to brighten the whole room. "I don't mean to seem ungrateful—"

"I wouldn't say ungrateful so much as resistant."

"I lived in New York City for the past dozen years," she told him. "I wasn't even on a first-name basis with most of my neighbors, and the biggest favor any of them ever did for me was to hold the elevator."

"Obviously moving to Pinehurst has been a big adjustment."

"My mother told me it was a different world. She encouraged me to make conversation with people I don't know, and she chided me for locking the doors of my van when it's parked in the driveway."

"You lock the doors of your vehicle in your own driveway?" he asked incredulously.

"When I first moved to New York , I lived in a third-floor apartment in Chelsea. Two weeks later, I wandered down to the little coffee shop on the corner without securing the dead bolt and by the time I got back with my latte, the place had been completely cleaned out."

"I can see how an experience like that would make anyone wary," he admitted. "But around here, neighbors look out for one another."

"Says the man who just moved into the neighborhood," she remarked dryly, turning the sandwich in the pan.

He grinned. "But I grew up in Pinehurst and I've lived here most of my life."

"And probably quarterbacked the high school football team to a state championship in your senior year," she guessed.

"Actually, I was a running back," he told her.

"Yeah, 'cause that makes a difference."

She removed one sandwich from the pan and dropped in another. Then she cut the first into four triangles, divided them between two plates and set them on the breakfast bar. She reached into the cupboard above the sink for two plastic cups, then maneuvered past him to the fridge for a jug of milk.

Though she moved easily in completing tasks she had no doubt performed countless times before, he was suddenly cognizant of the fact that he was just standing around.

"I'm in your way," he noted, moving aside so that he was leaning against the far stool at the counter, the baby still tucked securely in the crook of his arm.

She shook her head as she half filled the cups with milk. "If you weren't holding Pippa, she'd be screaming her head off, wanting her lunch, and I'd be juggling her and burning the sandwiches."

As she called the twins to the kitchen, he glanced down at the baby who had, in fact, shoved her fist into her mouth and was gnawing intently on her knuckles.

"Well, as long as I'm being useful," he said, his wry tone earning him a small smile from Georgia, and a wide drooly one from the baby in his arms.

The quick patter of footsteps confirmed that the boys had heard their mother's call, and they eagerly climbed up onto the stools at the counter.

Georgia moved back to the stove and flipped the next sandwich out onto a plate. She sliced it in half, then surprised Matt by setting the plate on the counter in front of him.

"Milk?" she asked. "Or did you want something else? I've got iced tea or juice or soda."

"Milk is fine," he said. "But I didn't expect you to feed me."

"It's just a grilled cheese."

"Which is much more appetizing than the cold pizza in my fridge at home."

She shrugged. "I figured a sandwich is a small price to pay for lawn maintenance."

"You might get the hang of small-town living yet," he told her.

"I'm trying."

The fact that she was making an effort gave him confidence that their fledgling friendship could lead to something more.

And though Jack's and Luke's warnings still echoed in the back of his mind, they were easily drowned out by the pounding of his heart when Georgia smiled at him.

## Chapter Three

Georgia waited until Matt's car was gone from his driveway before she okayed the boys' request to visit the neighbor's tree house. Over the past couple of weeks, they'd enjoyed several adventures in the treetop, but only when their new neighbor wasn't home.

It wasn't that she was avoiding Matt. Not exactly. There was just something about the man that set off warning bells in her head. Or maybe it was tingles in her veins.

He was friendly and great with the kids, and if not for the way her body hummed whenever he was near, she might have thought that they could be friends. But the sizzle of awareness was too powerful for her to be comfortable in his presence, so Georgia decided that it would be best to maintain a safe distance from him at all times—or at least until her post-pregnancy hormone levels were back to normal.

She carted Pippa over to the neighbor's backyard so that she could keep an eye on the boys while they played in the branches.

With the baby cooing happily in her playpen, Georgia settled in a folding lawn chair beside her. She smiled as she listened to the boys' conversation—or rather Quinn's animated chatter and Shane's brief responses. A few minutes later, she saw Shane's sneaker on the top step of the ladder.

"Be careful," she said, instinctively rising from her chair in the exact moment that his foot slipped off the next step. She was halfway to the tree, her heart lodged in her throat, when his body plummeted toward the ground.

Emergencies were par for the course for any doctor, and especially for one who worked in a hospital E.R. But when an emergency surgery was squeezed into a very narrow window between two scheduled procedures, it made an already long day seem that much longer.

After a quick shower, Matt decided to head to the cafeteria for a much-needed hit of caffeine. But then he saw Brittney—a much more effective mood booster than any jolt of java. He slung an arm across her shoulders and pressed his lips to the top of her head.

She, predictably, rolled her eyes. "A little professionalism, Dr. Garrett."

"My apologies, Miss Hampton," he said, not sounding the least bit apologetic.

Brittney Hampton was his former sister-in-law's only child and a student helping out in the E.R.—a co-op placement for which she'd applied without his knowledge, determined to secure the position on the basis of her interview and not because her uncle was a doctor on staff at the hospital. She was loving the experience, and he was pleased to see that she was so intently focused on the pursuit of her goals.

"Are you on a break?" he asked her.

She nodded. "Dr. Layton said I should take one now, while there's a lull in the E.R."

"A lull never lasts long," Matt agreed. "If you're heading to the cafeteria, can I buy you a cup of coffee?"

She made a face. "I hate coffee."

He smiled. "Hot chocolate? Coke?"

"Vitamin water?"

"Sold."

They settled at one of the tables by the window with their beverages.

"How was your morning?" Brittney asked him.

"In addition to the usual hip replacements, I put a plate and five screws in the ankle of a kid who took an awkward tumble on the soccer field."

She winced. "Sounds painful."

"Nah, we put him under so he didn't feel a thing."

She rolled her eyes. "I meant the tumble."

"I imagine it was," he agreed. "How was your morning?"

"I had a test on molecular genetics," she said.

"And?" he prompted.

She shrugged. "I think I did okay."

"So no worries that Northeastern is going to rescind their offer?" he teased.

"Not yet."

"Is Brayden going to Northeastern, too?"

"Brayden is old news," she told him.

"Oh. I'm…sorry?" Truthfully, he was relieved. On the few occasions that he'd met her boyfriend, he'd seemed like a nice enough kid but Matt had worried that the relationship with Brayden would distract Brittney from her studies and her ultimate goal of becoming a doctor like her uncle.

She smiled, at least a little. "It was a mutual decision."

"Then your heart isn't broken?"

"Not even bruised."

"Glad to hear it," he said.

"How's *your* heart?" she countered.

His brows lifted. "Do they have you working in cardiology now?"

She smiled again, but her eyes—when they met his—showed her concern. "Mom told me that Aunt Lindsay is having another baby."

"Yes, she is," he acknowledged, pleased that his voice remained level, betraying none of the emotions that churned inside of him whenever he thought about the family that his ex-wife now had with her new husband. He didn't resent the fact that Lindsay had everything he'd ever wanted, but he was painfully aware of how empty his own life was in contrast.

"You should get married again, too," Brittney said.

"Don't worry about me—I'm doing okay," he said. And it was true. Because he suddenly realized that, since moving in next door to Georgia Reed and her family, his life didn't seem quite so empty anymore.

"You need a family."

"I haven't given up on that possibility just yet."

"Mom was telling Grandma that you need a woman who can appreciate you for all of your good qualities," Brittney continued, "so I've been keeping my eyes open for—"

"I appreciate the thought, but the last thing I need is my sixteen-year-old ni—"

"*Seven*teen," she interjected. "Remember? You came by for cake and ice cream for my birthday last month."

"I remember," he assured her. In fact, he hadn't missed a single one of her birthdays in the past three years, and he was grateful that Brittney's mother had continued to include him in family events after the divorce. Of course, it probably helped that he and Kelsey had been friends long before he married her sister. "But the last thing I need is my *seven*teen-year-old niece trying to set me up."

"Well, I haven't found any candidates yet," she admitted. "Aside from my friend, Nina, who thinks you're really hot. But even I know how inappropriate that would be."

"And on that note," Matt said, pushing back his chair, "I think I should check in on my patient."

Brittney rose with him. "And I need to get back to the E.R."

But before she turned away, she gave him a quick hug.

He was as pleased as he was surprised by the impulsive gesture of affection. But it was the words she spoke—"You'll find someone, Uncle Matt"—that somehow shifted his thoughts to the beautiful widow living next door with her three children and made him wonder if maybe he already had.

Georgia didn't have a lot of experience with her kids and emergency rooms—thank God for small favors—but she knew that "the squeaky wheel gets the grease" was an adage that applied in hospitals as much as anywhere else. And when she finally managed to maneuver her family through the sliding doors, with Pippa fussing, Shane crying (and trying to hold a bag of now partially thawed frozen peas against his wrist), and Quinn shouting "Don't let him die!", she didn't even try to shush them. Or maybe she knew her efforts would be futile anyway.

After she gave the basic details of the incident and handed over her insurance information to the bored-looking clerk behind the desk, she was told—with a vague gesture toward the mostly empty seating area—to wait. But she didn't even have a chance to direct Quinn to an empty chair when a dark-haired girl in teddy-bear scrubs appeared with a wheelchair for Shane. Though the tag on the lanyard around her neck identified her as "Brittney" and confirmed that she was a member of the hospital staff, she didn't look to Georgia like she was old enough to be out of high school.

"I'm just going to take you for a walk down the hall to X-ray so that we can get some pictures of your arm," Brittney explained to Shane.

His panicked gaze flew to his mother. Georgia brushed a

lock of hair away from his forehead and tried not to let her own worry show.

"It's okay if your mom and your brother and sister want to come along, too," Brittney assured him. "Would that be better?"

Shane nodded.

Quinn shook his head vehemently. "I don't want Shane to get a X-ray. I wanna go home."

"We can't go home until a doctor looks at your brother's arm," Georgia reminded her son, holding on to her fraying patience by a mere thread. "And the doctor can't see what's inside his arm without an X-ray."

"*You* can make it better," Quinn insisted. "Kiss it and make it better, Mommy."

Georgia felt her throat tighten because her son trusted that it could be that simple, that she had the power to make it better because she'd always tried to do so. But they weren't babies anymore and Shane's injury wasn't going to be healed by a brush of her lips and a Band-Aid.

Just like when their father had died, there was nothing she could do to ease their pain. Nothing she could do to give them back what they'd lost or fill the enormous void that had been left in all of their lives.

"Unfortunately, that's not going to fix what's wrong this time," she told him.

"Does a X-ray...hurt?" Shane asked.

Brittney squatted down so that she was at eye level with the boy in the chair. "It might hurt a little when the tech positions your arm to take the picture," she admitted. "But it's the best way to figure out what to do next to make your arm stop hurting."

After a brief hesitation, Shane nodded. "Okay."

She smiled at him, then turned to Quinn and sized him up. "How old are you?"

"Four." He held up the requisite number of fingers proudly.

"Hmm." She paused, as if considering a matter of great importance. "I'm not sure if this will work."

"If what will work?" he immediately demanded.

"Well, hospital policy states that no one under the age of five is allowed to drive a wheelchair without a special license," she confided. "Do you have a license?"

Quinn shook his head.

Brittney rummaged in the pockets of her shirt and finally pulled out a small square of blue paper. "I have a temporary one here," she told him, and Georgia saw that the words TEMPORARY WHEELCHAIR LICENSE were printed in bold letters across the top of the paper. "And I can give it to you *if* you think you can steer the chair *slowly and carefully* all the way down the corridor to X-ray."

"I can do it," he assured her.

She looked to Georgia, who nodded her permission.

"Okay, then. But first I have to put your name on here—"

"Quinn Reed."

She uncapped a pen and carefully printed his name. "And the date?"

He looked to his mother for guidance on that one.

"May twenty-second," she supplied.

Brittney filled in the date, then recapped the pen and handed the "license" to Quinn. He studied the paper reverently for a moment before tucking it carefully into the pocket of his jeans and reaching up to take the handles of the chair.

"Just one warning," Brittney told him. "If you bump into anything or anybody, I'll have to revoke that license."

He nodded his understanding, and they set off toward the X-ray department.

Twenty minutes later, Brittney directed them into a vacant exam room with a promise that "Dr. Layton will be in shortly."

But one minute turned into two, and then five turned into

ten. And Pippa, already overdue for a feeding, made it clear—at the top of her lungs—that she would not be put off any longer.

Thankfully, Quinn seemed to have finally accepted that his brother wasn't in any immediate danger of dying, and he crawled up onto the hospital cot and closed his eyes. Shane was still crying, though there was only an occasional sob to remind her of the tears that ran down his cheeks. So Georgia eased Pippa out of the carrier and settled in a hard plastic chair to nurse the baby.

She tried to drape a receiving blanket over her shoulder, to maintain some degree of modesty, but Pippa was having none of it. Every time she tried to cover herself, her daughter curled her little fingers around the edge of the fabric and tugged it away, until Georgia gave up. Besides, she didn't imagine a nursing mother was either an unusual or scandalous sight in a hospital.

Of course, that was before Matt Garrett walked in.

In the few moments that Matt had taken to review the digital images before he tracked down the patient, he didn't manage to figure out why the name Shane Reed seemed familiar. Then he walked into exam room four and saw one little boy on the bed and an almost mirror image in the wheelchair parked beside it, and he realized Shane Reed was one half of the adorable twin sons belonging to his gorgeous neighbor. And sure enough, Georgia was seated beside the bed, nursing her baby girl.

The baby's tiny hand was curled into a fist and pressed against the creamy slope of her mother's breast, and her big blue eyes were wide and intent while she suckled hungrily. It was one of the most beautiful sights Matt had ever witnessed. And incredibly arousing.

"Mommy." It was Shane who saw him first, and he tapped his mother with his uninjured hand. "Mr. Matt's here."

Georgia's gaze shifted, locked with his and her pale cheeks filled with color.

"You're not Dr. Layton," she said inanely.

"Things are a little chaotic in the E.R. right now, so Dr. Layton asked me to take a look at Shane's X-ray."

Quinn sat up. "Are you a doctor, too?"

Matt nodded.

"You don't look like a doctor," he said accusingly.

"Quinn," his mother admonished.

But Matt was intrigued. "How does a doctor look?"

The little boy studied him for a minute. "Older," he decided. "With gray hair and glasses."

"I'm older than you," Matt pointed out.

"You still don't look like a doctor."

"Actually, I'm an orthopedist," he explained.

"See?" Quinn said triumphantly to his mother.

"An orthopedist *is* a doctor," she told him.

The boy looked to Matt for confirmation.

He nodded. "An orthopedist is a doctor who specializes in fixing broken bones."

"Is Shane—" Quinn swallowed "—broken?"

He managed to hold back a smile. "No, your brother isn't broken, but a bone in his arm is."

"I fell out of your tree house," Shane said quietly.

Matt winced. "All the way from the top?"

The little boy shook his head. "I missed a step on the ladder."

"And reached out with his arms to break his fall," Georgia finished.

He noted that she'd shifted Pippa to nurse from her other breast, and he quickly refocused his gaze on his patient. "And broke your arm, too," Matt told Shane. "Do you want to see the picture of your arm that shows the break?"

Shane sniffled, nodded.

Matt sat down in front of a laptop on the counter and tapped a few keys.

"This here is your radius—" he pointed with the tip of a pencil to the picture on the screen "—and this is your ulna."

Though the occasional tear slid down the boy's cheeks, his gaze tracked the movement of the pencil and he nodded his understanding.

"Do you see anything different about the two bones?"

"I do," Quinn immediately replied, as Shane nodded again.

"Well, since it's Shane's arm, I think we should let Shane tell us what's different," Matt said.

Quinn pouted but remained silent.

"What do you see, Shane?"

"The ra-di—" he faltered.

"Radius?" Matt prompted.

"It has a line in it."

"That line is the break, called a distal radius fracture."

"It hurts," Shane said, in a soft voice that was somehow both wounded and brave.

"I know it does," Matt agreed.

"Can you fix it?" Quinn asked. "You said you can fix broken bones."

He nodded. "Yes, I can, and I will."

Georgia tried to concentrate on what Matt was saying, but her mind was still reeling from the realization that her new neighbor wasn't just gorgeous and charming but a doctor, too. She couldn't have said why the information surprised her so much or what she'd expected.

While he was occupied with Shane, she took a closer look at him, her gaze skimming from his neatly combed hair to the polished loafers on his feet. This man certainly didn't bear any resemblance to the sexy gardener who had tended to her overgrown yard. If she'd taken a guess as to his occupation that day, she probably would have said that he was employed in some kind of physically demanding field, like construction work or firefighting. She certainly wouldn't have guessed that he was an M.D.

Maybe the Mercedes in his driveway should have been her first clue, though she'd never met a doctor who hadn't managed to reveal his profession within the first five minutes of an introduction. And she'd been living next door to the man for more than three weeks without him giving even a hint of his occupation. But as she watched *Dr.* Garrett now, she could see that he was completely in his element here.

As he explained the process of casting a broken bone, he used simple words that the boys could understand. Despite his careful explanation, though, Quinn remained wary.

"Is Shane going to die?" he asked, obviously terrified about his brother's potential fate.

Though Georgia instinctively flinched at the question, the doctor didn't even bat an eye.

"Not from a broken arm," he assured him.

Shane looked up, his dark eyes somber. "Do you promise?"

She felt her own eyes fill with tears when she realized that the question wasn't directed to her but to Matt. Which made perfect sense, since he was the doctor. But it was the first time since Phillip had died that either of the twins had sought reassurance from anyone but their mother, and emotionally, it cut her to the quick.

"I absolutely promise," he said.

And Shane's hesitant nod confirmed that he'd accepted the man's word.

"Can I ask you a question now?" Matt asked.

Shane nodded again.

"What's your favorite color?"

"Blue."

"Then we'll put a blue cast on your arm," the doctor announced, and earned a small smile from his patient.

He left the room for a few minutes, then came back with

Brittney and an older woman. The gray-haired nurse helped lift and maneuver Shane's arm while the doctor applied the cast and Brittney looked on, observing and providing a running commentary of the process to entertain the twins. When it was done, Matt tied a sling over Shane's shoulder and explained that it would help keep the arm comfortable and in place.

"Do you use your right hand or your left hand when you eat?" Brittney asked Shane.

"This one," he said, lifting his uninjured hand.

"Do you think you could handle an ice cream sundae?"

Shane nodded shyly, then looked to his mother for permission.

"They would love ice cream," she admitted to Brittney, reaching for her purse.

The girl waved a hand. "It's on Dr. Garrett—part of the service."

Matt passed her a twenty-dollar bill without protest.

"Does my wheelchair driver still have his license?"

Quinn pulled the paper out of his pocket.

"Then let's go get ice cream."

"Thanks, Britt," said Matt with a smile.

Georgia had mixed feelings as she watched her boys head out with the young nurse. They were growing up so fast, but they would always be her babies as much as the little one still in her arms.

"She's been wonderful," she said to Matt now. "I don't know that I would have survived this ordeal without screaming if she hadn't been able to engage the boys."

"It can't be easy, juggling three kids on your own on even a normal day."

"What is a normal day?"

He smiled at that. "I'm not sure I would know, but I'm sure it's not strapping three kids into car seats for a trip to the hospital."

"Mrs. Dunford did offer to look after Pippa and Quinn so I didn't have to bring them along but—" She knew there was no reason to feel embarrassed talking to a doctor about a perfectly natural biological function that women had been performing since the beginning of time, but that knowledge didn't prevent a warm flush of color from rising in her cheeks again. "But the baby was almost due for a feeding and Quinn was absolutely terrified at the thought of his brother going to the hospital."

"He has a phobia about hospitals?" he asked.

"They both do," she admitted.

"Any particular reason?"

She nodded. "Because their father—my husband—was in the hospital when he died."

"That would do it," he agreed.

"It was a heart attack," she explained. "He recognized the symptoms and called 9-1-1, but the damage was too severe. All the boys know is that he was alive when they put him in the ambulance and dead at the hospital."

"Now they think anyone who goes to the hospital is going to die," he guessed.

She nodded again. "I've tried to explain that it wasn't the doctor's fault—that it wasn't anybody's fault—but they don't seem to believe me."

"Which one is Mrs. Dunford?"

She smiled. "Across the street. Always outside at 7:00 a.m. in her housecoat, watering her flowers. She has a magic touch with geraniums."

"And gingersnap cookies," he said.

"She baked you cookies?"

"She wanted to welcome me to the neighborhood."

"More likely she wanted to set you up with her grand-daughter."

"Then she should have gone for chocolate chip—they're my absolute favorite."

"I'll be sure to let her know."

He shook his head. "I'd prefer to get my own dates—although even Brittney thinks I need some help in that regard."

"Brittney—the nurse who looks like she's fifteen?"

"She's seventeen."

"Then she's not a nurse?"

He laughed. "More like pre-pre-med. Actually, Brittney's a high school co-op student who also happens to be my niece."

"She's been fabulous with the boys."

"She plans to specialize in pediatric medicine."

"That's quite an ambition."

"She's very determined. And she's one of the most sought-after babysitters in town."

"I'll keep that in mind if I ever find myself in need of one," she promised, certain Brittney would have graduated from medical school before that would ever happen.

So she was more than a little surprised when Matt said, "How about Friday night so I can take you out to dinner?"

## Chapter Four

For a minute, she just stared at Matt as if he'd spoken in a foreign language. And with every second that ticked away during that interminable minute, he wondered if he should rescind his impulsive invitation.

He wasn't usually the impulsive type, a truth that was proven by the fact that he'd kept the condo he'd lived in with his wife and child for three years after they'd gone rather than take a hit on the downturned real estate market. Or maybe he just hadn't been ready to move on until now.

But he was ready now. And if Georgia agreed to go out with him—even just once for dinner—it would hopefully convince his niece to put her matchmaking efforts on hold.

"Are you asking me out...on a date?"

Except that her question, along with the skepticism in her voice, made him question whether he truly was capable of getting his own dates.

*It can be a nightmare if things don't turn out.*

He ignored the echo of Luke's words in the back of his

mind. While he trusted that his brother had his best interests at heart and believed that there was some legitimacy to
his warning, Matt couldn't deny the instinct that was urging
him to get to know Georgia a whole lot better.

"Let's not put a label on it," he said instead.

"So it's not a date?"

"It isn't anything until you say yes."

She considered for another few seconds, then shook her
head. "I can't."

"You can't have dinner with a friend? A neighbor?"

"I can't leave my kids with a stranger—even if she is one
of the most sought-after babysitters in town."

But he thought that, for just a minute, she'd been tempted.

"Quinn and Shane seem to like her just fine," he pointed
out.

"She's been great with the twins," she said again. "But
Pippa is another story. There are certain things that no one
but Mommy can do for her."

Okay, he didn't need to be hit over the head. At least, not
more than once. And if his gaze automatically dropped to her
breasts, well, he made a valiant effort to yank it away again.

Not so quickly that she didn't notice—as was attested by
the color flooding her cheeks.

"Okay, then, how about dinner at my place so you're not
too far away if you're needed?"

"Look, I appreciate the invitation, but I'm doing okay.
You don't have to feel sorry for me because I'm on my own
with three kids."

"Is that what you think—that I feel sorry for you?"

"I don't know what to think," she admitted. "But it's the
only explanation I can imagine that makes any sense."

"Maybe it did occur to me that a few hours away from
your responsibilities might be appreciated," Matt allowed.
"But I don't feel sorry for you. In fact, I think you're lucky to
have three beautiful children, and that they're lucky to have

a mother so obviously devoted to them." Because he knew from firsthand experience that there was nothing quite like the bond between a parent and child—and that nothing else could fill the void when that bond was broken.

"I am lucky," she said softly. "Although I don't always focus on how very lucky—and I don't always know how to respond to unexpected kindness."

"You could respond by saying you'll come to my place for dinner on Friday."

She shook her head, but she was smiling. "You're persistent, aren't you?"

"That's not the response I was looking for," he reminded her.

"I'll come for dinner on Friday," she finally agreed. "*If* Brittney is available—and willing—to watch the kids."

"Is seven o'clock good?"

"Shouldn't you check with the babysitter first?"

"Brittney will make herself available," he assured her.

"Then seven o'clock should be fine," Georgia said.

"Any food allergies or aversions?"

She shook her head.

"Favorite food?"

She smiled. "Anything I don't have to cook."

It was a long night for Georgia.

She gave Shane some children's acetaminophen to take the edge off of the pain, but she could do nothing to combat his frustration. He was usually a tummy sleeper, and he didn't like having to stay on his back with his injured arm elevated on a pillow, even if it was what "Dr. Matt" had recommended.

And she didn't have any better luck settling Quinn. While he'd been happy enough to wheel his brother around the hospital and indulge in ice cream, neither activity had succeeded in completely alleviating his worry about his twin.

But aside from checking on Shane and reassuring Quinn

and nursing and pacing with Pippa, what really kept Georgia awake through the night was second-guessing her agreement to have dinner with her sexy new neighbor.

He was a genuinely nice man who was wonderful with her kids, and if those were the only factors to consider, Georgia wouldn't have hesitated to accept his invitation. But Matt Garrett made her feel things she hadn't felt in a very long time—if ever before—and the stirring of those unexpected feelings made her wary.

Her mother had always said that falling in love was kind of like jumping into a pool without testing the water. And there was no doubt that Charlotte had always enjoyed that crazy sense of plunging into the unknown. Georgia had never been the type to leap without looking—she liked to gauge the temperature first and ease in slowly.

And that was the perfect analogy for her relationship with Phillip. She'd loved her husband, but their affection had grown over time along with their relationship. They'd started out as friends who'd shared common interests and values—and a mutual distrust of romance. Phillip had been engaged previously, but that relationship had ended when he found his fiancée in bed with his cousin. Georgia had, as a result of her mother's numerous relationships more so than her own experience, mostly steered clear of any romantic entanglements.

But Phillip had been as persistent as he was charming, and one date had led to another until, before Georgia knew what was happening, they were exchanging vows. They'd had a good relationship, a solid marriage. They'd been compatible enough, even if the earth hadn't trembled when they made love, and she had sincerely loved him.

When they'd decided to get married, she'd had no reservations. It wasn't that she couldn't live without him so much as she didn't want to—he was her best friend, the one person she knew she could always rely on, and the one person she always felt comfortable with.

She didn't feel the least bit comfortable around Matt Garrett.

She was thirty-one years old and a mother of three children, and she didn't have the first clue about what to do with these feelings that he stirred inside of her. She wished, for just a minute, that Charlotte was here so that she could talk to her about this inexplicable attraction. Four marriages—and four divorces—had given her mother a lot of experience with love—and heartbreak.

Except that Georgia didn't need to talk to Charlotte to know what her advice would be. "Go for it. Have fun—and make sure you have orgasms. Life's too short to fake it."

She smiled, almost hearing the echo of her mother's voice in her mind even as she chided herself for jumping the gun. After all, just because the man had invited her over for dinner didn't mean he was looking for anything more than that. Just because her heart pounded wildly inside her chest whenever he was near didn't guarantee that he felt the same attraction.

"I'll be glad when your Gramma's home tomorrow," she said to her daughter. Not that she expected her mother would be able to put the situation in perspective for her, but she would help out with the kids so Georgia could get some sleep. Because after more than a week of serious sleep deprivation capped off by an unexpected trip to the emergency room, she was starting to feel more than a little frazzled. But she was confident she could handle things on her own for twenty-four more hours.

The first few weeks after Pippa's birth had been pure bliss. The baby had slept and nursed and cried very rarely, and Georgia had been completely enthralled with her. And then, around four weeks, Pippa had started to get fussy. She still slept and nursed frequently, but the sleeping was for shorter periods of time, the nursing more frequent, and the crying much louder and longer.

After a thorough checkup, Dr. Turcotte had announced

that there was absolutely nothing wrong with her aside from "a touch of colic." He'd been sympathetic but unable to help. And though Charlotte had offered to cancel her annual trip with "the girls," Georgia couldn't imagine letting her do it. Because if she'd accepted that offer, it would be like admitting that she couldn't handle her own baby. Besides, Charlotte had already done so much for her daughter and her grandchildren.

When everything had started to fall apart in Georgia's life, her mother hadn't hesitated to invite her to come home. Not that Pinehurst, New York, had ever actually been *her* home. In fact, Charlotte had only settled in the picturesque upstate town about half a dozen years earlier, long after Georgia was living and working in New York City. But Georgia hadn't needed a familiar environment so much as she'd needed her mother. As she needed her now.

She was passing the kitchen when the phone rang, and she grabbed for the receiver automatically, forgetting for a moment that she didn't need to worry about the noise waking the baby because Pippa was already awake and snuggled happily—at least for the moment—in her carrier.

Georgia recognized her mother's voice immediately. "Hey, Mom, I was just talking to Pippa about you."

"How is my beautiful grandbaby girl?" Charlotte asked.

She always sounded upbeat, but Georgia thought she sounded even more so today. Not that it took much to make her mother happy—something as simple as winning a couple of hands at the blackjack table or scoring front-row seats to see Wayne Newton could be responsible for her joyful mood.

"She seems content enough right now," Georgia said, not wanting to let her mother know how difficult the last few days had been.

"Oh, I miss my grandbabies so much," Charlotte said. "Have you been givin' them all big hugs and kisses from me every day?"

"I have," she assured her mother. "But they're looking

forward to getting them directly from you when you come home tomorrow."

"Well, that's actually why I was callin'," Charlotte began, and Georgia felt a sinking sensation in the pit of her belly. "There's been a little bit of a change in my plans."

"What kind of change?" She tried to keep her voice light and borrow the brave face her mother always wore.

"I met someone." The excitement fairly bubbled over in Charlotte's voice again. "Oh, honey, I didn't think I would ever fall in love again. I certainly didn't expect it. I mean, I've already been so lucky in love—"

Lucky? Only Charlotte Warring-Eckland-Tuff-Masterton-Kendrick would think that four failed marriages somehow added up to lucky. On the other hand, her effervescent personality and unfailing optimism were no doubt two of the qualities that continued to draw men to her, in addition to the fact that she looked at least a decade younger than her fifty-four years.

Okay, Georgia thought, trying to be rational about this. Her mother had met someone. She certainly didn't have any philosophical objection to Charlotte having a romantic relationship—not really. But she did object to her mother, or anyone for that matter, believing that she'd fallen in love with a man she couldn't have known for more than a handful of days.

"—but the minute our eyes met across the baccarat table," Charlotte continued, "I felt a jolt as if I'd just stuck my finger in a socket."

Georgia had to smile at that. "I'm glad you're having a good time—"

"The *best* time," Charlotte interjected. "And after the ceremony last night, Trigger got us upgraded to the honeymoon suite, and I swear, I drank so much champagne my head is still spinnin'."

Right now, Georgia's head was spinning, too. Ceremony? Honeymoon suite? *Trigger?*

"Mom," she said, attempting to maintain a rational tone in the hope that it would calm the panic rising inside her. "Are you telling me that you married this guy?"

"Honey, when love comes knockin' on the door, you don't just open up, you grab hold with both hands and drag it inside."

Georgia banged her forehead softly against the wall.

"So yes," Charlotte finally answered her question. "I am now, officially, Mrs. Trigger Branston."

"His name is really Trigger?"

"Oh, his real name's Henry," she told her daughter. "But they call him Trigger 'cause he's so quick on the draw."

"Quick on the draw?" she echoed, fingers crossed that this whole conversation was some kind of bizarre waking dream induced by her own mental and physical exhaustion.

"With his gun," Charlotte clarified. "He's a *bona fide* member of the Cowboy Fast Draw Association and World Fast Draw Association and he's won all kinds of contests."

"That's...um...impressive?"

"You bet your cowboy boots it is," Charlotte said.

Georgia didn't remind her mother that the only boots she owned were of the snow-shoveling kind. What would be the point?

"So...this is what he does for a living?" she pressed.

Her mother laughed. "Of course not—the gun-slingin' thing is just a hobby. Trigger's ranch keeps him too busy for it to be anything else."

"Where is this ranch?"

"In southwestern Montana."

"You're moving to *Montana?*"

"Well, he can hardly bring the sheep and goats all the way to upstate New York," Charlotte pointed out.

Sheep and goats?

Georgia didn't want to imagine. Besides, she had a more pressing concern. "What are your plans for the house here?"

"Oh, I haven't even thought about that. But naturally you and my grandbabies can stay there as long as you want."

The statement was typical of her mother—equal parts impulsive and generous. And while Georgia appreciated the offer, her main reason for packing up her family and moving them to Pinehurst was that Charlotte was there.

But she bit her tongue. How could she do anything else when her mother sounded so happy and proud? What right did she have to begrudge her mother a new life just because her own had completely imploded?

So even while her eyes burned with tears, she said, "Congratulations, Mrs. Branston."

Her mother's laughter bubbled over the line. "I knew you'd be happy for me, baby girl."

And she was—at least, she really wanted to be. Because Charlotte Warring-Eckland-Tuff-Masterton-Kendrick-Branston had the biggest heart in the world and she deserved to be happy. But when Trigger Branston trampled all over that big heart with his Montana cowboy boots, Georgia thought ominously, he was going to answer to her.

Or maybe she was being too cynical. The fact that none of her mother's four previous marriages had worked out didn't mean that this one wouldn't. And really, who was she to judge? Just because Georgia didn't want to follow in Charlotte's footsteps didn't give her the right to condemn her mother's choices.

Maybe she had no interest in a steamy romance or a hunky man because she only wanted a few hours of sleep—preferably dreamless sleep. Because over the past couple of weeks, it seemed as if every time she closed her eyes, she couldn't help but dream about the sexy doctor next door.

Matt was wrapping potatoes in foil when the doorbell rang. Since it was just past six o'clock and, therefore, too early to be Georgia, he decided to ignore it. When he heard the door open and heavy footsteps in the foyer, he knew it had to be one of his brothers. An assumption that was proven accurate when Jack strolled into the kitchen.

His brother automatically reached for the handle of the fridge. "Do you want a beer?"

"No, thanks. But help yourself," Matt said dryly.

Jack did so and deftly twisted the cap off of a long-neck green bottle, his gaze zeroing in on the package of steaks. "Either you're really hungry or I picked the right night to stop by for dinner."

"You're *not* staying," Matt told him.

Undeterred, his brother dropped into a chair. "Why—you got a hot date or something?"

"As a matter of fact, I do."

Jack's bottle thunked down on the table. "You really have a date?"

"Is that so hard to believe?"

"Actually, yes."

Matt scowled as he tossed the foil-wrapped potatoes into the preheated oven. "I date."

His brother shook his head. "You've never invited anyone back to your place."

"It felt strange when I was still at the condo," Matt admitted. "Being with someone else there."

"Then you should have moved out of that place three years ago."

"Maybe I should have," he acknowledged. He'd known, long before the divorce was final, that his marriage was over. But he'd still been reluctant to leave the home that held so many memories of the little boy who had been his son for far too brief a time.

"So who is she?"

Jack's question drew him back to the present. "No one you know. Now finish your beer and get out."

"Maybe I should hang around to get to know her," his brother teased. "Maybe she'll like me better than you."

"You have enough women falling at your feet without homing in on mine."

Jack's brows lifted. "Is she? Your woman, I mean."

"It's a first date, Jack." And then, in a not-so-subtle effort to change the topic of conversation, he asked, "So what's going on with you?"

His brother shook his head. "It's the mom, isn't it? That's why you're trying to change the topic."

"I'm just curious as to why you're dateless on a Friday night," Matt hedged.

"Things were getting a little intense with Angela, so I decided to take a break from the dating scene for a while."

"I thought you really liked Angela."

"I did," he agreed. "And then I noticed that she was starting to stockpile bridal magazines."

"Someday you'll find the right woman and take the plunge again," Matt assured him.

Jack shook his head and reached for his beer. "I like to think I learned from my mistakes. One failed marriage is enough for me."

"Did you hear that Kelly Cooper's moving back home?"

"Yeah, I heard."

"I just wondered if that might be the real reason you decided to end things with Angela."

"Our youngest brother was the one who was always tight with the girl next door."

Matt couldn't help but laugh at that. "Because they were best friends—not because there was any kind of romantic connection."

Jack shrugged, but Matt knew that his brother's efforts to appear unconcerned only proved that he cared more than he wanted anyone to know.

"I always wondered why she never came home," Matt

mused now. "We all knew she was excited about going to school in Chicago, but no one expected that she would go from Chicago to Dallas to Seattle, or that she would stay away for so long."

"I'm sure she had her reasons."

"Would you be one of those reasons?"

Before Jack could respond, a knock sounded at the back door.

"I guess that's my cue," he said, picking up his almost-empty bottle to finish it off.

Matt didn't protest. The last thing he wanted was his brother hanging around all night. But he refused to let Jack off the hook so easily. "We'll get back to this," he promised.

But apparently Jack wasn't letting him off the hook, either, because instead of heading out the front—the same way he'd come in—he went to the back door as Matt was opening it to his guest.

"Hello, Georgia," Jack said.

"Oh, hi." She seemed taken aback by the other man's presence. "Jack, right?"

He smiled, pleased that she'd remembered his name. "It's nice to see you again."

"Jack was just on his way out," Matt said pointedly.

His brother shook his head. "I'm not in any huge rush," he denied.

Georgia's gaze shifted from Matt to Jack and back again. "Am I interrupting?"

"No, *you* were invited," Matt reminded her. "*He's* interrupting."

"He's right," Jack acknowledged. "And I promise I won't stay for long. I just wanted to meet my brother's mystery date."

"I didn't know that I was a mystery—or that this was a date," Georgia admitted.

"It's just a friendly dinner," Matt affirmed, shooting a

warning glance at his brother. "Did you want something to drink? I've got sparkling water or juice or—"

"Water would be great," Georgia said. "Thanks."

But before he even had a chance to pour her drink, Matt's pager went off.

He swore silently, but he couldn't ignore it. Not wanting the night to be a complete write-off for Georgia, he reluctantly left Jack in charge.

Then Matt headed toward the hospital, already devising a plan to secure a second date—and hopefully a first kiss.

## Chapter Five

Georgia was disappointed that Matt had to cancel their plans to go to the hospital, but she understood. She didn't understand why he'd insisted that she stay to enjoy the dinner he'd promised her, and she didn't know how to decline Jack's offer to barbecue without sounding rude. Her only hope was that Pippa would wake up and pitch such a fit next door that Brittney would call and demand that Georgia return home.

Of course, her cell phone remained stubbornly silent.

"Looks like Matt's taken care of everything," Jack told her, returning with the plate of steaks from the grill. "There's a green salad, baked potatoes and dinner rolls."

"He didn't have to go to so much trouble," Georgia said, feeling more than a little guilty that he wouldn't get to enjoy the meal himself. "I would have been thrilled with a burger."

"Obviously my brother thinks you're worth the trouble," he said.

Despite the compliment implicit in the words, something in Jack's voice warned Georgia that he wasn't so sure.

He set a steak on her plate. "Well done."

"I like my steak medium."

"Matt told me to cook it all the way through to ensure there's no risk of any bacteria."

Her smile was wry. "Does he try to take care of everyone?"

Jack dropped a spoonful of sour cream onto his baked potato. "He and Luke both—it's the nurturing-doctor thing."

"What's your thing?" Georgia wondered.

He grinned. "I'm the heartless lawyer."

She shook her head. "I don't believe that."

"I have a law degree to prove it."

"It's not the educational qualifications that I doubt—it's the claim of heartlessness."

"There are more than a few women in town, including my ex-wife, who would assure you it's true."

"You're close to, and protective of, your brothers," she noted.

He didn't deny it.

"And for some reason, you disapprove of Matt and I being friends."

"I don't disapprove of your friendship," he assured her.

"But?" she prompted.

"But—and I know Matt would kill me for saying this—he's vulnerable."

"And you think I'm going to take advantage of him in some way?"

"I don't know what to think," Jack admitted. "Because I don't know you."

"That's fair," she acknowledged. "Would it reassure you if I said that I'm not in the market for a husband or a father for my children?"

"Not really."

"Why not?"

"Because I know my brother and he doesn't give up on anything he wants."

"And you think he wants me?"

"I know he does," Jack told her. "Because he called dibs."

She set down her water glass. "Excuse me?"

"The day he moved in—the first time he saw you on the porch—he warned the rest of us to back off."

She wasn't sure whether to be amused or insulted. "I would think the three kids would be warning enough."

He shrugged. "It's all about balancing pros and cons. We're guys and you're hot—for most of our species, those factors outweigh everything else."

"I'm not sure how to respond to that," she admitted, blushing. "Thank you?"

"It was a compliment," he said, and grinned again. "And you're welcome."

"But I do think you're misreading the situation between your brother and me."

"I doubt it."

"Even if he might have been interested when we first met, I'm sure the brief interactions he's had with my kids since then have cured him of any romantic notions."

"If you really believe that, you don't know Matt at all."

"I'd be the first person to admit that I don't," she told him.

"Which is probably why he invited you for dinner tonight," Jack noted.

"He's been incredibly helpful and generous."

"Don't kid yourself into thinking that he doesn't want to see you naked."

"You are blunt, aren't you?"

He shrugged easily. "I believe in telling it the way it is. But as much as he does want to get you naked, I know he could easily grow to care for you, too, and that makes the situation even more complicated."

"I'm not looking for a relationship," Georgia said.

"Sometimes we don't know what we want until it's right in front of us."

"That's quite the philosophical statement from a man who claims to value a woman on the basis of her 'hotness.'"

He flashed that quick grin again. "I can't be philosophical and shallow?"

She sliced off a piece of steak. "I think you're not nearly as shallow as you want people to believe."

Jack just shrugged, but Georgia suspected there were a lot more layers to each of the Garrett brothers than they let anyone see. Which was just one more reason for her to steer clear of all of them.

Her life was complicated enough right now without adding a man to the mix, especially one who had the potential to send her life—and her heart—into a tailspin, as she suspected Matt Garrett had already started to do.

Matt had just finished pouring his first cup of coffee Saturday morning when his youngest brother walked in.

"What are you doing here?" he asked Luke.

"Jack told me about your date last night."

"It wasn't much of a date," Matt admitted, pouring a second cup of coffee for his brother and adding a generous splash of cream.

"Yes, he said that you were saved by the bell—or at least your pager." Luke accepted the proffered cup.

"What is it, exactly, that I was supposedly saved from?" Matt asked. "A few hours in the company of a beautiful woman?"

"Let's put aside the fact that she's a beautiful woman—and your neighbor—for just a minute," Luke suggested, "and focus on the fact that she has three kids."

"I like kids."

"I know—and I saw the look on your face when those two little boys scampered across your backyard."

"What look was that?" Matt lifted his cup to his lips again.

"Pain. Regret. Longing."

He snorted. "Really? You got all that from one look?"

Luke shrugged. "I know you, and I know what you've been through."

"Ancient history," he said dismissively. Because while the scars from his failed marriage and the loss of his son had not completely healed, they had started to fade—and even more quickly since he'd met Georgia and her kids.

"Your marriage is history and Liam is gone," his brother agreed. "But I doubt you've given up on wanting a family."

"If we're going to start talking about our feelings, I'm going to need something a little stronger than coffee," Matt told him.

"I get that you're lonely," Luke continued as if his brother hadn't spoken. "But zeroing in on the first woman who crosses your path—"

"Georgia's hardly the first woman to cross my path in the past three years," Matt chided.

"But she's the first one you've invited over for a home-cooked dinner."

"It was a couple of steaks on the grill, not a six-course meal."

Luke just stared at him over the rim of his mug.

"Okay," he finally acknowledged. "So I like her. What's the big deal?"

"The big deal is that you're setting yourself up for heart-break all over again. She was married to another man—presumably because she was in love with that other man—and her kids are that other man's kids."

"The situation is not the same," Matt denied, though he could understand why his brother might worry about the similarities. "Georgia is a widow."

"Which doesn't mean she's not still in love with her husband."

He knew it was true, but he also knew that there was a

definite crackle in the air whenever he was near Georgia, and he didn't believe he was the only one who felt it.

"I'm only suggesting that you expand your horizons," Luke said now.

Matt eyed him warily. "Expand my horizons—how?"

"Come out to Maxie's with us tonight."

"Maxie's? Are you kidding?" While he and his brothers had frequented the popular dance club when they were younger, the loud music and louder women didn't appeal to him anymore.

"It might be just what you need," Luke said.

"I doubt it."

"Come anyway," his brother cajoled. "If you don't have a good time, I'll back off and not say another word about your infatuation with your neighbor."

Matt snorted his disbelief.

"And I'll buy the beer."

"Well, in that case…"

Matt spent the afternoon framing the unfinished basement to divide the space into individual rooms. Although the house already had a lot of space, he thought it would be convenient to have a home gym so that he didn't have to head out whenever he wanted some exercise. And until the room was ready, he figured the construction itself was a pretty good workout.

The physical labor occupied his hands but not his mind, and he found himself wondering what Georgia was doing, if the twins were behaving, if Pippa was napping. He remembered those first few months with Liam, how he and Lindsay had struggled to meet the baby's needs and establish some routines. His life had never been quite as chaotic as it had been back then, and he was surprised to realize that he missed it. Of course, spending time with his neighbors had given him brief glimpses of that pandemonium again, and spending time in close proximity to Georgia had stirred his hormones into a frenzy. He hammered the final nail into a board and tried to push those thoughts from his mind.

He was covered in sweat and sawdust and heading for the shower—prompted by the text message Luke had sent to remind him of their plans (because his brother knew Matt would forget, or at least claim he'd forgotten, without such a reminder)—when the bell rang.

Since his brothers had already proven that they had no qualms about walking right in, he let himself hope that it might be Georgia at the door. And while a quick glance through the sidelight revealed a pair of shapely, tanned legs, the hem of a short skirt and a pair of slender arms wrapped around an enormous ceramic pot from which towered a plant with lots of glossy, green leaves, his hopes were dashed.

He opened the door, made a show of looking around the greenery. "I really need to find a landscaper who can deal with these weeds. They're out of control."

"It's not a weed, it's a schefflera."

"Kelsey?" He parted some branches, peeked between them. Maybe she wasn't the woman who had preoccupied so many of his thoughts over the past few weeks, but she was one of his best friends, and he was genuinely happy to see her. "Are you in there?"

His former sister-in-law shoved the pot at his midsection, causing the air to whoosh out of his lungs. "Happy housewarming."

He maneuvered back through the door and carefully set the pot on the floor. "It's a killer plant," he said, after he'd managed to catch his breath again. "Although chances are, I'll kill it first."

"It's low maintenance," she assured him. "But don't leave it by the door in the winter. And it needs lots of light, but not direct sunlight."

"Low maintenance like most women are low maintenance," he grumbled.

She just smiled as she kissed his cheek, then moved past him and into the foyer. "This is a great house."

"Why do you sound so surprised?"

"Because it's a house—and nothing at all like your condo. Even the furniture's different."

"I was ready for a fresh start."

She nodded, understanding, and continued toward the kitchen. "I'm sorry I didn't get a chance to stop by sooner," she said. "One of the cruise lines is having a summer sale and things have been crazy at the office."

"You know, a ticket for a cruise would have been a better housewarming gift than a plant."

"Except that you don't take vacations," she reminded him. "In fact, I don't think you've gone on a holiday since…"

"Since my honeymoon?" he guessed, when her words trailed off.

She winced. "I'm sorry."

"The divorce has been final for three years," he pointed out.

"I know," she admitted.

The sympathy and worry in her deep brown eyes made him realize that he'd given her cause for concern in those three years because he hadn't taken any concrete steps to prove that he was moving on with his life. Hopefully seeing him in his new home would prove to her that he was doing so now.

He opened the refrigerator, peered inside. "Beer, wine, soda, juice?"

"Juice sounds good."

He pulled out the jug of orange juice, filled a tall glass, grateful that she'd dropped the topic of his ex-wife—her sister.

"Am I going to get the grand tour?" she asked.

"Actually, you caught me just as I was about to hit the shower," he told her. "So you can wait fifteen minutes or poke around on your own."

"I'll wait," she said. "Unless this is a bad time, in which case I can just go. I should have called first, anyway."

He waved off her apology. "You're always welcome. But I really need to clean up."

"Another hot date tonight?" she teased.

"Yeah," he said dryly. "With my brothers at Maxie's."

"Maxie's?" She wrinkled her nose. "Aren't you guys getting a little old for that scene?"

"We're guys," he reminded her, though he didn't disagree with her statement. "Our maturity level always lags behind our physical age."

"Tell me something I don't know."

He didn't have to think long to fulfill her request. "Luke has eight puppies he's trying to place in good homes."

Kelsey groaned. "Remind your brother that, in the past five years, he's already conned me into taking two cats, a parrot and an iguana."

"And you love the whole menagerie."

"That doesn't mean I'm taking any more," she said firmly.

"Brittney's always wanted a puppy," he pointed out.

"Unfortunately, the residences at Northeastern have a strictly enforced 'no pets' policy, so she'll have to be satisfied with visiting yours when she comes home."

He shook his head. "I'm not taking one of Luke's puppies." He tried to sound firm—to ignore the voice in the back of his head that promised the twins would be absolutely overjoyed if he did. And when the twins were happy, Georgia was happy, and her smile did all kinds of crazy things to his insides.

"You were going to shower," Kelsey reminded him.

He nodded and turned away. He did need to wash away all of the sawdust and sweat—and he was hopeful that the chilly spray might finally help banish wayward thoughts of Georgia that continued to pop into his mind.

Georgia didn't let herself think twice. If she did, she would think of all kinds of reasons that walking across the yard and knocking on Matt's door was a bad idea. Then she'd convince herself not to do it and she'd end up eating two dozen freshly baked chocolate chip cookies all by herself. Besides, it was just a plate of cookies—it wasn't as if she was propositioning her neighbor. Even if there was something about the man that intrigued her, despite the fact that she didn't want to be intrigued.

He was more attractive than any man had a right to be, but it wasn't just his physical appearance that appealed to her. There was a warmth in his eyes that hinted at a kindness in his soul, and a twinkle in his smile that attested to a sense of humor. And when he looked at her, she felt some of the weariness in her bones fade away and an unexpected warmth spread through her belly. Which was just one more reason she should not be making the man cookies.

She'd meant what she'd said to Jack the night before—she wasn't interested in any kind of romantic relationship and she didn't want to send mixed signals. On the other hand, it was possible that Jack had misinterpreted his brother's intentions and that Matt wasn't even reading any of her signals. Just because the man gave *her* tingles didn't mean that *he* felt the same sizzle of attraction. After all, it was extremely unlikely the sexy doctor would ever be interested in a weary widow with a lot of kid-sized baggage.

The mental lecture didn't do much to reassure her, but she accepted that the truth needed to be faced. Her children were her priority right now, and it would be a very long time before she even considered adding a man into the equation. So resolved, she lifted a hand to press the buzzer.

A moment later, she heard light footsteps—much lighter than she would have expected from a man of her neighbor's size and build—then the door was opened.

"Oh. Um." Georgia wasn't expecting anyone but Matt to answer the door, and finding herself face-to-face with a stunningly beautiful brunette left her momentarily speechless.

"You're looking for Matt," the woman guessed.

"I was," Georgia admitted. "But I don't want to inter-rupt—"

"Please." The other woman laughed as she held up a hand to halt her apology. "You're not interrupting anything."

"Are you sure?"

"Matt is a very old and close friend and nothing more than a friend. I just stopped by to drop off a housewarming gift and to make sure he was getting settled," she explained, step-ping away from the door so Georgia could enter.

She held out the plate of cookies. "Actually, if I could just leave these with—"

"Georgia."

Before she could make her escape, he was there—fresh out of the shower, if his damp hair and the subtle scent of soap were any indication. And when he smiled at her, a smile filled with both warmth and pleasure, her heart actually skipped a beat.

"I'm sorry for just stopping by. I didn't know you had company."

"Kelsey's not company," Matt said, winking at the bru-nette.

The other woman rolled her eyes. "Didn't I tell you?"

Georgia smiled, then turned to offer the plate to Matt. "When you fixed up Shane's arm, you mentioned that you were partial to chocolate chip."

"I am," he agreed. "But I'm not sure I follow the connec-tion between the hospital and the baked goods."

"I wanted to thank you for last night," she said, then felt her cheeks heat. She glanced at Kelsey and hastened to explain. "For dinner, I mean." And then, to clarify further, "When I lived in Manhattan, I didn't socialize with the people in my building—to be honest, I didn't even know most of them—so this whole neighbor-helping-neighbor thing is all new to me. But you've been really great, and I thought baking some cookies might be a nice way to say thanks."

"It wasn't necessary, but I appreciate it." He breathed in deeply. "They smell fantastic."

"Well, I should get back," she said.

"How is Shane managing with the cast?" Kelsey asked.

Georgia must have looked startled by the question, because the other woman smiled.

"Brittney, your hospital assistant and babysitter, is my daughter," she explained.

"Your daughter?" Georgia was genuinely baffled by this revelation. "You don't look old enough to be the mother of a seventeen-year-old."

Kelsey laughed. "Oh, I *do* like you."

"Shane's doing okay," she said, in response to the original question. "Mostly because his brother is catering to his every whim. Although I suspect that will wear thin in another day or two."

"How's Pippa?" Matt asked. "Has she been sleeping any better?"

She shook her head again.

"Colic doesn't last forever," he told her.

"It only seems like forever," Kelsey warned.

"It already does," Georgia admitted.

"And yet," Kelsey mused thoughtfully, "somehow a woman who has her hands full with three small children, including a fussy newborn and a preschooler with a broken arm, still found the time to make cookies for her new neighbor."

"It took a lot less time to make the cookies than it would have to cut my grass, which Matt did for me the other day," Georgia explained, wanting to ensure that Kelsey didn't get any wrong ideas.

"So this is…tit for tat?"

Georgia wasn't sure if the emphasis on "tit" and "tat" was

deliberate, but the implication had her cheeks flooding with color again. "Something like that," she agreed lightly.

"Did you want some of these cookies and a cup of coffee? I could make decaf," Matt said, coming to her rescue again.

"Thanks, but I just had a cup of tea with Mrs. Dunford—and I've left her alone with the kids for too long already." She turned back to Kelsey. "It was nice meeting you."

"You, too," Kelsey said. "Next time, I hope you'll have time for that cup of coffee."

"That would be nice," Georgia said.

Matt followed her to the door. "Sorry about Kelsey."

Her lips curved. "Why are you sorry?"

"Because she's the sister I never wanted."

Despite the disclaimer, the tolerant affection she'd seen when Matt looked at Kelsey had been obvious. But when she glanced up now to find him looking at her, what she saw in his eyes wasn't tolerant affection but something hotter and more intense. And this time, the tingles that started low in her belly spread through her whole body.

She had to swallow before she could speak. "I really have to get back."

"Thanks again for the cookies."

"Thank you," she said. "For everything."

He smiled. "See? You're getting the hang of small-town living."

"I'm trying," she agreed.

"And from the neighbor-helping-neighbor thing, it's just a short hop, skip and a jump to friendship."

"I haven't had a chance to meet many new people since I moved here," she admitted. "I'd like it if we could be friends."

"I'd like that, too," he said.

Matt stayed where he was, watching until Georgia had disappeared through the back door and into her house.

In the few weeks since he'd moved in, he'd made more

progress with the beautiful blonde next door than he'd anticipated. She'd gone from being distant and wary to baking cookies for him, which gave him confidence that they were well on their way to becoming friends.

And from there, he was optimistic that it was just another hop, skip and a jump to something more.

# *Chapter Six*

Matt stayed out with Luke and Jack later than he'd intended. Not because he was having a good time, but he figured if he at least pretended he was, it might get his brothers off his back for a while. He had a couple of beers early in the evening, because Luke was buying, but then he switched to soda. It was rare for Matt to overindulge, he never had more than a couple of drinks when he was driving, and he didn't drink at all if he was on call.

By the time he left the bar, his head was pounding from the throbbing beat of the music, his muscles ached from the sawing and hammering he'd done in the afternoon, and he was exhausted. And when he pulled into his driveway at nearly 2:00 a.m., he was stunned to see Georgia carrying Pippa's car seat toward her own vehicle, with the twins—in their pajamas—shuffling along beside her.

He shifted into Park and turned off his vehicle. Even through the closed window of his car, he could hear the baby's cries. In fact, he wouldn't be surprised if she was screaming loud enough to wake Mrs. Dunford across the street—and she was almost 80 percent deaf.

As he exited the vehicle, he had to admire the baby's lung capacity. He lifted a hand in greeting, but Georgia didn't see him. And as she passed beneath the streetlight, he saw that Pippa wasn't the only who was crying. The wet streaks on Georgia's cheeks were his undoing. He forgot his own fatigue and crossed the patch of grass that separated their two driveways.

"What are you doing?"

She finished locking the car seat into its base, then made sure the boys were securely belted in their booster seats. Straightening, she wiped the telltale traces of tears from her cheeks. "I'm going for a drive."

"At 2:00 a.m.?"

"Is that a violation of street curfew?"

"No, just common sense," he told her.

She reached for the driver's-side door, but he scooped the keys out of her hand.

"What are *you* doing?" she demanded.

"You're too exhausted and emotional to get behind the wheel of a car," he said. "Especially with your infant daughter and two little boys in the backseat."

"I'm tired because Pippa won't sleep. Hopefully, a quick trip around the block will change that, then I can come back home and we'll all get some shut-eye."

He opened the passenger-side door and gestured for her to get inside. She just stared at him, uncomprehending.

"I'll drive," he told her.

She opened her mouth as if to protest, then closed it again without saying a word and climbed into the vehicle.

He knew she wasn't accustomed to having anyone look out for her, and that she was probably more suspicious than appreciative of his efforts, but tonight she was too tired to put up a fight.

He'd just turned onto Queen Street when he realized that she was right—the motion of the car had quickly succeeded in putting Pippa to sleep. A glance in the rearview mirror confirmed that both Quinn's and Shane's eyes were closed, too. He started to comment to Georgia on the obvious success of her plan, then saw that she was as deeply asleep as her children.

Matt continued to drive, with only the radio for company, because he was concerned that Georgia would wake up as soon as he pulled back into her driveway, and he knew that she needed the rest as much as—or maybe even more than— her daughter. But half an hour later, his eyes were starting to feel heavy, too, so he turned the vehicle back toward Lark-spur Drive.

Luckily, Georgia's house key was on the same ring as the van key, so he was able to let her sleep while he opened up the door and transferred the kids, one at a time, from the vehicle to their beds. He couldn't figure out how to unlatch Pippa's car seat, so he finally just unbuckled the belt and lifted the sleeping baby into his arms. She didn't stir. Obviously her sleepless nights were taking as much of a toll on the baby as they were on her mother.

When Pippa was settled in her crib, he went out to the van again to rouse Georgia. He touched her shoulder gently; she jolted.

"What— Where?"

"You're home," he told her.

She turned automatically to the backseat. "Where are the kids?"

"They're all inside, tucked into their beds."

Her eyes widened. "Really?"

He nodded. "Now it's your turn."

"Okay." She let him help her out of the car and toward the back door. "I didn't mean to fall asleep, too."

"Obviously you needed it."

"I guess so," she said, and lifted a hand to cover her yawn.

He steered her in the direction of the staircase. She automatically turned toward Pippa's room, but he guided her across the hall to what he assumed was her own. "Just go to sleep," he said softly.

"Pippa—"

"Is already in her crib."

"I should change her diaper."

"I checked it before I put her down."

She blinked. "You did?"

He smiled. "She's clean and dry and sleeping—you should do the same."

"Okay," she finally relented. Then she lay down on top of the covers, fully dressed, and closed her eyes.

"Sweet dreams, Georgia."

But she didn't respond, because she was dead to the world again.

Georgia awoke in a panic.

The sun was streaming through the partially open blinds and a quick glance at the clock on her bedside table revealed that it was 8:02 a.m.

She didn't believe it. The last time she'd nursed Pippa was around two, just before she'd gone out to the car to take her for a drive. But Pippa had never slept for six straight hours. She wondered if she might have awakened in the night and nursed the baby without realizing it, but her painfully engorged breasts immediately refuted the possibility.

Aside from the uncomfortable fullness, she felt good. Relaxed and rejuvenated. She crossed the hall to Pippa's room, a genuinely contented smile on her face.

The contentment and the smile disappeared fast when she discovered that her little girl's crib was empty.

She bolted across the hall to the twins' room and found it

was empty, too. She raced for the stairs, her heart hammering against her ribs. "Pippa?"

She couldn't have said why she was calling for her—she knew the baby wouldn't answer. But she wasn't thinking rationally. She wasn't thinking about anything except that her children weren't where they were supposed to be.

"She's here." Matt must have heard the panic in her voice, because he met her at the bottom of the stairs with Pippa in his arms and Quinn and Shane at his side.

Her breath rushed out of her lungs and her knees went weak. Matt reached out, catching her arm to hold her steady. "You okay?"

She nodded as she took Pippa, cuddling the little girl close to her chest. The baby cooed happily. "I am now."

"Why is Mommy crying?" Shane wanted to know.

She hadn't known that she was, and wiped hastily at her cheeks with her free hand, then touched his head. "I just got scared when I woke up and didn't know where you guys were."

"Pippa's a Who-dee-na, too," Quinn announced.

"Houdini," Matt corrected the boy automatically. Then, to Georgia, "I'm sorry. I thought I was doing you a favor by letting you get some sleep."

"You were. You did. I just didn't expect that you'd still be here, and when I saw that her crib was empty and I didn't hear the boys…" They wandered off now, back into the living room where she could hear their favorite cartoons on the television.

"You panicked. Understandably," he said. "And I'm sorry."

She wanted to be mad, but he was so genuinely contrite that she couldn't hold on to her anger. Especially not when he spoke again and asked, "Are you hungry? I hope you don't mind but I pilfered through your cupboards and was just about to make some French toast."

"No, I don't mind," she said. "Especially not if you're offering to make French toast for me, too."

"Absolutely," he assured her. "If for no other reason than to be able to tell my brothers that I had breakfast with my beautiful new neighbor."

She knew he was teasing, and she wasn't sure how she was supposed to respond to that. From their first meeting, he'd been friendly and flirtatious, but maybe he was just the type of guy who flirted with every woman who crossed his path. Because the idea that he could be interested continued to baffle her—and never more so than right now, as she suddenly remembered her wrinkled clothing, disheveled hair and unbrushed teeth.

"Do I have time for a quick shower?" she asked.

"Twenty minutes enough?"

She nodded and turned back toward the stairs.

"Are you planning to take Pippa into the shower with you?"

"No, but I figured she was overdue for a feeding," she said. Despite the fact that the baby certainly wasn't acting like it had been more than six hours since her last feeding, Georgia's aching breasts confirmed the fact.

"She had a bottle an hour ago," he said.

That stopped her abruptly in her tracks. "She had a bottle?"

"I found your stash of breast milk in the freezer."

Georgia was impressed, and more than a little surprised. Because on the few occasions that she'd tried to coax her daughter to take one, Pippa had refused to latch on to the artificial nipple. "She was okay with the bottle?"

"She was hungry," he said simply.

She couldn't help but smile as she secured Pippa into her bouncy chair. "You really do go above and beyond, don't you?"

"It wasn't a big deal," he assured her.

But to Georgia it was. Six hours of uninterrupted sleep was a very big deal—and she was very grateful. But now she wondered, "Where did *you* sleep?"

"Your couch, in the living room."

Having caught some quick naps there herself, she didn't recommend it. "I hope you don't have to work today," she said, wondering how he could get through a day at the hospital on only a few hours of sleep on a sofa.

"I work twelve-hour shifts for four days, then I'm off for four days, barring emergencies. This is one of my days off."

"Then you should be taking advantage of the opportunity to laze around in bed."

His lips curved. "Is that an invitation?"

"No!" She was shocked by the idea—and just a little bit tempted by the wickedly explicit thoughts that sprang to mind in response to his suggestion. "I only meant that you didn't have to hang around here taking care of my kids."

"I like your kids," he told her.

And they absolutely adored Matt, but that was hardly the point. She couldn't help but remember what Jack had said about his brother and worry that she was taking advantage of his generous nature. She hadn't asked him to help her out last night, but she hadn't objected to his offer, either. And she certainly hadn't asked him to spend the night so that she could get some sleep, but she was immensely grateful that he'd done so.

Matt took a step closer, lifted a hand to tuck an errant strand of hair behind her ear. "And I like you."

The contact was brief, casual. But the touch made her shiver; her heart started to pound; her throat went dry.

All he'd done was touch her, and her hormones had gone haywire. Was she so lonely, so desperate for human contact, that such a simple gesture could affect her so deeply? Apparently so, because not only was her pulse racing, her body was aching, yearning.

"Well, I'm going to go take that shower now," she said, and turned to make her escape.

What was he doing?

It was a question Matt had asked himself countless times

through the night and one that continued to plague his mind as he got breakfast under way.

He found a package of bacon in the fridge, started the meat frying on the stove while he gathered the rest of the tools and ingredients for French toast. The twins had been playing in the living room but, drawn by the sounds emanating from the kitchen, ventured into the room to investigate.

Quinn looked quizzical as he watched Matt turn the strips of bacon that were sizzling and popping. "Are you really gonna make breakfast?"

"Sure." He set a lid over the bacon to cut down on the grease spatters.

"Can I watch?"

"Sure," he said again. "You can even help, if you want."

The little boy's eyes went wide. "Really?"

"Why not?"

Shane, silent until now, frowned. "Daddies don't cook."

"Says who?" Matt challenged.

"My daddy."

The assertion, so firmly stated, gave Matt pause. He didn't want to contradict any memories the boys had of their father, but he couldn't imagine that Georgia wanted her sons growing up with the outdated assumption that the kitchen was strictly a woman's domain. "Your dad never scrambled eggs for you on a Sunday morning so your mom could sleep in?"

Shane shook his head. "Mommy doesn't sleep in."

Which was apparently a situation that had existed long before Pippa came along.

"She slept in today," Quinn pointed out.

"And we're going to make her breakfast today," Matt said.

"We could order pizza."

Matt had to smile. "For breakfast?"

"Daddy knew the best places to get pizza," Quinn said loyally.

"Well, I'm going to make French toast. And if you don't want to help, I'll crack all the eggs myself."

Shane shifted closer, looked up at him with solemn dark eyes. "I wanna crack eggs."

"Then let's get you washed up," Matt said.

He supervised the boys' washing their hands, or—in Shane's case—washing the only hand he would be using. Then he sat them at the table with a big bowl and gave them each three eggs while he took the bacon out of the frying pan and set it on paper towels to absorb the grease.

"Hey! You're not 'sposed to put the shell in the bowl."

Matt glanced over in time to see that Quinn's criticism had Shane's eyes filling with tears.

"It's hard with one hand," Shane said, his voice wavering.

"You're doing a great job," he assured the child. "And it's easy enough to fish the pieces of shell out again," he told Quinn. Then he gave Shane a spoon and showed him how to do it.

But Quinn was still scowling over his brother's clumsiness. "What if he doesn't get them all?"

"Then we'll have an extra dose of calcium with our breakfast."

"What's calsum?" Shane asked.

"It helps build strong bones and teeth."

"Like milk," Quinn said.

"That's right," Matt agreed. "Because milk is a source of calcium."

He poured a generous splash of it into the bowl with the eggs and let them take turns whisking the mixture. After reminding them that they should never go near the stove without an adult close by to supervise, he let them each dip a piece of bread in the liquid and then place it in the frying pan.

It was as much fun for Matt as it obviously was for the twins, and all the while, that same question echoed in the back of his mind: What was he doing?

But this time, the answer was obvious: He was getting too close.

Aside from the fact that she was a widow, he knew very few details about Georgia's life before she came to Pinehurst. Had her marriage been a happy one? Was she still in love with and mourning her husband? What did she want for her future?

Of course, he didn't know the answers to any of those questions. He only knew that he was extremely attracted to her—and totally captivated by her children. They were a family without a daddy, and he very much wanted to be a daddy again.

That, he knew, was his problem. He wasn't sure that he could separate his desire for Georgia from his affection for her children. And the closer he got to all of them, the more difficult it would be. He needed to take a step back, distance himself from the situation.

So that was what he was going to do—right after breakfast.

## Chapter Seven

Georgia did feel better after her shower. Fresh and well-rested, and completely in control of her wayward hormones. She could smell bacon and coffee as she made her way down the stairs and inhaled deeply, confirming that Matt had found the tin of French roast her mother kept in the freezer. Georgia had given up caffeine when she found out she was pregnant with Pippa and, more than a year later, it was the one thing she still craved. Unfortunately, Pippa's fussiness and sleeplessness ensured that it was something she continued to avoid.

"Mommy's coming!" She heard Quinn's excited whisper summoning his brother.

Shane appeared at the bottom of the stairs. He was still in his pajamas, but he bent at the waist in an awkward bow. "I'm your eksort."

"And a very handsome escort you are," she told him, and was rewarded with one of his shy smiles.

She took his hand and let him lead her to the dining room where the table had been set with mismatched plates on Mickey Mouse place mats with a centerpiece of wilting dandelions in a drinking glass. Georgia took in the scene in about two seconds, and that quickly, the firm grip she held on her emotions slipped.

During their eight-year marriage, Phillip had taken her to plenty of fancy restaurants with exclusive menus and exemplary service. But no Crepes Suzette or Eggs Benedict had ever looked as appealing to Georgia as the platter of overcooked bacon and slightly mangled French toast on her mother's dining room table.

She swallowed around the lump in her throat. "Somebody's been busy."

"We were!" Quinn said proudly. "We made it together—all of us."

She didn't—couldn't—look at Matt, because she didn't want him to see the tears that swam in her eyes. Instead, she focused on her boys. "Did you really?"

"'Cept for Pippa," Shane told her.

Georgia noticed that Matt had moved the baby's bouncy chair into the dining room so that her mother would be able to keep an eye on her while she had breakfast. Pippa kicked her legs and smiled now, as if she knew that she was the subject of their conversation.

"You did a wonderful job," Georgia said, and because Matt had spearheaded the effort, she lifted her gaze to meet his now. "Thank you."

"You're welcome." He pulled out a chair for her. "Now sit and eat before it gets cold."

The brusque command was exactly what she needed to keep the tears at bay. Following his direction, she sat and loaded up her plate. But before she could sample her own breakfast, she had to cut Shane's French toast. Then she turned to do the same for Quinn, only to find that Matt had already completed the task.

"Eat," he said again, though more gently this time.

So she sliced off a corner of the fried bread and popped it into her mouth.

"Do you like it, Mommy?" She heard the anxiousness in Shane's voice and wondered why it was that her youngest son worried so much about doing everything just right while his sibling always forged ahead without concern. Sometimes it was hard to believe they were brothers, never mind twins.

"It is the best French toast I have ever tasted," she assured him.

"That's 'cuz it's got extra calsum," Quinn told her. "From the shells Shane dropped in the bowl."

She sent a quizzical glance in Matt's direction. He just smiled and lifted one shoulder.

"That must be it," she agreed.

Georgia ate two slices of French toast and three strips of bacon and savored every bite. When the twins had finished their breakfast, they carried their plates and cups to the kitchen and went to wash up.

As she heard them clamoring up the stairs, she turned to Matt. "Thank you," she said again. "Not just for cooking breakfast, but for including the boys in the process."

"It was fun." He said it so simply and matter-of-factly, she knew he meant it.

"Can I ask you something?"

"Sure."

"Why aren't you married?"

The blunt question seemed to take him aback, and he lifted his mug for a sip of coffee before answering. "I was," he finally admitted. "Now I'm divorced."

She winced. "Excuse me while I take my foot out of my mouth."

"No need. The divorce was final more than three years ago. I'm over it. Mostly."

"Mostly?"

He shrugged. "It's always hard to accept the loss of something you really wanted."

A truth that she knew far too well. And though she knew it was a question she had no right to ask and none of her business anyway, she heard herself say, "Do you still love her?"

"No." This time he replied without hesitation and emphasized the response with a shake of his head. "Whatever feelings we'd once had for one another were gone long before the divorce papers were signed."

"Then why aren't you dating anyone?"

"How do you know I'm not?" he challenged.

"Because you spent Saturday night sleeping on my couch."

He smiled at that. "Okay, I'm not."

"Why not?" she asked again.

"I've been out with a few people—I just haven't met anyone who made me want to take the step from a few casual dates to a relationship."

"You're so great with my kids," she told him, "I'd have thought you had half a dozen of your own."

He looked away as he shook his head. "I don't."

And then, in an obvious effort to put an end to that topic of conversation, he reached across the table to tickle Pippa's bare toes. The baby kicked her legs and cooed joyfully in response to his attention.

"When she's happy, she's really happy, isn't she?"

Georgia smiled at her daughter. "Yeah. So much that I sometimes almost forget the hell she's been putting me through over the past few weeks."

He went to the kitchen to refill his mug of coffee, then returned to his seat across from her. "When did you say your mother would be back from Vegas?"

"The original plan was for her to come home yesterday."

"What happened?"

"She decided to go from Nevada to Montana."

He sipped his coffee. "Why Montana?"

"Because that's where her new husband lives."

His brows lifted. "When did she get married?"

"A few days ago."

"You don't approve of the man she married?" he guessed.

"I don't know him," she admitted. "In fact, *she* didn't know him before their eyes met across the baccarat table."

His lips curved. "She's a romantic."

"That's a more favorable word than the one I would have chosen," she admitted.

"I take it you're not a romantic?"

"I like to think I'm a little more...practical." It was so easy to open up to him, to tell him things she hadn't spoken aloud to anyone else—not even either of her sisters. In fact, if not for the way her body hummed whenever he was near, she might have thought that they could be friends.

But the awareness between them was too powerful for her to be completely comfortable in his presence. And when she glanced up to see him studying her, she was suddenly conscious that the awareness was sizzling even now.

"You've never been swept off your feet?" he challenged.

She shook her head. "I don't want a man to sweep me off my feet, although I wouldn't object to a man who was willing to sweep the floors every once in a while."

"I can sweep floors," he told her. "But I don't do windows."

She smiled. "I'll keep that in mind."

"No, you won't."

His blunt contradiction took her aback. "Excuse me?"

"You're so busy trying to do everything yourself that it doesn't occur to you to ask for help every once in a while."

"Maybe," she acknowledged. "But I'm learning to accept it when it's offered."

"That's a start," he said, and rose from the table to begin clearing the rest of the dishes.

Georgia gathered the napkins and cutlery and followed him into the kitchen.

"I don't like to feel inadequate," she finally admitted.

He turned and stared at her. "Are you kidding? You're juggling the responsibilities of a home, a job and raising three kids."

"Which is no more than a lot of women do."

"A lot of women have a partner to share the burden," he pointed out.

She dropped the napkins into the garbage and put the cutlery into the basket in the dishwasher. "Truthfully, even before Phillip died, he wasn't at home enough to share much of the burden." Then, because she didn't want to sound critical of the man she'd married, she felt compelled to add, "He was a good husband and father, but he had an incredibly demanding job. He worked a lot of long hours and weekends."

Too late, she recognized that she was making excuses about her husband to a man whose job as an orthopedic surgeon was undoubtedly more demanding and stressful than that of a trader. And yet, Matt didn't seem to have too much trouble making time for the things he enjoyed. Which was one of the concerns that had plagued her throughout her marriage: If Phillip really wanted to be with her, why had he chosen to spend so much time away from her?

She knew the situation wasn't that black-and-white, that her husband's drive originated from the hard lessons he'd learned in his life. And no matter what she said or did, she couldn't convince him that they should take time to enjoy what they had. It was never enough for Phillip—he wanted to work harder, earn more, buy more. In the end, he worked himself into an early grave, leaving his wife alone and his children without a father.

Her eyes filled again. Obviously she wasn't as in control of her emotions as she'd hoped, but this time she managed to hold the tears in check. "I'm sorry. I'm not usually such an emotional basket case."

"You don't have to apologize to me," he told her.

"Yes, I do. You've been nothing but helpful and kind, and I shouldn't repay you by crying on your shoulder."

"I'm not afraid of a few tears," he promised.

She managed a smile. "You're a good man, Matt Garrett."

"Don't say that too loud," he warned. "I have a reputation to protect."

"Believe me, every time I go into town I hear all about the string of broken hearts you left behind you in high school," she admitted. "Although rumor has it, you've matured into a responsible citizen since then."

"Just a nasty rumor," he assured her. "Don't believe it for a second."

This time, her smile came more easily.

However, before Georgia could respond, Shane ventured into the kitchen. "I built a hosp'al with my bricks," he told her.

Since his trip to the E.R. the previous week, he'd been understandably curious about hospitals and doctors and everything related to the medical profession, so his chosen project was hardly a surprise to Georgia.

"Did you want me to come take a look at it?" she asked.

He nodded, then glanced shyly at Matt and quickly away again. "Dr. Matt, too."

"I'd love to take a look at it," Matt said.

And when he held out his hand to the little boy, Shane hesitated less than half a second before he lifted his own and tucked it inside the doctor's much larger one.

Georgia stood rooted to the spot as fresh tears pricked her eyes. Shane was her introverted son—the little boy who hovered in the background while his brother basked in the spotlight. It was rare for Shane to make any kind of overture, especially to a stranger.

Okay, so Matt wasn't exactly a stranger, but being neighbors for a few weeks didn't make him a close acquaintance, either. Of course, the fact that he'd fixed up the little boy's broken arm might have helped the doctor breach Shane's usual guard, but Georgia suspected her son's ready acceptance of the man had more to do with the man himself. And that was something she was going to have to think about.

When she entered the living room, she saw that Matt was already hunkered down beside the twins to examine their construction projects. He admired the "fine craftsmanship" of Shane's hospital and the "creative design" of Quinn's fire station and commented that there were enough bricks left over to build a whole city.

"Do you want to help us?" Quinn asked.

But Shane was shaking his head before Matt even had a chance to respond.

"Daddies don't play," he reminded his brother, and the matter-of-fact tone of his voice made Georgia's heart ache.

Phillip had loved his children—she had never ever doubted that fact. But she'd never understood, until she'd seen how easily Matt interacted with the boys, how much the twins had missed out on by not having a hands-on dad. She knew they'd felt rebuffed when Phillip had been too tired to show much interest in whatever they were doing, and she'd tried to make it up to them. But no matter what she did, she couldn't be the father they needed.

"Some adults don't have time to play," Matt acknowledged. "But sometimes adults need to play—" he glanced up at Georgia and grinned "—just to prove they're still kids at heart."

"Are you a kid at heart?" Quinn wanted to know.

"Definitely," Matt said, and dug into the bin of bricks to prove it.

Georgia left the boys to their toys and set about cleaning up the kitchen. Matt and the twins had made a pretty good attempt at destroying her mother's stove, but the wielding of a scrubber with some serious muscle eventually succeeding in removing the last traces of egg from the ceramic cooktop.

Still, the cleanup was a small price to pay for everything Matt had done for her. Not only had he let her sleep through the night—and oh, what a glorious indulgence that had been!—he'd helped her boys make breakfast for her. And now, when she thought he would have been more than anxious to get back to his own house and his own life, he was playing with her children, giving them the male attention they needed more desperately than she'd guessed.

But as grateful as she was to Matt, she was also wary. It was obvious to Georgia that the boys already adored their new neighbor and she was worried that they would start to rely on him for too much. Because as great as Matt had been, he wouldn't stick around. Because no man in her life had ever stuck around.

If that was cynical, well, she had reason to be cynical. Her biological father had walked out before she was three years old, and not one of the three stepfathers who had passed through her life had stayed for much longer than that. The few casual and short-lived relationships she'd had as a teenager had done nothing to alter her opinion. It wasn't until she met Phillip that she let herself look to the future and trust that he would be there. But it turned out that she'd been wrong about that.

She knew that her husband hadn't chosen to leave her, and yet, the end result was the same. He was gone and she was alone. Well, not entirely alone. And she would forever be grateful to Phillip for their three beautiful children.

But as happy as they seemed most of the time—discounting Pippa's colic for the moment—she couldn't help worrying about them, about the void in their lives that only a father could fill.

Since Phillip's death, she'd sometimes found herself wondering if Charlotte's string of impetuous unions had been—even in part—an attempt to provide her daughters with a sense of family. Except that her daughters were all grown up now and Charlotte was still following her heart—wherever it might lead.

Georgia had no intention of following that same path, not for any reason and certainly not on the hunt for a substitute father for her children. She wasn't willing to risk her heart again, and she certainly wasn't going to risk theirs.

But as she heard the boys giggling in response to something Matt had said or done in the other room, she had to wonder if it wasn't already too late.

Matt made a conscious effort to keep his distance from his neighbor and her kids over the next week. Work at the hospital kept him busy enough for the first few days—it was his days off that caused him trouble.

In the space of a few weeks, he'd become accustomed to seeing Georgia and her kids almost every day, even if it only for a few minutes of conversation on the sidewalk. He missed Quinn's endless barrage of questions, Shane's intense focus as he listened to his responses, and the joyful light in Pippa's eyes whenever she saw him. But mostly he missed spending time with Georgia.

Every time he pulled into his driveway, his gaze automatically swung toward the house next door. More than once, he considered stopping by just to see how she was doing and to check if the shadows under her eyes had faded. Too many times, he'd started to head in that direction before his self-preservation instincts kicked in and turned him around again.

Instead, he did some more work in the basement. He hung drywall, taped seams, plastered nail holes. The physical labor kept his hands busy, but it didn't stop him from thinking about Georgia. He spent some time hanging out with his brothers and took a fair bit of ribbing for having struck out with the beautiful blonde next door. It was easier to accept their jabs than admit that he'd walked away from the plate before the first pitch had ever been thrown. He'd been nicknamed Mr.

Clutch in high school, because he'd always played his best in the biggest games. But if this was a game, it was the big leagues, and there was more at stake here than a score.

Georgia wasn't just a beautiful woman, she was the mother of three beautiful children, and they were a package deal. He couldn't take one without the other, and he was afraid to admit how much he wanted the whole package. And so, instead of stepping up to the plate, he'd walked away. Mr. Clutch had been face-to-face with what was potentially the biggest opportunity in his life, and he'd choked. And if his brothers knew the truth, he'd never hear the end of it.

So he let them think that he'd struck out and he tried not to think about Georgia while he listened to Jack boast about the clerk who had propositioned him in the judge's chambers. But when Luke started rambling on about the exploits of the puppies, he couldn't help but remember how totally enthralled the twins had been by them—and that those puppies had played a pivotal role in his first meeting with his neighbors.

It was readily apparent that Luke was trying to convince one or both of his brothers that their lives would not be complete without a canine companion. He'd found good homes for five of them, he admitted, and had decided to keep one for himself, which meant that there were only two left.

Jack, who was hardly ever at the penthouse apartment he paid an astronomical rent for, refused to be swayed. He didn't have the time or the energy that a puppy would demand, not to mention the havoc that an untrained animal would wreak on his designer furniture and hardwood floors.

So Luke gave up on Jack and focused his efforts on his other brother. Matt was able to tune out most of his arguments, but he couldn't forget the awe and excitement on both Quinn's and Shane's faces when they'd seen the puppies in his backyard. And he couldn't forget the stubbornness and longing in Shane's voice when he told his mother, "We *do* want a puppy."

And Matt knew he was fighting a losing battle, because he couldn't refuse anything that would put a smile on the boys' faces—and maybe Georgia's, too.

## Chapter Eight

## Chapter Eight

Matt was avoiding her.

Georgia didn't know why, but she knew it was true.

There was a part of her that insisted the "why" didn't matter. All that mattered was that Matt had done what she expected him to do—he'd walked away. But another part insisted that there had to be a reason for his withdrawal. And whether or not he wanted to be friends, they were neighbors, and she didn't want there to be any awkwardness between them when their paths crossed.

More than a week after he'd made her breakfast, on a rare night in which Pippa had actually settled down at a reasonable hour, she waited outside on her back porch to catch him when he came home from work.

She recognized the quiet hum of the engine as he pulled into his driveway, and her heart started to beat just a little bit faster.

She was unaccountably nervous, and already second-guessing her decision to confront him. Maybe he hadn't been avoiding her. Maybe he'd just been busy. Or—and this was a possibility that left her slightly unsettled—maybe he'd done some thinking after their breakfast conversation and had started dating someone. And wouldn't she feel like a complete idiot if she went over there now and he wasn't alone?

She decided that knocking on his door after ten o'clock at night, in the absence of an emergency, might make it look like she'd been waiting for him. And although she had been, she didn't want him to know it. A realization that only made her feel more ridiculous.

She had just turned to go back into the house when the light over Matt's deck came on and he stepped outside. Alone.

He dropped down onto the top step, his forearms on his knees, a beer bottle dangling from his fingertips.

Georgia hesitated. She was pretty good at reading body language, and the weariness in Matt's broad shoulders was visible even in the shadows from fifty feet away. He lifted the bottle to his lips, took a long swallow.

Her decision made, she ducked back into the house to make sure all of the kids were settled and sleeping, then she clipped the baby monitor onto her belt and made her way across the yard.

Despite his preoccupation, he must have heard her footsteps rustling in the grass, because his head came up and he peered into the darkness. She stepped into the circle of light.

"Georgia." She saw surprise flit across his face and heard the pleasure in his voice before he seemed to shut down all of his emotions.

It confirmed her suspicion—he had been avoiding her. For some reason, he was deliberately trying to put distance between them. But right now, she didn't care about any of that. All that concerned her was the look of abject misery on his face.

"Rough day?"

He just nodded.

Though he hadn't invited her to sit down, she did so anyway, settling onto the step beside him. "Can I do anything?"

He shook his head and lifted the bottle to his lips again.

The silence stretched between them, broken only by the chirp of crickets and the occasional hoot of an owl in the distance.

"Want to talk about it?"

He shook his head again. "Not really."

She waited another minute, hoping he would change his mind. He remained silent, and she pushed herself back to her feet.

"But I wouldn't mind if you stayed awhile," he said. "I thought I wanted to be alone, but that's not really a great place right now."

She glanced back at her own house. It wasn't really so far, but she didn't like to be away from her children, even when they were sleeping. "Can you bring your beer over to my step?"

"You want to be able to hear the kids," he guessed.

"I know it seems silly when I have this—" she tapped the monitor clipped on her belt "—but I feel more comfortable being close."

"It doesn't seem silly at all," he told her, rising to his feet. "In fact, I wish more parents were as concerned about their children as you are."

She sensed that his comment was somehow connected to his dark mood, and wondered what had happened at the hospital. He'd already said he didn't want to talk about it, and she didn't want to pry, but she wanted him to know that she was there for him—as he'd been for her when she needed him.

When they were settled on her deck, she decided to open up the channels of communication. Even if they didn't talk about what was bothering him, she thought it might help him just to talk.

"After living in Manhattan for so long, it took me a while

to get used to the sights and sounds outside of the city. It seems so quiet here—" she smiled wryly "—at least it is when Pippa's not screaming. At first, it seemed *too* quiet. But now, I sit out on the porch sometimes just to listen to the crickets, and I feel a sense of peace that I've never known anywhere else."

"I used to take it for granted," he admitted. "Growing up around here, I didn't really know anything else. But the years I spent away at college gave me a new appreciation for this town."

"I never thought I wanted anything like this. But now that I'm here, I can't imagine a more perfect place to raise my kids. I want to watch them run around the backyard, chasing butterflies and playing tag. I want to hear them giggle when they jump into piles of leaves we've raked up together."

"You'll have lots of leaves," he assured her, looking around at the towering maples that lined the back of her property. "Probably more than you want to rake."

"Luckily, I have this wonderful neighbor who's been a very big help with a lot of my outdoor chores."

"It's not as if I enjoy cutting the grass—actually, I do enjoy cutting the grass," he decided, sounding almost surprised by the realization. "The mindless physical work is a welcome diversion after a twelve-hour shift at the hospital."

"Then I'm sure raking leaves in the fall will provide similar benefits."

"And shoveling snow?"

She smiled. "If it works for you, I wouldn't want to deprive you of the pleasure."

"Believe me, there are other—and much more pleasurable—stress releases."

She felt her cheeks color, but refused to follow where his train of thought was trying to lead her. "Talking about the cause of stress also helps," she agreed.

"I wasn't talking about talking," he informed her.

"I know," she admitted. "But it can help. And if you ever decide you do want to talk, I'm happy to listen."

He was silent for a moment, considering her offer. She didn't expect he would actually open up to her. It had been apparent that whatever was bothering him wasn't something he wanted to discuss, but he finally said, "I performed surgery on a four-year-old girl with a spiral fracture tonight."

"What's a spiral fracture?"

"It's a break caused by twisting the bone—a common type of injury suffered by skiers. Their feet are tied into boots locked into skis, and when a ski twists around, the leg automatically twists with it."

"It seems unlikely that she was skiing anywhere around here in May."

"She wasn't. And it wasn't her leg, it was her arm."

It didn't take her long to make the logical jump. "She was abused?"

"The mother is denying it, but X-rays revealed that the child's arm had been broken before and healed improperly because it wasn't treated. So when I fixed the new break, I also had to rebreak and repair the previous injury."

Georgia's eyes filled with tears. "And she's only four?"

He nodded.

"I'd say that was a pretty rough day," she agreed.

"I'm doing okay now."

She touched her lips to his. Softly. Briefly.

He stilled. "What was that for?"

"A kiss to make it better," she said lightly. "Because you're hurting."

Georgia started to draw back, but Matt snaked his arm around her waist and held her close.

"I'm feeling a lot of things right now," he told her. "And hurt isn't anywhere near the top of the list."

Her eyes grew wide, her breath hitched, and he could see the pulse point at the base of her jaw fluttering.

"I think we're getting a little sidetracked," she hedged.

"Are we? Or are we finally back on the track that we've been heading toward all along?"

"How is it possible that we were heading anywhere in the same direction when you've been avoiding me all week?"

His lips curved, just a little. "Did you miss me?"

"Yes," she admitted, sounding piqued. "For almost three weeks, it seemed as if I couldn't step outside my door without tripping over you, and then, just when I got used to you being around—when I started looking forward to you being around—you disappeared."

"If it counts for anything, I missed you, too. All of you."

Her gaze softened. "The boys kept asking me why you didn't want to play with them anymore."

"I'm sorry," he said, and meant it.

"I don't want you to be sorry, I just want to know if it was something I said or did."

"No," he assured her. "It's all on me."

"Why?"

"Because I knew that if I didn't put some space between us I wouldn't be able to stop myself from doing this."

She knew he was going to kiss her. He could see the conflict in her eyes—the war between wariness and wanting. Not wanting to give her another second to worry or wonder, he dipped his head.

She held herself immobile and kept her eyes open, as if she was willing to tolerate his efforts but was determined not to participate. He kept his gaze locked on hers, his hand splayed against her lower back, as he brushed his mouth against hers. A soft sigh sounded in her throat and her eyelids flickered, just a little, proving she wasn't as immune to him as she wanted to believe.

Since the end of his marriage, he'd been with other women,

but sex without intimacy had left him feeling oddly unfulfilled. The problem with meaningless flings, he'd quickly discovered, was that they were meaningless. Truthfully, Georgia was the first woman he'd been sincerely attracted to in a long time, the first woman with whom he could imagine himself having a relationship rather than a one-night stand.

He also realized that he was probably thinking further ahead than she was. She was a young widow with three kids, and he knew he would have to take things slow until he was sure she wanted the same thing he did. Right now, she didn't seem to know what she wanted—but at least he knew he had her full attention.

His mouth cruised over hers again, savoring her texture and flavor. Her lips were soft, lush and deliciously seductive. He traced the shape with the tip of his tongue, and swallowed her soft sigh as her eyelids finally drifted shut.

He took his time, teasing her lips further apart, testing her response. She lifted her hands to his chest, and he half expected her to push him away. He would have been disappointed, but not really surprised. But then her hands slid over his shoulders to link behind his head, and she pressed herself closer, so that her breasts were crushed against his chest, her hips pressed against his.

She had to know he was aroused—there was no way she could think the erection throbbing inside the front of his pants was anything else—but she didn't pull away. His hand slid under the hem of her T-shirt, skimmed up her back. She shivered in response to his touch on her bare skin and moaned in pleasure. It was that low, sexy sound deep in her throat—proof that she wanted this every bit as much as he did—that nearly undid him.

He'd wanted to kiss her—and now that he had, he wanted so much more. But he'd promised himself that he would take things slow, which was a lot harder to do than he'd expected with his heart pounding so fiercely inside his chest and his blood pulsing hotly in his veins.

He eased his lips from hers but kept his arms around her to ensure she couldn't flee. Because he could see, even in eyes still clouded with desire, the first hint of panic beginning to set in. And her words, when she spoke, confirmed her worry.

"That was a really bad idea," she told him.

"I have to disagree."

"We're neighbors and, hopefully, friends."

"I'd say that's a good start to any relationship."

She shook her head. "I'm not looking for a relationship."

"Because you're still grieving for your husband," he guessed.

"Because I need to focus on my kids," she clarified. "And they don't leave me enough time or energy for any kind of romantic involvement."

"Okay—we'll put a hold on the romance portion of things."

"That includes the kissing portion."

"You kissed me first," he pointed out.

"Not like that," she protested.

"You didn't like the way I kissed you?"

She rolled her eyes. "Is your ego so fragile that you need to fish for compliments?"

"So you *did* enjoy kissing me," he surmised.

"It seems you're a man of many talents, Dr. Garrett."

"That kiss barely scratched the surface."

"That's what I'm afraid of," she admitted.

"There's something between us," he told her.

"It's a basic physical attraction."

"It's more than that."

She shook her head again. "I won't let it be anything more than that."

He smiled. "You think it's your decision to make?"

"Yes." Her tone was firm and unequivocal. "I make my

own choices, and I'm *not* getting romantically involved with you."

But he caught the slightest hint of desperation in her tone now and was torn between wanting to offer reassurance and challenge her conviction. Instead, he opted for a casual shrug. "Okay."

Her gaze narrowed suspiciously. "Okay?"

"You've obviously made up your mind," he acknowledged.

"I have," she confirmed. "And I appreciate that you're respecting my decision."

"I do," he agreed. "But that doesn't mean I'm not going to do everything in my power to change your mind."

"You'll be wasting your time," she warned.

He shrugged again. "I figure it's my time to waste."

Her sigh was filled with exasperation. "But why would you want to waste your time with me when there are any number of women in this town who would be thrilled to be with you?"

He grinned. "Any number, huh?"

"As if you didn't know that everywhere you and your brothers go, female heads swivel in your direction."

"It's been like that since high school," he admitted. "It's a curse."

"And how long ago was high school?" she asked, in what seemed to him an abrupt shift in the conversation.

"Almost twenty years," he admitted. "Why?"

"Because in the past few weeks, every time I go into town someone refers to me as the young mother from New York City who moved in next to Dr. Garrett—conveniently overlooking the fact that I was here before you. And on top of that, I've had at least half a dozen people tell me about the grand slam home run you knocked out of the park in the bottom of the thirteenth inning to bring home the district championship."

"Only half a dozen?" He frowned. "I guess my legend is truly fading."

She just shook her head.

"Did you ever play baseball?" he asked.

"Just in gym class at school or the occasional pick-up game at the park when I was a kid."

"Are you any good?"

"I was never the first one picked for a team, but I wasn't the last, either."

"Because we play a co-ed charity softball tournament on the Fourth of July and I'm putting together a team, if you're interested."

She shook her head. "I'm not playing any games with you—you're completely out of my league."

"I got to first base with you tonight," he teased. "And you didn't seem to have any trouble keeping up."

Her cheeks flushed. "It won't happen again."

He just grinned. "I guess time will tell."

"Matt," she said warningly.

"I'll see you soon," he promised.

His step was much lighter as he made his way across the grass to his own house, and he knew the sizzling kiss he'd shared with Georgia was only part of the reason. Another— maybe even bigger part—was just being with her.

He hadn't appreciated how much he'd missed having some- one to open up to at the end of a difficult day until she'd sat down beside him and invited him to talk. And she not only listened to him ramble about the stress of his day, she empa- thized with him. And then she'd kissed him.

True, it had been little more than a casual brush of her lips against his, but he figured it had to mean something that she'd made the first move.

He figured it meant even more that she hadn't balked—at least not too much—when he made the second.

A few days later, Matt had just walked into the house after a visit to his brother when his phone rang. Picking up the receiver, he was pleased to hear Georgia's voice on the other end of the line, and even more pleased when she said, "Have you had dinner yet?"

"No," he admitted.

"Because we just ordered a party tray of pizza and thought you might want to come over to share it with us."

"Why did you order a party tray?"

"Because it was the special of the day," she told him. "And because you've cooked for me—twice now—so it only seems fair for me to return the favor. I didn't actually make the pizza, but I thought I would earn some points by providing the meal."

"You're the only one keeping score," he said.

"Maybe, but the boys would like to share their pizza with you, if you don't have other plans."

Adding the kids to the equation obliterated any resistance. "I don't have other plans," he admitted. "And pizza sounds great, but would it be too much trouble if I asked you to bring it over here?"

"Not too much trouble," she told him, "but likely a lot of fingerprints you'll have to clean up around the house after."

"I'm not worried about fingerprints," he assured her.

"Then we'll be over in five."

As much as Georgia tried to convince herself that taking pizza over to Matt's house was just being neighborly, she knew that wasn't entirely true. One kiss had changed everything.

One unbelievably hot, mind-numbing, toe-curling kiss.

Since Matt had planted his lips on hers, all kinds of lustful thoughts had taken root in her mind. Thankfully, she wasn't just taking pizza but three kids, too, and she was grateful for the buffer that their presence would provide.

Maybe her hormones had been stirred up by that kiss, but she was confident that she still had enough self-control not to jump Matt's bones in front of her children. Because she'd meant what she'd said to him—she had neither the energy nor the inclination for a romantic relationship, even if she was suddenly, achingly aware that it had been more than a year since she'd had sex.

When Matt stepped out onto the back deck, the twins raced toward him, Shane, predictably, lagging a few feet behind his brother.

"We've got pizza!" Quinn announced.

"I hope it has pepperoni," Matt said, smiling as he took the long, flat box from him.

"Lots and lots of pepperonis," Shane chimed in. "'Cuz they're my favorite."

Matt winked at him. "Mine, too."

He glanced at Georgia, who had Pippa strapped against her chest, a diaper bag in one hand and a plastic bag in the other, then gave the pizza box back to Quinn with instructions to put it on the table in the dining room.

"Let me give you a hand," he said.

"Thanks."

"What have you got in here?" He took the grocery bag.

"Paper plates and napkins, veggies and dip, juice boxes for the boys."

"I do have plates and napkins."

"It didn't seem right to bring dinner then leave you with dirty dishes."

"I would have let you wash them," he assured her.

She smiled at his teasing, relieved that there didn't seem to be any evidence of the awkwardness she'd feared. "This way I don't have to."

When Georgia got Pippa settled on a blanket with her favorite toys, she saw that the boys were already seated at the table, eager to dig into dinner. She put a slice on each of their plates and added a few veggies—broccoli and carrots for Quinn and cucumber and red pepper for Shane.

Quinn wrinkled his nose. "Don't like veggies."

"Yes, you do," she reminded him.

He ignored the vegetables and picked up his pizza.

Matt reached into the box to take a couple of pizza slices. Then he looked at the boys' plates and, with more resignation than enthusiasm, he added some carrot sticks and cucumber slices. Georgia was grateful, because she knew that neither of the boys would protest any further about eating their vegetables if Dr. Matt was eating them, too.

She had just bit into her second slice of pizza when she heard a noise emanating from behind a closed pocket door that led to Matt's kitchen. She'd noticed the closed door earlier but had assumed he had a sink full of dirty dishes he didn't want guests to see. When the noise—a whimper?—came again, she suspected that he was hiding something much more significant than unwashed plates.

The boys were already finished eating—including their vegetables—when Matt confirmed her suspicions.

"Do you guys want to see what I've got in the kitchen?" he asked them.

"Is it ice cream?" Quinn asked hopefully.

"Sorry," Matt said. "It's not ice cream."

"I like ice cream," Shane told him.

He ruffled the little boy's hair, and Shane smiled shyly in response to the casually affectionate gesture. "Then I'll make sure I have ice cream for next time."

"Whatcha got this time?" Quinn wanted to know.

In response, Matt started to open the door. He'd barely slid the barrier a few inches when a tiny bundle of fur wriggled through the narrow opening. He held his breath, not entirely sure that this surprise would go over as well as he'd anticipated. Not that he doubted the twins' response, but their mother's reaction wasn't quite so easy to gauge.

"A puppy!" Quinn announced.

The boys were already on the floor, fussing over it. Georgia pushed away from the table to join her sons.

"Are you pet-sitting for your brother?" she asked Matt.

"No," he admitted.

Her eyes widened. "He's yours?"

"Actually—" he opened the door farther and picked up a second puppy "—they're both mine."

"Two?"

He shrugged. "Well, they were the only two left, and they're brothers."

She looked up at him, her blue eyes reflecting equal parts amusement and approval, and he felt as if his heart had actually swelled inside of his chest.

"You really are a softie, aren't you?" she said.

"I'm thinking 'sucker' is more accurate," he admitted, and bent to put the second puppy down on the floor with the first.

"What are their names?" Quinn wanted to know.

"I only just brought them home," Matt said. "I haven't had time to give them names yet."

"You hafta pick good names," Quinn told him. "Not like Fluffy or Buttercup." He wrinkled his nose in obvious disapproval of such choices.

"No Fluffy or Buttercup," Matt promised solemnly.

Shane giggled as a tiny pink tongue swiped his chin. "Finnigan," he said.

Matt's brows lifted, as surprised by the unusual suggestion as the fact that Shane had offered it.

"Finnigan?" he queried.

"And Frederick," Quinn declared.

"They're characters on a television show," she explained.

Shane looked up at him. "They're brothers."

"In that case," Matt said, "I guess the only question now is, which one is Finnigan and which one is Frederick?"

The boys were in complete agreement about the assignment of the names, and it warmed Matt's heart to see their enthusiasm about the puppies. Then he looked up and saw Georgia looking at him, and the small smile on her lips warmed every other part of him.

## Chapter Nine

Since bringing the puppies home, Matt had more than a few moments when he wondered, *What the hell was I thinking?* When he saw Quinn and Shane fussing over Finnigan and Frederick, he understood that he had been thinking of this exact moment. Not that he'd brought the puppies home just to score points with the little boys, but he couldn't deny that their apparent affection for the animals had been a factor in his decision.

"A tree house and puppies," Georgia mused. "My kids are going to be spending more time in your backyard than their own."

"That's okay with me," he said, dropping his voice so that the boys couldn't hear him. "Especially if their mom comes with them."

She picked up Pippa, who had begun to fuss. "Are you flirting with me?"

"Obviously I'm not doing a very good job of it if you have to ask."

"I just don't know why you'd bother when you know I have no intention of getting involved with you."

"I know that's what you said," he acknowledged.

She lifted a brow. "You don't think I meant it?"

"I think I can change your mind."

"I think you should take the puppies and the boys outside while I clear up in here," she countered, in an obvious attempt to change the topic of conversation.

"Don't worry about clearing up, I'll take care of it later."

"Okay, then, why don't you take the puppies and boys outside so I can feed Pippa?"

And he finally grasped that she hadn't been trying to change the topic so much as she'd been trying to get him out of the house so she could have some privacy. Not that he had any objections to the sight of a woman nursing her child, but he understood that Georgia might be a little self-conscious about baring her breast in front of him, especially now that she knew he wanted her in his bed.

"Matt?" she prompted.

"Take the boys and puppies outside," he agreed. "I can do that."

So he did, and he sat on the deck watching as the boys and their canine companions ran and jumped and wrestled in the grass. He tried to remember what Liam had been like at the same age, then felt a pang deep in his heart when he recalled that his son had been gone from his life before he'd celebrated his third birthday.

Matt shoved the painful memories to the back of his mind. He'd spent far too much time wishing for what he'd lost and wondering what might have been. When he'd finally sold his condo and bought this house on Larkspur Drive, he'd promised himself that he was finished living in the past and vowed to focus on the future. Now he found himself hoping that his future might include his beautiful neighbor and her three kids.

But convincing Georgia that she wanted the same thing was going to take some work.

Much to Quinn's and Shane's disappointment, the puppies tired out long before they did.

"How come he doesn't wanna play with me no more?" Quinn asked, stroking the soft fur of the puppy that had fallen asleep in his lap.

"He's just tired out right now," Matt told him. "He's still just a baby, even younger than your sister."

"Are the puppies gonna wake you up at night?"

"I hope not," he said fervently.

"What if they do?" Quinn pressed, followed by Shane's question, "Are they gonna sleep in your bed?"

"No." His response to the latter question was firm.

"I'd let him sleep with me," Shane said. "If I had a puppy."

"I think your mom might have something to say about that," Matt told him.

"She lets me sleep in her bed when I have a bad dream," Quinn said.

Matt didn't think that excuse was going to get *him* access to Georgia's bed, but he hadn't given up hope that he would be there. Preferably sooner rather than later, because he was getting tired of cold showers.

"I wish I had a puppy," Shane said wistfully.

"A puppy's a lot of work," Matt told him. "And your mom already has a lot to do, taking care of you and your brother and your sister."

"I'd take care of the puppy. She wouldn't hafta do nothin'," Quinn vowed.

Matt couldn't help but smile in response to the fervent promise that countless boys had used on their mothers over the years—mostly ineffectively.

"I think you'd have a better chance of convincing your

mother if she saw you were willing to help out with Finnigan and Frederick every once in a while."

"I'll help every day," Quinn promised.

"Me, too," Shane chimed in.

"Well, you'll have to check with your mom on that," Matt told them. "But if you can, I'd appreciate it."

"Does that mean we're friends again?" Quinn asked.

Not too much surprised Matt, but this question did. "I didn't know we stopped being friends."

"You stopped coming over."

The little boy's matter-of-fact statement made him appreciate that you could fool some people some of the time, but you couldn't fool a four-year-old. Obviously Georgia wasn't the only member of the Reed family who had recognized his avoidance.

"There was a lot of stuff going on at the hospital," he hedged.

"Did you fix more broken arms?"

He nodded. "A couple of those. A broken femur—" he tapped the little boy's thigh "—that's the bone in there, a hip replacement, some knee arthroscopies."

"What's arrow-scope-peas?"

Matt smiled. "Arthroscopy," he said again, enunciating the word more carefully. "It's an operation that uses a tiny camera to see what's inside the joint so that the doctor can fix whatever's wrong through little cuts in the skin."

Quinn drew back in horror. "You cut people?"

"Only when necessary," Matt assured him.

"You didn't cut me," Shane said.

"Because the X-ray let me see that the bone was only broken, not out of position, so we just had to put a cast on your arm to make sure the bone wouldn't move before it was healed."

The little boy considered this explanation for a minute,

then he said, "Mommy says we can't go back in the tree house till my cast is gone."

"She's probably worried that you might fall again."

"Maybe you could talk to her," Quinn suggested hopefully. "She'd listen to you, 'cuz you're a doctor."

"Nice try, but doctor's orders do not override Mommy's rules," Georgia said, stepping out onto the deck.

Matt noticed that she'd strapped on the infant carrier again and Pippa, obviously sated and happy, was snuggled inside.

Quinn let out a long-suffering sigh. "It was worth a try."

"And you get an A for effort," she told him. "But you don't go back to the tree house until *I* say so."

Shane pouted silently.

"Now take the puppies inside," she said. "It's time for us to go home so that you guys can have a bath before bed."

"Don't wanna bath," Shane said.

"I know, because you're a four-year-old boy and dirt is your best friend, but you're going to have a bath anyway."

Shane shook his head. "Quinn's my best friend, and then Finnigan and Frederick."

"Then you shouldn't mind getting rid of the dirt," Georgia said dryly, while Matt tried not to laugh at the little boy's solemn statement.

Quinn stood up, careful not to disturb the sleeping puppy in his arms. "It's okay," he told his brother. "We can come back and see the puppies tomorrow. Dr. Matt said so."

"I said *if* it was okay with your mom," he interjected quickly, before Georgia had to remind her sons again about doctor's orders and Mommy's rules.

Shane looked up at her pleadingly. "Can we, Mommy?"

"We'll figure that out tomorrow."

Quinn's lower lip jutted out.

"But if that's not acceptable, I can say 'no' now," she suggested.

Matt had to admire the quickness with which the boy

sucked his lip back so that it was in a normal position again before she'd even finished speaking.

"I guess that's acceptable then?" she prompted.

Both boys nodded as they carried the puppies back into the house.

Georgia waited until they were out of earshot before she said, "It looks like we'll be seeing you tomorrow."

"I'm already looking forward to it."

He stayed out on the deck, watching as they made their way back to their own house and wishing that they could have stayed. Not just for a little bit longer, but maybe even forever. Because somehow, over the past few weeks, he'd fallen head over heels for Georgia and her three adorable children.

He winced as tiny claws pressed down on his bare foot. He glanced down to see Finnigan—or was it Frederick?—trying to climb up his leg, wanting some attention. He scooped the puppy up and tucked him into the crook of his arm. Almost as soon as he had done so, his canine sibling appeared.

As Matt retreated back into the house with the puppies in his arms, he was consoled by the fact that he wouldn't be completely alone tonight.

Georgia didn't get much sleep that night, and she couldn't even blame Pippa because her baby girl had actually slept for almost five hours straight. Unfortunately, even while Pippa was sleeping, Georgia was tossing and turning—thinking about Matt Garrett. *Wanting* Matt Garrett.

She wasn't used to having her hormones all stirred up, especially not by someone who wasn't her husband. She wasn't sure what to do about it, or even if she wanted to do anything at all.

Matt was stirring her up on purpose—of that she had no doubt. To an outside observer, his treatment of her had been nothing but circumspect throughout the evening. He certainly hadn't done anything obvious or inappropriate. But when he led her to the table, he placed a guiding hand at the small of her back. When he sat in his own chair, he let his knee brush against her legs. When he wanted to get her attention, he'd touch a hand to hers. And every single touch, no matter how brief or casual, made her pulse jolt and her body yearn.

She didn't know if her response was specific to her neighbor or just a symptom of the fact that she'd been celibate for so long. She suspected it was specific to Matt, because no one—before or since her marriage—had ever affected her the way he did, and she didn't have the first clue what to do about it.

She could sleep with him. That seemed the most obvious and simple answer. *If you have an itch, scratch it,* Charlotte was fond of saying. But Georgia and her mother often had differing philosophies.

And there were a lot of reasons for Georgia not to get involved with her neighbor—one of them being that he was her neighbor. If they hooked up and things didn't work out, she still had to live next door to him.

But the primary consideration was her three children. Not only did their presence complicate the situation and decrease the likelihood of finding any alone time, she had to consider how any kind of romantic involvement would affect them. She didn't doubt that Quinn and Shane would be in favor of a relationship between their mother and "Dr. Matt" because they loved hanging out with him. But if things didn't work out, how difficult would it be for them to lose that connection? They'd been devastated by Phillip's death. For weeks after the funeral, they'd been plagued by nightmares; and for several more months, they'd frequently awakened Georgia in the night just to make sure she wasn't dead, too. They'd already grown so close to Matt, and she couldn't imagine what another loss would do to them. And because she didn't know, she wouldn't let herself risk the possibility of starting something that might only end with heartbreak—for her children and herself.

But what if things *did* work out?

Georgia wasn't sure she was willing to consider that possibility; she didn't want to look too far ahead. She didn't want a relationship—even if she was increasingly tempted to explore the chemistry between them.

As for what Matt wanted...she wasn't entirely sure. He'd admitted that he was attracted to her, so she was pretty sure he would go along with the sex thing. She just didn't know what—if anything—he wanted beyond that.

But the more time that passed, the more she thought about him, the more she wanted him. For a lot more reasons than the fact that his proximity made her all hot and bothered.

He was a good man. She knew that not all doctors had chosen the profession for benevolent reasons. But she didn't doubt that Matt had. It was his nature to help people, whether that meant fixing a broken bone or performing lawn maintenance or late-night taxi service. She knew he wasn't perfect—if he was, he wouldn't still be single. And while she couldn't deny a fair amount of curiosity about his marriage and divorce, she didn't feel it was her place to ask when they weren't really anything more than neighbors—even if the air fairly crackled whenever they were together.

But the physical attraction aside, he was innately kind and considerate, and he was great with kids.

He paid attention to her children. He looked at them when they were talking to him, he listened and responded to what they said, and he seemed to genuinely enjoy being with them. That alone was almost enough for Georgia to fall in love with him.

And the knowledge that she could fall in love with him was what terrified her.

If she thought she could scratch the proverbial itch and be done with it, she might have been more willing to take that next step. But she worried that scratching would only make the itch more intense—because the more time she spent with Matt Garrett, the more she wanted to be with him.

It turned out that the answer to Quinn's question was a resounding yes—the puppies did wake Matt up in the night. Three times, in fact. And each time that he was up, he noticed that there was a light shining in Pippa's room, so he knew Georgia was up, too.

A couple of times, he saw her shadow through the curtains as she passed in front of the window. He could barely keep his eyes open on night one with the puppies, so he could only imagine how exhausted she must be after more than four months of sleepless nights.

When he'd asked, Georgia told him that Pippa was sleeping better and her bouts of fussiness were less frequent and intense. Since Matt couldn't hear the baby crying, he figured that was probably true, but he still didn't think Georgia was getting much sleep.

A suspicion that was proven by the shadows under her eyes when he knocked on her door late the following morning.

"I was just going to take Finn and Fred for a walk and thought the boys might want to come with me," he said.

"We want to," Quinn responded before his mother could.

"Pippa's just gone down for a nap," Georgia told him.

"Why don't you do the same?" Matt suggested.

"You're going to take two boys and two puppies by yourself?"

"Don't I look capable?"

"It's not your ability I doubt, it's your desire."

Even before his lips curved, her cheeks filled with color as she realized how her statement could be interpreted.

"I thought we answered that question definitively the other night," he teased.

"I meant your willingness to take a walk with two boys and two puppies."

"I'm willing—and capable," he assured her. "And we won't be gone too long."

She looked down at the hopeful faces of her sons. "Go get your shoes."

The twins raced down the hall to the closet, and Matt took advantage of their temporary absence to dip his head and kiss their mother. It was a brief touch, barely more than a brush of his lips against hers. Certainly not enough to satisfy him, but enough to thoroughly fluster Georgia.

Before she could say anything, the boys were back.

"We're ready," Quinn said.

Matt took each boy by the hand. "Then let's go get the puppies."

Georgia intended to take advantage of the boys' absence to get some work done. But after checking her email and replying to the messages that needed replies, she found herself struggling to concentrate. And it was Matt Garrett's fault—even when he wasn't around, she couldn't seem to get him out of her mind.

She'd always been extremely focused and never, in her entire life, had she let herself be so easily and completely distracted by a man. Not that she was "letting" herself be distracted now—she just couldn't stop thinking about him.

And it wasn't just because she had let the twins go off with him. In fact, she wasn't the least bit worried about her children with Matt, because he'd proven that he was more than capable of looking after the boys and she absolutely trusted that he would do so.

But while she wasn't worried about her children, she was worried about herself. Because somehow, Matt Garrett had taken hold of her heart and she didn't have the first clue what to do about it.

The slap of the screen door against its frame jolted her back to the present.

"Mommy?"

"In the dining room," she said.

Quinn raced into the room, his brother on his heels and Matt right behind them, looking completely at ease with her children—and far too handsome and sexy for her peace of mind.

"We tired the puppies out," her son told her proudly. "Dr. Matt had to carry them home 'cuz they were too tired to walk."

"Then you guys must be pretty tired, too," she said, ruffling her son's hair.

"Nuh-uh," Shane said. "We're goin' for ice cream."

She lifted a brow. "Ice cream?"

"You haven't heard of it?" Matt teased. "It's a frozen dairy dessert."

She rolled her eyes. "I've heard of it. In fact, I've actually tasted it once or twice before."

"But have you experienced the bliss of Walton's ice cream?"

Georgia shook her head, thinking that there were a lot of blisses she would willingly experience with this man.

"You haven't really had ice cream until you've had Walton's," he told her.

She forced herself to ignore the clamoring of her suddenly hyperactive hormones. "It's almost time for lunch." She felt compelled to point this out to all of them.

"Walk on the wild side," he suggested, "and eat your dessert first for a change."

The low, sexy tone of his voice raised goose bumps on her flesh, but she ignored the physiological response of her body and focused on more practical matters.

"If the boys have ice cream now, they won't eat their lunch."

"A kiddie cone," Matt cajoled.

"Pleeeease," Quinn and Shane chorused.

She believed it was important for the boys to understand that there were rules to follow, but she wasn't so rigid that she would never bend those rules. And though she was tempted to bend this time, she shook her head. "Pippa isn't up from her nap yet, and when she wakes up she's going to need to be changed and fed."

As if on cue, the sound of Pippa babbling and cooing came through the baby monitor.

"Pippa's up," Quinn told her.

"It sounds like she is," Georgia agreed.

"Ice cream?" Shane said hopefully.

"Let me take care of Pippa, and then we'll go for ice cream."

Because that was one blissful experience she could justify, but personal fantasies about the doctor next door she could not.

## *Chapter Ten*

When Matt had agreed to take the remaining two puppies from his brother, he'd worried about how much time and attention they would need. Luke had somehow convinced him that having two puppies would be less work than one because they would be company for one another and content to play together. After a few days, Matt had found that was generally true. He'd also discovered that Finnigan and Frederick were never happier than when they were playing with Quinn and Shane—and the twins seemed equally enamored of their furry friends.

It was, to Matt's mind, a win-win situation. Or maybe it was a win-win-win situation, because when the boys were hanging out with the puppies, it gave him an excuse to hang out with Georgia. Since keeping a distance hadn't stopped him from thinking about her, he'd abandoned his campaign of avoidance for a new tack—spend as much time with her as possible in the hope that she would want him as much as he wanted her.

He knew she wasn't there yet, but he knew she was thinking about him. He saw it in the awareness in her eyes when he touched her, heard it in the huskiness of her voice when he stood close, and he'd definitely tasted it in the sweet softness of her lips when he kissed her.

Yeah, she was thinking about him, and hopefully—with just a little bit of a nudge in the right direction—she would be thinking about a lot more.

As they made their way toward Walton's, Georgia carrying Pippa in her baby carrier and Matt pulling the twins in their wagon, he considered that today just might be the day to give her that nudge.

"How did I not know this place was here?" she wondered, taking in the long row of freezers, the candy toppings displayed in glass containers and the list of menu items that stretched across the long wall behind the counter.

"You're new in town," he noted.

And because it was her first visit, she took her time surveying the offerings while the boys raced back and forth, pointing out one flavor then another.

Matt gave her a few minutes before he asked, "What looks good to you?"

"Everything," she said, and then she sighed. "But I'm going to have to pass."

He shook his head. "You can't come into Walton's and walk away from the counter empty-handed."

"Is that written into the local bylaws?"

"If it's not, it should be," he told her.

"I followed your advice and cut out dairy and it seems to have helped alleviate some of Pippa's colic. So as tempted as I am, I'm not going to sacrifice my sleep for a brief taste of sinful decadence."

But he heard the regret in her voice, and couldn't resist teasing, "Sinful decadence is the best reason I can think of to sacrifice sleep—but I'm not talking about ice cream."

The flush in her cheeks confirmed that she knew what he was talking about. "These days, I'm not sacrificing my sleep for *anything*."

He just grinned and turned her toward the freezer on the other side of the counter. "Nondairy sorbets."

She nibbled on her bottom lip, obviously tempted, as was he—but not for ice cream.

He might have been teasing when he'd responded to her comment about sinful decadence, but his desire for her was very real. There were all kinds of deliciously sinful things he wanted to do to her body, all kinds of decadent pleasures he wanted to share with her.

"The orange mango looks really good," Georgia finally said. "But so does the piña colada…and the raspberry…and the lemon lime."

"Raspberry gets my vote," Matt told her. "Or you could go for the sampler bowl and try three different flavors."

She shook her head. "I'll stick with the orange mango for today. I have a feeling the boys are going to want to come back here on a regular basis."

Matt ordered an orange mango cone for her and a raspberry for himself, while Georgia tried to help the boys narrow down their choices. Through the bits and pieces of conversation that he overheard, it sounded as if Quinn was vacillating between chocolate chip cookie dough, chocolate fudge brownie and chocolate peanut butter cup. Apparently the kid really liked chocolate. Surprisingly, Shane seemed to have already made up his mind.

"Two kiddie cones," Georgia finally told the teen behind the counter. "One chocolate peanut butter cup and one vanilla."

*Vanilla?* To Matt's way of thinking, that was almost as bad as not having any ice cream at all.

"Wait." He held up a hand to the server and turned his attention to Shane. "Vanilla? Really?"

Shane looked down at his feet, but he nodded.

"That's your absolute favorite flavor?"

"I like 'nilla," he said. But the quiet statement was hardly a rousing endorsement.

"Better than cotton candy or bubble gum or—" Matt looked at the Kids' Favorites labels "—superhero or alien invasion?"

*That* got the kid's attention.

Shane lifted his head. "What's alien 'vasion?"

Matt boosted him up so that he could see into the freezer case.

"It's lime sherbet with blueberry swirl and fruit juice gummies," the server said, then winked at Shane. "And one of my favorites."

The little boy nibbled on his bottom lip, considering.

"You want to give it a try or do you want to stick with vanilla?" Matt challenged.

The server scooped a tiny spoon into the bin and offered Shane a taste.

He looked to his mother for permission before accepting the spoon and cautiously sliding it between his lips. He hesitated for another minute, then pointed to the green ice cream. "That one. Please."

They decided to eat inside in the hope that Quinn and Shane might be able to finish their cones before they melted. Georgia seemed worried that, despite the sample, Shane would change his mind about alien invasion. But after a few more tentative licks, he pronounced it "the best ice cream ever" and she finally turned her attention to her sorbet—and had Matt's attention completely riveted on her.

Quinn gobbled his ice cream, as if he was afraid someone might try to take it from him. Shane—happy to have broadened his flavor horizons—worked at his cone methodically and steadily. Georgia savored every lick, closing her eyes and humming in appreciation as the sorbet melted on her tongue.

She somehow turned the consumption of a single scoop of sorbet into a blissful, sensual experience, making Matt wonder: If she was this passionate about dessert, how much passion would she exhibit in the bedroom?

"Doncha like it?"

Shane's question snapped Matt out of his reverie and back to the present.

"'Cuz you can share mine if you don't like yours," the little boy offered.

Matt shook his head. "Thanks, but I think I'll leave it up to you to gobble up all the alien invaders."

Shane smiled at that and took a bite of his cone.

The boys finished quickly—probably because they had as much ice cream on their hands and faces as in their bellies, the result of Quinn deciding to dig a peanut butter cup out of his cone in exchange for one of the gummy aliens from his brother's—and Georgia sent them to the washroom to clean up.

Though he knew it would only increase his own torture, he convinced Georgia to sample his raspberry, and nearly groaned aloud as he watched the tip of her tongue lap delicately at the sorbet. But when he tried to finagle a taste of her orange mango, she refused.

"You said the raspberry's the best," she explained. "Which implies that you've already tried every flavor."

It was true, but her obvious enjoyment of the orange mango made him suspect that it might taste better than he'd remembered. But since she wasn't sharing, he leaned over and touched his mouth to hers.

"Mmm." He swiped his tongue over her bottom lip. "Maybe that is better than the raspberry."

She drew back and when he shifted, as if to kiss her again, she stuck the cone between them to keep him at a distance.

He nibbled at her sorbet; she narrowed her gaze.

"You think you're clever, don't you? Tricking me into letting you taste my sorbet."

"The sorbet was my consolation prize—what I really wanted was a taste of you."

"You got that, too, didn't you?"

His gaze dropped to her mouth. "Not nearly enough."

Georgia and Matt finished their cones and they headed back outside. Pippa was still comfortably snuggled in her baby carrier, so as soon as the boys had climbed back into their wagon, they were ready to head out. She automatically reached for the handle of the wagon, only to find that Matt had beat her to it.

He kept telling her that she didn't have to do everything on her own, and Georgia was starting to believe it. But as nice as it was to have someone around who was willing to lend a helping hand, Matt had done so much for her already and Georgia didn't want to let herself rely on him too much.

She'd always prided herself on her independence. If she didn't count on anyone else, then she wouldn't ever be disappointed. But she found that she was starting to depend on Matt, not just because he helped her out in so many ways, but for his company and conversation. She liked having him around, just knowing he was there.

And the more time she spent with Matt, the more that growing attachment concerned her. And it wasn't only her own feelings that she was worried about.

"You're awfully quiet," Matt noted. "Something on your mind?"

She shook her head, unwilling to admit that *he* was the reason for her preoccupation. But after a moment, she realized there was something else bothering her, too.

"Shane always has vanilla," she said.

"Did I overstep by suggesting that he try something different?"

She shook her head again. "No. I'm just surprised that he was willing. His dad was strictly a vanilla guy," she admitted. "And I think one of the reasons Shane always had vanilla was a subconscious attempt to be more like his dad."

That maybe having something in common would cause Phillip to pay more attention to him. But of course she didn't say that part out loud. "He's always been so painfully shy, so much quieter than Quinn. Part of it, I suspect, is being Quinn's brother. My sister likes to joke that Shane doesn't talk much because he never has a chance to get a word in edgewise."

Matt glanced back at the wagon, where Quinn was entertaining his brother with a running commentary of one thing or another. "There might be something to that theory," he mused.

"Maybe," she acknowledged with a smile. "But he's talked more to you in the past three weeks than he's talked to anyone else in the past three months."

"Is that good or bad?" he asked cautiously.

"It's good." Now she looked over her shoulder at the boys in the wagon. "Spending time with you has been good for both of them."

"And yet you say that as if it's a bad thing," he noted.

She sighed. "I just don't want them to start expecting too much, depending on you."

"Because I'm not dependable?"

"Because they're not your responsibility."

"Why does it have to be about responsibility?" he demanded. "Why can't I just hang out with you and your kids because I enjoy hanging out with you and your kids?"

"You're twisting everything around," she protested.

He paused in the middle of the sidewalk. "*I'm* twisting things around?"

"Yes. I'm just trying to establish some boundaries—"

"And every time you throw up boundaries, you only tempt me to breach them," he warned, deliberately dropping his gaze to her mouth so she knew that he was thinking about kissing her again.

Georgia had spent more than enough time remembering every minute detail of their first kiss and, with her lips still tingling from the much briefer but more recent kiss in the ice cream parlor, she decided it would be smart to heed his warning.

"I'll keep that in mind," she promised.

Satisfied by her response, he started walking again.

Georgia fell into step beside him, as baffled as she was intrigued by this man. But it was a nice day for a walk, so she tried to concentrate on the scenery rather than her frustrating neighbor.

She'd always scoffed at the idea that people moved faster in the city. Life in New York hadn't seemed so fast when she was moving at the same frenetic pace as everyone else. Whenever she and Phillip had gone out anywhere, they'd rushed to the subway so the underground train could whisk them to their destination. They'd always been in a hurry to get where they were going. As odd as it seemed, she couldn't even remember just taking a leisurely stroll with her husband.

For a lot of reasons, she'd been reluctant to leave Manhattan. She hadn't wanted to take the boys away from everything familiar, but she'd felt so isolated and alone in the city. Maybe Phillip hadn't been a very hands-on dad, but he'd at least been there so she wasn't completely on her own. When he'd died, she'd become painfully aware of how truly alone she was. And with three-and-a-half-year-old twins and another baby on the way, she'd also felt completely overwhelmed.

When Charlotte left for Vegas, Georgia had been alone again, although not for long. Matt had moved in next door and suddenly she had a neighbor, a friend, a confidante… and maybe even more.

And she wanted more, even if she wasn't ready to admit it.

For the past year, she'd focused on being a mother to the exclusion of almost everything else. Being with Matt made her remember that she was a woman, with a woman's wants and needs.

She just hadn't yet figured out what, if anything, she was going to do about those wants and needs.

Five days later, Georgia still didn't have any answers. Since four of those days had been Matt's days at the hospital, she didn't see much of him. It was just like the man to get her all stirred up and then disappear, and she didn't doubt for a single minute that he'd done it on purpose. He was giving her time to think, to wonder, to want. She could no longer deny that she wanted.

But while she'd spent the better part of four days thinking about Matt, he'd apparently been busy planning a party, because when she took the boys outside late Saturday afternoon, there was quite a crowd gathered on his back deck. Even from a distance, she recognized both of his brothers and a woman that she thought might have been Kelsey, but most of the other guests were unfamiliar.

"Finnigan and Frederick are out," Quinn said, already heading in that direction.

Georgia caught his arm just before he raced past her. "I know you want to see the puppies but you can't just go over to someone else's house uninvited."

"Dr. Matt said we could go anytime," Quinn reminded her.

"I know that's what he said, but he has other company today and it isn't polite to intrude."

"I don't wanna be polite," her son protested. "I wanna see Finn."

She had to fight against a smile. No matter his faults, at least he was honest.

"I'm sure you'll see Finn tomorrow, and the day after that, and the day—"

"I wanna see him today!"

And apparently the puppy wanted to see him, too, because before Georgia could admonish her son, the puppy came tearing across the grass, racing as fast as his little legs could carry him. As usual, Fred was right behind him, neck-in-neck with a third puppy.

"Look, Mommy." Shane's eyes were wide. "Finn and Fred have a friend."

"I'm thinking he might actually be another brother," Georgia said.

Finnigan and Frederick were ecstatic to be reunited with their pint-sized playmates, and they jumped and danced around the twins while their companion went exploring. He put his nose deep in the grass and followed a trail—directly to Pippa's blanket.

Georgia watched as the baby and puppy eyed one another. Pippa lifted a hand, as if to touch him, and the puppy pulled back, out of reach. She dropped her hand, he moved closer, sniffed her face, then swiped his tongue across her chin. Pippa giggled.

The puppy licked her again; the baby giggled some more.

And then a strong arm reached down and scooped the puppy up and away. Pippa tipped her head up, wondering where her furry friend had disappeared to, and smiled when she saw him wriggling in Luke Garrett's hold.

"I'm so sorry," Matt's brother apologized. "I didn't think he would venture too far—or so quickly."

"No worries," Georgia assured him. "And he might not have ventured this way on his own, but he followed Finn and Fred."

"I should have been keeping a closer eye on him, so he didn't slobber all over your child."

She shrugged. "A little doggy spit never hurt anyone."

"I wish you could tell that to my date from last night."

Georgia's brows lifted. "She had a different opinion?"

"Oh, yeah," he told her. "When I took her back to my place after dinner—"

She held up a hand. "I'm not sure I want to follow wherever you're going with this."

Luke grinned. "Strictly *G*-rated. All that happened was Einstein licked her hand—not even her face, just her hand. And just once. And she jumped up screaming 'I've got dog germs' like Lucy in the old cartoons."

She couldn't help but smile at the image his words evoked. "First question—how did you end up dating a woman who doesn't like animals?"

"It was a blind date," he said. "I didn't know she didn't like animals."

She didn't even ask about the fact that he'd taken a woman, on a first date, back to his place. Obviously a lot of things had changed since the last time she'd been on a first date. Instead, she said, "Second question—Einstein?"

He sighed. "Because he's not."

"Having a little trouble training him?"

"More than a little," he admitted. "I have never met an animal so determined not to do what he's told."

"Wait until you have kids."

He shook his head. Emphatically.

"Not that I dislike kids," he hastened to explain. "And yours are great. I just don't see myself as a father—not anytime in the near future, anyway."

"That's because he's still a kid himself," Matt said.

Georgia hadn't seen her neighbor approach, and her heart gave a little jolt when he winked at her now. And she wasn't the only female affected—Pippa's eyes lit up and she gave him a gummy smile.

Matt picked up the little girl, who settled comfortably in his embrace, and Georgia realized that her boys weren't the only ones getting attached to "Dr. Matt." And she wondered again how it was that a man who so obviously doted upon children didn't have half a dozen kids of his own.

"Undeniably," his brother admitted with a grin.

"Then I would guess that's a family trait," Georgia noted. "As common as the broad shoulders and brown hair."

"We're not as similar as people think," Luke denied. "Matt's the smart one, Jack's the charming one, *I'm* the good-looking one."

She chuckled at that. "I think you all got more than your fair share of brains, charisma and looks."

"And they're all heartbreakers," Kelsey warned, joining their conversation.

Matt tugged on the end of her ponytail. "Don't you be telling tales out of school," he warned.

"I wouldn't dream of it," she said sweetly. Then she spotted the puppy in the crook of Luke's arm. "Ohmygoodness— he is such a sweetie."

"You had your chance to take one," the vet told her.

"I've already taken enough animals off of your hands," she retorted, stealing the puppy from him—at least for the minute. "Is this one Finnigan or Frederick?"

"That one's Einstein," Luke said.

"He's sooo adorable." She tore her gaze away from the puppy for a minute to explain to Georgia, "Brittney was dying to see Uncle Matt's puppies, so I brought her over and crashed the party."

"It isn't a party," Matt protested.

"Tell that to the dozen other people hanging out on your back deck."

"I didn't invite any of those people," he denied.

"I did," Luke admitted. "Think of it as an impromptu housewarming."

Georgia glanced over at Matt's deck. "None of those people look like Brittney."

"She's in the house, on the phone with her ex-boyfriend, attempting to remind him of the 'ex' part," Kelsey told her.

Georgia winced. "That's awkward."

"Yeah. Almost as awkward as not inviting your neighbor

to a backyard barbecue," she said with a pointed glance in Matt's direction.

"I would have invited my neighbor if I'd been planning a barbecue," he retorted, before turning to Georgia to say, "Apparently I'm hosting an unplanned barbecue."

"Apparently," she agreed, trying to hold back a smile.

"So—" he nudged her playfully, caused tingles to dance down her spine and toward all of her erogenous zones "—do you want to come over for a burger?"

When he looked at her the way he was looking at her now, she was almost ready to admit that she wanted a lot more than a burger. But she wasn't going to get into that kind of conversation in front of his family and friends.

Instead, she forced herself to match his casual tone and said, "Yes, I think I do."

He held her gaze for another minute, then turned to call out to Shane and Quinn. "Come on, boys. Let's go get lunch."

## *Chapter Eleven*

The twins were racing across the yard before Matt finished speaking.

"I remember when Brittney was that young—and that active—and wishing I could figure out a way to bottle that energy," Kelsey said to Georgia.

"I wish the same thing," she agreed. "Every single day."

Matt wanted to be part of her every single day—to share the joys and responsibilities of raising a family with her. But as much as he wanted it, the prospect also scared the hell out of him.

After the failure of his marriage, he'd thought he might never heal, and he'd vowed that he would never give his heart to anyone again. Somehow, over the past few weeks, Georgia and her kids had stolen it away from him. And he didn't know whether to be frustrated or grateful that she didn't seem to have a clue.

Luke's elbow jamming into his ribs severed his wayward

thoughts. "Since you've got your arms full of adoring female, I'll take Finn and Fred back to the house."

Matt nodded and glanced down at the little girl in his arms. He didn't know if she was adoring, but she was absolutely adorable, and gazing up at him with big blue eyes just like her mother's. And just like her mother, she had firmly taken hold of his heart.

Luke and Kelsey headed back across the yard with the puppies, while Georgia gathered up Pippa's supplies. By the time she and Matt made their way across the yard, Jack had the food line moving. Hot dogs and hamburgers were available at the barbecue and an assortment of potluck dishes were set out on the picnic table. Brittney—having finally ended her conversation with Brayden—held Shane's plate so that he could load it up. Like his brother, he opted for the hot dog with a side of macaroni salad and homemade baked beans.

"Beans are awesome!" Quinn declared. "They make you fart real loud!"

Though everyone chuckled—even Adam, the baker of the beans—Matt saw the color rise in Georgia's cheeks, the natural blush making her eyes look even bluer than usual and somehow more beautiful.

By the time she settled Pippa in her bouncy chair and they joined the food line, the boys were half finished with their meals. Matt introduced Georgia to various guests who passed by: Adam Webber and Melanie Quinlan; Tyler Sullivan; Tyler's brother, Mason, and Mason's wife, Zoe, and their kids; Gage and Megan Richmond and their three-year-old son, Marcus.

"And there's Megan's sister—"

"I'm never going to remember everyone," Georgia warned him.

"—Ashley Turcotte and her husband, Cameron."

But she smiled as the couple drew nearer. "I'll remember those names, because Dr. Turcotte is our new family doctor."

"I'm only a doctor when I'm wearing the white coat," Cameron said, protesting her use of his formal title.

"Or when there's a scraped knee in the vicinity," his wife added, offering her hand.

"I'm Georgia Reed."

"The city girl with the three kids who moved in next to Dr. Garrett," Ashley noted.

"He moved in next to me," Georgia pointed out, with just a hint of exasperation in her tone.

The other woman chuckled. "I know, but the rumor mill always orbits around the locals."

"Which is just one more reason to be glad you're an import," Matt told her. Then, to Ashley, "Where are Maddie and Alyssa?"

"Our daughters discovered your tree house."

"Have they eaten?" Cameron asked.

"Maddie said that they needed to go exploring to work up an appetite first," his wife explained.

"Those are my boys," Georgia told Ashley, pointing out the twins who were seated on a blanket with Brittney. "They always seem to have an appetite."

"But their mom needs to eat, too," Matt said, nudging Georgia toward the barbecue where Jack had a long-handled spatula in one hand and his own burger in the other.

"Make sure you try Zoe's broccoli salad," Ashley advised.

Matt and Georgia loaded up their plates and found a couple of empty chairs near Brittney and the twins. A few minutes later, Kelsey and her husband, Ian, joined them. And when everyone had a plate, Jack finally abandoned the grill and came over.

"Hey, Britt, I heard Matt talked you into playing on our softball team for the Fourth of July tournament," he said.

"Despite my protests and against my better judgment," she said. "Which I'll remind you again when I strike out for the umpteenth time."

"We've got three weeks to practice—we'll get you hitting the ball," he said confidently.

The teen shook her head. "I really suck, Uncle Jack."

"I'm sure you're not that bad." Kelsey tried to assure her daughter.

"Actually she is," Luke said, dropping onto the blanket beside the twins.

Brittney wadded up her napkin to throw it at him—and missed her target by a mile.

He winked at her. "Thanks for proving my point."

"You can show her how it's done at practice tomorrow," Matt told his brother.

"Three o'clock at the park," Jack confirmed.

"There's swings at the park," Shane said.

"And monkey bars!" Quinn added.

"Do you guys want to go to the park?" Brittney asked.

They both nodded enthusiastically.

She looked at their mother. "Do you mind if I take them over there for a while?"

"They would be thrilled and I would be grateful," Georgia told her.

"Why don't we round up all the kids and I'll go with you?" Luke offered. He looked at Jack, as if he expected to rope him into babysitting duty, too.

Jack shook his head. "I'm going to check the food supply, make sure no one goes hungry."

Ian stood up. "Actually, I could go for another burger."

"Me, too," Matt said, then he turned to Georgia. "Do you want anything?"

"Brittney to live with me so she can keep the boys entertained 24/7?" she asked hopefully.

"You'll have to talk to her mother about that," he said, heading back toward the barbecue.

Georgia turned to see Kelsey was already shaking her head. "Sorry, but Northeastern has dibs."

"But not until September, right?"

"Not until September," she agreed, then sighed. "Damn, I'm going to miss her."

"I can imagine," Georgia admitted. "The boys are only starting kindergarten in the fall, but already I'm thinking about how quiet the house will seem when they're at school."

"Don't blink," Kelsey warned. "Because before you know it, they'll be packing their bags for college."

Georgia watched the boys, each one holding on to one of Brittney's hands, with a trail of other kids behind them. They were in their glory, not just because they had Brittney's attention but because there were other kids to play with, too.

"I'm not accustomed to anything like this," she told Kelsey.

"Like what?"

"Big, noisy get-togethers. Growing up, it was just my mom and my sisters and I. Obviously, I didn't know what I was missing."

"You mean the chaos and confusion?" Kelsey teased.

Georgia smiled. "No, that came along with the twins. What I meant was the camaraderie, and the sense of comfort that comes from knowing that there's always someone there. Matt and his brothers might argue and tease one another mercilessly, but there's no doubt that each one would go to the wall for the others."

"And they have," Kelsey confirmed. "You don't have that kind of relationship with your sisters?"

Georgia shook her head. "Maybe it's geography—I'm here, Virginia's in Texas and Indy's in Alaska."

"That's a lot of distance," the other woman noted.

"I sometimes wonder if we went our separate ways because we never had a sense of belonging anywhere."

"It makes a difference," Kelsey agreed. "Matt and Jack and Luke all went away to school, but they all came back to Pinehurst in the end."

"How about you?" Georgia asked.

The other woman shook her head. "My sister was the one with wanderlust. I never wanted to be anywhere else."

"I had mixed feelings about moving to Pinehurst after my husband died. But now, I'm so glad that I did. This is what I want for my children—a home in a community where everyone looks out for their neighbors."

"Is that a diplomatic way of saying 'where everyone butts into everyone else's business'?"

"That thought never once crossed my mind."

Kelsey laughed, because she saw right through the lie. "So tell me, now that you've accepted we're all busybodies, what has Matt said or done that has you worried?"

Georgia wasn't usually the type to confide in a woman she barely knew, but she didn't know many people in Pinehurst and she desperately needed someone to talk to. And Kelsey seemed a more logical choice than the elderly Mrs. Dunford.

"He kissed me," she admitted.

"And that surprised you?"

"Maybe not the kiss itself," she admitted. "But the intensity of it."

"Matt's never been the type to do anything by half measures," Kelsey said. Then, after a beat, she asked, "How was it?"

Just the memory of that kiss had Georgia's blood humming. "Beyond spectacular."

The other woman grinned. "Go Matt."

"That's the problem," Georgia said. "I don't know if I'm ready for this…attraction…to go anywhere."

"You're deluding yourself if you think you can stop it."

Georgia frowned at that.

"You're thinking about the kids," Kelsey guessed. "'What if I get involved with this guy and things don't work out?'"

She nodded, surprised that a woman she barely knew could be so attuned to her thoughts and concerns. Except that Kelsey was a mother, too, so maybe it wasn't surprising at all.

"Pippa's probably young enough that you don't have to worry about her too much, but the boys are already looking at Matt as if the sun rises and sets in him, and what will happen if things don't work out and he's not part of their lives anymore?"

She blew out a breath. "You're good at this."

Kelsey shrugged. "I'm a student of human nature—and I can see the situation a little more clearly because I'm not personally involved.

"I can also tell you," she continued, "that Matt isn't the type of guy to play fast and loose with anyone's heart. Despite my teasing, he wouldn't have invited you here tonight, with his family and his friends, if this wasn't where he wanted you to be."

"Or maybe he just figured I'd be less likely to complain about the music if I was invited to the party."

"You really don't see it, do you?"

"See what?" she asked warily.

"How completely smitten he is."

"He's been a good friend—"

Kelsey snorted.

"—and he's absolutely terrific with the kids."

"I've never known a man better suited to being a father or more deserving of a family," the other woman said. "Which is why I know Matt would never risk everything we just talked about if he wasn't sure he wanted a future with you."

"I think you might be reading too much into the situation."

Kelsey just smiled. "He already loves your kids, Georgia. When are you going to figure out that he's more than halfway in love with you, too?"

"No." She shook her head. "Now you're definitely reading too much into things."

"And that instinctive panicked reaction is probably why he hasn't told you how he feels," Kelsey said.

Then she gathered up the empty plates and headed up to the house, leaving Georgia alone to think about what she'd said.

She decided that just because Kelsey and Matt were good friends didn't mean that the other woman knew what was in his heart. Certainly he'd never given any indication that he was "halfway in love" with her, or even "completely smitten." Sure, he flirted with her, and he'd kissed her once—okay, a few times, but the more recent kisses had been too quick to really count, even if she'd felt tingles all the way down to her toes—but he hadn't given any indication he wanted to take things any further than that.

She wanted to put Kelsey's words out of her mind, but her gaze kept zeroing in on Matt as she watched him mingle with his friends, and she couldn't help but admire his easy manner. She also couldn't help but admire the way his shorts hugged his spectacular backside, and felt that now-familiar throbbing in her veins. There was no doubt about it, Matt Garrett was a fine specimen of masculinity.

It was only Pippa's fussing that succeeded in tearing her attention away from the doctor next door, and she ducked into the house to find a private corner to nurse her. When the baby was finally sated, Georgia rejoined the group that had gathered on Matt's back deck. With all the other kids at the park with Brittney and Luke, Pippa was the star attraction, and she was happy to let herself be passed from one set of arms to another, charming all with her big blue eyes and even bigger smile.

Georgia was chatting to Adam Webber—a fifth-grade teacher at the school the boys would be attending in the fall—when Matt made his way back to her. Adam, catching a look from the host, excused himself to grab another drink. When he did, Matt stepped into the space his friend had vacated and slipped an arm around Georgia's waist.

She eyed him warily. "You're going to give your friends the wrong idea about us."

He nuzzled her ear, and she couldn't quite suppress the delicious shiver that skated down her spine. "I'm trying to give you the *right* idea about us."

"You haven't listened to anything I've said, have you?"

"I've listened to a lot of things you've said," he countered. "But all your protests about not wanting to get involved can't override how right you feel in my arms. Or the fact that your body's instinctive reactions contradict your verbal responses."

She just sighed. "I don't know what to do about you."

"I have a few ideas," he teased. "But I'm not sure you're ready to hear them just yet."

"We're *friends*," she said firmly.

"Believe me, I'm feeling very friendly right now."

She shook her head, but she couldn't help smiling. "You are far too charming for your own good."

"The Garrett curse," he lamented.

"I'll bet it is."

Somehow, Georgia was still there when the rest of Matt's guests had cleared out. The twins had played for hours outside—first with the puppies, then at the park with Brittney and the other kids, then with the puppies again—until they were as tired out as their four-legged friends. Georgia had wanted to take them home to get them ready for bed, but they'd balked at that idea. When Matt suggested they could go inside to watch TV, they'd jumped all over that offer with both feet.

Pippa was awake again, but happily playing with the soft toys attached to her bouncy chair. Her fussy nights finally seemed to be a thing of the past, for which Georgia was immensely grateful. But while Georgia was getting more sleep, she wasn't feeling any more rested because her sleep continued to be disturbed by erotic dreams starring one very handsome doctor.

"I didn't think they would ever leave," Matt said, as the last car pulled out of the driveway.

"You have an interesting group of friends," she noted. "Have you known them all very long?"

"Most of us go back to grade school," he admitted.

"Really?"

"Why do you sound so incredulous? You must keep in touch with friends you went to school with."

She shook her head. "There were too many schools to keep track from one year to the next. In fact, it was rare for me to walk out of class in June at the same school I'd started in September."

"Was your father in the military?"

"No, my mother was following her bliss."

"Really?"

"She's settled down in recent years—or so I thought until I got the phone call informing me that she'd found husband number five."

"Where's your dad?" Matt wondered.

"Somewhere in Atlanta."

"Is that why you're named Georgia?"

She nodded. "And I have a half sister named Virginia and another half sister named Indy."

"Short for Indiana?" he guessed.

"No, she was actually named for the Indy race circuit. Her father was a member of one of the pit crews and we traveled so much from track to track that summer, Charlotte couldn't be sure whether the baby had been conceived in Wisconsin or Iowa, so she decided to go with Indy."

He smiled. "A good choice, considering the other options."

She nodded her agreement. "Charlotte always said the only

crime in life is in not following your heart wherever it wants to lead."

"And you disapprove of that philosophy?" he guessed.

"I didn't see that following her heart ever led to anything more than heartache."

"Did you never follow yours?"

She glanced away. "I believe the desires of the heart need to be balanced against the reason of the mind."

"How long did it take you to balance the desires of your heart with the reason of your mind when your husband proposed?" he teased.

"He never actually proposed."

"He never proposed?" Now Matt was the one who sounded incredulous.

"The topic of marriage came up in conversation and we decided it was what we both wanted, so we got married. The formalities weren't as important as being together to either of us."

He shook his head. "Next you're going to tell me that you got married at city hall."

"What's wrong with that?"

"Not a thing—if that's what you wanted," he said.

She'd told herself that it was, that she didn't need a white dress or a bouquet of flowers. She wasn't the type to be influenced by romantic trappings or swayed by amorous words. She wasn't like her mother.

But there had been a few occasions—usually other people's weddings—when she found herself wishing they'd done things a little differently. Not that she'd ever admitted it to anyone, and she wasn't going to do so now. Instead, she stood up. "I should check on the kids."

She'd set the twins up in the living room to watch a program on the Discovery Channel, but now they were both fast asleep.

"I hope this isn't a premonition," she murmured to Matt, who had followed her into the house.

"Of what?"

"Their attention span for educational instruction. I don't want them falling asleep in class when they start kindergarten in September."

"I don't think you need to worry. They just crashed because they had an incredibly busy day."

She nodded, acknowledging the point. "But regardless of how exhausted they were, if I'd put cartoons on TV, they'd still be awake."

"Which is obviously why you didn't put cartoons on."

But now that they were asleep, she was second-guessing her choice. Because Quinn and Shane were supposed to be her chaperones, and she was suddenly conscious of being *un*-chaperoned with her sexy neighbor. "I should get them home."

"You're going to wake them up to take them home so they can go to sleep?"

"They should be in their beds," she insisted.

"They seem comfortable enough," he noted.

Looking at her boys cuddled up with the puppies, Georgia couldn't disagree. But that didn't make her any less uneasy.

They moved into the kitchen, where their conversation wouldn't disturb the kids, and Matt said, "I should have considered that you might be tired. How are you holding up?"

"I didn't do anything all day. Your brother cooked the burgers, your friends supplied the rest of the food, Brittney occupied the boys, and everyone else took turns with the baby." She looked up at him and smiled. "In fact, I was thinking we should do it again tomorrow."

The implication of her words registered too late, and she immediately tried to backtrack.

"I didn't mean to imply... I mean, I don't expect you to spend all of your free time hanging out with me and my kids,"

Matt just shook his head. "When are you going to figure out that I like hanging out with you and your kids?"

"It's starting to sink in," she told him.

"Maybe this will help," he said, and lowered his mouth to hers.

## *Chapter Twelve*

Matt prided himself on being a patient man. When he'd decided that he wanted Georgia—about three minutes after their first meeting—he'd accepted that it would probably take her some time to come to the same realization. He also figured there was no harm in nudging her in that direction.

He braced his hands on the counter, bracketing her between them, and brushed his lips over hers softly, slowly. Her eyes fluttered, closed. He traced the shape of her mouth with just the tip of his tongue. She breathed out a sigh.

Apparently she didn't need as much nudging as he'd anticipated, because when he swept along the seam of her lips, they parted willingly. His hands moved from the counter to her hips; her palms slid over his chest, her hands linking behind his neck.

He deepened the kiss, stroking the inside of her mouth with his tongue. He didn't demand a response but coaxed it from her. Their tongues danced together in a sensual rhythm of advance and retreat that had all the blood rushing from his head. Part of him felt as if he could go on kissing her for hours, but another part refused to be satisfied with kissing.

His hands moved up her rib cage, over her breasts. She moaned and pressed closer. This was exactly how he wanted her—warm and willing in his arms. His hands curved around her bottom, pulling her tight against him. He was rock hard and aching with wanting her, and she was rubbing against him, her movements so natural and sensual she nearly pushed him to the brink.

Determined to regain control of the situation, he eased his lips from hers to trail kisses across her jaw, down her throat. He nipped at the nape of her neck, and she shuddered against him. His tongue traced over her collarbone, then along the edge of the lacy cup of her bra. Her skin was so soft, her breasts so perfect and round, and when he nuzzled the hollow between them, he could feel her heart racing.

He brushed his thumbs over her nipples, and she shuddered again. But when he reached for the clasp at the front of her bra, she pushed his hand away, shaking her head.

Reminding himself that he'd promised to be patient, he didn't push back. Instead, he cupped her face in his hands.

"What are you afraid of, Georgia?"

"I'm not sure," she admitted.

"I'm not going to push for more than you're ready to give," he promised.

Her smile was wry. "Maybe that's what I'm afraid of. Because there's a pretty big disparity between what my body wants and what my brain is thinking."

He brushed his lips against hers. "Would it be wrong for me to encourage you to listen to your body?"

"Believe me, my hormones are clamoring loudly enough without any encouragement."

"At least you're no longer trying to deny the chemistry between us."

"That would be hypocritical, considering the way I was pressed up against you less than a minute ago."

"I liked the way you were pressed up against me," he assured her. "In fact, feel free to press up against me anytime."

She shook her head. "That was a temporary state of mindlessness induced by an overload of hormones after more than a year of celibacy."

"Is that what you think it was?" He had to fight to keep his voice level, his tone casual. "Just a combination of factors that really had nothing to do with you and me?"

Her gaze shifted away. "It seems like the most reasonable explanation."

"Then let's be unreasonable," he suggested, and lowered his head again to nibble on her bottom lip.

His efforts were rewarded by a soft moan low in her throat.

"I can be unreasonable," she agreed.

Which sounded like a green light to Matt.

He allowed his hands to stroke over her shoulders, down her arms, while he continued to kiss her. Deeply. Hungrily. And she responded with equal passion.

His hand slipped down the front of her shorts, dipped inside her panties. She gasped as his fingers sifted through the soft curls in search of her womanly core. He had to bite back his own moan when he found her hot and wet and oh-so-ready.

He slid a finger deep inside of her, and let his thumb zero in on the tiny nub of her most sensitive erogenous zone. She moaned again but made no protest as he slowly and inexorably coaxed her closer and closer to the pinnacle of her pleasure.

She was mindless now, writhing and panting. He didn't disagree that hormones played a role in what was happening here, but he knew that it was more than that. And he wanted more than hot, meaningless sex—he wanted intimacy. From the first, he'd sensed that deeper level of connection with Georgia, and he'd be damned if he'd let her dismiss what was between them as nothing more than a transitory urge.

He slid his finger in again, then two fingers. In and out, deeper and faster now, while his thumb continued to stroke her nub. He felt the clamp of her inner muscles around his fingers in the exact moment that her teeth sank into his bottom lip, the unexpected shock of erotic pleasure nearly bringing him to climax. He clamped his other arm around her waist, holding on to her, while the shudders racked her body.

She eased her lips from his and dropped her head against his chest. But several minutes passed before she said anything, and then it was only, "Oh. My. Wow."

He managed to smile, though his own body was screaming for its own release. And when she reached for the button of his shorts, her fingertips brushing the top of his aching erection, it took more willpower than he knew he possessed to stop her.

But he caught her hands in his, held them at her sides. "It's late. You should be getting home."

She just stared at him, stunned. "But don't you want to... finish?"

"What I want," he told her, "is to take you upstairs, slowly strip every piece of clothing away, and spend hours touching and kissing you all over until you're begging for me."

She swallowed. "So why...are you sending me away?"

"Aside from the fact that your screams of pleasure might wake your kids?"

Her cheeks flushed. "I guess that's a good reason."

"But the main reason," he continued, "is that I'm not going to make love with you until I know it's what you want, too. Not because you need a release, but because you want *me*."

She glanced away, but not before he saw that her eyes had filled with tears. Cursing himself, he put a hand on her arm.

Not surprisingly, she shrugged away from his touch.

"Should I thank you for taking the edge off?"

Except that there was still an edge—he could hear it in her voice.

"It wasn't all for you," he said, because it was true. "Touching you was definitely my pleasure."

But she turned away, proving that his words hadn't swayed her. "I need to get the kids home."

He held back a sigh. After all, he was the one who had reminded her it was getting late.

"You take Pippa, I'll bring the boys."

She opened her mouth as if to protest, because even now, she didn't like to accept help from anyone.

"Unless you really want to make three trips," he said.

"Thank you—I would appreciate your help." Except that her sharp tone and narrowed gaze contradicted her words.

She slung Pippa's diaper bag over her shoulder and lifted the bouncy chair with the baby securely fastened and contentedly slumbering in it. It was a little more awkward for Matt to juggle the twins without waking them up, but he managed.

He kicked off his shoes inside the front door and carried the boys upstairs to their bedroom while Georgia changed Pippa. He ignored the pajamas that were neatly folded at the foot of each bed and laid Quinn gently on top of his mattress.

He'd done this before—tucked a sleeping child into his bed. And while the memories of his son usually tore at his heart, tonight—with Georgia's little boy cuddled up against his chest—he was able to smile at the remembrance.

Then he eased Shane down onto his pillow and carefully tucked the covers around him. He brushed away a lock of hair and impulsively touched his lips to the child's forehead.

"Night-night, Daddy."

Matt froze.

He'd always wanted to be a father, and even after he'd lost Liam, he'd been confident that he would have other children someday. But he hadn't realized how much he wanted to be a father to Georgia's kids until he heard the word *Daddy* slip from Shane's lips. He knew the little boy was asleep, and that the words had been murmured subconsciously, but that knowledge didn't prevent them from arrowing straight to his heart.

He took a moment to compose himself before he moved back to Quinn's bed, tucked his covers around him and kissed his forehead. He wasn't sure if he was relieved or disappointed when this twin didn't stir.

Georgia was just leaving Pippa's room when he stepped into the hall. She followed him down the stairs.

"Thank you," she said formally. "For helping with the boys and for inviting us to dinner."

"You're welcome," he said.

And because he couldn't resist, he touched his mouth to hers, softly, fleetingly.

She kept her lips tightly compressed, but her lack of response didn't faze him. Because he knew now, without a doubt, that she wanted him as much as he wanted her.

Now he just had to wait for her to come to the same realization.

He was driving Georgia insane.

Six days after Matt had given her an up-close-and-personal glimpse of the stars and the heavens, he was acting as if absolutely nothing out of the ordinary had happened. Then again, maybe arousing women to the point of climax in his kitchen wasn't out of the ordinary for him. But it had been an extraordinary experience for her—and an incredibly frustrating one.

She hadn't meant to insult him when she'd tried to explain away the sizzle between them as a basic physiological response to their proximity. It made sense to her that more than twelve months of celibacy in combination with post-pregnancy hormones would fuel an attraction to the sexy doctor. But Matt had taken exception to her reasoning and endeavored to prove that what she wanted wasn't just sex but sex with him.

And he was right, damn it. Because when she went to

sleep that night, she didn't dream about hot, sweaty sex with nameless, faceless partners, she dreamed about hot, sweaty sex with Matt Garrett. And she woke up craving his kiss, aching for his touch, yearning for the fulfillment she knew only he could give her.

Since Phillip had passed away, she'd been a mom first and foremost. She'd been dealing with the twins' grief and her own pregnancy. She hadn't missed sex—in fact, she hadn't even thought about it. For more than a year, it was as if every womanly urge in her body had simply shut down. And then Matt Garrett had moved in next door.

Being around him stirred all kinds of wants and needs inside of her. He made her feel like a whole woman again. Except that, in the past six days, nada. Not one kiss, not the brush of a single fingertip on her skin, nothing.

Not that he was avoiding her. In fact, she was practically tripping over him every time she turned around. He was solicitous and helpful and he continued to spend a lot of his free time with the boys. He'd even taken it upon himself to make a trip to the local garden center and arranged for a delivery of sand to fill the empty box at the back of her mother's yard. And he was out there with the boys now, driving dump trucks, bulldozers and cement mixers through the sand right alongside them.

Yeah, he was having a great time with the boys, and he hadn't made a single move to touch her or kiss her in six days. At first she'd thought he was punishing her, then she started to wonder if he'd lost interest, maybe he'd decided that she wasn't worth the effort. Except then she'd catch him looking at her, and the intense heat of his stare certainly didn't telegraph disinterest.

Stepping outside, she called to the boys. "Quinn, Shane— lunch is ready."

The boys jumped up, wiping their sand-covered hands on their shorts before they raced toward the house. Matt followed behind them, at a more leisurely pace. While the boys went inside to wash up, she waited for her neighbor.

"I made a pot of chili, if you wanted to join us."

"Thanks, but I've got some things I have to do."

She stepped in front of him, blocking his path. "Are you going to stay mad at me forever?"

"I'm not mad at you," he told her.

"Then why haven't you kissed me in six days?"

The corner of his mouth tilted up in a half smile. "You've been counting the days?"

She lifted her chin, met his gaze evenly. "Have you changed your mind about wanting me?"

The answer was evident in his eyes before he spoke. The glint of amusement in his gaze immediately replaced by desire—hot and hungry and unrestrained. "No," he said slowly. "I haven't changed my mind."

"So why haven't you kissed me?"

"Because I was afraid that if I started, I wouldn't be able to stop."

She swallowed. "Maybe I wouldn't want you to stop."

He took a step back. "Let me know when you can make that statement without the 'maybe.'"

"I'm sorry," she said with a sigh. "I'm not playing hard-to-get. At least, not on purpose."

His smile was wry. "I know."

And then he pressed a quick kiss to her lips.

It was almost too quick, and he was walking away before the fact even registered in her brain. But it had certainly registered in her body, zinging through every nerve ending from the tip of her head to the soles of her feet and everywhere in between.

If she thought about it, she might have worried that her response to the casual touch was too much. But in the moment, all she could think was that she wanted much more. That she wanted him to kiss her and touch her and never stop.

But she wasn't ready to say the words out loud. And even if she was, it was too late.

He was already gone.

A few days later, Georgia decided to reward herself for finishing her reports on three slush pile submissions with a trip to the park. Since the boys had mostly behaved and let her focus on her work, she decided to take them with her. It wasn't until they got to the park and she saw Matt in the outfield that she knew his team—the Garrett Gators—was practicing today.

While the boys played—Shane no longer encumbered by the cast that had been removed the day before—she put Pippa on her blanket on the grass. Her daughter had recently learned to roll from her stomach to her back and vice versa, and she happily spent a lot of time practicing her new skill. While Georgia was proud of her daughter, she was also a little wary. Pippa's increased mobility required even greater diligence because Georgia knew that if she turned her back for a moment, the baby might roll out of sight. For the moment, however, she seemed content just to go back and forth.

"Heads up!"

Georgia spun around to see the ball pop high into the air and over the backstop of the baseball diamond. Instinctively, she cupped her hands and snagged the ball before it dropped near the baby. There was a smattering of applause from the field as she tossed the ball back to the catcher.

"Sign her up!" somebody yelled from the field.

Georgia ignored the commentary and turned back to Pippa who had, in her mother's brief moment of inattention, rolled all the way to the edge of the blanket. With a mock admonishment, she scooped up the baby and set her in the middle of the quilt again.

"Mrs. Reed?"

She glanced up to see Brittney jogging toward her. Georgia smiled at the girl. "Another practice for the Fourth of July tournament?"

"Yeah," the teen responded with a complete lack of enthusiasm. "And I still completely suck. Unfortunately, there are strict rules about the number of men and women you can have on each team, and uncle Matt's team needed another female body on the field."

"I'm sure you'll do just fine," Georgia told her.

Brittney shook her head. "After half a dozen practices, it's still my instinct to get out of the way when the ball's coming toward me. I haven't fielded a single hit and I haven't hit a single pitch past the pitcher's mound."

"Why are you telling me this?"

"Because when that ball came at you, you didn't even think about it—you just reached out and grabbed it."

"A mother's instinct," she explained. "I was protecting the baby."

"Still, it proved that you'd be a much better asset to the team than I am," Brittney told her.

"Matt asked me if I wanted to play, but—" she gestured to the boys on the climber and Pippa on the blanket under the tree "—I can't sit them in the bleachers and expect them to stay put."

"I'd be happy to hang out with the kids if you took my spot at second base. No, I'd be *thrilled*," the girl amended.

Still, Georgia hesitated. "I haven't played baseball in more years than I care to admit."

"Give it a try now," Brittney urged, offering her glove.

And that was how Georgia found herself playing second base for the Garrett Gators on the Fourth of July.

The local sports complex had been turned into a carnival for the holiday, including a family fun zone with an enormous ball pit, a twenty-foot inflatable slide, a puppet theatre, and face painting and balloon animals for the little kids. For the bigger kids, there was a midway area with thrill rides and games of chance and skill. And since everyone in attendance had an appetite, food vendors offered everything from hot dogs, popcorn and snow cones to perogies, schnitzel and sushi. But one of the biggest draws of the day was the Sixth Annual Co-ed Softball for Sick Kids Hospital Tournament.

Brittney's best friend, Nina, had offered to help out with the kids, but Georgia still couldn't help worrying that the twins and Pippa would be too much for the girls over the course of the day. And she was feeling more than a little guilty that she wasn't able to spend the day with her family. But the twins were happy to wander off with the teens, who pushed Pippa along in her stroller, leaving Georgia with nothing to do but play ball.

There were two divisions of three teams in the tournament, so every team played a five-inning game against each of the others in its division to determine standings. Then the two first-place teams played for the championship trophy.

Georgia nursed Pippa between games and made sure that the girls had enough money to keep the twins occupied and supplied with snacks. At the end of the first round, it was announced that the Garrett Gators would be facing off against the Sullivan Swingers for the hardware.

"A rematch of last year's final," Ashley Turcotte said, in a tone that warned Georgia that game had not ended well for the Gators.

"What happened?" she asked.

"Tyler Sullivan cranked a solo home run over the right field fence to win it for the Swingers in the bottom of the ninth."

"Ty got lucky on that one," Luke grumbled.

"And for months afterward by retelling the story to any female who would listen," Jack chimed in.

"We've got a better team this year," Matt said confidently.

"So do they," Karen, Luke's receptionist and their right

fielder, noted. "They finished with a better run differential, so they're the home team again."

"Then let's get ready to bat," Matt suggested.

Matt had always loved baseball. Hardball or softball, windmill or slo-pitch, it was a fun game. And while the annual charity tournament didn't have quite the same intensity as the high school state championship, there was definitely a rivalry between the Gators and the Swingers, and Matt really wanted payback.

This year's game, just like the previous one, was a close contest. The Gators would go up by a couple of runs in the top of the inning, then the Swingers would catch up when they batted in the bottom. And just like the previous year, the game was on the line in the bottom of the ninth when Tyler Sullivan stepped up to the plate with two outs. But this time, he didn't need a big hit. With his sister-in-law at third base, he only needed a single to score her and tie the game.

In center field, Matt pulled his ball cap lower and focused his attention on the plate. Tyler took a big swing at the first pitch, fouling it back and out of play. When the second pitch came off of his bat, Matt immediately knew by the crack of the bat that it had made contact right at the sweet spot.

Cursing under his breath, he watched the ball fly...straight at Georgia. As if in slow motion, she lifted her glove and the ball disappeared inside its pocket.

The umpire held up his closed fist to signal the final out; Tyler dropped his bat in disgust; the spectators went crazy. Matt stood still, stunned.

Georgia barely had time to toss the ball back toward the pitcher's mound before she was lifted off her feet and swung around. Jack, from his position at shortstop, had reached her first, and when he finally put her feet back on the ground, he planted a kiss right on her mouth. Luke, who had been on first, was next in line. Following his brother's example, he gave her a smack on the lips, too.

Adam Webber showed a little more restraint. After high-fiving her, he said, "I'm just glad the ball wasn't hit to third. I mean, I like all these guys, and I don't mind them patting my butt, but I draw the line at kissing."

"I draw the line at kissing you, too," Jack told him.

There were more high fives all around, and then the Gators lined up for the post-game handshakes with the Swingers.

After the trophy had been presented and the crowd began to disperse, Matt saw Tyler Sullivan approach Georgia to ask, "So what are you doing next Fourth of July?"

She just chuckled. "I don't make any plans that far ahead."

"So you're not on the Gators' permanent roster?" he pressed.

"Back off, Sullivan," Matt growled.

Tyler just grinned. "Can't blame a guy for trying."

"Are you trying to steal my second baseman or snag my woman?"

Georgia seemed as startled by the question as Tyler.

"Your woman?" she echoed.

Tyler, sensing that the fireworks might start hours ahead of schedule, held up his hands in a gesture of surrender and backed off.

Matt slipped his arm around Georgia's waist. "Any woman who can snag a line drive for the final out in the bottom of the ninth and go three-for-four at the plate is the woman for me."

"The ball was hit right into my glove and it's pretty hard to strike out when your own team is pitching to you."

"Cam managed to do it," Luke said. "Twice today."

"They were foul tips," Cam pointed out in his defense. "They don't count as a third strike in real baseball."

Ten-year-old Maddie, who had been their bat girl, patted his shoulder. "You're still a hero to me, Daddy."

He kissed the top of his daughter's head. "That's all that

matters to me." Then he draped an arm over his wife's shoulders. "That, and scoring when I get home."

Ashley shook her head, but she was smiling as they walked away.

"Speaking of scoring," Karen said, winking at Georgia. "I have to admit that I'm curious. Now that you've been kissed by all three of the Garrett brothers, which one would you score the highest?"

Georgia's cheeks filled with color, but she responded lightly, "I'm not the kind of girl who kisses and tells."

"At least tell me this—is their reputation warranted?"

She smiled. "Absolutely."

## Chapter Thirteen

Thankfully, before Georgia could be pressed for more details, Quinn and Shane came running onto the field. She bent down to receive their hugs and kisses. As sweaty and dirty and exhausted as she was, just holding her boys was enough to make her forget everything else.

"You were awesome, Mommy!" Shane's voice was filled with admiration, and her heart swelled with pride.

"Better than the Yankees!" Quinn declared, because that was undoubtedly the highest praise he could think of.

"A performance that definitely warrants ice cream," Matt noted.

"Ice cream?" Quinn said hopefully.

"Well, don't you think your mommy deserves a reward after that terrific game?"

Shane nodded. "Me, too."

Matt grinned. "You bet. Ice cream for everyone. Go tell Brittney and Nina that they're invited, too."

Georgia held back a groan as the twins raced away again.

"You, too," Matt told his brothers. "If you want to join us."

But Jack shook his head regretfully. "I've got a huge file to review before a trial on Monday."

"And I just got a call from Peggy Morgan asking me to take a look at Southpaw."

"She still has that old cat?"

"Probably not for much longer," Luke said. Then, to Georgia, "Make him spring for a double scoop—you more than earned it today."

"I guess it's just you and me," Matt said to Georgia when his brothers had gone.

"And two teens, two preschoolers and an infant," she added. And then, more hopefully, "Or you could let me beg off, too."

"You don't want ice cream?"

"Right now, I just want to go home, wash all the sweat and dust from my body and crawl into bed."

"That sounds even better than ice cream," he said.

"Alone," she said pointedly.

His smile never wavered. "A doctor knows all the muscles in the human body. I'd be happy to help you work out some of the kinks."

"A tempting thought, but I think I'll pass." She tossed him the baseball glove she'd borrowed.

He caught it against his chest, then took a step closer. "Is it?" he wanted to know. "A tempting thought?"

"If you're asking if I've thought about your hands on my body, the answer is yes."

His eyes darkened. "I should have known you'd make that admission at a time and place where I can't do anything about it," he grumbled.

She smiled sweetly. "It seemed safest."

He stepped closer. "Do you want to see the fireworks tonight?"

She lifted a brow; he grinned.

"That wasn't some kind of secret code," he assured her. "The town puts on a fabulous fireworks display back here after dark. I'm sure the boys would love it."

"They probably would," she agreed. "But I don't know about Pippa."

"Brittney could keep an eye on Pippa and the puppies at my place."

"She's been watching my kids all day."

"She owes me, for bailing on the team."

"I thought you said you owed her a 'thank you' for that," she reminded him.

"I'll thank her tomorrow," he promised. "After she baby-sits tonight."

Of course, Georgia wouldn't really disappoint her boys by bailing on a trip for ice cream, so they all piled into her van and made the short drive to Walton's. Unfortunately, the lineup at Walton's was not short, and she suspected that everyone who'd been at the game had the same idea as Matt. But they finally made their way to the cashier and placed their orders: s'mores sundae for Brittney, hot fudge with nuts for Nina, a chocolate chip cookie dough kiddie cone for Quinn, alien invasion again for Shane—apparently he had a new favorite—lemon-lime sorbet for Georgia, and the colossal banana split for Matt.

By the time they polished off their treats and headed back home, the boys could barely keep their eyes open and Georgia knew there was no way they would stay awake for the fireworks show. In fact, she still had doubts about whether *she* could stay awake, but she owed it to Matt to make the effort.

While he went home to shower and change, she steered the boys into the bathroom and filled the tub. When they were clean and dry, she instructed them to put their pajamas on and brush their teeth while she took her turn in the shower. By the time she finished, Pippa was hungry again, so Geor-

gia sent the boys downstairs with Brittney and Nina while
she fed the baby, promising them a story when she was done.


Matt returned to find the twins hanging out with the teens,
waiting for their mom to read them a bedtime story. When he
suggested that he could read the story, the boys exchanged
wary glances.

"Mommy tells the bestest stories," Shane told him.

"But you can read to us now," Quinn said, handing him
the book he'd picked out. "'Cuz Mommy's busy with Pippa."

"All right, then," Matt agreed, and opened the book.

"Upstairs," Shane told him.

"It's not a bedtime story if we're not in bed," Quinn explained.

"I don't know what I was thinking," Matt said, and followed them up to their room.

When the boys were settled with Matt sandwiched between
them—in Shane's bed tonight, because apparently they alter-
nated and it was his turn—he opened the book again. It was a
story about a funny, furry monster that had the boys giggling
out loud at various parts, sometimes even before Matt read
the words on the page, so he knew it was a story they'd heard
several times before. By the time he got to the last page, both
boys were snuggled in close and struggling to stay awake.

When he closed the cover, Shane tilted his head back to
look up at him. "Maybe you could be our new daddy."

It was the hopeful tone even more than the words that
squeezed Matt's heart. And he wanted, more than anything,
to agree with the little boy's suggestion. But it wouldn't be
smart to get Shane's hopes up—or his own—until he knew
that Georgia was on board with the idea, too.

"If you were our daddy, then me and Shane could take care
of Finnigan and Frederick for you all the time," Quinn said.

Matt had to clear his throat before he could speak. "Well,
that's definitely something to consider."

"But you'd hafta marry Mommy to be our daddy," Quinn continued.

He was mildly amused and incredibly humbled by their reasoning. "Is that how it works?"

Both boys nodded.

"You do like her, doncha?" Shane asked.

"Yes, I like her," he admitted, fighting against the smile that wanted to curve his lips. "And I like you guys, too."

"That's good, 'cuz we like you, too."

Georgia paused just outside the door of the twins' bedroom. She hadn't intended to eavesdrop—she hadn't even known that Matt was back until she heard his voice down the hall. And she hadn't overheard much of their conversation, just enough to get the impression that they were having a meeting of the mutual admiration society.

But when Quinn said, "That's good, 'cuz we like you, too," she saw Shane shake his head. And her heart broke, just a little, when her shy son looked up at him and said, "I love you, Dr. Matt."

She'd worried that she was making a huge mistake in allowing herself to get close to Matt; she'd been even more worried about the twins. And just as she'd suspected, her boys had already given him their fragile, trusting hearts. Now she stood frozen in the doorway, waiting for him to respond to her son's heartfelt confession.

Matt lifted a hand and gently tousled Shane's hair. "I love you guys, too," he said, his voice husky with emotion.

And Georgia's heart tumbled right out of her chest to land at his feet.

Over the past couple of months, she felt as if she'd gotten to know Matt Garrett fairly well. She knew he was a dedicated surgeon who cared about his patients, a brother with close ties to his siblings, a neighbor always willing to lend a hand, and the man who made her heart beat faster whenever he was near. He was good with kids and kind to animals—and he kissed like there was no tomorrow. He was smart and sexy and far too charming. But he was also steadfast, reliable and trustworthy.

She pressed a hand to her rapidly beating heart and prayed that she wasn't wrong about that part. Because she'd decided that she was finally ready to prove that she trusted him, with her body *and* her heart.

But first she had to get her kids to sleep.

Obviously Matt was thinking along the same lines, because he said, "Now let's get you both tucked into your own beds before your mom comes in to check on you."

Quinn climbed out of his brother's bed and into his own, pulling his sheets up under his chin and closing his eyes tight.

"Well, look at this," she said, stepping into the room. "My two handsome boys with their jammies on and teeth brushed, all snuggled down and ready to go to sleep."

Quinn's eyes popped open and he exchanged a guilty glance with Shane.

"You did brush your teeth, didn't you?"

Of course she knew that they hadn't, because she'd checked their brushes on her way past the bathroom and found they were still dry.

"We forgot," Shane admitted.

"Then you better go do it now," she advised.

"But I'm already in bed and I'm really tired," Quinn protested.

"Then the hot dogs and cotton candy and ice cream on your teeth will be a delicious feast for the cavity monsters who come out when you're asleep."

She held back a smile as the boys scrambled out of bed and raced to the bathroom.

While they were brushing, she crossed the room to where Matt was standing and kissed his cheek. "Thank you."

"For what?"

"Being so great with the boys."

"They're great boys," he said, with an ease that assured her he meant it.

"I think so," she agreed, then smiled. "Most of the time, anyway."

The boys raced back into the room, stopping in front of Georgia and opening their mouths for the ritual inspection to ensure there wasn't anything left for the cavity monsters to snack on in the night.

"Looks good," she said approvingly.

Then there was a round of hugs and kisses and she tucked them into bed again. Matt glanced at his watch as he followed her into the hall, and she knew he was eager to head back over to the park. But when they made their way down the stairs and into the empty living room, he frowned.

"Where did Brittney and Nina go?"

"I sent them home." She hoped she sounded more confident than she felt, because now that they were really alone, her stomach was in such a mess of knots she didn't think they'd ever untangle.

"I thought we were going back to the park to see the fireworks."

"I changed my mind."

"Don't I get a vote?"

She shook her head. "No, but you have a choice."

"What choice is that?" Matt asked her.

She lifted her arms to link them around his neck. "You can go back to the park for the fireworks—" her fingers cupped the back of his head, drew it down towards hers "—or we can make some of our own right here."

And then she kissed him.

To his credit, it didn't take him long to catch on to the change in their plans. In the space of a heartbeat, surprise had given way to seduction. He didn't respond to her kiss so much as he took it over—and she let him, because she'd never known anyone who kissed like Matt Garrett, with singular purpose and intense focus.

His lips were firm and masterful, confident and seductive. His tongue slid between her lips, stroked the roof of her mouth. Tingles of anticipation danced over her skin, desire shot through her veins. She wanted this—wanted him—more than she'd realized. And as glorious as it was to be kissed by Matt Garrett, she wanted more. She slid her hands over his chest, where she could feel the beat of his heart beneath her palms—strong and steady. Just like Matt.

She wanted to touch him, to feel the warm texture of his skin beneath her hands. Intent on her goal, she started to tug his shirt out of his pants, and nearly whimpered in protest when he caught her wrists in his hands and held them at her sides.

She eased her mouth from his and looked up at him, her gaze steady and sure. "I want you, Matt. Now. Tonight."

His eyes darkened, as much she suspected with satisfaction as with desire, but she didn't care. He could be as smug and self-righteous as he wanted, so long as he was with her.

"No doubts?"

She shook her head. "No doubts."

His lips hovered over hers again, tantalizingly close and oh so far away. "Are you going to let me strip every piece of clothing off your body, then touch you and kiss you all over until you're begging for me?"

Georgia wondered how she'd so quickly lost control of the situation. She'd set out to seduce him, and with just a few well-chosen words spoken in that low, sexy voice, he practically had her on the brink of climax. It made her wonder what would happen when he finally touched her—and made her desperate for his touch. But before that could happen, she had to make one thing clear. "I don't beg."

He grinned. "We'll see."

He captured her mouth again, kissing her so deeply and thoroughly she wanted to beg him to never stop. He finally released his hold on her wrists, skimming his fingers up the length of her arms to her shoulders, over her collarbone. Her skin burned everywhere he touched, and her body yearned everywhere he didn't. He traced the V-neckline of her blouse, raising goose bumps on her flesh. Then his thumbs brushed over nipples, and she moaned as sharp arrows of pleasure shot to her core.

His hands immediately dropped away. "Did I hurt you?"

"No." She shook her head and grasped his wrists, drawing his hands back to her breasts. "I love the feel of your hands on me."

"Good. Because I want to touch all of you. I want to explore every inch of your satiny skin, every dip and curve of your exquisite body." As he spoke, his hands moved over her, from her shoulders to her breasts to her hips and her thighs, making her shudder.

"Are you planning to do all of that in the middle of my living room?" she asked.

"I guess a room with a door would be a better option."

"Upstairs," she said.

"I know," he said, and scooped her into his arms.

He knew because he'd taken her to her bed once before. At the time, she'd been practically comatose and unable to appreciate having a strong, handsome man at her disposal. She was definitely going to appreciate him tonight.

And despite having told him that she never wanted a man to sweep her off her feet, she couldn't deny that there was something incredibly romantic about being held against a solid, masculine chest with a pair of strong arms around her.

He set her on her feet just inside the room, then turned and closed the door with a soft click. Then he waited, as if giving her one last chance to change her mind. She took his hand and led him over to the bed.

Her heart was racing and her knees were shaking, not because she was afraid but because she'd never wanted anyone as much as she wanted this man now. He laid her down gently on the mattress and lowered himself over her. Then he kissed her again, and she sighed in blissful pleasure.

She wasn't aware that he'd unfastened the buttons of her shirt until he pushed the fabric over her shoulders and down her arms. Then he dipped his head to kiss the hollow between her breasts before he unclipped the front of her bra and parted the lacy cups. She tensed, because her breasts were ultra-sensitive as a result of nursing Pippa, and nearly lost it when he touched his tongue to her nipple.

He continued to focus his attention on her breasts, alternately licking, kissing and suckling until she was very close to begging. And then his mouth moved lower, raining kisses over her rib cage, the curve of her belly, and lower still. She tensed, her hands fisted in the covers, as he removed her jeans.

His fingers trailed along the soft skin inside her thighs, coaxing them to part. Then his tongue followed the same path to the apex of her thighs, and with the first touch of his tongue to her center, she simply and completely shattered.

"Matt." His name was both a whimper and a plea, but not even Georgia knew if she was begging him to stop—or not.

He didn't alter course. With his lips and his tongue and his teeth, he continued to tease and torment her, driving her higher and higher, ever closer to another pinnacle of pleasure. She bit down hard on her lip to keep from crying out. She wouldn't have thought it was possible, but somehow the second climax was even more explosive than the first.

"Now. Please now."

He paused only long enough to take care of protection, and her body was still pulsing with the aftershocks when he finally levered himself over and into her. She cried out as another wave of pleasure crashed over her. She didn't think it was possible, that she'd had anything left to give, but Matt proved her wrong once again. As her body found its rhythm in concert with his, she was flooded with new sensations, unimaginable pleasures.

She arched beneath him, lifting her legs to hook them over his hips, drawing him even deeper inside her. His groan mingled with hers, and he began to thrust faster, harder, deeper. Her fingers dug into his shoulders, the short nails scoring his flesh, as her body tensed again.

This time he rode the wave with her, crest after crest, until he finally shuddered his release into her.

Matt had dreamed of Georgia, hot and naked and screaming his name. But as vivid as those dreams had been, they paled in comparison to the reality of the woman in his arms. Making love with her had transcended all of his expectations. She was passionate and playful, and the result was an experience both gloriously intense and unexpectedly fun.

But the best part about making love with Georgia was that even after his body was sated, he still wanted to be with her. He wasn't proud to admit it, but he'd had a few interludes after which he couldn't wait to put his clothes back on and go home. And that, he'd finally understood, was the difference between meaningless sex and true intimacy. Both served a purpose, at least with respect to satisfying basic physiological needs, but he'd quickly grown bored of attraction without affection. Thankfully, with Georgia, there was plenty of both.

When he finally managed to catch his breath, he propped himself up on an elbow and couldn't resist teasing, "You begged."

One bare shoulder peeked out from the sheet as Georgia shrugged. "It seemed to matter to you."

"Oh, yeah?" He touched a fingertip to that bare shoulder, traced a path down below the sheet, over the curve of her breast to circle a taut nipple. "That was the only reason?"

"That and the fact that—" her breath caught when he gently tweaked her nipple "—you made my knees weak and my head spin."

He frowned, feigning concern as he shifted his attention to her other breast. "Sounds like a serious medical condition. Maybe you should see a doctor."

She smiled at that. "You don't really expect me to let you play doctor with me, do you?"

"I don't care what you call it—" he replaced his hand with his mouth, gently licking and nibbling until she was writhing and panting "—so long as you let me play."

"I can't think...of any...immediate...objections."

His hand slid over the gentle curve of her belly to the center of her femininity. And smiled with satisfaction when Georgia's breath whooshed out of her lungs and her eyes drifted shut.

"In fact...I can't think...at all."

"I like when you don't think," he told her.

She bit down on her lower lip. "Part of me wonders if I should be insulted by that remark."

"And the other part?" he prompted.

"All the other parts are too aroused to care."

"Are you going to beg again?"

"Make me," she challenged.

And because he'd never been able to resist a challenge, he did.

## *Chapter Fourteen*

Georgia had known that Matt would be a good lover. He was too attentive and thoughtful in every aspect of his life to be otherwise in the bedroom. Not that she had much experience for comparison. She'd never been with anyone but Phillip, and she didn't know if that was the kind of admission she should have made to a potential lover.

She didn't know what Matt's expectations were when he took a woman to his bed. All kidding aside, the man did have a reputation. He'd dated a lot of women, probably slept with a lot of women—women who were likely more sophisticated and experienced than she. And women whose bodies didn't bear the evidence of having carried three babies.

She wouldn't trade any one of her children for anything in the world, but that didn't stop her from wishing—at least in the moment—that her hips were a little less round and the skin on her belly a little more taut. But Matt didn't seem to have any issues with her body during their two intense rounds of lovemaking. Which might explain why she was so thoroughly exhausted—three games of baseball followed by energetic bedroom activities would wear out anyone.

Georgia stretched her arms up over her head, trying to ease some of the kinks out of her body. Rolling over to face the other side of the bed, she was surprised to find it empty.

Obviously Matt had decided to go home, and while she was undeniably disappointed, she figured it was for the best. They really hadn't talked too much before they'd fallen into her bed, so it was probably wise for them both to take some time to think things through and reestablish boundaries. Because there had been absolutely no boundaries when she'd been naked in his arms.

After a quick trip to the bathroom, she noticed that soft light was spilling out of Pippa's partially closed doorway. Tiptoeing closer to peek into the room, she saw Matt in the rocking chair, feeding Pippa a bottle.

He'd pulled on his pants but not bothered with a shirt, and the sight of her baby girl cradled against his solid, masculine chest took her breath away. He should have looked ridiculous—a half-naked man in the midst of all the ultra-feminine décor; instead, he looked perfect—as if he belonged there.

"I raided your freezer stash again," he explained, whispering so as not to startle the baby.

"I can't believe I didn't hear her fussing."

"She didn't make too much noise," he assured her.

"You should have woken me up."

"I figured it was at least partly my fault that you were so exhausted, and I wanted to let you sleep."

Even before tonight, even before she'd watched him with her boys, she'd been more than halfway in love with him. But she'd refused to admit it, so sure that she could control her emotions. Then she'd made love with him, and she'd tumbled the rest of the way.

Now, seeing him here with Pippa, looking every bit as if he belonged there, made her wish that Matt Garrett could be a part of her life—and her children's lives—forever. Except that there had been too many stepfathers in and out of her life for Georgia to let herself even hope. Nothing was forever, and the sooner she put an end to such foolish fantasies, the better.

As he rose to put the sleeping baby back in her crib, Georgia turned away so he wouldn't see the shimmer of her tears. But he was somehow attuned to the change in her mood, because he followed her into the hall and tipped her chin up, forcing her to meet his gaze.

"What's going on, Georgia?"

She shook her head. "Nothing. You're right—I'm just really tired and...I think you should go now."

He seemed more amused than offended by her impulsive suggestion. "Where do I have to go?"

"Home."

"Why?"

The gentle patience in his tone made her want to scream. How could he be so calm when she was on the verge of a full-scale panic?

"Because it's late," she snapped.

He smiled at that. "I don't have anyone waiting up for me."

"The puppies," she suddenly remembered, seizing upon the excuse. "Don't you have to let them out?"

"I already did," he told her.

"Won't they be scared, alone in the house without you?"

"They'll be fine," he insisted, and drew her into his arms. "What I want to know is why you're suddenly scared to have me in your house with you."

"I'm not scared," she lied. "I just think we should take a step back."

His amusement faded. "You want to take a step back?"

She nodded. "Sex is sex, but sleeping together implies a certain level of intimacy."

"Yes, it does," he agreed. "And I intend to spend the night

with you, Georgia—to sleep with you in my arms and wake up with you in the morning."

She wanted that, too, far more than she should. Because if she let him stay tonight, she would want him to stay the night after that and the night after that, and eventually she would start to count on him being there.

"Do you want me to beg?" His tone was deliberately light, but she could tell by the intensity of his gaze that he understood this was a big deal to her.

"Would you?" she wondered.

His gaze never wavered. "I would do anything for you, Georgia. Don't you know that by now?"

"I guess I do," she finally said. "And maybe that's what scares me."

"Have there been so many people in your life who have let you down?"

"Each of my mother's four husbands, including my own father. Every single one of them claimed to want her and her kids, and every single one of them dropped out of our lives."

"And then your husband did the same," Matt noted with surprising insight. "Not that it was his choice, but the result was the same. He promised to be with you forever, and then he was gone, leaving you alone and your children without a father."

She nodded.

"And if even he didn't stick around, why should you trust that I will?"

She nodded again. "And before you point it out, yes, I know that I was the one trying to push you out the door."

"Because then it would be *your* choice," he noted.

Even she hadn't consciously understood the rationale behind her actions, but now she realized he was right. Every time her mother had walked out on one of her husbands, it had been Charlotte's choice, and her daughters had no option but to follow her out the door.

"Okay, you get to decide," he said. "Do you want me to stay—or do you want me to go?"

She should have been relieved that he was letting her choose, because her choice was already made. Except that somehow, during the course of their conversation, she'd started to question the wisdom of her decision to push him away. He'd proven that he understood her as no one else ever had, and he wanted to be with her anyway. And the fact that he had enough faith in her to put the choice in her hands gave her the courage to trust her heart.

She reached for his hand and linked their fingers together. "Stay."

Matt understood how hard it was for Georgia to say that single word. Because while it might have seemed like an easy response to a simple question, he knew that it was much more than that.

For Georgia, admitting that she wanted him to stay was the equivalent of putting her heart directly in his hands. And he was both grateful and relieved that she'd found the courage to do so, because whether she knew it or not, his heart was completely in hers.

This time when he took her back to bed, he showed her with his hands and his lips and his body the words he knew she wasn't ready to hear. And in the morning, when he woke with her in his arms, he had absolutely no doubt that this was how he wanted to wake up every day for the rest of his life.

Over the next several days, they resumed their normal routines with only a few minor adjustments—the puppies' bed was moved into Georgia's kitchen in the evening, he spent the nights in Georgia's bed, and she'd stopped pretending that she didn't want him there.

But as much as he enjoyed the new physical aspect of their relationship, he also enjoyed just being with her. There was so much he didn't know about her, so much he wanted to learn, and they often stayed awake late into the night just talking.

One night, after filling her in on the exploits of Finnigan and Frederick during a recent trip to Luke's office for their nine-week checkup, Georgia commented, "You've got a great relationship with your brothers, but I've never heard you mention any other family."

"That's because both of my parents died a few years back."

She winced. "I'm sorry—I shouldn't have pried."

"It's hardly a big secret," he said, and certainly not in comparison to the other, bigger secret that he'd yet to confide. Not because he didn't want to tell her, but because he knew that the time and place of the telling were crucial to ensuring her understanding, and this was not the time or the place.

*Then when?* the nagging voice of his conscience demanded.

Followed by Georgia's question: "Can you tell me what happened?"

It took him a second to comprehend that she was referring to the loss of his parents and not the failure of his marriage. "After my dad retired, they decided they wanted to see the world—the Great Wall of China, the Australian outback, the Serengeti—and they were having a great time. Then they decided to sail around Cape Horn, but the captain's years of experience were no match for the storm that capsized their boat. My parents—and all the crew—drowned." She took his hand, a silent gesture of comfort and encouragement.

"That must have been horrible for you and your brothers— losing them both at the same time," she murmured.

He nodded. "It was hard to find solace in anything under those circumstances, but once we'd started to get over our frustration and grief, we were able to take some comfort in the fact that they were together. Because we knew that, after almost forty years of marriage, neither one of them would have wanted to go on without the other.

"Losing them so unexpectedly was tragic," he continued.

"But we were lucky to have been witness to such an example of a strong and stable marriage, to have seen, day in and day out, the evidence of their deep love and enduring affection for one another."

"My mother has never found that kind of forever-after love," she told him. "And not for lack of searching. Yet she still believes it exists."

"It does," he said, and lowered his head to press a soft kiss to her lips.

"Did you think you'd found it with your wife?"

He leaned his forehead against hers. "Are you trying to kill the mood?"

"I guess I'm just curious," she said. "I can't imagine that you would get married without believing it was forever, and—believing it was forever—I can't imagine you ever giving up on your vows. At least not easily."

"It wasn't easy," he admitted, resigned now to spilling the whole sordid story of his ex-wife's deception.

Except that the puppies suddenly broke into a chorus of yelps and howls.

Georgia froze. Matt threw back the covers and swung his legs over the edge of the mattress, but she grabbed his arm, halting his movements.

In the midst of all the frantic puppy sounds, the muttering of a female voice could be heard. Matt couldn't actually make out the words, but he thought they sounded like, "You'd think she could have told me about the dogs."

"You stay here," Georgia said, reaching for her robe. "I'll go."

He shook his head, baffled that she would even suggest such a thing. "There's someone in the house, and there's no way—"

"It's not just someone," she interrupted. "It's my mother."

Georgia had faced more than a few curveballs in her life, and having Charlotte Warring-Eckland-Tuff-Masterton-

Kendrick-Branston show up unannounced and in the middle of the night was only the latest one.

The puppies heard the creak of the stairs before Charlotte did, and they happily abandoned the unfriendly stranger in favor of the human who occasionally fed them dinner and took them for walks. Georgia bent to pat them both on their head, reassuring them that they were excellent watchdogs, before she addressed her mother.

"This is a surprise, Mom."

Charlotte kissed each of her daughter's cheeks in turn before she offered a smile that was wide, and just a little bit forced.

"Well, that was my plan—to surprise you. But I didn't mean to wake you up, baby girl," she said, a note of apology in her voice. "And actually, I don't think I did, it was the dogs. Why didn't you tell me that you were turnin' the house into a kennel?"

"It's only two puppies, and they're not mine."

"Then why are they here?"

"I'm helping out a friend," she hedged. "Why are you here?"

"As far as I know, this is still my house."

"You know it is," Georgia agreed. "But why are you showing up here at two o'clock in the morning?"

"Because it's nearly a three-hour drive from the airport," she said, as if that explained everything.

"Okay," Georgia said, trying not to lose patience. "Why did you choose to make the trip from Montana at this particular point in time?"

"I was just missin' my grandbabies so much I simply couldn't wait another day to put my arms around them, so Trigger bought me a plane ticket and here I am."

There was something about Charlotte's explanation that struck Georgia as a little off, or maybe it was the deliberately casual tone that tripped her radar. Whatever the reason,

Georgia was suddenly convinced that there was more to this impromptu trip than her mother needing a baby fix. And she was pretty sure she knew what it was.

"You left him, didn't you?"

"What are you talkin' about?"

"Trigger—your husband. The one who made you feel a jolt as if you'd stuck your finger in a socket," Georgia reminded her.

Charlotte pressed a perfectly manicured hand to her chest, right over her heart. "It was just like that," she agreed.

"So where is he now?"

"At his ranch, of course. He couldn't just abandon his animals 'cause I had a whim to see my baby girl and her babies."

"You're actually sticking to that story?"

"Really, Georgia May, I don't understand why you're being so confrontational."

Upstairs, she could hear Pippa starting to fuss, wanting to be fed, and Georgia was eager to get to the baby before her mother decided to trek up the stairs.

"I'm sorry. Maybe we should continue this conversation in the morning—or rather, at a more reasonable hour in the morning."

"Sounds good to me," Charlotte agreed. "It's been a long day and I could definitely use some shut-eye."

Georgia nodded, though she didn't expect that she would get to sleep any time soon. First she'd have to feed and change Pippa, then when the baby was settled back down and she was sure that Charlotte was asleep, she'd have to get Matt out of the house. She didn't doubt he would balk at being shoved out the back door but even though she was thirty-one years of age, Georgia still wasn't willing to risk her mother catching a man in her bed.

Another soft coo drifted down the stairs, followed by a chattier babble that was the little girl's version of a conversation. Which meant that Matt had heard the baby and, knowing that Georgia was occupied downstairs, had gone in to Pippa's room to check on her.

"Oh, the baby's awake," Charlotte said, her voice filled with genuine pleasure. "I have to take just a little peek—"

"Why don't you wait until morning?" Georgia suggested. "If she sees you now, she won't settle down again."

Charlotte waved a hand dismissively as she started up the stairs. "Don't be silly. She'll settle down just fine if she's tired."

Short of physically restraining her mother, Georgia knew there was no way to prevent Charlotte from going into Pippa's room. Which meant there was no way that she wasn't going to cross paths with—

"Matthew Garrett," Charlotte said, her voice tinged with both surprise and approval. "I was wonderin' whose size-thirteen shoes I nearly tripped over downstairs."

"Well, that wasn't as awkward as I thought it might be," Matt said, after Georgia had finished nursing the baby and Charlotte had gone back to the main floor master bedroom.

"It felt plenty awkward to me," Georgia told him.

"You're just embarrassed because your mom gave you two thumbs up before she said good-night," he teased.

"The fact that she approves of our involvement does make me wary," she admitted. "My mother has notoriously bad taste in men."

"Are you saying that because her exes were of questionable character or because the relationships were unsuccessful?"

"I'm not sure the distinction really matters."

"Sure it does. If she truly made poor choices, then you should be wary. But if they were good men, then there could be any number of reasons that things didn't work out."

"Like her habit of bailing whenever a relationship hits a snag rather than trying to find a solution?" she suggested.

"That could be an issue," he agreed.

"I don't think she's here for a visit," Georgia finally said. "I think she left Trigger."

"Wouldn't she have told you if that was the case?"

She shook her head. "No. Not until she's figured out a way to spin it so that it isn't her fault."

"That's kind of harsh, don't you think?"

She sighed. "Maybe. And maybe I'm wrong. I honestly I hope that I am, because if she did walk out on her marriage, her heart is completely shattered but she won't let anyone know it."

"I guess that proves you come by your tough demeanor honestly enough."

"You think I'm tough?"

"On the outside," he said. "On the inside, you're all soft and gooey like a marshmallow." He lowered his head to kiss her, softly, deeply. "And very, very sweet."

"Mmm." She hummed her approval as she linked her arms around his neck. "You're trying to distract me, aren't you?"

He slid his hands beneath her shirt and unfastened the front of her bra so that her breasts spilled into his hands. Her breath hitched; her nipples pebbled. He rubbed his thumbs over the taut peaks, making her moan. "Is it working?"

Her breath shuddered out between her lips as he nibbled on the lobe of her ear. "Is what working?"

Smiling, he lowered her onto the bed.

Matt got called in to the hospital early the next morning, leaving Georgia to face her mother's barrage of questions and unsolicited advice alone. And Charlotte didn't disappoint. In fact, Georgia had barely begun cracking eggs into a bowl when her mother said, "You picked a good man, baby girl."

Considering that Matt hadn't moved in until after her mother had left for Vegas, she had to ask, "How do you know?"

"There's no disputing the Garrett boys were all players in

their youth, but everyone in town agrees that they've grown into fine, upstanding citizens. Or at least Matt and Luke," her mother clarified, a slight furrow in her brow. "There seems to be some difference of opinion with respect to Jack."

"That's your source of information—town gossip?"

"News—good and bad—travels fast in Pinehurst. And I've heard nothin' but good things about Matt Garrett." Charlotte dropped her voice, as if revealing confidential information. "Did you know that he's a doctor?"

She focused on whisking the eggs and ignored the fact that her mother actually thought Georgia might sleep with a man without knowing something as basic as his occupation. "Yes, I know he's a doctor. In fact, he put the cast on Shane's arm when he broke it."

Her mother nodded. "Smart, charming and very handsome. It's almost too much to hope that he'd also be good in bed."

"Mom!" Georgia felt her cheeks burn hotter than the skillet on the stove.

Charlotte smiled. "Well, well. My baby girl's discovered that there's passion in her blood."

"A true revelation after having three children delivered by the stork," Georgia said dryly.

"The earth doesn't have to move for a woman to get pregnant," her mother pointed out as she gathered plates and cutlery for the meal. "And while I never doubted that Phillip was a good man, I did wonder if he was a good husband."

Georgia was baffled by the statement. "Why would you ever wonder about that?"

"Because I never saw him look at you the way Matt looks at you—and vice versa."

Georgia hated to admit that it was probably true. In so many ways, she and Phillip had been well suited, but while they'd shared a certain level of attraction, they'd never generated any real sparks. Certainly nothing that could compare to the kind of sparks that flew whenever Georgia and Matt were together, but acknowledging that fact—even to her mother—seemed disloyal somehow. "I loved my husband."

"I know you did," Charlotte said. "But do you love Matt?"

She pushed the eggs around in the pan. "I've only known him a couple of months."

"I only knew Trigger a couple of days," Charlotte reminded her. "But that was long enough to know that I wanted to spend the rest of my life with him."

Except that, for some inexplicable reason, she was here and her husband was in Montana. But Georgia wasn't going to get into that with her mother today. Instead, she only said, "I'm not ready to make that kind of leap."

"Well, don't wait too long," Charlotte advised. "If you don't snap up that sexy doctor quick, another woman will."

"If he let himself be snapped up that easily by someone else, then maybe I'm better off without him."

Charlotte huffed out a breath, unable to dispute her daughter's logic, and Georgia took advantage of her momentary silence to call the boys to the table.

They were just settling down to eat when the doorbell rang. Not just once but three times in rapid succession, and then, before Georgia could even push her chair back, a fist was pounding on the door.

A quick glance across the table revealed that her mother's face was whiter than the napkin she'd twisted around her fingers. Since she obviously had no intention of going to the door, Georgia did, pulling it open to a tall, broad-shouldered cowboy, complete with hat and boots. "Can I help you?"

The man on the porch swiped the Stetson from his head, revealing neatly trimmed salt-and-pepper hair. "I'm Henry Branston. I'm here to get my wife."

## Chapter Fifteen

"Your driveway's starting to look like a rental-car agency," Matt commented to Georgia when he got home from the hospital later that afternoon.

"I know. I walked to the grocery store with all the kids today because it was easier than moving three vehicles around. That and it allowed me a brief opportunity to escape from the drama."

"You can always stay at my place," he offered. "If you want some extra space."

"I might take you up on that if they don't go back to Montana soon, because after all the accusations and tears were done and they'd kissed and made up, they went straight down the hall to her bedroom and locked the door. And then I heard *noises*." She shuddered at the memory.

"Does that mean they've worked things out?" he asked cautiously.

"I think so. But what's even more bizarre, from what I

overheard of their argument, I think I understand why she left. I don't agree with her decision, but I understand."

"Want to explain it to me?"

"My mother felt as if she was the only one who made any kind of sacrifice when they got married. She left her home and her family and moved to an environment completely unfamiliar to her in order to be with the man she loved. And the more time she spent in Montana, the more she recognized that his life hadn't changed at all.

"She didn't necessarily want him to make any changes, she just wanted to know that he loved her enough to be willing to do so. The fact that he dropped everything to follow her halfway across the country to take her back home seemed to prove to her that he did love her enough."

"And now everything's okay?"

"Apparently."

"So when are they heading back to Montana?"

"Probably not soon enough," she said.

He chuckled. "As long as they're not leaving today, then I don't have to change our plans for tonight."

"Our plans?"

"Last night, when you were nursing Pippa, your mom offered to babysit the kids so that I could take you out on a real date."

She lifted a brow. "Have we had fake dates?"

He nudged her with his shoulder. "You know what I mean."

"Actually, I'm not sure that I do," she admitted. "What is a real date?"

"Dinner in a restaurant that doesn't have a kiddie menu, a movie that isn't a cartoon."

"Those things are beyond my realm of experience," she warned.

"Are you willing to give it a try?"

"We could," she allowed. "Or we could order pizza with spicy sausage, hot peppers and black olives, and watch a movie on the TV in your bedroom."

"You're assuming I have a TV in my bedroom," he pointed out.

Her lips curved. "If you don't, I'm sure we could find something else to occupy the time."

He decided to go with her plan, but upgraded it a little by setting the table with candles and champagne flutes filled with sparkling grape juice. And for dessert, he picked up some miniature pastries from the Bean There Café.

After the pizza had been eaten, Matt asked Georgia if she had any update on her mother's plans.

"They want to stay for two weeks," she told him, making the "two weeks" sound like "forever."

"Charlotte misses her grandchildren," he guessed.

"I think she does, but it was actually Trigger's idea to stay for a while, to get to know his new family." But she didn't sound very enthusiastic about the prospect.

"And you're afraid that if you get to know him, you'll like him, and if your mother walks out a second time, you might never see him again."

"That's certainly been the history," she admitted. "But honestly, I think Trigger is different. I think my mother could walk out a dozen times, and he'd track her down and take her back, because he loves her."

"Does that mean you now believe they did fall in love over a baccarat table?"

"It seems that I do."

"Then it wouldn't be completely out of the realm of possibility that a man could fall in love with his next-door neighbor after only a couple of months?"

She picked up her juice, sipped. "I guess not, but I'm hardly an expert on the subject."

"Okay, as a non-expert, do you think there's any chance that she might someday feel the same way?"

She nibbled on her lower lip for what seemed like an eternity while he waited for her response.

"I think it's possible that she already does," she said, and he was finally able to release the breath he'd been holding.

"I know you probably think I'm rushing things—even I thought I was rushing things," he admitted. "But Charlotte convinced me that sometimes the heart just knows what it wants."

"You're taking relationship advice from a woman who's been married five times and divorced four?"

"It takes courage to follow your heart."

"Then she has to be the bravest woman I know."

"She probably is," Matt agreed.

"And you think I'm a coward."

"I think you're wary," he said. "And I understand why you would be."

"My kids are my priority."

"I don't have a problem with that," he assured her. "And I don't think your kids have any problem with us being together."

"They don't, because they want you to be their new daddy. But they've already lost one father—how will they feel if things don't work out?"

"I'm thirty-eight years old and long past the stage of wanting to sow any wild oats. I wouldn't be with you—I wouldn't risk getting close to your kids—if I wasn't serious." He put his hand in his pocket and closed his fingers around the box from Diamond Jubilee. He set it on the table in front of her. "Very serious."

Georgia's breath caught when she recognized the logo. Matt hadn't opened the lid, but that didn't matter. She didn't care if he'd chosen a diamond solitaire or a cluster of cubic zirconias, it was the significance of the box itself that had her mind reeling.

"This isn't how I planned to do it," he told her. "But I couldn't let you continue thinking this is just a fling, because it's not. Not for me."

"I kind of liked the idea of a fling," she said, keeping her tone light and her hands clasped together. "I've never had one before."

"Because you're not the type of woman to share your body without giving your heart. At least, I hope you're not."

That heart was pounding frantically now, though she didn't know if it was with excitement or apprehension. "I'm also not the type of woman who believes that an intimate relationship has to lead to a walk down the aisle."

"And I've never felt compelled to propose to a woman just because I slept with her," he pointed out. "But I've been married before and if the failure of that marriage taught me nothing else, it at least taught me that there are no guarantees in life.

"After the divorce, I learned to appreciate every moment—and I vowed that if I was ever lucky enough to find someone with whom I wanted to share those moments, I would never let her go." He reached across the table and linked their hands together. "I want to share all of my moments with you."

The heartfelt words brought tears to her eyes. And while she could appreciate that he was putting it all on the line, she was too cowardly to do the same.

"I wasn't ready for this," she protested. "I'm *not* ready for this."

He released her hands and tucked the box back into his pocket. But removing it from the table didn't make her feel any less pressured, because now she knew it was there.

"I wasn't pushing you for an answer. Not right now," he said. "I just wanted you to know that I was looking toward a future for us—all of us—together."

"And I was looking forward to tonight—just the two of us."

She could tell that he was disappointed in her response, but she didn't know what else to say. Or maybe she was afraid to admit what was in her heart. She wasn't just wary—she was terrified, because what she felt for Matt was so much bigger than anything she'd ever felt before.

"Then let's start with tonight," he said, and led her upstairs to his bedroom.

Georgia wouldn't have thought it was possible, but she was almost more nervous now than the first time they'd made love. Because then she'd had no hopes or expectations beyond that single night. And when one night had become two, she'd still been content to live in the moment.

*I want to share all of my moments with you.*

As Matt's words echoed in the back of her mind, Georgia knew without a doubt that she wanted the same thing. From this moment to forever.

He paused in the act of unbuttoning her shirt. "You're trembling," he noted.

She could only nod.

"It can't be nerves," he said, in a gentle, teasing tone. "Because I've seen you naked at least once or twice before."

"But I never knew it wasn't just a fling before."

"But you know it now?"

She nodded again. "You matter to me, Matt. And I don't want to screw this up."

"You won't," he assured her.

"How do you know?"

"Because we're in this together, and I won't let anything screw this up for us." He kissed her then, softly, deeply, thoroughly. "I love you, Georgia."

She wasn't sure if it was the kiss or his words, but suddenly her head was spinning and her knees were weak. Her fingers curled into the fabric of his shirt, holding on. "Show me."

So he did. With each kiss, every touch and every caress,

with his lips and his hands and his body, he showed her the depth and truth of his feelings. She had never felt more treasured or cherished. Her pleasure was his pleasure. He gave and gave until she couldn't take any more, until she didn't want anything—not even her next breath—as much as she wanted him inside of her.

And when their bodies finally joined together, Georgia knew that their hearts and souls were equally entwined.

Afterward, when she was snuggled against his chest waiting for her heart rate to return to normal, she appreciated that this was one of those moments he'd been talking about. A moment that she wanted to share with only Matt. Not just because they'd had earth-shattering sex together, but because, when she was in his arms, she felt as if she truly belonged there. And because there was nowhere else in the world that she would rather be.

And along with that certainty came the courage to finally admit what she wanted. "Was there really a ring in that box you pulled out earlier?"

"You want to see it, don't you?" His lips curved, just a little. "It's always about the bling, isn't it?"

"No, I don't want to see it," she denied. "I want to wear it. But only if I hear a proper proposal." It really hadn't mattered to her that Phillip had never formally proposed. But he was her past and Matt was her future—and she wanted this time to be different. She wanted this time to really be forever.

His brows quirked. "Does that mean I have to get dressed?"

She shook her head. "It only means you have to ask."

He leaned over the edge of the mattress, searching for the pants that had been discarded on the floor to retrieve the box from the pocket. He fumbled a little, trying to open the lid, but she covered his hand.

"The proposal," she reminded him.

"Now *I'm* nervous," he admitted.

She smiled, relieved to know that she wasn't the only one. "Would it help if I told you that I'm probably going to say yes?"

"*Probably?*" he echoed. "That's not very reassuring."

"Well, I can't say anything until you ask the question."

"I really didn't plan to do it like this. I wanted to have all the right words to tell you how much you mean to me, how just knowing you has changed my life and made every day a little bit better."

"That sounds pretty good so far," she said.

"Being with you makes me happy," he told her, "and the only way I could imagine being any happier would be with you as my wife. But I don't just want to be your husband, I want to be your partner in every aspect of your life. I want to share your hopes and dreams, to help raise your children, to celebrate with you when you're happy and hold you when you're sad. I want to share every moment of the rest of your life, and that's why I'm asking, Georgia Reed, will you marry me?"

She blew out a shaky breath. "I don't have any words that can top that."

"There's only one word I want to hear," he said.

"Yes." She pressed her lips to his. "Yes, Matthew Garrett, I will marry you."

"You haven't even looked at the ring," he chided.

Because it seemed so important to him, she dropped her gaze to the box in his hand. And this time when her breath caught in her throat it was because she was absolutely stunned by the enormous princess-cut diamond set in a platinum band.

"So it's not about the bling?" he teased, slipping the ring onto her finger.

She couldn't deny that she liked the way the diamond sparkled on her finger, but far more precious to her was the love in his heart. A love that matched her own.

"No," she said, and kissed him again. "It's all about the man."

Georgia had hoped to keep the news of their engagement on the QT for a while—at least until she had a chance to get used to it herself. She didn't count on the fact Charlotte could sniff out a diamond at twenty paces. Georgia had barely walked into the kitchen the next morning when her mother let out a squeal of delight and snatched up her daughter's hand for a closer inspection.

"Look at the size of that rock," she said approvingly. "If that doesn't say 'I love you,' nothin' does." But then her gaze narrowed. "So why is it that your cheeks are glowin' but there's worry in your eyes?"

"I guess I'm just feeling a little like I'm venturing into new territory."

"You were married once before," Charlotte reminded her.

"I know, but everything was different with Phillip. I felt safe with Phillip."

"You're feelin' vulnerable," her mother guessed.

She nodded.

"Every time you put your heart out there, you put it at risk," Charlotte acknowledged. "You just have to trust that it's worth the risk."

"I loved Phillip, but it was a comfortable kind of love. What I feel for Matt is so much more intense, so much more all-encompassing. So much more...everything."

"Love can be scary," her mother agreed. "It's both exhilaratin' and terrifyin', much like those roller coasters you enjoyed so much as a kid."

"That was Indy," Georgia reminded her. "I *hated* roller coasters."

Charlotte chuckled. "That's right. You used to scream

bloody murder whenever your sister convinced you to strap yourself into one."

"She didn't convince me—she bribed me." Usually by offering her share of the cotton candy or caramel corn Charlotte had bought for them. Georgia would happily devour the treat—and then promptly throw it up again when she got off the ride.

And she couldn't help wondering if she was making the same mistake now. The idea of a future with Matt was like a trip to the carnival—both thrilling and terrifying. She had never loved anyone as she loved him, which meant that no one had ever had so much power to break her heart.

But when she was in Matt's arms, she had absolute faith that he wouldn't do so. He was like the safety bar that held her tight, that would keep her in the car, protect her through all of the ups and downs and corners and curves. He would be the partner who shared not just her life but her hopes and her dreams, and a father for her children.

When Phillip died, she'd mourned for her children even more than she'd mourned for herself. She'd cried for her sons who had absolutely doted on their father, and who had been devastated to know that he was never coming home again. And she'd cried for her unborn child who would never even know her daddy. But she hadn't cried for herself, because the truth was, she'd been living life on her own for a long time before she buried her husband.

"So when's the weddin'?" Charlotte asked.

"We just got engaged," Georgia reminded her.

"Which means it's time to start thinkin' about a weddin'," her mother insisted. "Better yet, let's go out today to find you a dress."

"I'm not rushing into anything," Georgia protested.

"But it would mean so much to me to see my baby girl happily married before I go back to Montana."

She shook her head. "There's no way I'm planning a wedding in two weeks."

"You don't need to do a lot of plannin'," Charlotte said, her eyes twinkling. "You and your fiancé can just fly down to Vegas—"

"No."

Her mother frowned. "Why not?"

"Because I don't want to get married by a second-rate Elvis impersonator in some tacky chapel..." She felt the flood of color in her cheeks as her brain finally halted the flow of words from her mouth. "I'm sorry. I didn't mean—"

Charlotte waved off her apology. "Most of those chapels are tacky, but some of those Elvises are real good. Not the one who married me and Trigger, mind you, but I didn't care about the settin' so much as the vows." Then she winked. "And the weddin' night."

Georgia cringed. "Too much information."

"Honestly, Georgia May Reed, I don't know how any daughter of mine grew up to be such a prude."

"Did you know that the word 'prude' provides the root of the word 'prudence,' meaning the exercise of sound judgment?" she asked, undaunted by the criticism.

"Nothin' would show more sound judgment than movin' forward with your life with that sexy doctor," Charlotte told her. "And I'd feel so much better about goin' back to Montana if I knew you were settled and taken care of. But if you won't do it for me, do it for your children."

Georgia narrowed her gaze. "Don't you use my children to manipulate me."

"I'm just askin' you to consider how happy they'd be to have a full-time daddy in their lives again. Especially the twins, since they'll be startin' kindergarten soon." Her mother refilled her mug with coffee, added a heaping teaspoon of sugar. "When they're asked to draw those pictures of their family, I'm sure they'd like bein' able to put a daddy in the scene."

It was, as Charlotte had to know, the only argument that could sway Georgia from her conviction not to rush into anything.

Matt was surprised but not opposed when Georgia suggested a date for their wedding that was less than two weeks away. And he was determined that doing it on short notice didn't mean they couldn't do it right. While Georgia went shopping with her mom for a dress and made arrangements for a minister, flowers and cake, he enlisted the aid of his brothers to get the upstairs bedrooms ready for the kids.

He'd let the twins decide what they wanted for their room and was pleased with the sports-themed border and green paint they selected. Since the room had been empty, he ordered new furniture for them, too—a set of bunk beds, and dressers and desks. Georgia picked out the paint for Pippa's room and lace curtains for her window and pitched in with the decorating whenever she could spare a few minutes in between taking care of the kids and dealing with wedding details.

They were both so busy that they rarely had any time alone. And when they did manage to steal a few minutes of private time, they usually only stayed awake long enough to make love and then fall asleep in one another's arms. But as the date of the wedding drew nearer, Matt knew they needed to find time to talk. Except that now, with the wedding only a few days away, he couldn't help but worry that he'd already waited too long.

He was in the midst of hanging the border in the twins' room when he remembered that he needed a utility knife. When Georgia walked in to check on his progress, it seemed logical to ask her to get the knife out of the top drawer of his desk. It wasn't until she'd started down the stairs that he remembered the photo that was in that same drawer.

Panic clawing at his belly, he dropped the border and raced after her, desperate to get to her before she opened that drawer. But when he reached the doorway, he saw that he was already too late.

Georgia stood behind the desk, the utility knife in one hand and a wallet-sized photograph in the other. He couldn't see the picture from where he was standing, but the image was burned into his mind. A six-year-old boy with dark hair, dark eyes and a broad grin, wearing a mortarboard and gown and holding a rolled-up scroll. Liam's kindergarten graduation photo.

He took a tentative step into the room. "Georgia?"

She looked up at him, and his heart broke to see the doubts and confusion swirling in her eyes. "Who is he?"

He blew out a breath. "His name's Liam.... He was my son."

## Chapter Sixteen

Georgia could only stare at him, uncomprehending. She thought he'd said "my son" but that wasn't possible. There was no way he could have a child he'd never mentioned. But the expression on his face—a combination of guilt, regret and remorse—was silent confirmation of his words.

She sank into the chair behind the desk. "You have...a child?"

"I did," he said. "For almost three years."

Three years? But that didn't make any sense either, because the boy in the photo was clearly more than three years old.

"Maybe you could fill in some more details," she suggested, still trying to wrap her head around this sudden and unexpected revelation.

He nodded, but he didn't say anything right away, and she knew that he was struggling to find the right words to explain the situation.

"I married Lindsay because she was pregnant," he finally

said. "And because she told me the baby was mine. It turned out that he wasn't."

Though his words were casual, she heard the tension—and the hurt—in his tone, and her heart ached for him. She could only imagine how he'd responded to the disclosure. And because she knew Matt fairly well now, she knew he wouldn't have just felt hurt and betrayed, he would have been wrecked. "How did you find out?"

"Liam's real father finished his tour of duty in Iraq and decided to track down his ex-girlfriend, only to find that she'd married someone else less than two months after he was deployed."

"Did he know that she was pregnant?"

"No. Apparently Lindsay didn't even know when he left. And even when she knew she was going to have his baby, she didn't want to tell him because she was convinced he would never make it home. Instead, she decided to find another father for her baby."

As a mother, Georgia understood wanting what was best for her children, and she would—without question—do absolutely anything to protect them. But she couldn't imagine any woman being as coldly calculating as Matt was describing this woman to be.

"And I was the perfect patsy. She'd known me for years, because of my friendship with Kelsey. We'd even gone out a couple of times in high school, but it had never gone any further than that. Then suddenly she comes back from California after several years away, spinning this tale about how she never stopped thinking about me. She was beautiful and determined, and I let myself be flattered and seduced."

"She knew you would do the right thing," Georgia guessed. And it made her furious to think that this kind, generous, wonderful man had been ruthlessly targeted for those qualities.

He nodded. "I never even hesitated. I wasn't in love with her but I already loved the baby we were going to have together, and I believed our affection for one another would grow during the course of our marriage."

"I'm so sorry, Matt." And she was, her heart aching for everything he'd gone through.

Having witnessed firsthand how effortlessly he'd connected with her children, it was all too easy to imagine the deep and immediate bond he would have formed with a baby he believed was his own. And when the truth came out, he would have been absolutely devastated.

But he still wouldn't have turned his back on the child. Blood ties or not, in every way that mattered, he had been the little boy's father. His next words confirmed it.

"When Lindsay told me that she wanted a divorce so that she could take Liam back to California to be with his real dad, I was stunned and furious. So much that I thought about suing for custody.

"Although I wasn't Liam's biological parent, Jack assured me that I had a good chance of success, that the courts wouldn't look kindly on Lindsay's blatant deception and might believe that maintaining the status quo was in the child's best interests."

"What changed your mind?" she asked, though she suspected she already knew the answer to that question.

"Seeing the three of them together. It was immediately obvious to me that Lindsay and Jarrod loved one another in a way that she and I never had. And when he first saw Liam, when he realized that he was looking at his son—" Matt cleared his throat. "I just couldn't deny them the chance to be a family."

"Even though it broke your heart," she said softly.

He didn't deny it.

"Do you see him anymore?"

"Not since they moved back to California. Lindsay sends a card and a picture every once in a while, but Liam—" his gaze shifted to focus on the watercolor on the wall behind her "—he doesn't even remember me."

Georgia knew that was likely true. Even the twins' memories of their father were starting to fade. She knew they wouldn't ever forget Phillip—she would make sure of that—but their recollections would dim. For her, that sad truth had been countered, at least in part, by the pleasure of watching her sons bond with Matt.

She looked down at the photo again, her heart aching for the little boy who had been a pawn in his mother's game, thoughtlessly shifted from home to home, from father to father. As a result, Matt had lost his son. And then he'd moved in next door to a woman with three children who had lost their father. But the implications of that were something she wasn't ready to examine too closely just yet.

"This was his kindergarten graduation," she guessed.

He nodded.

She had to moisten her lips before she could ask, "How long ago was that?"

"A few weeks."

So much for thinking that the photo had been in the drawer for so long he'd forgotten about it. He'd only received it a few weeks earlier, and she didn't—couldn't—understand why he'd never mentioned it to her.

"I know I should have told you," Matt began.

And she waited, wondering what explanation he could possibly come up with that might make sense of the whole situation for her. He'd told her about his marriage—no, he'd only told her about his divorce, she realized now. When she'd asked him why he wasn't married, he'd only said that he was divorced. He'd never given her any details and he'd certainly never mentioned that his wife had given birth during the course of their marriage.

Even if it had turned out that the child wasn't his, it was a pretty significant omission. And it made her wonder why he'd been so closemouthed about the situation. In the beginning, okay. She hadn't spilled all the details about her marriage the first time they'd met. But as they'd grown closer, she thought he'd opened up to her. For God's sake, he'd asked her to marry him, their wedding was only three days away, and he'd never given her the tiniest glimpse into this part of his life.

Maybe she should have asked. Certainly his ease with her children, especially with Pippa, should have been a major clue that he had experience with kids. But when she'd questioned why he didn't have half a dozen children of his own, he'd never mentioned that he'd once had a son. He hadn't said anything at all.

Just like he didn't say anything else now, and Georgia finally understood that he wasn't going to. He wasn't going to explain why he hadn't told her about the beautiful little boy who had been his son. She knew it couldn't be easy for him to talk about Liam, to remember the child he'd loved and who had been ripped from his life. She could understand that experience would leave a huge hole in anyone's heart. But this wasn't just anyone, it was Matt—the man who claimed to love her.

And now she couldn't help but wonder if his affection for her was real, or if he just missed being a father.

He'd always been so good with her kids—forging a deep and enduring connection with each of them. At first, it had worried her, how quickly and easily the twins had taken to their neighbor. And Pippa hadn't been far behind. The little girl had never known her father, but she lit up like a neon sign whenever Matt walked into the room.

But Georgia's wariness had slowly faded and she'd been

grateful that she'd fallen in love with a man who so obviously loved her children. *I wasn't in love with her, but I already loved the baby we were going to have together.*

As Matt's words echoed in her mind, she had to wonder what had been the precipitating event in their relationship: his attraction to her or his affection for her children?

"Say something, Georgia, please."

She searched for words—any words—to describe the chaos of emotions churning inside of her. In the end, she only said, "Yes, you should have told me."

And she handed him the utility knife and walked out.

Georgia had introduced Trigger to the twins as Henry, not wanting to explain the origin of his nickname, but as soon as they found out he was married to Gramma, they decided that made him their Grampa. The boys had never had a Grampa before and Trigger had seemed so pleased with the designation that she didn't bother to nix the boys' decision.

And Gramma and Grampa were more than happy to look after the kids while Georgia ran some errands. At least that was the excuse she gave for going out again as soon as she'd returned from next door. And she probably did have errands that she needed to run, but in the moment, she couldn't remember any of them with all the doubts and insecurities churning in her mind.

She needed to talk to someone—she needed to vent and cry and try to figure out what Matt's revelation meant for their future. But she still didn't know very many people in Pinehurst and the one person she might consider talking to— Kelsey—had been Matt's friend for a long time.

*She'd known me for years, because of my friendship with Kelsey.*

That part of his explanation hadn't really registered at the time. In comparison to all of the other details, it had hardly seemed significant. But now Georgia knew that Kelsey might be the one person who had some of the answers she so desperately needed.

She walked down Main Street, past Emma's Flower Shop and Beckett's Sporting Goods until she found herself in front of Postcards from the World—Travel Agents & Vacation Planners.

Kelsey spotted her as soon as she walked through the door and waved her over. "Matt said you guys weren't going to plan a proper honeymoon until you'd weaned Pippa, but I had some ideas...." Her excited chatter faded away as Georgia got closer. "Obviously you're not here to inquire about vacation destinations."

"No, I'm not," Georgia agreed. "And I probably shouldn't have just dropped in, but I was hoping you might have a few minutes."

Kelsey looked around the mostly empty room. "Right now I have a lot of minutes. Did you want a cup of tea?"

Georgia nodded. "That would be great."

There was a small kitchen in the back, and Kelsey gestured for her to sit while she filled the kettle and put out a plate of cookies. When the tea was ready, she took a seat across from Georgia and said, "What did he do?"

Georgia wasn't surprised that the other woman had so quickly zeroed in on the heart of the problem, and the bluntness of the question encouraged her to respond equally succinctly. "He forgot to mention that he had a son."

"Are you saying that he didn't tell you until today?"

"He didn't tell me at all. I found a graduation photo of a little boy in his desk."

Kelsey winced. "Sometimes I wonder how that man ever got through medical school with only half of a working brain." Then she sighed. "Of course, he's not really an idiot, he just leads with his heart instead of his head sometimes.

That's why it was so easy for Lindsay to manipulate him. She played her cards exactly right to get what she wanted from Matt."

"Sounds like you knew her well," Georgia commented.

Kelsey paused with her cup halfway to her lips. "What did he tell you about my connection to his ex-wife?"

"He just said that he knew her because of his friendship with you. I assumed that meant you were a friend of hers, too."

The other woman shook her head. "Lindsay is my sister."

Now Georgia felt like the idiot. "I should have realized... I know Brittney calls him 'Uncle Matt,' but I thought that was just because you and he were such close friends."

"She refers to Jack and Luke as 'uncle' for that reason," Kelsey acknowledged. "But there's a real family connection to Matt through his marriage to my sister."

Georgia sipped her tea and tried to assimilate all of this new information.

"What are you thinking?" Kelsey asked gently.

"I don't know what to think. My head is spinning with so many questions and doubts that I don't know if I can articulate any of them."

"I can understand the questions, but what are you doubting?"

"Matt's reasons for wanting to marry me."

"The fact that he's head over heels in love with you isn't enough?"

"Is he?" Georgia asked, finally speaking her greatest fear aloud.

Kelsey looked startled by the question. "Do you really doubt it?"

"He married Lindsay to be a father to her baby," she reminded the other woman. "How do I know he isn't marrying me to be a father to my kids?" It was a possibility that tore at Georgia's heart.

"Ask him," Kelsey said. "That's the only way you can be sure."

It was good advice. Georgia certainly agreed that she and Matt needed to do a lot more talking, but first she went home to nurse her baby and hug her boys. Being with her children always helped her put things in perspective, through all of the best and worst times in her life. Since Matt had come into their lives, they'd enjoyed some of the best, and losing him, if that were to happen, would be one of the worst.

A short while later, Charlotte tracked her down in the laundry room where she was folding clothes.

"Did you pick up your wedding dress while you were out?"

Georgia shook her head. "No, I forgot."

"Forgot?" Her mother laughed. "How could you forget when you're gettin' married in three days?"

"I don't know if there's going to be a wedding," she admitted.

"Don't be silly," Charlotte chided. "Of course, there's goin' to be a weddin'. The church is booked, the flowers and cake have been ordered, and I know two very handsome boys who are lookin' forward to walkin' their mama down the aisle."

Georgia's eyes filled with tears. "This is all happening too fast. I knew Phillip three *years* before we got married—I've barely known Matt three *months*." She swallowed around the tightness in her throat. "And as it turns out, I'm not sure I really know him at all."

Charlotte waved a perfectly manicured hand. "You're just havin' some pre-weddin' jitters. Not to worry—every bride does."

"Mom, I'm not a virgin bride fretting about my wedding night," Georgia said, frustration evident in her tone. For once she wished her mother could be her mother, not the cliché-spouting Southern Belle that she played so well.

"Then tell me what it is about."

So, with no small amount of reservation, she did.

Charlotte was silent for several minutes after Georgia had finished talking, and when she finally spoke, it was only to ask, "Do you love him?"

"It's not that simple," she protested.

"Do you love him?" her mother asked again.

"You know I would never have let him put a ring on my finger if I didn't."

Charlotte nodded. "But do you know that marriage is a leap of faith as much as a testament to love?"

"How am I supposed to trust a man who hasn't been honest with me?"

"He should have been more forthcomin'," Charlotte agreed. "But I don't think you can say he was dishonest. I mean, he never actually told you he didn't have a son, did he?"

"That doesn't make it okay."

"I'm not sayin' it's okay." Her mother's tone was placating. "I'm just sayin' that you need to cut him some slack. No one's perfect, baby girl, and if you expect him to be, you're just goin' to be disappointed."

"You're right," Georgia finally said, because it was easier to agree with her mother than to expect that she might ever see things from her daughter's perspective.

"I understand why you might question his motivations," Charlotte said now. "But you might also consider that he's been so focused on his future with you that he wasn't thinkin' about the past. His ex-wife and her little boy are his past, you and your children are his future.

"You can postpone the weddin'—cancel it even, if that's what you feel you have to do," her mother continued. "But before you make that decision, make sure you think about all of the consequences."

"The boys would be so disappointed," Georgia admitted.

Charlotte shook her head. "Though you're right that puttin' off the weddin' would likely break their hearts, this isn't about my grandbabies. It's about you and about why you said yes when he proposed to you in the first place."

"Because I love him," she admitted.

Her mother looked her in the eye. "And are you willin' to spend the rest of your life without the man you love?"

\* \* \*

After her conversation with her mother, Georgia had gone next door to talk to Matt, only to find out—from his brother Jack, who was cursing as he attempted to assemble bunk beds—that he'd been called in to the hospital. So she went back to her mother's house, but she kept peeking out the window to watch for his return.

It was late when she saw his headlights turn in the driveway, but their conversation couldn't wait any longer. Knowing his routine, she slipped on a pair of sandals and went out the back door. Sure enough, Matt was out on the back deck, watching the puppies run around on the grass. The sky was black, but the moon and the stars gave off enough light that she was able to navigate her way across the yard.

The puppies spotted her first and greeted her with a cacophony of ecstatic barks, jumping at her heels as she made her way to where Matt was sitting.

"Hey," he said, trying for casual, but she heard a world of uncertainty in that single syllable.

She sat down beside him. "Hey, yourself."

Finnigan and Frederick were jumping all over one another, vying for her attention, so she took a moment to play with them while she tried to find the right words to say what she wanted to say.

But Matt broke the silence first, cautiously asking, "Are you still mad?"

She considered the spectrum of emotions that had churned through her system over the past twelve hours. "Mad isn't even part of what I was feeling," she told him. "Unless you count being furious with your ex-wife for what she did to you."

"I wish there was something I could say or do to explain," he said, "but I honestly don't know that there's any explanation."

"You're an idiot?" she suggested.

He managed a smile. "You've been talking to Kelsey."

Georgia nodded.

"I am an idiot," he agreed. "Because the absolute last thing I ever wanted to do was to keep anything from you."

"Then can I ask you something?"

"Anything," he promised.

"Why did you ask me to marry you?"

He shifted so that he was facing her. "That's your question?"

She nodded again.

"I screwed up even worse than I thought if you don't know how much I love you."

"I know you said you do," she acknowledged. "But I need to know that you want to be with me and didn't just see the widow next door and her fatherless kids as an opportunity to have a family again."

"Obviously you know how much I care about Quinn and Shane and Pippa, but as completely as your children won my heart, I never would have proposed to you if I didn't want to be with *you*.

"We've both been married before," he reminded her. "And I don't know about your vows, but I'm pretty sure that mine included something like 'so long as we both shall live' and not 'until the kids grow up and go off to college.'"

She had to smile at that. "The difference this time being that the kids aren't an obscure concept but an immediate reality."

"I couldn't love Quinn and Shane and Pippa any more if they were my own, but I wasn't thinking about them when I proposed to you," he assured her. "When I asked you to marry me, I wasn't thinking about teaching Quinn to throw a curveball or watching Shane knock it out of the park or even about the huge princess party we're going to throw for Pippa's first birthday."

"Although you've obviously given all of those ideas some thought."

"Because when I think of the future with you, it encompasses everything that I've ever wanted, but none of it matters without you." He took her hands, linked their fingers together. "I asked you to marry me because when I thought about my future, I couldn't imagine it without you. The kids are a bonus—I won't deny that—but it's you that I want by my side for the rest of my life."

The sincerity in his tone, the depth of emotion she could read in his eyes, brought tears to her own.

"But if you want to reschedule the wedding, that's okay," he told her. "Just don't push me out of your life. Give me a chance to prove how much I love you. Please."

"Do *you* want to reschedule?"

"No," he replied without hesitation. "I want to spend the rest of my life with you, and I want the rest of our life together to start as soon as possible. But if you've got any doubts at all…"

She shook her head, because she didn't. Not anymore. "I don't want to postpone the wedding," she said. "I want to marry you because I love you, and I want the rest of our life together to start as soon as possible."

He hauled her into his arms and kissed her firmly. And then he drew back to say, "In the interest of full disclosure—"

Georgia instinctively tensed. "Is this another secret from your past?"

"No, it's an idea for our future."

She exhaled. "Okay."

"I just wanted you to know that I've thought about someday adding to our family."

"You'd want more children?" She hadn't considered the possibility. Maybe because Pippa was still just a baby, the idea of having another baby had never crossed her mind. But now that Matt had mentioned it, she knew that she would love to have another child—Matt's child.

"Only if you do," he hastened to assure her. "I just thought, we've already got two boys, it might be nice for Pippa to have a sister."

It was the *we* that had her eyes filling with tears, the ease with which he'd spoken that one word that made her accept the truth of his feelings for her. He hadn't put the ring on her finger to make them a family—they already were a family. The ring really was about his love and commitment to her.

"Why don't we hold off any discussion about another baby until I've finished nursing this one," Georgia suggested.

"That sounds fair," he agreed.

"Besides, we have more important things to do right now if we're going to move into your house after the wedding in three days."

"I finished hanging the border in the twins' room," he told her. "Do you want to see it?"

"You're just trying to get me upstairs, conveniently down the hall from your bedroom," she guessed.

He smiled. "Am I that transparent?"

She framed his face in her hands so that she could look into his eyes and clearly see his love for her shining through.

"Yes, you are," she said, and touched her lips to his.

"I love you, Georgia Reed."

"And I love you, Matt Garrett," she told him. "Now, let's go check out that border."

He took her hand and led her into the house that was no longer his own but the home they would share—just like their future—together.

## Epilogue

The day of the wedding wasn't very different from any other day that Matt had experienced since moving in next door to Georgia and her kids—which meant that it was pretty much chaos from beginning to end.

He knew it was his own fault, since he'd convinced his bride-to-be to let the twins spend the night at his house. He'd been confident that he could handle the routines of two little boys and get them ready for church the next day. Besides, he had backup in the form of Jack and Luke.

When the boys were fed and washed and dressed—and looking way too darn cute in their little tuxedos, despite the fact that Quinn kept complaining the shoes were too tight—they wanted to play. But all of their toys were next door, so he put cartoons on the TV. That occupied them for all of about thirty minutes, after which he finally agreed they could go outside with the puppies *so long as they didn't get dirty.*

Both Quinn and Shane nodded their understanding of the rule, and Luke went outside with them to ensure they followed it. Unfortunately, no one could have anticipated that Finnigan would find "something stinky and dead" (as Quinn later described it) in the yard and decide it would make a tasty snack, but not so tasty that he didn't later throw it up on Shane's pants.

Luke—the expert on all kinds of puppy puke—brought them back inside for cleanup. It was shortly after that when Jack discovered Quinn's shoes in the toilet of the downstairs bathroom. Apparently Mommy never let him put wet shoes on his feet for fear he'd catch "new-moan-ya," so he'd stuffed them in the toilet to get them wet and unwearable.

When Matt rounded everyone up for a last inspection before they headed off to the church, he decided that the boys' tuxedos didn't look too bad with running shoes. Then he made the mistake of reminding the twins that they were going to walk down the aisle on either side of their mom to give her away. He said the words without thinking, and both Quinn and Shane burst into tears, protesting that they didn't want to give away their mommy, they wanted to keep her forever and ever.

By the time he dried their tears, clarified their role in the ceremony and confirmed that they were *all* going to be together forever and ever, his head was throbbing.

A grinning Luke handed him a glass of water and a couple of Tylenol. Jack followed that up with a tumbler of scotch.

But all the drama was forgotten as soon as he saw Georgia. Wearing a sheath-style dress of cream-colored lace and carrying a bouquet of red roses, she completely took his breath away.

It seemed to take forever for her to reach the front of the church—which might have been because Quinn and Shane were almost literally dragging their feet—but when the minister instructed them to join hands, Georgia's were steady and warm. And in her eyes, he couldn't see any evidence of lingering doubts, just love and joy shining in the beautiful blue depths.

But as a reminder, in case the vows hadn't been enough, he whispered to her, "I love you, Mrs. Garrett."

"I know," she said. "I love you, too."

And when his lips brushed over hers, he heard Quinn clearly announce, "We gived her away, but she's still our mommy."

As soft chuckles sounded from the gallery, Georgia drew back to look at him, silently questioning.

Matt could only shake his head. "Let's just say that the only thing that got me through the last few hours on my own with those boys was the knowledge that, after today, I would always have you by my side."

"Always," she promised.

As Georgia and Matt made their way back down the aisle, they were flanked by Shane and Quinn with Pippa in her mother's arms.

Now, officially, a family.

* * * * *

**He brought her closer. "I'm glad I met you. I'm even glad I lost my memory."**

"I'm glad we met, too. But you shouldn't say that about having amnesia."

"It's giving me a chance to start over."

"This isn't starting over, J.D. It's a break from your other life."

"I don't care about my other life."

"You shouldn't say that, either. It's important to care about who you are."

How could he care about something he couldn't remember? They didn't talk anymore, and he was grateful for the silence. He didn't want to disturb the bond. He wanted the luxury of knowing her in this way. He was in the moment. He was part of it. John Doe and Jenna Byrd, he thought.

He danced with her as if his amnesia depended on it, the heat between them surging through his veins.

This was a memory he would never forget.

# THE TEXAN'S
# FUTURE BRIDE

### BY
### SHERI WHITEFEATHER

First published in Great Britain 2013
by Mills & Boon, an imprint of Harlequin (UK) Limited,
Eton House, 18-24 Paradise Road, Richmond, Surrey TW9 1SR

© Sheree Henry-Whitefeather 2013

ISBN: 978 0 263 90117 7
ebook ISBN: 978 1 472 00492 5

23-0613

Harlequin (UK) policy is to use papers that are natural, renewable and recyclable products and made from wood grown in sustainable forests. The logging and manufacturing processes conform to the legal environmental regulations of the country of origin.

Printed and bound in Spain
by Blackprint CPI, Barcelona

**Sheri WhiteFeather** is a bestselling author who has won numerous awards, including readers' and reviewers' choice honors. She writes a variety of romance novels for Mills & Boon. She has become known for incorporating Native American elements into her stories. She has two grown children who are tribally enrolled members of the Muscogee Creek Nation.

Sheri is of Italian-American descent. Her great-grandparents immigrated to the United States from Italy through Ellis Island, originating from Castel di Sangro and Sicily. She lives in California and enjoys ethnic dining, shopping in vintage stores and going to art galleries and museums. Sheri loves to hear from her readers. Visit her website at www.SheriWhiteFeather.com.

To Judy Duarte and Crystal Green
for supporting my dreams
and always believing that they will come true.

# 20% OFF*

with code
**THANKSJUN**

Visit www.millsandboon.co.uk today to get this exclusive offer

Ordering online is easy:

- 1000s of stories converted to eBook
- Big savings on titles you may have missed in store

Visit today and enter the code **THANKSJUN** at the checkout today to receive **20% OFF** your next purchase of books and eBooks*. You could be settling down with your favourite authors in no time!

MILLS & BOON

JUN1

# Chapter One

W hat the—?

As Jenna Byrd steered her truck toward the Flying
B, she noticed a man walking along the private road
that led to the ranch. Or stumbling was more like it. He
didn't look familiar, but he didn't seem out of place, either. His dusty jeans, plain T-shirt and battered boots
were typical small-town Texas attire. He was missing
a hat, though. Had he lost it somewhere? His short dark
hair was decidedly messy.

Jenna frowned. Clearly, he was snockered in the middle of the day. Cowboys could be a hell-raisin' breed.
Of course she didn't dally with that kind. Although she
was hoping to find a cowboy to call her own, she was
attracted to well-behaved men, not rabble-rousers who
could barely put one foot in front of the other. He was
ambling toward her pickup instead of away from it.

Good grief. She couldn't just leave him out here. The Flying B was about five miles down the road, and in his condition, he would never make it. And why he was heading toward the ranch was beyond her.

She stopped her truck and sighed. She knew he wasn't a Flying B employee. She'd made a point of meeting everyone on the payroll. Jenna owned a portion of the ranch. She and her sister and their cousin had inherited equal shares of the Flying B, and they were going to turn it into a B and B.

She rolled down her window and said, "What are you doing out here?"

He looked at her as if he wasn't really seeing her. His deep brown eyes were glazed. He didn't respond.

She repeated the question.

He blinked at her. He was probably around her age, thirty or so, with tanned skin and striking features—handsome, even in his wasted state.

Curious, she tried to figure him out. Maybe he was a whiskey-toting hitchhiker. Or maybe he was affiliated with another ranch in the area and after he'd tied one on, he'd mistakenly taken the wrong road. There had to an explanation for his disorderly presence.

Hoping to solve the dilemma, she asked, "Who are you?"

"Who are you?" he parroted.

This was going nowhere. "You've had too much to drink."

He squinted. "I have?"

"Yes."

"I don't think so."

Easy for him to say. He was too drunk to know the

difference. While she debated how to handle the situation, he staggered a little more.

"I feel funny," he said.

*No kidding,* she thought.

"I've got a headache." He rubbed the back of his head. When he brought his fingers forward, the tips were red.

Her pulse jumped. He was bleeding.

She parked and leaped out of her truck. Had he gotten into a brawl? Overly intoxicated men were prone to that sort of behavior. But whatever he'd done, it didn't matter. All that mattered was getting his wound treated.

"My cousin's fiancé is a doctor. He lives at the ranch where I live, and I think he's home today. If he isn't, I'll take you to his office."

"No. That's okay." He wiped his hands on his pants. "I'm better now."

Obviously, he wasn't. She slipped her arm around him and realized that he didn't smell of alcohol. Most likely, he hadn't been drinking, which made his condition a bigger cause for concern. He was probably dazed because of the injury.

"Come on. Let's get you into the truck."

Shouldering his weight wasn't easy. He was about six feet, packed with lean muscle mass. At five-five, with a slight build, she was no match for him.

He lagged against her, and she held him tighter. Nonetheless, he kept insisting that he was fine, which clearly wasn't the case. He was definitely confused.

Once he was seated, she eased away from him and closed the door. She got behind the wheel and reached for her cell phone. She called Mike Sanchez or "Doc" as he'd become known in these parts. He was at the ranch. She asked him to meet her at the main house and told him that she was bringing an injured man with her.

"The back of his head is bleeding." She glanced at her passenger. He was staring out the window with those glazed eyes. She lowered her voice. "I don't know much about these things, but I think he has some sort of concussion. I found him wandering along Flying B Road."

"Don't worry, Jenna," Doc replied. "Just stay calm and get him here."

"I'm on my way." She ended the call, then started the engine and headed for her destination.

The cowboy turned to look at her. "Are we on a date?"

Yikes. Talk about befuddled. His condition was worse than she thought. "I'm taking you to see a doctor, remember?"

"Your hair is pretty." He reached out as if he meant to grasp a loose tendril of her wavy gold locks.

Jenna's heartbeat skittered. He didn't make contact, but she could almost imagine how his tortured touch would feel.

Almost. She focused on the road.

"Very pretty," he said.

She gripped the wheel, and to keep him from reaching for her hair again, she redirected his thoughts.

"What's your name?" she asked, rephrasing her original "Who are you?" question.

He furrowed his brows. It wasn't a trick question, but he didn't appear capable of a response. He didn't know his own name.

"It's okay," she said. "That's why I'm taking you to see a doctor." Besides, all they had to do was look at his ID to see who he was. Everyone carried identification with them. Still, not knowing something as simple as his name wasn't a good sign.

He leaned against the window, then closed his eyes. She hoped that he wasn't going to pass out. That wouldn't be a good sign, either.

She increased her speed, bumping along the road, her truck flanked by green pastures and grazing cattle.

Finally, as the main house came into view, she breathed a sigh of "thank You, God" relief.

The dashing young doctor was waiting for her on the wraparound porch. Tammy, her equally fetching cousin, was there, too. Jenna had only met Tammy recently, when all of the inheritance whoopla had begun. None of the heirs had grown up on the Flying B or visited when they were kids because their families had been estranged from each other. So, when they'd gotten called to their ailing grandpa's bedside, and when he'd died, they'd wept for a man they'd just begun to know.

She glanced at the cowboy beside her. Now wasn't the time to think about men she barely knew. Or death. Or anything bad.

Jenna stopped the truck, and Doc opened the passenger side and escorted the patient into the house.

Once Jenna exited the vehicle, Tammy approached her, and they went inside, too.

Doc didn't waste time. He was already examining the stranger, who sat on the edge of a sturdy leather sofa, looking as confused as ever.

Jenna stood back and frowned. "Do you recognize him?" she asked Tammy. "Do you know if he's from around here?"

"No."

"Me, either." But dang if he didn't make her tongue stick to the roof of her mouth. She couldn't get his tortured attempt to touch her out of her mind.

Just a few feet away, Doc was telling the patient that he was going to need a couple of stitches. In fact, Doc was preparing to patch him up. But the cut itself was incidental. What obviously concerned Doc were his other symptoms.

Apparently Jenna was right. Indeed, he had a concussion.

Thing was, his identity was still unknown. He wasn't carrying any form of identification; Doc checked his person.

"What do you think is going to happen?" Jenna whispered to Tammy.

"I don't know."

Neither did Jenna. But it was clear from the examination that he had no recollection about himself or how he'd gotten hurt.

After his cut was sanitized and stitched, Doc made arrangements for him to be treated at the local hospital. He spoke gently to the patient, then explained the situation to Jenna.

"I'm going to order a CT scan," he said. "At this point, it's impossible to know the severity of his trauma."

"What's the worst-case scenario?" she asked, making sure the stranger was out of earshot.

"Bleeding in the brain."

She shivered.

Doc concluded, "But let's not get ahead of ourselves. Let's get a thorough diagnosis first."

"I want to go to the hospital with him." She was unable to bear the thought of abandoning him.

"That's fine. A police report will have to be filed, too, since we don't know who he is or what triggered the injury. He'll be admitted as a John Doe."

Jenna didn't like the impersonal sound of that. But she didn't like any of this. She preferred to have her ducks in a tidy yellow row, with carefully laid plans, no matter what aspect of her life it concerned. She'd even created a list of the type of qualities she wanted her future husband to have, a man who would be nothing like her father. She used to be disappointed in her dad, but these days she was downright ashamed of him. A humiliating skeleton in his closet had surfaced.

She glanced at the stranger. Did he have skeletons in his closet, too? Even if he did, it was none of her concern. She was going to see him through this injury and forget about him.

Doc and Tammy took him to the hospital, and Jenna followed them in her truck.

She sat in the waiting room while he underwent the CT scan. Was she going to be able to forget about him? Already she was feeling oddly attached, as if she was responsible for him somehow.

She glanced over at Tammy, who occupied the seat next to her. "Thanks for keeping me company."

"It shouldn't take long. Rather than wait for a written report, Mike is going to look at the scans himself, along with the radiologist, of course."

"It's nice having a doctor in the family."

Tammy quirked a smile. "Very nice." She stood up. "Do you want some coffee?"

"Sure."

"How do you take it?"

"Cream and sugar."

"Coming right up."

Jenna watched her cousin head for the vending machine. She was a petite brunette, thriving on newfound love. She and Jenna formed a bond when Jenna had helped her with a makeover that had caught the doctor's eye. Tammy was a tomboy turned hot tamale. She could still ride and rope with the best of 'em, but she also looked darn fine in feminine attire. The girl could cook up a storm, too. Soon the Flying B cook would be retiring and Tammy would be taking over as the down-home B and B chef.

Tammy returned with two cups and handed Jenna one. She took a sip. It tasted better than expected.

Jenna said about the stranger, "I can't help but wonder who he is. What his name is, what his family is like."

"Hopefully he'll remember soon."

"I just hope the scan comes out all right." She drank a bit more of her coffee. "He said some weird things when we were in the truck. He told me that he liked my hair, then he asked me if we were on a date."

"That must have been awkward."

"It was." She frowned. "What sort of treatment do they do if someone is bleeding in the brain?"

"I have no idea, but you shouldn't be dwelling on that."

"I know. But I'm the one who found him."

"Finders keepers, losers weepers?" Tammy put her cup beside a dog-eared magazine. "Did you ever say that when you were a kid?"

"All the time. But I hope that doesn't apply to this situation."

"Like someone is left behind weeping for him?"

Jenna nodded, and they both fell silent. But it seemed better not to talk. Other people had just entered the waiting room with somber looks on their faces, as if they were afraid that they might be left weeping for whoever they were there to see.

Time ticked by.

Then Tammy looked up and said, "There's Mike," as her fiancé strode toward them.

Jenna got to her feet, with Tammy on her heels.

Doc said to them, "The results were normal, but we're going to keep him overnight for observation."

"Then what?" Jenna asked.

"Then we'll reevaluate his condition in the morning."

"Do you think his memory will return by then?"

"It's possible. Oftentimes these sorts of lapses only last a day or two. But it could continue for a while. It's hard to say."

"Can I see him?"

"Once we check him into a room, you can visit him."

By the time that happened, the stranger was asleep. Doc and Tammy went home, and Jenna sat in a stiff plastic chair beside his bed and watched him. She used the opportunity to study his features: dark eyebrows, a strong, sharp nose, cheekbones a male model would envy, medium-size lips with a bit of a downward slant. That made her curious about his smile. Was it bright? Crooked? Brooding? She noticed that he was harboring a five-o'clock shadow. The sexy scruff made him look even more like the cowboy she assumed he was.

The hospital gown, however, didn't; it robbed him of his edge.

He stirred in his sleep, and she frowned. Although he had a semiprivate room and the curtain was drawn, the TV of the older man next to him sounded in her ears. A game show was playing, a program that had been on the air since she was a kid. She'd never actually seen it, not all the way through. But she'd gotten used to hearing the noisy show in the background when her dad used to watch it, much like she was hearing it now.

Tuning out the sound, she studied the stranger again. Because she was tempted to skim his cheek and feel the warmth of his skin, she kept her hands on her lap. She even curled her fingers to keep them still. Being this close to him while he slept wasn't a good idea. She should go home, but she stayed for as long as the hospital would allow, already anxious to return the following day.

In the morning, Jenna had breakfast with her sister in the main house, surrounded by retro-style gingham accents in the kitchen. Unfortunately it was too early to head over to the hospital. With the exception of spouses and significant others, visiting hours were limited.

She'd barely slept last night, wondering if the stranger would recoup his memory today.

She glanced across the table at Donna, but her sister didn't look up. She was busy texting, in between sips of fresh-brewed coffee and bites of a Spanish omelet, courtesy of the soon-to-retire cook.

Jenna continued to study Donna. They'd always been different from each other. Jenna, a certified horseback riding instructor, loved everything country, and Donna, a magazine writer turned marketer, loved everything city. As soon as the B and B was off the ground, Donna would be returning to New York, where she lived and worked. Jenna, on the other hand, planned to stay at the ranch and help run the B and B with Tammy.

Donna finally glanced up. "What?" she said.

"Nothing."

"Then why were you staring at me?"

"I was just thinking about how opposite we are."

"We're siblings, not clones."

"Yes, but you'd think that we would have more in common. Or look more alike or whatever." Although both were blonde, Donna was a year older, three inches taller and wildly curvy. She had the figure of a 1940s pinup, while Jenna was small and lean.

Donna shrugged and went back to texting, and Jenna considered how distant their relationship was. Her sister had trouble connecting with people on an emotional level, but Jenna could hardly blame her. They'd been raised in a go-your-own-way environment.

Tammy entered the room, and Jenna immediately said, "Hi."

"Hello, yourself." Their cousin sat down and greeted Donna, as well. Then she turned back to Jenna and said, "Mike left a couple of hours ago to check on our patient."

Her stomach fluttered. "He did? Any word?"

"From Mike? No. But I'm sure he'll call when he can."

Donna quit texting. "What patient? Who's sick?"

Jenna answered, "I found a man yesterday. He was wandering around on the road with a concussion." She went on to explain the details. "Hopefully he'll be better today."

"Wow," Donna said. "Can you imagine losing your memory?"

No, but Jenna wouldn't mind forgetting about the mess their dad had made of things. But he'd been notorious for disappointing her, even when she was a child. He'd never been there when she needed him. He'd been too busy with his corporate job. He rarely attended parent-teacher conferences or planned birthday parties or took his daughters to the movies or engaged in the types of activities that would have made them seem more like a family.

She glanced at Donna. Funny thing about her sister. Before the skeleton in Dad's closet had surfaced, Donna used to idolize him. He'd been her hero, the person she often emulated, particularly with her workaholic, career-is-king habits. Not that Donna would ever admit how deeply he influenced her. But Jenna was keenly aware of it.

Clearing the Dad-clutter from her mind, Jenna said to Tammy, "I was planning on going to the hospital later, but maybe I should wait for Mike to call."

"It might take him a while to check in," her cousin replied. "He has a lot of rounds to make. Why don't you head over to the hospital now and look in on the man? I can tell you're still worried about him."

"I can't see him until noon."

"Says who?"

"The hospital visiting hours."

Tammy waved away the rules. "They probably won't notice if you slip in a little early."

"I think it would be better if I went at noon." She

wasn't comfortable taking liberties. She preferred to play by the book.

Tammy didn't push her out of her comfort zone and neither did Donna. They allowed her to be her regimented self.

When the time rolled around for her to get ready, she donned classic Western wear: a broomstick skirt, a feminine blouse and a nice pair of boots. She freshened up her face and fluffed her hair, too. Not that it should matter what the stranger thought of her appearance. If he was better today, this would probably be the last time she saw him.

She arrived at the hospital at twelve o'clock sharp and went to the nurses' station, where she inquired about the patient's condition. They informed her that he was awake and coherent, and once everything was in order, Dr. Sanchez would be releasing him.

So, he *was* better.

She thanked them for the information and continued down the hall. A moment later, she stalled. She was nervous about conversing with him.

Pushing past the trepidation, she proceeded. She entered his room and passed the TV-watching patient. Today he was engaged in a sitcom from the seventies. He didn't glance her way, and she left him alone, too.

She moved forward and came face-to-face with the stranger. He was sitting up in bed. His gaze zeroed in on hers, and her heart went bumpy.

"Good morning," she said, keeping a calm voice.

"You're the girl from yesterday."

"Yes."

"The blonde I thought I was dating. I'm sorry about that."

Dang. Did he have to go and mention it? "It's okay. You were out of it."

He nodded, and she took the seat next to his bed, the same spot where she'd watched him sleep. "You look healthier." Still a bit worn-out, she thought, but an improvement nonetheless. "I heard that Doc will be releasing you."

"Yes, but I'm supposed to take it easy."

"You can't go kicking up your heels just yet?"

"No. Not yet." He smiled a little.

It was sinfully crooked. The *bump-bump* in her chest returned. "I'm Jenna, by the way. Jenna Byrd."

"Thank you for what you did. Jenna," he added softly.

The bumping intensified. "I'm glad I was there to help." She scooted to the edge of her chair. "So, what's your name?"

He furrowed his dark brows. "I don't know. I still can't remember anything, aside from you bringing me to your ranch and coming here."

She gaped at him. "Your memory hasn't recovered? Then why is Doc releasing you?"

"Because I'm not dizzy or confused, and my vital signs are good. I have what's called retrograde amnesia, but they can't keep me in the hospital for that. Besides, my memories are supposed to return. It's just a matter of when."

She didn't know what to say. He was still as much of a stranger as he was before.

He said, "The sheriff was here earlier. He took a report. He took my fingerprints, too." He held up his hands and gazed at them. "If I'm in the system, they'll be able to identify me that way."

He might have a criminal record? That wasn't a comforting thought. "Do you think you're in the system?"

"I don't know." He lowered his hands. "But the sheriff doesn't want Dr. Sanchez to release me until the results are in. So we're waiting to hear. I guess the police want to be sure that there isn't a warrant out for my arrest before they put me back on the streets."

"Do you mind if I wait until you hear something?"

"Why would you want to do that?"

Because she still felt responsible for him. Or was it because she was so doggone attracted to him? That wasn't a comforting thought, either. Confused and covering her tracks she said, "I'm interested in knowing who you are." And hoping that he was an upstanding guy.

"At the moment, I'm no one."

"That's not true. Everyone is someone."

He glanced away. Obviously her comment hadn't made a dent in his amnesiac armor. She wanted to reassure him, but how could she, especially since he might be wanted by the police?

Just then, double sets of footsteps sounded, and Jenna turned around in her chair. The stranger shifted in the direction of the approaching people, too.

It was Doc, making a crisp-white presentation in his lab coat, and next to him was a tall, stocky lawman.

As the air grew thick with anticipation, the stranger shot Jenna a quick glance.

Trapping her in the moment they'd been waiting for.

## Chapter Two

Amid the silence, Doc caught Jenna's attention. She expected him to ask her to leave, but he merely nodded an acknowledgment. Maybe it was going to be okay. Maybe there was nothing to be concerned about.

The lawman said to the patient, "I'm Deputy Tobbs. The sheriff assigned your case to me."

"Do I have a record?" the stranger asked bluntly.

The deputy shifted his weight. "No, you don't. Your fingerprints aren't on file, but I'm going to investigate further. I'll do my best to uncover your identity and discover what happened to you. I'll be questioning everyone in the area, in case you work around here or were visiting someone."

"Someone who hasn't noticed that I'm gone?"

"It could have been a surprise visit and you never made it to your destination. It could have been a number of things. I'm inclined to think that you were assaulted and robbed, possibly carjacked, which would account for you wandering around on foot. But we'll have to wait and see what turns up."

The stranger tugged a hand through his hair, stopping short of his injury. "It could be worse, I guess." He addressed Doc. "Are you going to sign my release papers now?"

"Yes, but first we need to figure out where you're going to go."

The stranger replied, "Is there a homeless shelter in the area?"

The deputy answered the question. "There's one in the next county, about thirty miles from here."

"Then that will have to do, if they'll take me."

"I can give them a call," the deputy said.

*No way,* Jenna thought. She wasn't going to let him go off like that. She would worry about him. Still, did she have a right to intervene? Regardless, she couldn't seem to hold back.

She said to the stranger, "You can stay at the Flying B until you regain your memory or until Deputy Tobbs finds out who you are. We're turning the ranch into a B and B, and we have guest rooms and cabins on the property."

"I can't stay there."

Jenna persisted, especially now that she'd made up her mind about saving him, or whatever it was she was trying to do. "Why not?"

"I just can't. I shouldn't."

"Sure you can," Doc said, supporting her idea. "It would be a good place for you to recover."

"I don't know."

Jenna frowned. "What's not to know? Just say yes."

He frowned, too. "Are you always this insistent?"

Was she? "Sometimes." Considering from the time that she and Donna were kids, the one lesson their father had always taught was to go after what they wanted. "But Doc agrees with me, so you're outnumbered."

"Consider it part of your treatment," Doc said. "I could keep a better eye on you, and being surrounded by fresh air would be a heck of a lot nicer than being holed in a homeless shelter."

The deputy interjected. "Sounds like you've got it worked out."

"We do," Jenna assured him.

"Then I'm going to take my leave." He placed his card on the rolling stand beside the bed. "Call me if you have any questions," he told the man with amnesia. "And if I need to reach you, I'll stop by the Flying B." The deputy turned to Jenna. "You should introduce him to everyone at the ranch. It's possible that someone there will recognize him."

"I will, just as soon as he's feeling up to it."

He turned back to the patient. "You take care."

"Thank you," came the polite reply.

Deputy Tobbs said goodbye to everyone and left the room, a hush forming in his absence. Jenna wondered if Doc was going to depart, too. But he stayed quietly put.

She said to the stranger, "You're going to need another name, other than John Doe."

His dark gaze caught hers. "Some people have that name for real."

"I know. But it's doubtful that you do."

"Then you can pick one."

"You want me to name you?"

"Somebody has to."

Jenna glanced at Doc. He stood off to the side, clutching a clipboard that probably contained "John Doe's" charts. Anxious, she crossed her arms over her chest. Doc's silent observation created a fishbowl-type effect. But he had a right to analyze his patient's reactions.

Was he analyzing her, too?

She'd been bothered by the John Doe reference from the beginning, but now that she'd been given the responsibility of changing it, she felt an enormous amount of pressure.

Could Doc tell how nervous she was?

She asked the stranger, "Are you sure you don't want to come up with something yourself?"

"I'm positive."

He sounded as if it didn't matter, that with or without a makeshift name, he still considered himself no one.

Reminding her of how lost he truly was.

As he waited for the outcome, he thought about how surreal all of this was. He felt like a ketchup jar someone had banged upside the counter, with memories locked inside that wouldn't come out.

Emptiness. Nothingness.

His only lifeline was the pretty blonde beside his bed and the doctor watching the scene unfold.

"What do you think of J.D.?" she asked.

"The initials for John Doe?"

She nodded. "I always thought that using initials in place of a name was sexy."

He started. Was she serious? "Sexy?"

She blushed, her cheeks turning a soft shade of pink. "I didn't mean it like that."

Intrigued, he tilted his head. She'd gone from being aggressive to downright shy. "How did you mean it?"

"That it's mysterious."

"Then I guess it fits." Everything was a mystery, right down to his confusion about dating her. Was she the type he would've dated in the past? Or did he even have a type?

"So we can start calling you J.D. now?" she asked, obviously double-checking.

He nodded.

"And you're going to stay at the Flying B?"

He nodded again, still feeling reluctant about being her houseguest or cabin guest or whatever. As far as he was concerned, a homeless shelter would have sufficed.

She said, "When I first saw you, I assumed that you were a cowboy, maybe an employee of a neighboring ranch. I hadn't considered a carjacking, but I wondered if you might be a hitchhiker. I'm glad the deputy is going to talk to everyone in the area about you. Then we'll know for sure." She glanced at his clothes, which were hanging nearby. "You were certainly dressed like a local cowboy, except that you didn't have a hat. But I figured that you'd lost it somewhere."

He followed her line of sight. The T-shirt, jeans and worn-out boots he'd been wearing were as unfamiliar as the day he'd been born. "I don't have a recollection of doing ranch work."

"You don't have a recollection of anything," she reminded him.

"I know, but wouldn't I have a feeling of being connected to ranching? Wouldn't it be ingrained in me if that's what I did for a living?" He turned to the expert. "What do you think, Dr. Sanchez?"

"I think it's too soon to be concerned about that. You just need to rest and let your feelings fall into place when they're meant to." He smiled. "I also think you should start calling me Doc."

"Okay, Doc." He preferred less formality, too, and already he'd gotten used to hearing Jenna say it. A moment later, he shifted his gaze back to his unfamiliar clothes.

Jenna said, "You put some miles on those boots."

"I must have thought they were comfortable." He noticed that the toes were starting to turn up. "I guess I'm going to find out if I still like wearing them."

"Yes, J.D., you are," Doc said, using his new name. "In fact, you can get dressed now, if you want. I can send a nurse in if you need help."

"No, I can handle it."

"All right. Then I'll go get your papers ready, and Jenna can step out of the room and come back when you're done."

J.D. got a highly inappropriate urge, wishing that he could ask her to stay and help him get dressed. He even imagined her hand on his zipper.

*Hell and damnation.*

He should have insisted on going to a shelter. Clearly, being around Jenna wasn't a good idea.

She and the doctor left, closing the curtain behind them. J.D. got out of bed and walked over to the closet, still thinking about Jenna.

He cursed quietly under his breath, stripped off the hospital gown and put on his Western wear. He grappled with his belt. He fought the boots, too. They felt odd at first, but he got used to them soon enough.

Curious to look at himself in the mirror, he went into

the bathroom. He didn't recognize his reflection, with him wearing the clothes. He was still a nowhere man.

Luckily, the hospital had provided a few necessities, like a comb, toothpaste and a toothbrush. Still standing in front of the mirror, he combed his hair straight back, but it fell forward naturally, so he let it be. They hadn't provided a razor, so he had no choice but to leave the beard stubble. It was starting to itch and he wanted it gone. Or maybe it was the image it created that he didn't like. It made him look as haunted as he felt, like an Old West outlaw.

J.D. the Kid? No. He wasn't a kid. He figured himself for early thirties. Or that was how he appeared. But he could be mistaken.

Blowing out a breath, he returned to his room and opened the curtain, letting Jenna know that she could come back.

She did, about five minutes later, bringing two cups of coffee with her.

"It's from the vending machine," she said. "But it's pretty good. I had some last night when I was waiting for your test results." She handed him a cup. "It has cream and sugar. I hope that's okay."

"It's fine. Thanks. I don't have a preference, not that I'm aware of, anyway." He sat on the edge of the bed, offering her the chair. "You've been putting in a lot of time at this place, hanging out for a man you barely know."

"I'm starting to get to know you." She smiled. "You obviously like coffee."

"So it seems." He drank it right down. "I had orange juice with breakfast, but this hits the spot."

"We have gourmet coffeemakers in the guest cabins. You can brew yourself a fancy cup of Joe tomorrow morning."

"That sounds good, but maybe I shouldn't stay there. You don't need the burden of having a guy like me around."

"You can't back out. You already agreed. Doctor's orders, remember?"

Yes, but his recovery didn't include the stirrings she incited. Even now, he wanted to see her blush again. He liked the shy side of her.

"When this is over, I'll repay you for your hospitality," he said.

"Just get better, okay? That will be payment enough."

"You're a nice girl, Jenna."

"And you seem like a nice man."

"You thought I was drunk off my butt when you saw me stumbling around. I remember you telling me that I had too much to drink."

"I retracted that when I saw that your head was bleeding. How is your head, by the way?"

"Still hurts a little."

"How about your feet?"

He squinted. "My feet aren't injured."

"I was talking about your boots. How do they feel?"

*Oh, yeah. The boots.* He glanced down at the scuffed leather. "Fine." He motioned to hers. "You've got yourself a fancy pair."

"These are my dressy ones. Sometimes I go dancing in them, too."

"I have no idea if I know how to dance."

"You can try the two-step and see."

"Right now?" He teased her. "Up and down the hospital corridor?"

She laughed. "Later, smarty, when you're up to par."

Were they flirting? It sure as heck seemed as if they were. But it didn't last long because he didn't let it.

He knew better than to start something that he was in no position to finish. She seemed to know it, too. She turned off the charm at the same instant he did.

Tempering what was happening between them.

As a bright and bouncy nurse wheeled J.D. out to Jenna's truck, he said, "I'd rather walk."

"It's hospital policy," the chipper lady said. "Everyone leaves in a wheelchair."

He made a face, and Jenna smiled to herself. Machismo. He certainly behaved like a cowboy.

She stopped smiling. She was actually taking this man home with her, and she knew darn well that he was as attracted to her as she was to him.

But they weren't going to act on it. They were both cautious enough not to let it take over. So it would be fine, she assured herself. He would be a recuperating guest, a patient of Doc's, and nothing more.

She turned on the radio, and they listened to music instead of talking.

Finally, when they were on the private road leading to the ranch, he glanced over at her and said, "Déjà vu," making a joke about repeating his car-ride experience from yesterday.

She tried to make light of it, too. "Your first encounter with it."

"That I'm able to remember. I probably had déjà vu in my old life."

His old life. That made it sound as if he'd become someone new. She supposed that, at least for now, he was a different person. But since she didn't know who he was before, she couldn't compare the old with the new.

"I wonder if I should put you in the dream cabin."

"The cabins have names? Is that part of the B and B thing?"

"No. The dream cabin is what everyone on the ranch has been calling it, for years, amongst themselves. So we call it that, too. It has an old feather bed that used to belong to our great-grandmother. She had the gift of second sight, and her visions came in the form of dreams while she was sleeping in it."

"Interesting family history."

"The bed is magical."

He openly disagreed. "Your great-granny having visions in the bed doesn't make it magical."

"Other people have had vision-type dreams while sleeping in it, too. Tammy had dreams about Doc. Then later, he had a life-altering dream about her, and he wasn't even at the cabin when it happened to him. But we figured that her dreams triggered his, so the feather bed was still part of it."

"Maybe you shouldn't put me in that cabin."

"Why? Don't you want to have a dream that might come true?"

"It just seems like something that should stay within your family."

"Doc wasn't in our family until he and Tammy got engaged."

"I'm not going to get engaged to anyone."

Their discussion was barreling down an uncomfortable path. She struggled to rein it back in. "I wasn't insinuating that you were."

"I don't understand the point of me sleeping in the bed."

"You might have a dream that will help you regain your memory."

"I can't imagine that."

She parked in front of the main house. "Anything is possible. Wait here and I'll get the key to the cabin." She went inside, wondering why he wasn't more interested in the bed. Didn't he want to regain his memory?

She returned with the key, and he sat in the passenger seat, looking tired and confused.

He said, "I don't mean to offend you, Jenna, but I don't know if I believe in magic."

Ah, so that was it. He was a skeptic. "You just need to recover, J.D. and let the rest of it happen naturally."

"Magic isn't natural."

"I didn't used to think so, either. But I've become open-minded about it since Tammy and Doc had their dreams."

He didn't respond, but it was just as well. She didn't want to discuss the details of Doc and Tammy's romance with him.

She took him to the cabin. They went inside, and she showed him around.

"This place was locked up for a long time," she said. "But we aired it out and put some modern appliances in it."

"Like the gourmet coffeemaker?"

She nodded. "Eventually we're going to use it as one of the rental cabins. We think people will be fascinated by the magic associated with the bed. Of course we can't guarantee that they'll dream while they're here."

"You can't make that guarantee for me, either."

"No, but I think it's worth a shot."

They entered the bedroom, and since the bed had already been presented as a focal point, it stood out like a sore thumb, even though it had been designed to look soft and inviting. The quilt was a soft chocolate-brown, with a sheepskin throw draped across it.

He ran his hand across the sheepskin. "Have you ever slept here?"

A sinful chill raced up her spine. Suddenly she was imagining sleeping there with him. "No."

"If you believe in the bed's magic, why haven't you tried it yourself?"

"There's nothing I need to dream about. Besides, there's another story about someone who stayed here that's been bothering me."

He frowned. "Who?"

Jenna winced. She should have kept her mouth shut. "Someone named Savannah Jeffries. She was my uncle's girlfriend when they were younger." She was also the woman who'd had a scandalous tryst with Jenna's father, but she wasn't about to mention that part.

"Did she dream while she was here?"

"I don't know. Tammy accidentally discovered a secret Savannah was keeping, though, and now my family has been talking about hiring a P.I. to search for her."

"Why? Did she go missing?" He wrinkled his forehead. "Was there foul play involved?"

"No. She left town on her own. When Tammy first discovered her secret, all of us girls—Tammy, my sister Donna and I—tried to find out things about her on the internet, but nothing turned up."

"Sounds like you want to find her."

"I'm curious about her, but I'd just as soon let sleeping dogs lie." She purposely changed the subject. She wasn't prepared to discuss Savannah's secret or the possible ramifications of it. "Doc will have my hide if I don't let you rest, so I'm going to get going. But I'll come back and bring you something to eat. I'll bring some extra groceries and stock the fridge for future meals, too. Oh, and I'll see if I can drum up some clothes that will fit you." She motioned to his rugged ensemble. "You're going to need more than one shirt and one pair of jeans."

"You don't have to fuss over me."

"I don't mind."

"You're going above and beyond."

"I want you to get well." She left her cell-phone number on the desk. "Call if you need anything."

"How long are you going to be gone?"

"Probably a couple of hours. You should try to nap while I'm gone." She walked to the door and glanced over her shoulder at him.

He stood beside the feather bed, looking like a man in need of magic.

## Chapter Three

After Jenna left, J.D. didn't know what to do with himself. He didn't want to take a nap, even if he was supposed to be resting. He glanced around the room, then eyed the landline phone.

Already he felt like calling Jenna and telling her that he needed something. But what?

*Companionship,* he thought. He was lonely as hell.

He sat on the bed, then went ahead and reclined on it. Damn. The feather mattress was heavenly.

J.D. considered his whereabouts. He was hellishly lonely on a heavenly bed? Talk about an odd combination.

The amnesia was odd, too. He couldn't remember anything about himself, but he knew what year it was, who was president, what the world at large was like.

He closed his eyes, and unable to resist the bed, he dozed off.

He awakened hours later, the red-digit clock glaring at him. He hadn't dreamed. His subconscious hadn't created any thoughts or images.

He got up and waited for Jenna to return.

She arrived with a light knock at the door. He answered her summons eagerly.

Her hands were filled with grocery bags.

"I'll take those." He lifted the bags and carried them to the kitchen.

She went out to her truck and came back with containers of fried chicken and mashed potatoes.

"I'm not much of a cook," she said. "This came from the diner in town. I picked it up when I got the groceries."

"I hope you're going to join me. It looks like there's plenty for both of us."

"Sure. I'll eat with you." She walked into the dining room to set the table.

After the plates and silverware were in place, she returned to her truck for the rest of the stuff she'd promised. He could see her from his vantage point in the kitchen.

Upon reentering the house, she called out to him. "The clothes belong to a ranch hand who, I think, is about your size. I'll put them on the sofa for you. There's a nice little satchel with toiletries, too. Donna had them made up for the guest rooms and cabins. She's handling the marketing end of the B and B. She's been redecorating, too."

Interested in talking to her, he crammed the grocery bags in the fridge and met her in the dining room.

"What do you do, Jenna?"

"I'm a horseback riding instructor. It was my profession before I came to the Flying B. I've always been a country girl, even when I lived in the city. I grew up in Houston."

"I assumed you grew up here."

"No. Tammy, Donna and I inherited the ranch from our grandfather, and Tammy's brothers inherited some undeveloped land on the west side of the property. All of us were rewarded money, too, with stipulations of how it's to be used. The girls are supposed to keep the ranch going, which we decided includes the inception of the B and B. And the boys are supposed to take advantage of the mineral rights that go with the land, so they'll be commissioning a survey. Our grandfather left us a portion of his legacy, but we barely got to know him before he passed away. Our families were estranged from him and each other."

They sat down to eat. Curious, he asked, "Who was estranged, exactly?"

"Our dads. They're twin brothers. They hadn't spoken to each other or to Grandpa since…"

She didn't finish her statement, and he wondered if the rift had something to do with Savannah Jeffries and why she'd left town.

He said, "Who knows who my family is or if I even have one."

"Everyone comes from somewhere."

"Yes, but I forgot who they were. I mean, how important can they be?"

"You have a head injury. That's not your fault."

He popped open a soda can. "It still feels personal."

"Your life will be back on track before you know it."

Would it? At this point, he couldn't see past his amnesia. He couldn't imagine who he was. "I fell asleep while you were gone."

Her eyes grew wide. "Did you dream?"

"No."

She seemed disappointed. "Maybe you will tonight."

He didn't reply.

A short time later, they finished their meals and went into the living room. They sat on the sofa, and he checked out the clothes, which consisted of a handful of shirts and a couple of pairs of Wrangler jeans. He noticed a package of unopened boxer shorts, too. "Where did these come from?"

"I bought those at the emporium in town. I took a chance that you wore that type. I took a chance on the size, too." She paused, a sweetly shy expression on her face. "I hope it wasn't too forward of me." She quickly added, "I got you socks, too. Did you see those?"

"Yes, thank you." But buying him socks wasn't nearly as intimate as buying him boxers. "I appreciate everything you've been doing for me."

"I borrowed the clothes before I went into town, and then, while I was shopping for groceries, it hit me that you might need those other things, so I made a quick trip to the emporium."

"I feel badly that you've been spending money on me."

"It wasn't that much."

He begged to differ. He knew how expensive it was to live these days. He returned his attention to the clothes, glad they hadn't cost her anything. "These should fit. What's the ranch hand's name who loaned them to me?"

"Caleb Granger. He isn't aware of the loan, though.

He's out of town on a personal matter, but he left some of his things behind."

"You borrowed them without his consent?"

"I didn't. The foreman did. When I mentioned that I needed clothes for someone who was about the same size as Caleb, he went into Caleb's cabin and got them for me. I never would've done that. I don't know Caleb very well."

"You noticed how he was built."

"He's tall and muscular, like you. Women notice those sorts of things."

Curious about this Caleb character and the comparison she'd just made, he asked, "Are you interested in getting to know him better?"

"Oh, my goodness, no. The last I checked, he had eyes for my sister. But I don't think she's aware of his interest in her, and now that he's out of town, it doesn't matter anyway."

"It might when he gets back."

"For him, maybe. But for her? I doubt it. I can't see Donna dating a ranch hand. She's Ms. New York. Not that I have a right to criticize her."

"Why? Are you a fussy dater, too? Are you as picky about your men as your sister is about hers?"

She glanced away and started fidgeting. He'd obviously struck a chord. He should have left it alone, but he was too damned curious to drop it.

"Come on, Jenna. Fess up."

"There's nothing to fess."

He frowned, suddenly imagining her in a bad relationship. "Did someone hurt you? Did you get your heart broken?"

"Oh, no. It's nothing like that."

He felt immediately better. She'd been so kind to him, he didn't want to envision someone being unkind to her. "Then what is it?"

"I guess it won't matter if I tell you. But you're probably going to think it's dumb." She blew out a breath and continued, "I made a list of the qualities I want in a man, and I'm following it to the letter."

Well, then. That certainly wasn't what he expected. "I hope you find what you want."

"Me, too."

In the next curious instant, he wondered what sorts of qualities she was after. "Maybe you can show me the list sometime."

"I don't think that's a good idea."

"Why? Do you have sexual things on it?"

She straightened her spine, looking like a sweet little prude. "I can't believe you asked me that."

"Hey, you're the one who gave me a sexy name, remember?"

"I already explained that I didn't mean that literally."

"I know." He shot her a smile. "I was just teasing you."

"You have a wicked sense of humor."

He wondered if a sense of humor was on her list, but decided not to push the issue or tease her anymore about it.

Still, he couldn't get the list out of his mind. Sooner or later, he would probably ask her about it again.

He set Caleb's clothes aside and picked up the toiletry satchel. "Is there a shaving kit in here?"

"Truthfully, I've never taken inventory of what Donna puts in those, but she's a really thorough person, so I'm betting there is. I grabbed that from the supply room. I didn't even tell her that I was taking it."

"Let's see how thorough she is, shall we?"

"Sure. Let's see."

He opened the bag and started removing the items, placing them on the coffee table and reciting them, one by one. "Soap. Shampoo. Conditioner. Lotion. Toothpaste and mouthwash. Ah here we go. Shaving cream and disposable razors."

"Donna came through."

"Yes, she did." He reached into the satchel again. "There's a small box of some kind. It's wedged at the bottom." He dug it out of the bag and as soon as he held it up, he wanted to shove it back inside.

Condoms.

He looked at Jenna and she stared back at him. He couldn't think of a thing to say.

And apparently neither could she.

Jenna wanted to strangle herself for not checking out the items ahead of time. She wanted to strangle Donna, too, for being far more thorough than necessary.

Before the silence swallowed them alive, she managed a lame comment. "I guess my sister really did think of everything."

"She sure did." He seemed relieved that Jenna had broken the ice. He even smiled.

She was relieved that the moment had passed, too, but she struggled to summon a smile. Her heart was still beating with a quick cadence.

He put the condoms next to the razors. "Are you close?"

"What?"

"You and your sister?"

Funny he should ask. "No. I was just mentioning that to her this morning. How unalike we are. How we don't communicate all that well to each other."

"Did you discuss why?"

"No, but it's because of our family dynamics when we were growing up. Our parents got divorced when we were little, and we lived with our mom. Then she died when I was eight and Donna was nine."

"I'm sorry."

"It was ovarian cancer. I still miss her—Mom and I were close. Donna never bonded with her, or anyone, for that matter. But I think Donna wished she'd been closer to Mom. Sometimes, after Mom died, I used to catch her gazing at Mom's pictures in the most horribly sad way, but then Donna would look away, as if she didn't want me to know how badly she was hurting."

"What happened to you and Donna after your mom passed away?"

"We went to live with our dad. But he worked a lot, and we learned to fend for ourselves. I always wondered about my grandfather and his ranch. Secretly I wanted to meet him. But I knew Dad was estranged from his family, so I didn't talk to him about it. Dad isn't easy to talk to."

"You are."

She felt her cheeks go warm. "Really?"

"I'd tell you about myself if I knew who I was."

"The way I'm blabbing? Somehow, I doubt that."

"You're not blabbing. I asked you about your family and you're answering my questions."

*In way too much detail,* she thought. But it felt good

to get some of it off her chest. "The American dream was lost on my family."

"How common is that, really? How many people get to live that kind of life?"

"I don't know. But someday I want to create a family of my own, one that will be bonded and true to each other."

"Husband, kids, picket fence?"

She nodded. "I want a man who shares my love of the country. I feel blessed that I inherited part of this ranch. It's everything to me now, and I want it to be everything to my future husband."

"That stands to reason." He paused. "So, what was your grandfather like?"

"He went by the name of Tex. He was an ornery old guy, but charming, too. I regret not having the opportunity to know him better, but I'm grateful that he welcomed me into his life when he did." She thought about everything that had transpired recently. "Doc was his private physician. That's how he and Tammy met."

"And then they had dreams about each other that came true?" He glanced toward the bedroom. "If you don't mind me asking, what were those dreams?"

She'd avoided mentioning them earlier, but she supposed it didn't really matter since Doc and Tammy spoke openly about their experiences. "Tammy dreamed that she and Doc had a romantic evening in this cabin before it actually happened."

Clearly, J.D. wasn't impressed. "That's not very groundbreaking."

"Tammy worked hard to catch Doc's eye. In fact, I helped her with a makeover. She was a tomboy for most of her life and didn't know how to doll herself up."

"Doc doesn't seem like he's from around here."

"He isn't. He's originally from Philadelphia, and he came here to pay a debt to the man who put him through medical school, and that debt involved caring for our grandfather." She shifted on the sofa. "Doc was planning on leaving afterward and going back to his life in the city, then he fell in love with Tammy. He dreamed that they were happily married with three kids."

He frowned. "That's not a magic dream. They're not even married yet, and there aren't any kids."

"They're going to be married, and the kids will come later. Besides, they both dreamed about the same little dark-haired girl."

"Really?" He was obviously surprised.

"Yes, and someday that little girl is going to be born to them." Jenna was certain of it.

J.D. didn't respond, but she was glad that they'd had this discussion. Offering him a break, she said, "You should probably rest again."

"I won't be able to take another nap."

"You can watch TV."

"I don't like TV."

"So you do know something about yourself."

"I'm only saying that because when I turned on the TV in the hospital, it bored me."

"Then it probably bored you before you got amnesia, too."

"I don't know, but the man next to me sure liked to watch it."

"Yes, he did. I didn't care for his taste in shows." Especially the game show that reeked of her childhood. Jenna had always been sensitive about her youth, but even more so now that she was dealing with the Savannah Jeffries issue and her dad's part in it.

"What do you watch?" J.D. asked.

She pulled herself back into the conversation. "The news mostly. I like Animal Planet, too. Sometimes I watch romantic comedies."

"Is that what's called chick flicks?"

She nodded.

He got up and stood beside the living-room window. "So, how long have you had that list of yours?"

*Dang. He was back to that.* "Awhile."

"How long is awhile?"

"Since I was twenty-five, and I'm thirty now."

"Five years? That is awhile. Have you been refining it?"

"I added a few things about the ranch since I came here."

"About your future husband loving this place?"

"Yes." Restless, she reached for the clothes she'd loaned him. "But the list is mostly the same as it was five years ago. I knew what qualities I wanted in a man then, and I still want him to have those same qualities now."

"I couldn't begin to make a list. I don't know what I expect out of myself, let alone someone else."

"You'll know all about yourself once your memory comes back."

"I still can't imagine making a list."

"Then you're probably not a type-A personality like I am."

"I suppose not." He motioned to the clothes. "Is that part of your type-A nature?"

She glanced down. Apparently she'd been folding and refolding the same pair of jeans. "I'm just…"

"What?"

*Nervous,* she thought. But she said, "I'm just trying to help you get organized." She quickly folded each article of clothing, then went after the toiletries, dropping them back into the bag. She made sure the condoms went first, keeping them out of sight and out of mind. "I'll put all of this away for you."

"Sure. Okay. Thanks." He smiled a little. "I was going to leave everything there until I needed it."

So much for blocking the condoms from her mind. He wouldn't need those while he was staying at the Flying B, would he? Not unless he found a local girl to mess around with once he started feeling better.

Jenna frowned and headed for the bedroom.

He tagged along. "What's wrong?"

"Nothing."

"You seem flustered. If I'm too much work for you, just leave that stuff, Jenna. I'll take care of it."

"I'm not flustered." She just didn't like envisioning him with another woman.

As opposed to him being with her? She reprimanded herself. She shouldn't be entertaining those sorts of thoughts. J.D. could have sex with whoever met his fancy.

Trouble was, he met the physical requirements on her list. Of course she knew that being sexually attracted to someone wasn't enough to sustain a relationship. Every piece of the puzzle had to fit.

While she put his borrowed clothes in the dresser, he sat on the edge of the bed.

"You should stay in this cabin after I'm gone," he said.

"Why?"

"So you can sleep here." He patted the bed.

Her pulse went haywire. "I already told you there's nothing I need to dream about."

"I was talking about the comfort factor."

"I have a comfortable bed in my room."

"Do you have an old feather mattress?"

"No."

"Then I'll bet it doesn't compare. I sank right into this bed. It's pretty darn amazing."

She glanced away. "I'm glad you like it."

"It's interesting that you don't think you have anything to dream about."

She turned to look at him again. "What do you mean?"

"Seems to me that you'd want to dream about the man you're hoping to marry."

"I don't need to see him in a dream. I'll know who he is when I meet him in person."

"You'll recognize him from the list? That must be some list."

"It is to me. But most people probably wouldn't think much of it."

"Where do you keep it?"

"I have a file on my computer. But I keep a copy in my purse, too."

"You carry it around?" He flashed his lopsided grin. "That's over the top."

His cavalier attitude annoyed her. "Keeping it close at hand helps me to stay focused."

"So you can checkmark it when you're on a date?"

His grin got even more crooked. "I feel sorry for the poor saps who take you out, having to live up to whatever your expectations are."

"Your sense of humor is wearing thin, J.D."

"Sorry. It's just that I've never met anyone like you before."

"How would you know if you've ever met anyone like me?"

"I wouldn't, I guess. But logic tells me that you're one of a kind."

"You think I'm weird." She tromped into the bathroom to put his toiletries away.

Soon she felt his presence behind her. She sensed that he was looming in the doorway, watching her. She ignored him. The condoms were the last items she put away. She placed them in the cabinet under the sink, stood up and turned in his direction.

He said, "I don't think you're weird. I think you're sweet and beautiful and unique."

He was looking at her with tenderness in his eyes, and now she longed to reach out and hold him. "Thank you. That was a nice thing to say."

"I meant every word."

The bathroom was small already, and now the walls were closing in.

"I should get going," she said.

"You don't have to leave yet."

She glanced at her watch. "It's getting late."

"But I want you to stay." He didn't move away from the doorway, trapping her where she was.

J.D. scrambled for an excuse to keep her there. "I need you to help me put the groceries away."

"You already put them away."

"I just put the bags in the fridge. I didn't unload them."

"Oh, my goodness. Really? There was frozen food in those. And canned goods and…" She shook her head. "You should have unpacked them."

"So help me do it now."

She made a *tsk-tsk* sound. "Who doesn't look in a grocery bag to see what's in it?"

He smiled. "A guy recovering from a concussion?"

She returned his smile, and he realized he'd just charmed her. It made him feel good inside, but a bit anxious, too. He shouldn't be asking her to spend more time with him.

"Come on," she said. "Let's put the food away properly."

He cleared the doorway, allowing her to pass by him. As her body breezed by his, he got a zipper-tugging sensation. He took a rough breath and followed her to the kitchen. While he was walking behind her, he checked her out. She was lean and gently toned. Had he always been partial to small-framed girls?

She made a beeline for the fridge and removed the bags. Together, they unloaded them. She'd gotten him a variety of stuff to choose from: frozen pizza, fresh fruit, ready-made salads, boxed macaroni and cheese, sandwich fixings, canned chili, soup and crackers, pudding cups, cereal and milk.

*Meals designed for a bachelor,* he thought. "Thank you again for everything you've been doing for me. I really do intend to repay you."

"All I want is for you to get better," she said, repeating what she'd told him earlier. "That will be payment enough."

"I'm glad you didn't get anything that requires cooking skills. I don't think I'd be very good in that regard."

"We have that in common."

He nodded. She'd already mentioned that she wasn't much of a cook.

After they completed their task, he said, "Will you sit outside with me before you go?" He was still looking for excuses to keep her there, and since the cabin was equipped with a quaint little porch, it provided a cozy atmosphere. "We can have some pudding."

She accepted the invitation, and they settled into mismatched chairs. The air was rife with something sweet. Honeysuckle, maybe. Foliage grew along the sides of the building.

As he spooned into his dessert, he looked at Jenna, impressed with how beautifully she fit into the environment. Her hair caught the setting sun, making it look even blonder. He couldn't explain why her hair was a source of fascination. Was it because his was so dark? His skin was a lot darker than hers, too.

"I wish I could cook," she said, her mind obviously back in the kitchen.

"You could learn, couldn't you?"

"I don't know. Every time I try to make something, it tastes awful. Maybe I'll ask Tammy if she can give me some pointers."

"The way you gave her pointers about dolling herself up?"

Jenna smiled. "It might be a good trade."

"Sounds like it to me." He studied her again. She certainly knew how to make herself look pretty. Whatever she was wearing on her lips created a warm, kissable effect. "You can use me as a guinea pig if you want."

"For my cooking?"

*Or kissing,* he thought. "Yes, cooking."

"You're already suffering from a head injury. I don't want to poison you, too."

"I'm sure I'd survive it."

"I'd rather not take the chance."

"I probably won't be here long enough anyway." No poison food. No soft, sweet, poison kisses, either. He needed to stop thinking about how alluring she was.

"Do you like the pudding?" she asked.

He glanced at his cup. He'd only taken a few bites. He'd been too busy admiring her. "Yes, it's good."

"Butterscotch is my favorite."

He noticed that she'd barely made a dent in hers, either. "You're not gobbling it up very quickly."

"I'm savoring it."

"So am I," he lied, when in fact, he'd been savoring her.

"This is nice, sitting out here with you."

"Thanks. I think so, too." He couldn't envision anything nicer. Well, actually he could, but he'd warned himself not to obsess about kissing her. "We're becoming friends."

*Friends and only friends,* he reiterated.

While a soft Texas breeze blew, he asked, "What's the name of this town?"

"Buckshot Hills. I'm surprised no one told you before now."

"It must have slipped their minds."

"It slipped mine. I wonder how long it will take for Deputy Tobbs to start questioning the locals about you."

"Soon, I hope."

"Once you're feeling better, I can take you on a tour of the Flying B and introduce you to the people who work here, like Deputy Tobbs suggested."

"Wouldn't it be ironic if I was on my way to visit someone at the Flying B when I got hurt?"

"It would certainly solve the mystery, and quickly, too."

There was a mixed-up part of him that wished he'd been on his way to visit her, that she'd been his agenda. No matter how hard he tried, he couldn't seem to control his attraction to her. He even worried that he might have an intimate dream about her tonight, with or without a so-called magic bed.

After they finished their pudding, she said, "I really should go now."

He didn't try to stop her. It was better to have some distance between them.

She left, and he watched her go.

About an hour later, someone rapped at the door, and he jumped up to answer it, wondering if she'd returned.

But it was Doc, with his medical bag.

The other man said, "Jenna told me that she put you up in this cabin. How do you like it?"

"It's fine. But I don't believe that the bed is magical. I know you do, though."

"I'm a man of science, but I've learned that sometimes logic doesn't apply."

J.D. didn't respond, and the subject was dropped. Regardless, the feeling remained. He was still concerned that he might have a sensual dream.

Doc examined him and recommended more bed rest.

J.D. followed orders and went to sleep early that night.
He didn't dream about Jenna.

Much to his shock, he dreamed about himself, with
an emotion-packed glimpse of who he was as a child.

## Chapter Four

Jenna looked across the table at Donna. They were having breakfast together again, and today Donna was paging through wallpaper samples that were stacked beside her.

"We really should stop meeting like this," Jenna said.

Her sister glanced up and rolled her eyes. But she smiled, too, lightening the moment.

After their mom died, they rarely shared a meal. They would just grab their food and go. Actually, they hadn't dined together all that much when Mom had been around, either. She'd been depressed over the divorce, then she'd gotten sick.

"Our childhoods sucked," Jenna said, thinking out loud.

Donna crinkled her face. "This isn't a discussion we should be having."

"Why not?"

"Because sitting around wallowing in the past isn't going to change anything."

"I wasn't wallowing." She was trying to have a meaningful conversation. "It wouldn't hurt to talk things through once in a while."

"I don't see the point in crying over spilt milk. We need to focus on the B and B and making it a success."

"That's what we've been doing."

"Then let's not lose sight of it."

Jenna considered her sister's determination. A failed business venture had put a dent in Donna's bankbook, damaging her self-esteem and putting her glamorous life at risk. The B and B was her chance to make up for it.

Donna lifted a paisley-printed swatch. "What do you think of this for the bedroom that overlooks the garden?"

"What garden?"

"The one I'm designing with the landscaper. I told you about it before."

"No, you didn't."

"Oh, I'm sorry. I thought I did. It's going to have a redwood gazebo and a boatload of flowering perennials. Daisies in the summer, Texas bluebonnets in the spring. It'll be a perfect spot for weddings and special events."

"It sounds beautiful, and I think the wallpaper is pretty, too."

"I don't know." Donna gave the swatch a critical eye. "Maybe I should use a Western pattern. My goal is to create an idyllic atmosphere but without infringing on the natural environment."

"You're doing a great job so far."

"Thank you."

"I've always admired your sense of style." Jenna hadn't been born with a gift of flair, not like her sister. "I learned how to put myself together from watching you."

"Really?" Donna seemed surprised, maybe even a little embarrassed by the praise. "Well, you know what? You did a spectacular job of helping Tammy with her makeover. She looks like a million now."

"It was fun, and she nabbed the prize, too."

"The Prince Charming doctor? You'd never catch me playing the role of Cinderella."

For a moment, Jenna was tempted to tell Donna about Caleb's interest in her, but she figured it was pointless since it wouldn't go anywhere, anyway. She said instead, "I gave J.D. one of the toiletry satchels you created for our guests."

"Who's J.D.?"

"The man with amnesia. That's what we're calling him until we know his real name. It's the initials for John Doe. I offered to let him stay at the ranch until his memory returns or until the police uncover his identity."

"I wonder which will come first."

"I don't know. I put him in the dream cabin."

"Did he like the toiletries? I labored over what brand of shampoo and conditioner to order."

"I'm sure the shampoo and conditioner will be just fine, when he's able to use them. For now, he isn't supposed to get his stitches wet." But that was the least of Jenna's concern. "Why did you include condoms in those bags?"

"Because other top-notch establishments provide prophylactics to their guests. Actually, I was thinking that I should use little baskets to display everything instead of the satchels. What do you think?"

"Baskets would definitely be better. No surprises. I nearly died when J.D. pulled the condoms out of that bag."

Donna furrowed her delicately arched brows. "Don't tell me you have a crush on him."

"What?"

"Why else would you want to die over a box of condoms?"

"Because I barely know him."

"Are you sure that's all it is?"

"Yes."

"Good. Because Flying B romances are chock-full of trouble."

"That isn't a very nice thing to say about Tammy and Doc."

"I wasn't talking about them. It's nice that Tammy is walking around all shiny and new."

"So, you were talking about Savannah Jeffries? Maybe it's time for us to have a discussion about her."

"I'd rather not." Although the detachment in Donna's voice was evident, so was the vulnerability. "Savannah Jeffries has nothing to do with our future."

Jenna wasn't so sure about that. Already Savannah was affecting them. "We can't ignore it forever. We're going to have to vote on the P.I. issue."

"Not at the moment, we don't."

True. The rest of the family had to decide, as well—the rest of them being Tammy and her brothers, Aidan and Nathan.

The fathers were being excluded from the vote, mostly because Jenna and Donna didn't want their dad to have a say in the mess he'd made. As for Uncle William, Tammy said that he preferred to be left out of it anyway, as he just wanted the whole thing to disappear. *The way Savannah had disappeared,* Jenna thought.

Suddenly her cell phone rang. She glanced at the screen and saw the landline number from the dream cabin. She walked away from the table and answered it.

"J.D.?" she said.

"I hope I'm not disturbing you."

"No, not at all. How are you feeling?"

"Truthfully? I'm overwhelmed. The bed worked, Jenna. I dreamed about myself last night. A memory dream. Do you want to come by and I'll tell you about it?"

Her heart struck her chest. "Yes, of course. I'm on my way."

The call ended, and she approached table. "I have to go," she told Donna.

Her sister turned in her chair. "Is everything all right?"

"Yes." At least she hoped it was. J.D. didn't say if his dream was good or bad. *Overwhelmed* could apply to either.

She left the house and climbed in her truck. The cabin was within walking distance, but only on a leisure day. She wanted to hurry up and get there.

She arrived within a matter of minutes, and he was waiting for her on the porch.

She ascended the steps and they stood face-to-face. He was clean shaven, and without the stubble, his strong-boned features were even more pronounced.

He was wearing one of Caleb's shirts, but he'd left it unbuttoned. The jeans were Caleb's, too, and they fit him a little snugger than his own. She assumed that he had a pair of the new boxers on underneath.

"Do you want to talk out here or go inside?" he asked.

"It's up to you." Where they conversed didn't matter. She was distracted by him: his abs, his navel, the frayed waistband of his borrowed jeans. Even his bare feet seemed sexy.

He said, "Let's stay out here."

Normally the outdoors soothed her. But being around J.D. was turning her into a jumble of hormones. She'd lied to Donna about not having a crush on him.

Instead of taking a chair, he sat on the porch steps. She had no choice but to sit beside him, far closer than a chair would've allowed.

"Was it a good dream?" she asked quickly.

"Yes, but it was troubling, too. I saw myself as a boy. I was about ten. I was in a barn, grooming a sorrel mare. I grew up around horses, Jenna. I could feel it during the dream."

"Why is that troubling?" She thought it was wonderful. She'd pegged him as a cowboy from the beginning.

"I was the only person in the dream. I didn't get a feeling about my family. For all I know, I could have been a foster kid who was too old to get adopted."

That struck her as an odd thing for him to say. Was it a memory struggling to surface? "Were you sad in the dream?"

"No. But I was with the mare, and I felt a connection to her. She made me happy."

Horses always made Jenna happy, too, but they gave a lot of people joy. His bond with the mare didn't prove or disprove what type of childhood he'd had. His foster care/adoption comment was too specific to ignore, though. "Maybe the dream will continue on another night."

"Maybe."

She studied his chiseled profile. "What did you look like as a ten-year-old?"

"Why does that matter?"

"I just want to know." To see him through his own eyes.

"I was on the small side, a skinny kid, and my hair was sort of longish. A little messy, I suppose." He shrugged, but he smiled, too. "I was wearing a straw cowboy hat, and I had sugar cubes in my shirt pocket for the mare."

She smiled, as well. She liked envisioning him as a youth and she liked the boyishness that had come over him now. He seemed wistful. If he hadn't made the foster-child remark, she would've assumed that he'd had a solid upbringing. But he had made the remark, and it weighed heavily on her mind.

"Tell me more about the dream," she said. "Were you in Texas? Is that where you grew up?"

"I don't know. I didn't get a sense of the location."

"What was the barn like?"

"I couldn't tell how big it was, but it was well maintained."

"Did you get a sense of how long you'd lived there?"

"No."

"But you sensed that you'd been raised in an equine environment?"

"Yes."

"So if you were a foster child, then all of the homes

you'd been placed in had horses? How likely do you think that is?"

"I have no idea." He changed the subject. "So, why don't you tell me about the horses on the Flying B?"

"We have plenty of great trail horses that Tex used to favor and that anyone on the ranch can use at their leisure, but I'm still acquiring school horses."

"For your riding instruction?"

She nodded. "They have to be able to accommodate any level of rider. I'll need a string of them for group lessons, but I'm being extremely cautious, hand-selecting each one. I have two wonderful geldings, so far."

"Will you take me to see them?"

"Today?"

"Yes, now. Today. I want to know how being around horses makes me feel in person. You can introduce me to the employees on the ranch, too, and see if any of them recognize me."

"I think I better check with Doc before I take you on a tour. You've only been out of the hospital for a day."

"I feel fine."

"I still think I should talk to him." She removed her phone from her purse and called Doc, but she got his answering service. "He's supposed to call me back."

"When?"

"As soon as he's able."

J.D. stood up. "I'm going to get ready."

He went into the cabin and came back, carrying his socks and boots. Jenna couldn't blame him for being anxious, but what if he was jumping the gun?

"Doc might not think you're ready for an outing," she said.

"He will if you tell him about my dream. Besides, I'll go stir-crazy just sitting around here."

After his boots were in place, he buttoned his shirt and tucked it into his pants.

"I forgot my belt." Off he went to retrieve it.

She took a moment to breathe, as deeply as she could. Watching him get dressed was making her warm and tingly.

He returned with the belt halfway threaded through his belt loops. She should've turned away, but like the smitten female she was fast becoming, she trained her gaze on his every move.

This was crazy. Now she felt as if she had a concussion, and she hadn't even taken a hit to the head. Not literally, anyway. Figuratively, she'd been struck and struck hard.

Determined to keep her wits, she thought about her list. Aside from his physical attributes and his newly discovered connection to horses, he didn't meet her requirements. First and foremost, the man she chose had to be as marriage-minded as she was, and J.D. didn't seem like the husband type. Nor was she foolish enough to believe that he was going to dream himself into that role.

He sat beside her, pulling her out of analytical mode and back into a heap of emotion. His nearness caused a chemical reaction.

Fire in her veins. Pheromones shooting from her pores.

Before the silence grew unbearable, she said, "If you were raised around horses, then I'll bet you're a skilled rider."

He shot her a half-cocked grin. "Give me a bucking bronc to ride and we'll see."

She laughed, albeit nervously. She hadn't recovered from his nearness. "All I need is for you to get tossed on your head. Doc would accuse me of trying to kill his patient."

Finally the doctor in question called, and Jenna spoke with him.

Afterward, she told J.D., "He said it was fine, as long as you don't stay too long or wear yourself out."

"I knew he would agree." He reached over to give her a hand up.

Being touched by him didn't help her condition. She was still fighting fire, pheromones and everything else that had gone wrong with her.

"Are we going to walk?" he asked.

"I think it would be better to take the truck."

He glanced out in the distance. "How far is it?"

"Not that far. But too far for a man with a head injury," she amended. "Doc said not to tax your energy."

"Did he specifically say that I shouldn't walk?"

"No, but I'm saying it." For the second time that day, she avoided a leisurely stroll.

After they got in the truck, he turned toward her. "Thanks, Jenna."

"For what?"

"Putting up with me. I know I'm taking up a lot of your time."

"It's okay. I want to help you through this." And once he was completely well, she could try to resume some order in her life. "Look at the progress you've made already."

"Because of you and your family. You really should

stay in the cabin after I'm gone, even if it's just for one night."

"The bed in my room is fine."

"The bed in your room doesn't induce dreams."

She repeated what she'd told him before. "I don't need to rely on magic. Things will happen for me when they're meant to."

"But you seem tense."

She started the engine and headed toward the stables. "There's a lot going on in my world."

"Like the Savannah Jeffries issue?"

"Yes."

"If you need a sounding board, I'll lend you my ear."

"I tried to talk to my sister about it this morning."

"But she didn't want to discuss it?"

"No."

"I'm here, if you need me," he reiterated.

There was a part of her that wanted to tell him the whole sordid story, to lean on his shoulder and let him wrap her in comfort. But relying on him wasn't the answer, especially with her troubled attraction to him.

She parked in front of the stables and introduced him to the ranch hands who were nearby. None of them recognized him. Neither did Hugh, the loyal old foreman who'd snagged Caleb's clothes. But she didn't expect Hugh to recognize him, especially since she'd already described J.D. to him.

"You can meet everyone else on another day," she told J.D.

He agreed, and she took him to the barn that housed the school horses.

"This is Pedro's Pride," she said as a tobiano paint

poked his head out to greet them. She opened the gate and they went into his stall. "But I just call him Pedro."

J.D. approached the horse, and it was love at first sight. Man and beast connected instantly. Jenna stood back and marveled at the exchange.

"He's big and flashy," J.D. said, "But he has manners, too."

As he roamed his hands along the gelding's sturdy frame, the horse stood patiently. Jenna wasn't quite so calm. Seeing J.D. this way heightened her feelings for him.

He said, "If Pedro carries a rider the way you say he does, then you found a gem."

"You look as if you found a gem, too. In yourself," she clarified. "I can tell that you're in your element."

"I am. It feels right." He tapped a hand to his chest. "Here, where it counts."

*In his heart,* she thought. "That's how I feel every time I come out here."

"You're lucky that this is your life's work."

"It's probably yours, too. You just can't remember the who, what and where."

He remained next to the gelding. "How long will Caleb be out of town?"

"I think he's scheduled to come back next month. Why?"

"If you need someone to fill in for him until he gets back, maybe you can hire me. Then I can repay your kindness by working it off."

Yesterday, he'd been unable to acknowledge that he might be a cowboy, and today he was offering to be a ranch hand. But given the circumstances, his offer made sense. "I'll have to talk to Hugh about it, and to Doc, too, of course. You can't start working until he gives you a clean bill of health." She added, "And you'll get the same wages as everyone else. Repaying my kindness doesn't mean that you'll be working for free."

"I won't let you, Hugh or Doc down. I'll do a good job."

"I'm sure you will." But it was only temporary, she reminded herself.

J.D. wasn't going to be part of the Flying B forever.

J.D. glanced at Pedro, then at Jenna. He felt perfectly at ease around the horse. But around the woman? Not so much. The zip-zing between them jarred his senses.

He wanted to do right by her, to work at the ranch and make himself useful. But somewhere in the pit of his stomach, he wanted to run to the nearest bus stop and leave Buckshot Hills, Texas, far, far behind.

He'd seen the way she'd looked at him when he'd gotten halfway dressed in front of her. True, he'd been antsy about meeting her horses, but he shouldn't have buttoned his shirt or zipped his jeans in her presence, especially since it had been a fantasy leftover from the hospital.

"How are you feeling?" she asked.

He blinked. "What?"

"I want to be sure you're feeling well enough to continue."

"I'm doing fine." Except for his bad-to-the-bone hunger for her.

"Then let's go to the next stall."

They proceeded, and she introduced him to Duke, her other school horse, whose original owner, a lover of old Westerns, had given him the same nickname as

John Wayne. He was a friendly sorrel with a blaze and three white socks. J.D. approached the gelding, anxious to get close to him.

"He resembles the mare in my dream. His markings are similar." And it made J.D. feel like the boy he once was. "If I had a sugar cube, I'd give him one."

"You can spoil him next time. And Pedro, too."

"I wish I could ride him."

"Next time," she said again.

"How old were you when you started riding?" he asked.

"Ten."

"The same age I was in my dream."

She nodded. "I was one of those kids that collected horsey stuff—pictures, books, toys, stuffed animals—but other than a few pony rides, I wasn't around them. Then, two years after Mom died, I asked Dad if I could take riding lessons. He agreed, but he didn't take an active part in it. He didn't drive me back and forth or watch me during my lessons. He hired a babysitter for that, and once I got old enough to go on my own, I hung out there all the time, before and after school, on weekends, in the summer. It was a magnificent equestrian center. My home away from home."

"So, what did you look like when you were ten?" he asked, interested to know the same thing about her that she'd wanted to know about him.

She smiled. "I was a skinny kid with longish hair."

He smiled, too. She'd stolen his line. "Did you favor straw hats?"

"Are you kidding? I still do."

"I haven't seen you in a hat yet."

"You will. Speaking of which, you're going to need

one once you start working here. I can give you one that
belonged to my grandfather."

"You don't have to do that."

"Tex wouldn't have minded. He probably would have
given you one himself. I think your dream would have
fascinated him."

He thought about his unknown family. "Do you think
I was a foster kid?"

"I don't know. But your comment about possibly
being too old to be adopted gave me pause."

It gave him pause, too. "Most people want babies or
toddlers, not older kids." He frowned. "Don't they?"

"I don't know anything about adoption, J.D."

He searched her gaze. "Would you ever consider raising someone else's child as your own?"

"Truthfully, I've never really thought about it before. But I love children, so if it was something my
husband wanted to do, I would certainly consider it.
What about you?"

"Me?" He took a cautionary step back. "I don't think
I'd make a very good dad, adoptive or otherwise. I'd
have enough trouble dealing with myself, let alone being
a parent."

"My future husband is going to be father material.
That's one of the most important qualities on my list. I
want him to bring our children presents, even when it
isn't their birthdays. I want him to help me read to them
at night. I even want him to dress up as Santa Claus and
sneak past the tree on Christmas Eve."

Surprised that she referred to the list she'd been protecting, he said, "I wouldn't be able to do any of that."
Even now, he felt as if he were on the brink of a panic
attack. "Marriage, babies, birthdays, Christmas."

"I wasn't implying that you should."

"Neither was I." He fought the panic, forcing his lungs to expand. "I was just making conversation."

"About how different we are? I already figured that out."

*Of course she did,* he thought. She analyzed the men she was attracted to. She weighed them against her list.

She said, "After your identity is restored, you can return to whatever type of lifestyle suits you."

He nodded, knowing that was exactly what he would do. Nonetheless, it didn't give him comfort. The fact that Jenna found him lacking made him ache inside.

An ache he couldn't begin to understand.

## Chapter Five

A week passed without J.D. having any more dreams and without the police uncovering any information about him. But at least Doc said that he was well enough to work. And ride, which he'd done, but only minimally. He hadn't had the opportunity to spend a lot of time in the saddle yet. Mostly his work entailed maintenance in and around the barn.

As for Jenna, his hunger for her was getting worse. In spite of the fact that they were completely wrong for each other, he felt like a thunderstruck kid.

Today he was mucking out stalls, and she was reorganizing the tack room. Every so often, as he moved about the barn, he would catch sight of her in the tack room doorway, and his heart would dive straight to his stomach.

"J.D.?" a male voice said, drawing his attention.

He turned to see Manny, another ranch hand, coming toward him. By now, J.D. had met all of the other employees on the Flying B., including the household staff. Manny, he'd learned, had a thing for one of the maids, a girl he talked incessantly about. J.D., however, hadn't said a word about his forbidden interest in Jenna.

Manny flashed a youthful grin. He was all of twenty-two, with curly brown hair and a happy-go-lucky personality. J.D. wished he knew how to feel that way, but the more time that passed, the more he sensed that his emotions had been screwed up long before Jenna had found him and brought him here.

Manny said, "A group of us are getting together at Lucy's tonight. You ought to join us, J.D. It might do you some good to get out."

"Who's Lucy?"

"It's a place, not a person. Lone Star Lucy's. The local honky-tonk. So, do you want to go?"

"Sure, okay. Thanks." He didn't have anything else to do.

Manny grinned again. "Some of the household staff is going, too."

J.D. cracked a smile. The other man's infectious energy seemed to demand it. "I take it that means the gal you're hot for will be there?"

"Heck, yeah. And I'm going to stick to her like glue. You just watch me."

"I don't doubt that you will." J.D. couldn't seem to stop from asking, "Are any of the Byrds going?" He wanted Jenna to be there. He wanted to see her as badly as Manny wanted to see the maid.

"No."

"Why not?"

"Nobody thought to invite them, I guess. We haven't mingled with them outside the ranch."

"Then maybe it's time."

"You can ask them to come, if you want. I wouldn't count on the prissy one showing up, though. She wouldn't fit in." Manny chuckled. "What's her name? Dana?"

"Donna. I met her briefly, a few days ago." A quick introduction when Jenna had taken him inside to meet the household staff. "She doesn't seem easy to get to know." Which had given him a clearer understanding of the lack of closeness between the sisters.

"I've seen her walking around, dodging manure and sniffling from the hay. I'm surprised she's lasted as long as she has."

"I'll invite all of the Byrds to keep from being rude." And to keep it from seeming as if he only had Jenna in mind. "It would be nice to see Doc and Tammy out on the town."

"Yeah, Tammy is country folk, and Doc is getting there, too. Make sure you don't forget about Jenna, not after everything she's done for you. I think you should buy her a drink."

"I agree. I'll do that, if she accepts the invite." He tried to seem casual. "She told me that she likes to dance so maybe I'll two-step with her, too, if I can keep up." He still wasn't sure what kind of dancer he was, but he was willing to find out if it meant having Jenna as his partner.

"Great. Sounds like a party to me. I can give you a ride. Let's say, about eight? I'll swing by your cabin."

"All right. See you then."

Manny returned to work, and J.D. put down his rake

and walked over to where Jenna was. He entered the tack room, and she looked up from the bridles she was hanging on wooden pegs.

He got right to the point. "Manny asked me to join him and some of the others at Lucy's tonight. It would be nice if you, Tammy, Doc and Donna wanted to meet us there."

"Donna would never go to Lucy's."

"Yeah, that's what Manny figured. How about you? Do you want to go?"

"I don't know if it's the right place for me, either. From what I've heard, it caters to a wild crowd."

Hoping to thwart her concern, he said, "I'll protect you from the crazies."

"You will, huh?" She laughed a little. "And who's going to protect me from you?"

"If Doc and Tammy go, Doc can keep me in line. He can tranquilize me if I get too rowdy."

She laughed again. "Then I'll make sure they come along."

Damn, but he liked her. "I thought maybe you and I could dance. Or I'd like to give it a try anyway."

"That sounds nice."

"We're leaving around eight. You can head over about the same time if you want."

"I'll do my best."

Before he overstepped his bounds, he said, "I should get back to work now."

"Me, too." She made a show of jangling the bridles in her hand.

"Bye, Jenna."

"Bye."

He walked away, dreading the day he had to say

goodbye to her for real. But at least for now, he had the chance to hold her while they danced.

Jenna walked into Lone Star Lucy's, where scores of people gathered. Doc and Tammy couldn't make it, so she'd ventured out on her own—clearly a stupid thing to do, especially at a bar like this.

She didn't have a clue where J.D. or the Flying B employees were. Everyone looked alike in the dimly lit, sawdust-on-the-floor, tables-crammed-too-close-together environment. Most of the men were bold and flirtatious, with their hats dipped low and their beer bottles held high, and most of the women wore their makeup too heavy, their hair too big and their jeans too tight.

As she made her way farther into the room, she noticed the dance floor. A digital jukebox provided the music. Way in the back, she caught a glimpse of pool tables.

J.D. had said that he would protect her from the crazies, but already she was getting hit on.

A cowboy with slurred speech leaned over his chair and grabbed her shirtsleeve. "Where are you going in such a hurry?"

She tugged her arm away. "I'm looking for someone."

"I can be your someone," he replied.

*It is time to leave,* she thought. She turned around and ran smack-dab into J.D. He stood there, like a wall of muscle.

"Is that guy bothering you?" he asked.

Her pulse went pitter-pat. "He was, but he isn't anymore."

Slurred Speech had gone back to his beer.

"Where's Doc and Tammy?" J.D. asked.

"They had other plans."

"You should have let me know you were alone. You could have ridden with us."

"You and Manny?"

"And some of the other guys."

"A truckload of testosterone? I don't know about that."

"We would have made room for you, and you could have sat up front with me."

She envisioned herself squeezed in the middle, practically sharing the same seat with J.D. "Taking my own truck was fine."

"I'm just happy you're here. You look damn fine, Jenna."

"Thank you." Her boot-cut jeans were as tight as every other cowgirl's in the place. She'd gone easy on the makeup, though, aside from the crimson lipstick that matched her fancy silk blouse. She hadn't overdone her hair, either. She wore it loose and soft.

He kept looking at her with appreciation in his eyes, and his dark gaze whipped her into a girlish flutter. She'd wanted to impress him, and she had.

"Come on," he said. "I'll take you to our table."

He put his hand lightly on the small of her back, and as they weaved their way around other patrons, he never broke contact. His gentle touch heightened her girlish reaction to him.

He motioned with his free hand. "Over there."

She saw the Flying B group, with Manny smiling big and bright amongst his peers.

There were nine people in all, including her and J.D.

He'd saved a seat for her. He'd saved seats for Doc and Tammy, too. But as soon as it became apparent that they weren't being used, they were quickly snatched up by people at another table.

Jenna was greeted by the Flying B employees. The other women in attendance were part-timers from the housekeeping staff. Their names were Celia, Joy and Maria, and they looked a lot different here than they did at work. Celia's boobs were busting out of her top, Joy had eyeliner out to there and Maria's dress hugged her curvaceous hips. They smelled of the same flowery perfume, too, a telltale sign that they'd gotten ready together, sharing a bottle of whatever it was. Overall they seemed like nice girls who'd gone into Lucy's mode for the night.

J.D. turned to Jenna. "Would you like a drink? I'm buying."

"You shouldn't spend your money on me." She knew he'd gotten an advance on his pay, but it wasn't much.

"Are you kidding? I owe you more than a drink."

She offered a smile. "You owe me a dance, too."

His smile matched hers. "First a drink."

She considered white wine, but changed her mind. "I'll take a longneck." She motioned to his bottle. "The same kind you're having."

"I'll get it from the bar. It'll take the waitress forever to work her way over here." Before he left, he finished his beer, which apparently had been almost gone. One last swallow.

He stood up, and she watched him walk away. He had an awfully cute butt. But before someone caught her admiring his backside, she turned her attention to the people she was with and noticed that Manny had eyes for Maria. She seemed flattered by the attention, leaning toward him when he talked and laughing at silly things he said. Now she understood why Manny had orchestrated this get-together. He wanted to make something happen with Maria.

J.D. returned with Jenna's beer. She thanked him and noticed that he'd gotten himself another one, too.

She hoped that he didn't overindulge. It was bad enough that she'd assumed he was drunk when she'd first seen him, lest it come true this evening. She still knew very little about J.D and his habits. Of course he knew little about himself, too. Each day was a new exploration.

Earlier, he'd joked about having Doc tranquilize him, and she'd laughed at the time. But it wouldn't be funny if he got carried away.

Luckily, he didn't. He sipped his second drink slowly.

"We should share a toast," he said.

"To what?"

"Us spending the night together."

She blinked at him. She also felt her skin flush. Suddenly, she was racked with heat. Her nipples shot out like bullets against her bra, too. "We're not spending the night together."

"That isn't what I said."

"Yes, it is."

"No, it isn't," he countered. "I said that we were spending the night *out* together."

"You left off the *out* part."

"I did? Are you sure?"

She nodded. She knew the difference.

"It's noisy in here. Maybe you misheard me."

"You goofed up, J.D." He'd made a Freudian slip or whatever mistakes like that were called.

"I'm sorry. I didn't realize…" He fidgeted with his beer.

Now she wished that she would have kept quiet. "I'm sorry, too. I shouldn't have pointed it out."

The subject was dropped, but that didn't ease the moment.

Just when she thought it couldn't get any worse, Manny glanced across the table and said, "When are you guys going to dance?"

"In a while," J.D. responded.

"You don't look like you're having a very good time." Manny cocked his head. "Either of you."

Jenna piped up. "We're just being quiet while we finish our drinks."

"Liquid courage," J.D. said. "I'll probably suck out there."

Manny replied, "You should have done a test run at the ranch and danced around the cabin."

J.D. made a face. "Now how stupid would I have looked?"

"Pretty dang dumb." The other man grinned. "But at least you would've known if you were any good."

"I don't think it would have been the same without a partner. I won't know until I try it for real."

"We're going to dance later, too," Manny said, and moved closer to Maria. "We're waiting for the songs we picked to play."

He turned back to the rest of the group, leaving J.D. and Jenna to their silent agony. Heaven help her, but she wanted to spend the night with him, to make love, to sleep beside him in the dream cabin. But she knew that being with him would create emotional havoc. Dallying with a man who was destined to disappear from her life wasn't part of her get-married-and-have-babies plan.

"Should we pick some songs, too?" he asked. "It might help us relax."

She appreciated his attempt to make things better. "Sure. Let's give it a try."

He stood up, and like a knight in shining armor, he pulled back her chair. "Chivalry" was one of the husband-requirements on her list. She frowned to herself. As always, her list was tucked away in her purse.

They proceeded to the digital jukebox and waited for the people in front of them to make their selections.

When their turn arrived, he said, "I like the old-style jukes better."

"Me, too. But we live in a digital world now."

"Some things should remain the same."

*Like chivalrous men,* she thought, fighting another frown. Tonight, of all nights, she shouldn't be referring to her list, especially since J.D wasn't in the running.

He scanned the songs. "The jukebox might be new, but at least the music is classic country."

She stood beside him. "Oh, I love this song." She gestured to "Breathe" by Faith Hill.

"That's a romantic one."

"I wasn't suggesting that we dance to it. I was just saying that it's a favorite of mine."

"Do you like this one, too?" He pointed to Faith's duet with Tim McGraw called "Let's Make Love."

"Now you're being smart." And making a naughty joke about his Freudian slip. "You and that wicked sense of humor of yours."

He flashed a dastardly smile. "Are you brave enough to dance to it with me?"

Was she?

"Are you?" he asked again.

*Why not?* she thought. At this point, it seemed better to acknowledge their chemistry than try to avoid it. "Go ahead and push the button. But we'll probably smolder on the dance floor and make everyone jealous."

"If I don't step all over your feet."

"That would certainly ruin the ambience."

"I can't guarantee it won't happen." He chose the song. "Any more?"

"I think one is enough, considering. Don't you?"

"Yeah. We probably shouldn't bite off more than we can chew." They stepped away from the jukebox and he said, "Did you know that Manny has a thing for Maria?"

She looked across the room and toward their table. "Yes, I noticed that he's into her. She seems to like him, too. They'll probably start dating after tonight."

"That will make Manny happy. Who knows how long it will last, though?"

"They're young. They have lots of time to find who they're meant to be with."

"Do you think everyone is meant to be with someone?"

"No. But only because some people seem happier when they're single."

"I can't imagine being married. Just thinking about it makes me panic."

Absolute proof that they were wrong for each other. "It has the opposite effect on me. The thought of being married makes me feel calm."

"Do you have the ceremony planned out in your

mind? The style of dress you'll wear and whatever else women daydream about?"

"Actually, I don't. I purposely haven't done that. Otherwise the wedding becomes more important than the marriage."

"That's a grounded way of thinking."

She appreciated his praise and even preened a little. "Thank you."

"Look at you. All pretty and smug. I still think your list is goofy."

"You're just miffed because I won't let you see it."

"Has anyone seen it?"

"I showed it to Tammy after she and Doc got together." She'd needed to confide in someone, and Tammy had been the logical choice. Sharing it with Donna would have been way too awkward.

"Can you blame me for wanting to see it? How am I supposed to leave the Flying B without knowing what type of man Jenna Byrd wants to marry?"

"You can come back someday and meet my husband."

"And tell him that we danced to 'Let's Make Love'? You should pick that for your wedding song."

"Ha, ha. Very funny. And for the record, we haven't danced to it yet."

"We will. But if I'm a lousy dancer, it's going to ruin the song for you."

*Maybe having it ruined would be better than feeling its sensual effect,* she thought.

Just then, "Save a Horse (Ride a Cowboy)" came on, adding a bit of fuel to the fire. What timing. The crowd exploded with hoots and hollers and country wildness.

J.D. gestured to the table. "Hey. Manny and Maria are getting up."

She followed his line of sight. Sure enough, the younger couple was headed toward the dance floor.

"They must have picked this song," J.D. said.

"So it seems."

"Can't say as I blame them. They'll probably have a great time with it."

Jenna nodded. No doubt they would.

He kept watching. "Yep. There they go."

She watched, too. They were definitely having a great time. Whenever Maria would bump her hips, Manny would flash a big happy grin and mimic her movements. Jenna couldn't fathom scooting around to the song, while she was in the presence of the cowboy she'd vowed *not* to ride.

"Should we go back to the table?" he asked.

She nodded, and they resumed their seats. Then J.D. leaned over and quietly asked, "Do you think it's becoming obvious that we're attracted to each other?"

"Obvious to whom?"

"Whoever is around us."

She glanced at the Flying B employees who were left at the table. "I'm sure it will be when we dance. We're going to smolder, remember?"

"If I don't blow it."

"You won't."

"They'll probably talk about us."

"It doesn't matter." Instead of fretting about the curiosity that would ensue, she justified being gossiped about. "It's just an innocent flirtation. It's not as if we're going to go home together tonight."

He turned quiet, and the anxiety of waiting for the song they'd picked was almost too much to bear.

Then, about fifteen minutes later, it happened. The first melodic chords of "Let's Make Love" began to play.

Their gazes locked. Hard and deep.

It was time for them to dance.

## Chapter Six

**J.D.** reached for Jenna's hand. "Ready?" he asked, even if he wasn't sure if he was ready himself.

"Yes." She accepted his hand and they walked onto the dance floor.

He took her in his arms and drew a blank. Here he was, holding a beautiful woman, and he still didn't know if he could dance. He couldn't seem to move, so he simply stood there, locked in position.

"Are you all right?" she asked.

"I'm more nervous than I thought I'd be."

"Do you want to forget it? You're under no obligation to—"

"No. I want to try." He listened to the melody, the lyrics, the singer's voice, letting those elements guide him. Slowly, he began to relax and dance with her.

A gentle, heart-stirring two-step.

Mercy, they were good together. Beyond good. Beyond imagination. They gazed at each other the entire time.

"You absolutely know how to do this," she said.

So did she, but her skills were never in question.

As they rocked and swayed, the other dancers barely existed and neither did the bar. Everything was out of focus, melding into misty colors and scattered light. All he saw was Jenna, her fair skin and golden hair.

He brought her closer. "I'm glad I met you. I'm even glad I lost my memory."

"I'm glad we met, too. But you shouldn't say that about having amnesia."

"It's giving me a chance to start over."

"This isn't starting over, J.D. It's a break from your other life."

"I don't care about my other life."

"You shouldn't say that, either. It's important to care about who you are."

How could he care about something he couldn't remember?

They didn't talk anymore, and he was grateful for the silence. He didn't want to disturb the bond. He wanted the luxury of knowing her in this way.

He was in the moment. He was part of it. *John Doe and Jenna Byrd,* he thought. He danced with her as if his amnesia depended on it, the heat between them surging through his veins.

This was a memory he would never forget.

When the song ended, his vision cleared and the bar came back into focus. But it didn't put him on solid ground. He longed to kiss Jenna, to taste her ruby-red lips.

"I need some air," he said. "How about you?"

"Definitely." She looked as dazed as he felt.

He escorted her outside, and they stood in front of the club, with a view of the parking lot. Other people were out there, too, standing off to the side and smoking, the tips of their cigarettes creating sparks.

Speaking of sparks...

J.D. was still feeling the fire. Apparently so was Jenna. Her voice vibrated. "I warned you that we were going to smolder. I've never danced with anyone like that before."

"I doubt I have, either." He struggled to put it in perspective. "How long do you think that song was?"

"Three, maybe four minutes."

"That's nothing in the scheme of things."

"I know. But it was beautiful." Her eyes drifted closed.

"Maybe you really should use it as your wedding song."

She opened her eyes. "I could never do that, especially not after dancing with you to it. That wouldn't be fair to my husband."

"Would it be fair to him if I became your short-term lover?" He couldn't help it. He wanted to have a dazzling affair with her. "I'd be good to you, the best lover I could be."

"I'm sure it would be amazing." She crossed her arms over her chest, and the protective gesture made her look achingly vulnerable. "But if we slept together, it would complicate my feelings for you, and I would miss you even more after you're gone."

Her reaction made him feel guilty for suggesting the affair. But he still wanted to be with her. Regardless, he said, "You're right. It wouldn't work. It wouldn't solve anything. We need to focus on being friends, like we agreed on from the beginning."

She nodded, but she didn't uncross her arms. She still looked far too vulnerable. He wanted to reach out and hold her, but he refrained from making physical contact. He'd done enough damage for one night.

He glanced at the smokers. They kept puffing away. As he shifted his attention back to Jenna, the headlights from a departing car shined in his eyes. He blinked from the invasion.

"I've never actually had an affair," she said.

He blinked again. He hadn't expected her to offer that kind of information.

She continued, "I've only been with two men and they were my boyfriends. Neither of them was right for me, though."

"They weren't husband material?"

"I thought they were at the time, but I misjudged them. That's part of why I created the list. I needed something definitive to use as a guide. I've always had specific ideas about family, considering how messed up mine was, and writing everything down was the best way I knew to stay focused on my priorities."

He considered the time line. She'd told him that she'd started the list when she was twenty-five and she was thirty now. "You haven't dated since then?"

"Yes, but just casually."

"So, you've been celibate for five years?"

"I'd rather wait for the right man. Besides, I haven't been overly attracted to anyone, not until…"

Dare he say it? "I came along?"

"Yes."

He blew out a gust of air from his lungs. She did, too, only in a softer manner. Still, they were mirroring each other.

Then, awkward silence.

The smokers stamped out their cigarettes and returned to the club, making it quieter.

More awkward silence.

"Maybe we should go back inside, too," he said.

A strand of hair blew across her cheek, and she batted it away. "I think I should go home, J.D."

*And get away from him and their madly wrong-for-each-other attraction,* he thought. "I'll walk you to your truck."

"Thanks." She led the way.

They didn't speak. The only sound was their booted footsteps.

Once her pickup came into view, she stated the obvious. "We're here." She hit the alarm button on her key fob.

If they were dating, this would have been the time to kiss her.

He made a point of keeping his distance. "Be safe."

"I will." She got in her truck and started the engine.

As she drove away, he gazed into the dark, feeling much too alone.

Jenna paced her room and finally ended up in the kitchen, heating milk in a pan on the stove. When she was little, her mother used to give her warm milk and now she thought of it as comfort food.

She poured it into a coffee mug and wandered the halls in her pajamas. It was after midnight, and she didn't expect to run into anyone else at this hour.

She was wrong. She noticed that one of the empty guest-room doors was open and a light was on. Jenna poked her head in and saw her sister.

She crossed the threshold and said, "What are you doing?"

Donna spun around, her hand flapping against her heart. "You scared the daylights out of me."

"Sorry, but it's not daylight." A dumb thing to say, she supposed, since that was a technicality of which they were both aware.

A beat of silence passed before Donna replied to her original question. "I have too much work on my mind to sleep."

"Is this the room that's going to overlook the garden?"

"Yes, and in my sleep-deprived state, I'm still debating on what wallpaper to use."

Jenna replied, "I couldn't sleep, either. Or relax or sit still. But I guess you already figured that out."

"What are you drinking? I hope it's not coffee. You'll be wired all night if it is."

"It's warm milk."

Donna didn't react. But to do so would have opened the door to a discussion about Mom, and Donna was apparently more cautious than that.

"I went out earlier," Jenna said.

"Where to?"

"Lone Star Lucy's."

Donna crinkled her nose. "That yee-haw bar? Whatever for?"

"Some of the ranch hands and maids were meeting there, and J.D. invited me, too. He invited all of us, you, me, Tammy and Doc, but I was the only one who could go."

"No one told me that I was invited."

"Would you have gone?"

"Not a chance."

"Then what would have been the point in telling you?"

"Protocol. I would have declined the invitation myself." Donna took a chair near the window. "Did that place live up to its reputation?"

Jenna sat on the edge of the bed. "Nothing crazy happened while I was there." Nothing except the way J.D. made her feel. "I left early, though."

"You weren't having a good time, I take it."

"Actually, I was enjoying myself." *Far too much,* she thought.

"Why is that a reason to leave early?"

"Because I danced with J.D. and then he suggested that we have an affair."

"You said that you didn't have a crush on him. I should have known you were lying."

Donna's reaction actually made her seem like a big sister. Or heaven forbid, a mother.

Jenna replied, "I'm not going to sleep with him."

"Right."

"I turned him down. I swear I did." She'd never confided in Donna about things like this before. Girl talk between them was a foreign concept. But she continued, hoping it was going to get easier. "I told him that it wasn't a good idea, and he agreed that we shouldn't."

"I'll bet he only agreed because you turned him down. If you would have said yes, you'd be doing it right now instead of roaming around in your pajamas.

Be honest, Jenna, you're having trouble sleeping because you want to climb into bed with him."

"Of course I want to. But I'm smart enough to know when to keep my pajamas on."

"They're pretty, by the way. A bit of silk, a bit of lace."

Jenna clutched her cup. She suspected that Donna had more to say about her sleepwear.

She did indeed. The older sibling added, "They're actually pretty enough to wear on a stroll down to his cabin and crack open those condoms I inadvertently provided."

"You're supposed to be talking me out of being with him, not tempting me to do it."

"I already tried to talk you out of it. I warned you that having a Flying B romance would be trouble, but you didn't listen. You danced with him anyway, a dance that prompted him to suggest an affair."

"He took it back."

"Uh-huh. Well, go traipse down to his cabin and see how quickly he jumps your bones."

Jenna scowled. Girl talk with her know-it-all New York sister sucked. "I'm going back to bed."

"Alone?"

"Yes, alone." Jenna stood up, preparing to stomp off.

Donna rolled her eyes. "You're acting like you did when we were kids."

"I am not."

"Yes, you are. You were always melodramatic."

"You mean like this?" For the heck of it, Jenna stuck out her tongue.

Donna shook her head, and they both laughed. Jenna

got a surge of warm and fuzzy, of the closeness that had been missing between them all these years.

But before she could bask in it, the moment ended and Donna withdrew again. She said a quiet good-night, and when she turned away, she stared out the darkened window. Was work the real reason she couldn't sleep? Or did she have something else on her mind?

Jenna went back to her room. Figuring out Donna was impossible when she could barely figure out herself.

She walked over to the mirror and gazed at her reflection. No way was she going to go to J.D.'s cabin dressed like this. Besides, he was probably still at the bar. Not that his whereabouts mattered.

She ditched her milk and got into bed, pulling the covers up around her ears. She was staying away from him for the rest of the night.


The following morning, Jenna finished up some work in the barn, but she didn't come across J.D. She didn't see him anywhere. Curious, she checked the schedule and discovered that it was his day off. She glanced at her watch. She planned on taking Pedro out for a trail ride, and if she brought J.D. along, he could ride Duke. Both horses needed to get away from the barn, and it would be good to take them out together.

Was that an excuse to see J.D., to spend time with him?

Maybe, but it was also important for her lesson horses to get accustomed to the trails. So why not kill two birds with one stone? It would be nice to pack a picnic, too, and enjoy a long leisurely ride.

She suspected that J.D. was anxious to put time in

the saddle, and this would be a great opportunity for him to do that, if he didn't have other plans for the day. The only way to know would be to ask him.

As she walked to his cabin, her heart started to pound, mimicking the erratic motion it had made when she'd danced with him. If only she could keep her attraction to him in check. But at least she'd had the good sense to refuse his offer of having an affair.

She arrived at his place, but instead of approaching the cabin, she sat on the bottom step, hoping to quiet her mind. But it didn't work. In that lone moment, she thought about Savannah Jeffries and her connection to the cabin. How could Savannah have had affairs with two men, brothers no less, when Jenna could barely contain her feelings for one man?

"Jenna?"

She stood up and spun around. J.D. stood in the doorway, gazing at her.

"Hi," she said, feeling foolish for getting caught off guard.

"What are you doing?" he asked.

Aside from wondering about Savannah? "I was just sitting here for a minute, before I came to see you. What are you doing?"

"I was planning on going for a walk."

She didn't ascend the steps. She stayed where she was. "Would you like to go for a ride instead? On horseback," she clarified so he didn't think she was inviting him to go somewhere in her truck. "I can ride Pedro, and you can ride Duke. We can take them out by the creek."

"Are you kidding? I'd love to. When?"

"We could go now, but I was thinking that we could

have lunch on the trail. I can head over to the main house and throw something together before we leave."

"Mind if I tag along?"

"Not at all. It would be nice to have the company."

He closed the cabin door and joined her.

While they walked beside each other, she asked, "How long did you stay at the bar last night?"

"Until it closed. I would have left earlier, but that's how long everyone else stayed and I didn't have a ride back."

She forged ahead into her next question. "Did anyone say anything?"

"About us? Everyone at the table did, especially Manny. He asked me if we were going to hook up, but I told him no, that it was just a dance. It was an easy explanation."

"Do you think he bought it?"

"Why wouldn't he? It was the truth."

It wouldn't have been the truth if she'd agreed to sleep with him, but she kept that to herself. "I'm glad it's over."

"The explanation or the dance?"

Her heart thumped. "The explanation. The dance, too, but not because I didn't like it."

"I know you liked it, Jenna. We both did. But we probably shouldn't talk about it anymore."

*Or think about it,* she reminded herself.

Once they were in the kitchen, she opened the fridge. "Is ham and cheese okay, with lettuce, tomatoes and peperoncinis? That's about as fancy as I get."

"Sounds good to me. But my culinary skills aren't any better than yours." He watched her set everything on the counter. "Are you going to ask Tammy to teach you to cook?"

"Actually, I think I am. I'd feel better about being a wife and mother if I could offer my family some home-cooked meals now and then. Plus there's that old saying, 'The way to a man's heart is through his stomach.'"

"I'm still willing to be your guinea pig. I can give you an honest opinion and tell you if your lessons are working." He flashed his lopsided grin. "And if they aren't, Doc can pump my stomach."

"All in the name of helping me nab a husband? Oh, gee. That's mighty gentlemanly of you."

"It's the least I can do since I messed up your wedding song."

"That was never intended to be my wedding song." She jabbed his shoulder in a playful reprimand. "And we're not supposed to be talking about the dance, remember?"

His grin resurfaced. "Sorry. My bad."

"Very bad." But she understood his need to flirt. She was doing it, too, even if she knew better.

He offered to help, and they built the sandwiches together, working well as a team, unskilled as they were.

She snagged a pepper and ate it. "I love these."

He snagged one, too. "Spicy and sweet, like a girl I know."

More flirting. "You wish you knew her."

"A guy can dream."

"In the dream cabin? Those aren't the kinds of dreams that are supposed to happen there."

"Then I'm safe because I haven't done that yet."

*Yet?* She decided it was time to change the subject.

"We should get going or we're going to be starving by the time we make it to the creek."

He tossed a couple of apples into their lunch sacks. "I'm ready."

So was she. They went to the barn, saddled the horses and packed their saddlebags with food and water.

They rode for hours. The weather was perfect and the ever-changing terrain was riddled with towering trees, fallen branches, stony surfaces, grass, weeds and wildflowers.

J.D. was a magnificent horseman. He looked strong and regal on his mount. Jenna had to keep stopping herself from admiring him too deeply.

Upon reaching the creek, they set up their picnic, using a blanket they'd brought.

"This is beautiful," he said as a butterfly winged by.

"It's my favorite spot on the trail." She sat across from him. "Heaven on earth, as they say."

He unwrapped his sandwich. "I appreciate you sharing your favorite spot with me."

"That's what friends are for." She just wished that the platonic stuff was easier. "It's nice having a male friend to talk to."

"About finding a husband?"

"And other things." She removed the wrapping from her sandwich, too. "I was thinking about Savannah Jeffries earlier. That's what I was doing when you came out of the cabin and saw me. I think about her a lot."

"You actually haven't told me much about her, other than she was your uncle's girlfriend and Tammy discovered that she was keeping a secret."

"I can tell you the whole story now." Suddenly this seemed like the right time, the right place. "It's sordid, though." She steadied her emotions and started at the beginning. "Tammy first learned of Savannah when she overheard some of the household staff talking about her. Employees who've been around the Flying B a long time. Not like the young maids we socialized with at Lucy's."

He nodded in understanding.

She continued, "According to what Tammy overheard, Savannah didn't just sleep with Tammy's dad. She slept with mine, too."

"Damn," J.D. said.

Jenna's thoughts exactly. "Savannah was Uncle William's girlfriend when he was at Texas A&M, and that's why she was staying at the ranch. He was on summer break from university. He'd been in a car accident, and she came here to help him mend. My dad was home that summer, too."

"Giving Savannah the opportunity to mess around with him, too? That's some heavy stuff."

"It gets worse."

"I'm listening."

"Tammy uncovered an old grocery list in the cabin. It was from the time when Savannah was staying there."

"Why is that relevant?"

"It had an E.P.T. pregnancy test on it."

J.D. started. "That was her secret when she left town? She was pregnant?"

Jenna put her sandwich aside. "She might have been. But there's no way to know for sure. That's why we need to decide if we should hire a P.I. to search for her."

"The family vote?"

She nodded. "If Savannah was pregnant and she gave birth, then the child could belong to either man. Of course he or she wouldn't be a child anymore. They would be the oldest of all of us."

"I think you should hire the P.I."

"Really? Because I was going to vote no. As much as I want to uncover the truth, I'm afraid it will open a can of worms we're not prepared to deal with."

"I understand your concern, but I think it's important to know if there is another member of your family out there. Just think, Jenna, you could have another brother or sister. Or another cousin. That's epic."

*Too epic,* she thought.

He asked, "Are your dad and uncle going to vote on it, too?"

"No. Just the kids. Donna and I don't want our dad having a stake in it, so that means leaving Uncle William out of it, too. But he made his position clear. He would just as soon never see Savannah again. He's not trying to influence our vote, though. He'll accept whatever all of us decide."

"Does your dad want to see Savannah again?"

"I have no idea, and I don't intend to ask him. Donna and I are no longer on speaking terms with him."

He frowned. "So what's the holdup? Why haven't you voted yet?"

"We're waiting for Tammy's brothers to come back to the ranch. They went home after Tex's funeral and are scheduled to return next week. They have their own business. They're general contractors, and they've been busy with work. When they have time, they're going to help do some renovations around here."

"For the B and B?"

"Yes." She glanced at the body of water and the

way it shimmered. "Are you absolutely convinced that I should vote yes?"

"I would if I were you."

"Because family is important? You keep saying that yours doesn't matter because you can't remember them."

"That's because I don't think I have anyone."

She felt lonely for him, but confused for herself, too. Was he right? Should she vote yes?

"Tex hired a P.I. to keep an eye on all of us," she said. "He felt badly about not knowing his grandchildren, so he used someone to find out about us and report back to him."

"That's nice that he cared so much about you. I wonder if he would've condoned the use of a P.I. to find Savannah now that there's a possible child involved."

"I don't know." She pushed the P.I. out of her mind and moved on to a new topic. "Do you want to take a road trip with me this weekend? There's an equestrian center north of Houston that has some school horses for sale."

"Sure, that sounds great. Is it affiliated with the center where you used to work?"

"No. But it's a nice place, and they have some horses that are worth seeing. There's only one motel near there, so I'll book us a couple of rooms ahead of time."

"I can sleep in the truck."

Spoken like a true cowboy. "Humor me, J.D., and accept a room." She smiled. "Way far away from where mine will be."

He laughed. "On the other side of the motel, huh? It's a deal, if you let me buy you dinner while we're there."

"As long as there's no dancing involved."

"There won't be, I promise."

"Then it's a deal for me, too." She was determined to keep their upcoming trip friendly and light.

With absolutely no distractions.

## Chapter Seven

The trip was long, but interesting. J.D. enjoyed Jenna's company. She was a hell of a woman: smart, pretty, funny, sweet. She knew how to handle a rig, too. She was driving a Dodge dually and gooseneck horse trailer that had belonged to her grandfather, with the Flying B brand prominently displayed.

They arrived in the evening, too late to go to the equestrian center. But they knew ahead of time that they would be cutting it close, so they'd already made arrangements to see the horses in the morning.

"Let's check into the motel, then get some dinner," she said. "In fact, there's a diner there where we can eat. Then we don't have to go back out again."

"Sure. That will work." He didn't blame her for wanting to stay put for the night. She'd been behind the wheel for hours.

The motel was a typical roadway-style place, located in a rural area. The restaurant next to it was a rustic building with a yellow rose painted in the window, and across the street was a gas station with a little convenience store.

She parked the truck and trailer. "The equestrian center is just up the road. It'll be easy to head over there in the morning."

"I'm sorry I wasn't able to help with the driving. You must be beat."

"I'm a little tired, but it's nothing a hot meal can't cure." She glanced over at him. "Besides, you'll be able to drive once your identity is restored and you have access to your driver's license. I wonder how long it will be before the police uncover anything."

"I don't know, but Deputy Tobbs is probably right about me having been carjacked and robbed. That scenario seems to make the most sense."

"Do you remember how to drive?"

"I have a sense of it. I'm sure that when I get behind the wheel it will feel natural."

They exited the truck and went into the rental office. The middle-aged woman behind the counter greeted them, and J.D. realized that they probably looked like a couple, as if they would be staying together. That was quickly dispelled. Jenna asked for two rooms.

Afterward, she handed him his key card. "Your room is next to mine."

For lack of a better response, he made a joke. "What happened to putting me in a room far, far away from yours?"

She smiled. "What can I say? It would have been weird. The clerk would have thought you were a leper."

"I'm just an amnesiac. That's not nearly as bad." He smiled, too. "You can't catch my forgotten memory."

Her expression turned somber. "Sometimes I wish I could."

He assumed that she was referring to the Savannah Jeffries scandal. "I'm sorry you're at odds with what's going on with your family."

"It helped talking to you about it."

"I'm glad you trusted me with your feelings."

"You're turning into a really good friend, J.D."

"So are you, Jenna."

A beat of intimacy passed between them, but she filled it quickly. "Are you ready to eat? We can bring our luggage into our rooms after dinner."

He nodded. His luggage was a duffel bag he'd borrowed from Manny, and hers was an airline-style carry-on with a push-button handle and wheels.

They entered the diner. It had the same rustic appeal inside as it did on the outside, with battered wood booths and antler light fixtures.

A hostess took them to a small corner booth, and they scooted in beside each other. J.D. studied the menu, but Jenna only glanced at hers.

"I already know what I want," she said. "I've got a hankering for a burger and fries. A chocolate milk shake, too."

"That sounds good. I'll get the same thing." He set his menu down. "But with a root-beer float."

The waitress arrived, and they placed their orders.

While they waited for the meals, he asked, "Where in Houston did you grow up?"

"It's about sixty miles from here. Mom stayed in our

old house after the divorce, and Dad got himself a new place, but it was in the same neighborhood."

"A suburban area?"

She nodded. "Near shopping malls and schools and everything else a family might want, I guess. I prefer the country. Always have, always will."

He glanced out the window. "I like this area. It has a great view."

"That's the Sam Houston National Forest in the distance."

"It's impressive."

"Yes, it is." She frowned. "My dad was named after Sam Houston. Sam Houston Byrd. My uncle's full name is William Travis Byrd. But less people know who William Travis is than Sam Houston. Dad got the biggie."

She always scowled when she mentioned her father, but he understood why, considering the Savannah situation. Still, he wished it wasn't troubling her so badly. "You should discuss the details with your dad."

"The details?"

"About what happened all those years ago."

"I don't want to hear about his dirty little fling with his brother's girlfriend."

"I'm talking about the impact it had on his life and the family rift it caused, not the physical stuff between him and Savannah."

She set her jaw. "I know what you meant."

Dang, she was stubborn. "I'm just saying that maybe you should try to make things right with your dad."

"I'm not going to right his wrong."

"There are two sides to every story."

"His side isn't a story I care to hear."

He decided to drop it for now, with the intention of

broaching the subject another time. The way this was gnawing at her wasn't healthy.

During the lapse in conversation, their food and drinks arrived. She dived in, as eager as a bear coming out of hibernation.

"I'm sorry for getting testy," she said.

"You'll feel better now that you're getting some chow in you."

"It's yummy. The milk shake, especially." She sipped from a red-and-white-striped straw.

"My root-beer float is good, too."

She smiled. "Sugar highs."

He could get high on her smile, if he let himself. Let himself? Hell, he already was.

As a distraction, J.D. looked out the window again, where the view erupted into hills, valleys and scores of trees.

She followed his line of sight. "I hope you didn't get the impression that I'm at odds with the real Sam Houston. It's not his fault that my dad ended up with his name."

"I didn't think you disliked *Colonneh*."

"What? Who?"

He blinked, as confused as she was. He didn't know why he'd said *Colonneh*. Not until his thoughts jumbled into a feeling, a memory, and struck him like a warrior's arrow. "Oh, God, Jenna, I'm related to him."

"I don't know who you're talking about."

He turned to look at her. "Sam Houston."

He gaped at him. "*The* Sam Houston?"

"Well, not him, exactly. But to the band of Cherokee that adopted him."

Another gape. "You're Cherokee?"

"Part. A quarter," he added, amazed by how quickly this information was tumbling into his mind. "That's how I'm registered with the tribe."

"And you're certain that you're affiliated with the band that adopted Sam?"

"Yes. This stuff just hit me, memories that zoomed into my head." And it made him damned proud, too. "Pretty cool, huh?"

"I'll say." She studied him with awe. "Was *Colonneh* Sam's Cherokee name?"

He nodded. "It means The Raven."

"Oh, that's right. His other name was Raven. All Texans should know that. But to actually know someone whose ancestry is connected to his..." She paused. "Do you recall anything else about yourself? Like who told you about your heritage?"

"No. But I'm from Texas. I'm not sure what part I hail from, but it's my homeland." He smiled, feeling a bond with the Lone Star State, with Sam, with the Cherokee blood running through his veins.

"I'm happy for you, J.D."

As she leaned toward him, his heart knocked against his chest. She was almost close enough to kiss. All he had to do was make his move to close the deal. He studied her mouth, then lifted his gaze. She was staring at him, too.

"We aren't supposed to be doing this," she said.

"We aren't doing anything but looking at each other."

"But we want to do more."

"We've wanted that since the beginning."

"We can't."

"We could," he corrected. "But we agreed that we wouldn't."

Regardless, they were damn close to breaking their agreement. She even wet her lips. Unable to help himself, so did he. But then Jenna moved away from him and grabbed her milk shake, sucking viciously on the straw. Unfortunately, her diversion didn't help. It only managed to give him a wildly sexual feeling, worsening his urges.

After their meal ended, they got their luggage from the truck and proceeded to their rooms. But they didn't unlock their doors. They just stood there, trapped in their attraction.

"We better go," she said.

He motioned with his chin. "You first."

She fumbled for her key card, digging around in her purse. She found it and gripped the plastic a little too tightly. "I'll see you in the morning."

"Okay." He didn't trust himself to say anything else. He was still thinking about her mouth on the straw or, more accurately, about kissing her senseless.

She went inside, and he waited until she closed the door before he blew out his breath.

And wished that he was spending the night with her.

Jenna stood in the middle of her room, wondering how long it would take J.D. to enter his. *This is crazy,* she thought, *absolute insanity.* She wanted to forgo their friendship pact and become lovers.

Then why not do it? Honestly, what did she have to lose?

Her heart, for one thing. If she fell in love with him, she would be setting herself up for a world of pain. It wasn't as if J.D. was going to stick around and marry her.

But he wasn't even husband material, so what was the likelihood of falling in love with him, anyway? There was nothing wrong with uncommitted sex. True, it wasn't Jenna's style, but maybe she needed to rethink her immediate priorities. Later, she could find a man who had the qualities on her list. Later, she could walk down the aisle with Mr. Right. But at the moment, *Mr. Right Now* was *right* next door.

Still, she stalled.

Needing more time to contemplate the issue, she stripped off her clothes and drew a hot bath. Determined to relax, she pinned up her hair and soaked in the tub. She even closed her eyes. Then she lost all sense of reason and conjured an image of J.D. pulling her into his arms. So much for contemplating the issue. She knew darned well that she was going to cave into temptation.

Should she invite him to her room or go to his? Jenna didn't have any experience at this sort of thing.

She sat upright and scrubbed clean, careful not to get amorous with the soap. Touching herself wouldn't help her cause.

After drying off, she moisturized her skin. She brushed her teeth, refreshed her face and let down her hair, too.

Maybe it would be better to invite him over. That way she didn't have to get dressed. She could wrap herself in her robe and stay naked underneath.

What if he rebuffed her advances?

Oh, sure. As if that was going to happen. She knew that J.D. wanted this as badly as she did.

She slipped on her robe, a silky garment that caressed her flesh. Better though, would be the sensation of J.D.'s hands.

Without further hesitation, she dialed his room.

He answered on the second ring. "Hello?"

"It's me," she said, instead of reciting her name. Who else would be calling him at the motel? "I was wondering if you wanted to come over and hang out."

A slight pause. "For how long?"

*Here goes,* she thought. "All night. I want to be with you, J.D."

His voice turned graveled. "Are you sure?"

Her nerves jangled. "Yes."

"I just got out of the shower." His voice remained rough, anxious, sexy. "I need to get dressed."

Was he fully naked? Or did he have a towel tucked around his waist? She didn't have the courage to ask. Instead, she said, "I just got out of the bath. And I'm in my robe." Fair warning, she decided. No surprises.

"Damn. I'll hurry. But first I have to run across the street to the convenience store."

Obviously he intended to buy condoms. The motel didn't provide them, not like Donna had done for the guest accommodations at the ranch.

"I can't believe this is going to happen," he said. "Are you sure you're not going to change your mind?"

"I'm positive." She didn't have the strength to back out. She needed him, more than anything. "I'll see you soon."

They ended the call with eager goodbyes, and she returned to the bathroom to check her appearance. She even opened her robe and looked at her naked self in the mirror.

Her nerves went nuts. What if he found her lacking? What if he thought her hips were too bony or her breasts were too small? Dang it, why hadn't she been blessed with a figure like her sister's?

Jenna closed her robe and tied the belt. She couldn't do anything about her body. She was what she was.

She headed for the bed and sat on the edge of it. He'd said that he would hurry, but it felt like forever.

Finally, a knock sounded on the door.

She leaped up and answered it. There stood J.D. with a small paper bag in one hand and a plastic yellow rose in the other. Their gazes locked, and he extended the rose.

He said, "It's not the prettiest flower, but it's all they had."

She accepted his gift, assuming that the convenience store was selling them as souvenirs. "I think it's wonderful that you thought of me." And she would cherish the rose, simply because he gave it to her. "Come in, J.D."

He crossed the threshold and closed the door. Silence sizzled between them. He glanced down at her robe, particularly at the area where it gapped in front, revealing the hint of flesh between her breasts.

She didn't make an effort to close the material. Nor did she feel self-conscious about her lack of cleavage. He obviously liked what he saw.

He said, "Promise me that you won't have regrets later."

"I promise."

"What about the comment you made before?"

She considered his question. "You mean on the night we danced?"

He nodded, repeating her words and making them clear. "You said that if you slept with me, you would get attached and it would only make my leaving more difficult for you."

She replied as honestly as she could. "That crossed my mind tonight. I even considered how terrible it would be if I fell in love with you. But it's become more difficult wanting you than not having you, so I'm not going to worry about the future. All that matters is the here and now."

He reached out to touch her cheek. "Someday you'll find the man you're meant to marry."

"I'm counting on it."

But that didn't mean that she didn't appreciate him, exactly as he was, at this very moment. His hair was damp from the shower and although he'd combed it back, stray pieces fell on to his forehead. His hasty attire consisted of jeans, an untucked shirt, no belt and his usual battered boots.

He removed the condoms from the bag and opened the box. "I'm going to put these beside the bed for when we need them."

She handed him the flower. "Will you put the rose there, too?"

He set everything on the nightstand and returned to her. Then he took her into his arms and kissed her. The kiss she'd been waiting for. The kiss he'd been hungry to give her. Their lips met softly at first, but he deepened the contact quickly, using his tongue to intensify the feeling.

She flung her arms around his neck, and he held her body close to his. She could smell a citrus aroma—the customary soap from the motel—on his skin. She'd bathed with the same type of soap, and somehow that made their union seem even more sensual.

J.D. released the tie on her robe and the garment drifted open. He stepped back to look at her, and her heart thudded in her ears.

"Take it all the way off," he said.

Suddenly she went shy, her self-consciousness kicking in. But she did his bidding and removed the robe so he could fully see her.

"I should have put the lights on low," she said.

"No. It's perfect like this. You're perfect. Turn around."

She made what she hoped was a ladylike pirouette. When she faced him once again, he was smiling. She smiled, too. His crooked grin was infectious.

He anxiously led her to bed.

She watched while he discarded his clothes. They reclined on the mattress and started kissing again. Only now, caressing was involved. He roamed his hands along the lines of her body, making her skin tingle. She stroked him, too, gliding over flesh and bone and strong male muscle.

"I can't remember being with anyone else," he said. "But I'm glad I can't. I want this to be my first intimate memory."

His words affected her as deeply as his touch. "You certainly haven't forgotten how to entice a woman."

"You make me want to entice you."

He climbed on top, pinning her hands above her head and making her his willing prisoner. She studied his features. Now that she knew about his Cherokee roots, his heritage seemed magnificently obvious.

"Being with you is everything I imagined," she said.

"For me, too." He released her, but only because he

was moving down her body and making a moist path with his tongue.

She arched and closed her eyes. He did things a man had no right to do, things that ignited a fire, things that made her melt all over him. By the time she opened her eyes, she could barely see straight.

He reached for the protection, ripped into a packet and sheathed himself. He was impatient, but so was she. She didn't want to wait another second.

He entered her, and their lovemaking took flight, with Jenna matching his glorious rhythm. As she moved her hips in time with his, prisms of colors spun in her mind, binding them together, almost as if they were one.

But they weren't, she told herself. This was a pleasure-only affair. No heartstrings, no commitment, no ties. J.D. wasn't hers to keep.

And he never would be.

## Chapter Eight

J.D. couldn't keep his eyes off Jenna. He wanted to devour her in every way imaginable. The experience was so new, so exciting.

He said, "Have you ever heard someone say that sex is overrated? Well, that's not true. Not when it makes you feel this way."

In lieu of a response, she wrapped her legs around him, and the experience got better and better.

He glanced down at her, intrigued by the sinuous manner in which she moved. Her skin was creamy and smooth, soft and fair and so unlike his. The wonderment was almost too much to bear, but she seemed as fascinated by him as he was by her.

She said, "I'm so glad you remembered something about yourself tonight."

"At least I know that I'm from Texas."

"Not only are you from here, you have a connection to Sam Houston. That makes the yellow rose you gave me even more special."

"Next time it will be a real flower. I'd give you hundreds of roses if I could."

"I always imagined rose petals on my honeymoon. All over the bed."

"Don't put fantasies like that in my head."

"You're not interested in marriage, J.D."

"No, but I like the flower-petals idea. It sounds sexy."

"And romantic."

"That, too." He covered her mouth with his. He also slipped his hand between them and heightened her pleasure.

Heat. Beautiful urgency.

He ached to give her a release, to shower her with everything she needed, everything she desired. They weren't a couple, nor were they on their way to becoming one, but for now they belonged to each other, and that was an aphrodisiac neither of them could deny.

Enthralled, he watched her, and with carnality bursting at the seams, she shuddered and climaxed. Unable to hold back, he lost himself in the passion, too.

Spent, he fell into her arms and stayed there for a while, allowing her to bask in the afterglow. She nuzzled his chest, her hair tickling his skin. In a deliberate show of affection, he skimmed a hand down her spine.

After they broke apart, he went into the bathroom to dispose of the condom.

He returned to find her sitting up in bed, with the quilt tucked around her. She looked sweetly tousled. Well-loved.

No! Not loved. He frowned at the mind slip. Making love wasn't love. In this case, it was miles apart.

Before she noticed his unease, he softened his expression and approached her. "Do you want a cup of tea? They have the herbal stuff."

"That sounds good."

He used the coffeepot to heat the water. He didn't brew himself any. He didn't drink hot tea. In fact, he wasn't sure why he'd offered some to her. Was it to keep his mind in check? Or was there someone from his past who favored tea? He honestly didn't know. In spite of his Sam Houston breakthrough, the bulk of his memories remained blocked.

"Cream and sugar?" he asked.

"Sugar. One packet."

He fixed the drink and brought it to her. "It's chamomile. It's supposed to be soothing."

She took the cup and tasted the fragrant brew. "It's just right. Thank you."

He sat beside her, his thoughts drifting back to the flower conversation, as well as to something she'd previously said. "You told me that you haven't planned any of your wedding details. But you have."

"The rose petals on the bed? I saw that in a movie, and it appealed to me. But we shouldn't do it. It wouldn't be right for our affair."

Because it would make their affair seem like a honeymoon? "I agree that we shouldn't."

She made a perplexed expression. "Funny, how we're always talking about what we shouldn't do."

"That's because we're being noncommittal."

She nodded, then clutched the tea with both hands,

as if she needed an extra dose of warmth. Was she thinking about the man she was destined to marry and wishing he was here instead? Or was J.D. the only man on her mind?

Either way, he said, "If you want to snuggle, I can hold you tonight while you sleep."

"That would be wonderful." She leaned against his shoulder. "I like to spoon."

"Me, too. I think." He tossed out a smile. "I can't remember. But I'm sure I'll like it with you."

Soon they settled in for sleep, extinguishing the lamp and taking the aforementioned spooning position, with the front of his body pressed against the back of hers. He slipped an arm around her waist, creating a cozier connection.

She sighed, the feathery sound proof of her contentment. Grateful that she was satisfied, J.D. whispered a gentle, "Good night."

"You, too," she responded, using an equally soft voice. She tugged at the covers, getting more comfortable.

Although he closed his eyes, he wasn't able to sleep, at least not right away. He could tell when Jenna drifted off, though, mostly by the change in her breathing. Her limbs seemed looser, too.

Finally he joined her, and in the morning, he awakened before she did. With dawn peeking through a space in the drapes, he sat up and gazed at his lover.

*Such delicate repose,* he thought, tempted to touch her. But he kept his hands at his sides. He didn't want to rouse her. He wanted to see her while she was unable to see him. He realized that it was his way of shielding his confused self from her, of continuing to hide behind his amnesia.

And taking an odd sort of comfort in it.


As Jenna awoke, she sensed that she was being watched. She squinted, struggling to get her bearings. Then she saw J.D. sitting next to her, the sheet draped around his waist, his dark gazed fixed on hers.

"Morning," he said, skimming his thumb along her cheek, as if he'd been waiting all morning to do that.

"Hi," she replied quickly, reminding herself not to get attached. Thing was, she wanted to grab him and never let go. But what woman wouldn't feel that way, considering how affectionate he was?

He took his hand away. "You still look sleepy."

She sat up and clutched her portion of the sheet, shielding her nakedness, more out of caution than shyness. "I suppose I am. What time is it?" She couldn't see the clock from her side of the bed.

"A little after six."

"Dang. I hadn't planned on getting up this early. We're keeping rancher's hours, even on a road trip. But I guess it stands to reason, considering we live on a ranch."

"I don't live at the Flying B, Jenna."

"You live there for now." Everything was temporary: his job, his living arrangements, their affair.

"You're right. I do." He leaned closer. "Can I kiss you? Or is it too early for that?"

Her pulse spiked. "It's never too early for a kiss."

He reached for her, and she released the sheet, allowing it to fall to her waist. Their mouths met and mated, and she slipped deeper into the moment.

There was no denying it; she was getting attached. But she would do her darnedest to cope with his departure when the time came.

Sweet and tender, the kiss continued. J.D. had a way of making her feel special, even if it wasn't meant to last.

He pushed the sheet completely away, making it easier to roll over the bed and take her with him. She landed on top, and he smiled. He obviously wanted to make love in this position.

But so did Jenna. She desired him in all sorts of ways. Her heart pounded from the want, the need, the anticipation.

He secured a condom, and the shiny packet glittered. He opened it and concentrated on his task. She suspected that they were going to go through the protection quickly.

"I'm glad we have more of those back at the ranch," she said.

He glanced up and smiled again, a bit more devilish this time. "That's for sure. Now let's get you seated, nice and tight."

He circled her waist, giving her a boost while she straddled him. She impaled herself, and the sensation nearly knocked her for a loop.

With a powerful grip, he lifted her up and down, setting a rocking horse rhythm. "You look like a cowgirl."

She latched on to his shoulders, mesmerized by his broad strength. "I feel like one, too."

"We're good together." He kept her within his grasp. "And it's good that there aren't any future worries between us."

"You mean no plans to stay in touch after you leave?" *No phone calls, emails, texts,* she thought.

He nodded, morning shadows playing against his skin. "You're still okay with that, right?"

"Yes." She was determined to accept it, the best she could. After he was gone, she would accept the blessing of having known him and move on with her life. "All I want right now is to make this happen."

He kissed her hard and rough. "Then do it. Make it happen."

Quickening the pace, she rode him with every ounce of hunger she had, bucking wildly, and leaving them both breathless when it was over.

J.D. took a minute to collect his thoughts, then he said to Jenna, "You blow me away."

"Likewise. Sex with you packs a punch." She climbed off his lap and sagged like a rag doll.

"Relax and I'll be right back." He got rid of the condom and returned to her. "Do you want me go to the diner and get some breakfast?"

"Sure. I'll shower while you're gone."

"I need to shower, too, and shave. But I left my bag in the other room."

"You can do that before you get breakfast. It will probably take me longer to get ready than you, anyway."

"Women and their hair and makeup." He twined his fingers around her golden locks. "I like you the way you are."

"Messy from going cowgirl?"

"Definitely." He noticed that her mouth was swollen from his kisses. Talk about hot. And sinful. And beautiful.

After a beat of soul-stirring silence, she pushed at his chest. "You better go. Before we end up ravishing each other again."

"Good thinking. Or else we'll never leave this bed."

"They'd find us, dead from exhaustion."

He laughed. "With a plastic rose and a box of condoms beside us. How embarrassing would that be?"

She laughed, too. "Proof that we need to control ourselves."

"And eat and be normal?" He climbed into his rumbled clothes. "What should I bring back for you?"

"Ham and eggs, with any kind of toast. It doesn't matter."

"How do you like your eggs?"

"Scrambled is fine."

He gave her a quick kiss, but it didn't satisfy the urges stirring inside him. He wanted to linger, to get his second wind, even after the jokes they'd made.

He headed for the door instead. He was too damned eager to have her again. But what did he expect? He couldn't remember being with anyone but Jenna.

He glanced back and saw that she was watching him. She even chewed her swollen lips, pulling the bottom one between her teeth. Neither of them had the affair down pat. She seemed overwhelmed, too, and possibly on the verge of telling him to forget breakfast and come back to her.

But she didn't give in. And neither did J.D.

He went to his room, and after he showered, shaved and donned clean jeans and a fresh shirt, he walked to the diner and ordered their meals.

Food in hand, he returned to Jenna and noticed that the door was ajar. She'd obviously left it that way for

him. He entered the room. She was fully dressed, crisp
and pretty in a Western blouse and jeans, with her hair
in a ponytail.

"That's a good look on you," he said.

"Thank you."

*The certified riding instructor,* he thought. She definitely fit the part. The whole purpose of this trip was
to shop for lesson horses, not have lust-burning sex.

He put the food on the dining table, which was po-
sitioned by the window and equipped with two padded
chairs. "Okay if I open the drapes and let more light in?"

"Oh, of course. I meant to do that." She glanced at
the takeout containers. "Which one is mine?"

"They're both the same. Ham and eggs was the special, with home-fried potatoes. I got wheat toast and lots
of jelly to go with it. Ketchup and salt and pepper, too."

"I made coffee while you were gone. Do you want
a cup?"

"Sure." He could use some caffeine. "Did you drink
yours already?"

"No. I was waiting for you to come back." She
poured two cups and set them on the table, along with
the little basket that contained powdered creamer, sugar
and the accompanying stir sticks.

They sat across from each other and fixed their coffee. Next, they opened the plastic utensils he'd gotten
from the diner and doctored their meals. He squeezed
ketchup on his eggs, and she used it on her potatoes.
Both were generous with the pepper and light on the
salt. She favored the grape jelly, and he went to town
on the strawberry.

Would this be considered post-sex compatibility?
*No,* he thought. *Not quite.*

She took deliberately small bites. She wasn't as ravenous as she'd been at dinner last night. Either that or she was trying to behave properly. He was, too, still mindful of his hunger for her.

She lifted her coffee and studied him from beneath the rim of her cup. "I wonder if you know any other Cherokee words besides Sam Houston's Raven name."

"It's possible, I suppose. Who knows what's locked inside my brain? But I should probably count my blessings that I remember how to speak English, let alone my ancestor's language."

"My ancestors are from Sweden. On my mom's side. The Byrds are Texans, through and through, but they originated from England, with a little gypsy tossed in. I didn't know about the gypsy part until Tex told us about our great-grandmother and the feather bed."

"It was foolish of me not believe in your great-grandmother's magic when you first mentioned it to me. The Cherokee believe in magic, in dreams, in visions. It's part of my culture, too. A medicine man is a called *di da nv wi s gi,* and it means 'curer of them.'"

"So you *do* know more Cherokee words."

"Well, damn. Listen to me." He grinned, stunned and pleased that it came so easily. "I guess I do."

She reached across the table to touch his hand. "It's nice to see you looking so happy."

"It's nice for me, too." And so was her caring touch.

"You know what, J.D.? I don't think you were a foster child. I think someone in your family taught you about your culture, and I think you were surrounded by it."

"You could be right. If I was a foster kid, I would probably be missing the Cherokee side of myself instead of recalling it in such a positive way."

As their hands drifted apart, she said, "It's still odd, though, that you seem to have knowledge of the foster-care system and how the older kids rarely get adopted."

"Maybe I knew someone else who grew up in that world."

"Someone who must have been important to you."

The tea drinker, perhaps? If there was such a person. "I don't know. It's all a bit weird. If I had a family, parents who nurtured me, maybe even brothers and sisters, then why do I get the sense of not having anyone in my life?"

"Maybe you just haven't remembered them yet."

"Or maybe something went wrong with my relationship with them. Maybe they turned away from me or I turned away from them. The positive connection I feel to my heritage doesn't mean that other aspects of my life aren't screwed up. Maybe I'm holding on to my heritage so tightly because it's all I have."

"I agree that there's something going on with your family. Otherwise you probably wouldn't be advising me to vote in favor of finding Savannah and the child she might have had. And you wouldn't be trying to encourage me to give my father a chance."

"Are you having a change of heart? Are you going to take my advice?"

"I'm considering the vote."

"But not squaring things with your dad? Sleeping with his brother's girlfriend was a lousy thing to do. But judging him without hearing his side of the story isn't fair, either."

"There's nothing he could say that would make me feel okay about what he did."

"Then forgive him to lessen the burden on yourself."

"I wish I could, but I can't." She moved a forkful of eggs around, mixing them with her potatoes. "If only my mom was still alive. I would talk to her about this if I could." She paused, apparently considering how the conversation would go. "If she were here, I think she would tell me to stay away from Dad and just let him be."

"Why do you think she would say that?"

"Because she never pushed Donna to open up. She accepted that my sister was distant, like Dad in that regard."

Curious, he asked, "Does Donna favor him in her appearance, too? Because I envision that you look more like your mom. And since you and Donna don't really resemble each other, I figure each of you took after a different parent."

"You got that right. I'm my mother's daughter."

He hadn't meant to imply that she didn't have anything in common with her father. "What does your dad think about you and Donna turning the ranch into a B and B?"

"He hasn't given us his opinion. But we don't want him butting into our business or trying to talk to us."

"When's the last time you saw him?"

"At Tex's funeral."

"If I were him, I would be proud of you and your sister. You make a hell of a team. And Tammy. The three of you are going to make the B and B a tremendous success."

Her eyes lit up. "Thanks. That means a lot to me. And thanks for caring about my feelings. Even if I don't follow your advice, I appreciate your motives." She motioned between them. "You and I make a good team, too. I'm glad I brought you on this trip and that you're going to check out the horses with me."

"So am I." He was eager to go to the equestrian center and help her in any way he could, and he couldn't agree more—they were a damned fine team.

In and out of bed.

# Chapter Nine

Jenna hit the jackpot. She'd purchased two wonderful geldings and now she and J.D. were almost home, traveling down the Flying B Road and heading toward the ranch.

She glanced at the man she'd spent the night with. They'd behaved in a professional manner at the equestrian center. No hand-holding, no public display of affection, nothing that indicated that they were lovers.

"What's going to happen now that we're back?" she asked. "How are we going to handle this?"

"What do you mean?"

"Our affair. Are we going to sneak around and keep it a secret? Or let everyone know that we're together?"

"I'll do whatever you're comfortable with."

"What would you prefer?" Before she went out on a

limb and expressed her feelings, she desperately wanted to know how he felt.

"Truthfully? I'd like to be open about it. We're both consenting adults and have a right to be together. We don't have anything to hide, not as far as I'm concerned. But if you would rather go the secret route, I'll respect your wishes."

He'd said exactly what she'd hoped he would say. "I completely agree. Sneaking around seems cheap, and it would make me feel cheap. I don't want to call dirty attention to ourselves, and if we have a secret affair and get caught, it will seem too much like what my dad did with Savannah. Even if the circumstances aren't the same, it would affect me that way."

"I'd never want to do anything that would make you feel badly about yourself." He leaned over and kissed her cheek. "This is a nice thing we've got going."

She smiled. "Very nice."

They arrived at the ranch, and she drove to the barn. Although it was still daylight, dusk would be closing in soon. As they prepared to unload the first gelding, Manny and Hugh, who'd been working nearby, moseyed on over to greet them, obviously curious about the horses she'd purchased.

Jenna got a little nervous. She knew that she shouldn't, not after she and J.D. agreed that they had every right to disclose their affair, but now that they were actually in the company of Flying B employees, she wasn't sure how to act.

J.D. behaved in a perfectly natural way. He unloaded the horse and talked to Hugh and Manny about both geldings and what great finds they were. By the time the second horse was unloaded and placed in his stall,

Jenna was able to relax, too. She realized that J.D. was going to handle it.

He said to the other men, "Normally I wouldn't bring something like this up, but I'm concerned about ranch gossip. Jenna and I are dating now. So if you notice us hanging around together or Jenna coming and going from my cabin more often than she did before, please treat the situation with respect."

Hugh replied, "I understand. People talk, and you can't stop their tongues from wagging. But you don't want them talking out of turn." He addressed Jenna. "I'll admit that I've done my share of talking over the years. But never in a hurtful way. And I won't do that to you, either."

"Thank you." She couldn't be more pleased with his reaction. Hugh was as honest as they come, and he'd been around since the Savannah days, witnessing the devastation firsthand.

Young Manny was another story. The Savannah situation had occurred long before he'd been born. No doubt he'd heard about it, though, especially since the past had been unearthed. But Manny only seemed concerned with the here and now.

A cheeky grin broke out on his face, and he said to Jenna, "I knew you two were going to hook up. Maria and I are seeing each other now, too. We should go on a double date sometime."

"Sure." She smiled at him. "Maria seems like a nice girl."

"She's the best. I'm right crazy for her."

Jenna hoped J.D. was feeling the same sense of boyish craziness for her, regardless of how short-lived their affair proved to be. She glanced over at him, and he winked, making her heart spin.

Hugh nudged Manny. "Let's go. It's about quitting time."

Manny was still grinning. To the new lovers, he said, "See you guys."

After the old foreman and the young ranch hand were gone, Jenna spoke to J.D. "Thanks for taking care of that."

"You're welcome. I figured that we needed to get it out there, better sooner than later." He reached for her hand. "Do you want to stay with me tonight? Or are you planning on sleeping in your own bed?"

"I'd like to stay with you, as long as you don't think it's too soon."

"Too soon for what? We already went public with it. In fact, maybe you should just move in with me."

Stunned, she stared at him. "Move in?"

"To the cabin. It would be nice to have you there every night, and now that my memory is starting to improve…"

"You only remembered a few things. Granted, they were really important things, but it was just bits and pieces."

"Yes, but look how quickly it happened. It's probably just a matter of time before everything comes rushing back. And then I'll be leaving."

"So we should cram in as many days together as we can?"

"It works for me."

It worked for her, too. She wanted as much of him as she could get and for as long as she could get it. Still, it wasn't something she'd expected. "I'll move in with you, but I need time to prepare. I want to talk to Donna and Tammy first."

"About us?"

She nodded. "I can't go skipping off to stay with you without explaining it to them."

He laughed. "Skipping?"

She play-punched his arm. "You know what I mean."

"Yes, I believe I do." He kissed her, long and slow, and she wrapped her arms around him.

After the kiss ended, she said, "Will you take my luggage to the cabin? There's no point in me hauling it back to the house. I should probably pack a few more bags if I'm moving in with you." She paused to ponder the situation. "God, that sounds weird. Us living together."

"I know, but I figure it's going to be more like a vacation since it's probably going to be so short."

"That's a good way of looking at it."

"It will be fun. A romantic adventure."

"I think so, too." One more kiss, and they parted ways.

As she exited the barn, the horses she'd just purchased whinnied, calling out to each other and adjusting to their new home. Jenna was making an adjustment, too.

She walked to the house with an emotionally cluttered mind. She came to the porch and ascended the steps, grateful that she owned a piece of the ranch. If J.D. was the type who wanted to settle down, she could easily imagine sharing her home with him.

But he wasn't, and it was pointless to entertain those types of imaginings. Someday she would meet the man from her list. J.D. wasn't him, and all of the wishing in the world wouldn't change the nature of their relationship. She had no choice but to accept it.

She opened the front door and saw Donna, sitting on the sofa, tapping away on her iPad. Although she was dressed casually, she managed to look elegant, as always.

Tammy was in the living room, too, paging through a magazine. She looked lovely, as well, and appeared to be dressed to go out. On the floor beside her was her purse.

Jenna approached both women. She was glad that she'd come across them together, rather than having to summon a meeting or speak to them separately.

Tammy glanced up first. "Hey," she said. "You're home from your trip. How did it go?"

Obviously Jenna had plenty to say about the subject, but she started off simple. "I bought some new lesson horses."

"That's great. Maybe I can see them tomorrow? I don't have time tonight. I'm waiting for Mike to call— we're meeting in town for dinner."

"Tomorrow would be fine. I'd like for you to see them." She didn't make the same offer to Donna. Her sister's allergies acted up whenever she went near the stables.

But that didn't stop Donna from sensing there was more to the conversation than met the eye. She asked, "What else is going on? Besides the horsey stuff?"

"A lot." Jenna sat beside her, with Tammy directly across from them. "I took J.D. on the trip with me, and we're lovers now. But it's just an affair."

Tammy frowned. "There's no commitment involved?"

"He isn't the right man for that."

Donna put the iPad down. "I figured that you'd end up sleeping together. It was obvious how much you wanted him."

"As long as you don't get hurt," Tammy put in.

"I won't. After he leaves, I'll go on with my life and he'll go on with his." She dropped the rest of her bomb. "But we're going to live together for the duration of his stay. I'm moving into the dream cabin with him, and we're going to treat it as a vacation, of sorts."

"That sounds too easy," Donna said.

Before a feeling of sadness crept in, Jenna shoved it away. "Actually, J.D is getting closer to recouping his memory." She relayed the Sam Houston/Cherokee information. "He thinks it's only a matter of time before the rest of it comes tumbling back."

Tammy scooted to the edge of her chair. "That's fascinating. Okay if I tell Mike? He should know."

"I'm sure that would be fine. I think J.D. would appreciate you passing it on to Doc. Come to think of it, J.D. should probably inform Deputy Tobbs, too. The more information the sheriff's department has, the better their chances are of uncovering his identity. In case he doesn't remember everything on his own."

After a stream of silence, Tammy said, "This is off topic, but I already told Donna while you were on your trip, and it concerns the three of us. I heard from my brothers this morning. They'll be here on Wednesday, so if that fits into your schedule, we should plan on having the vote that day."

Jenna's stomach went tight. The P.I. Savannah. The possible child. "J.D. thinks I should vote yes. He thinks it's important to know the truth and embrace it."

Tammy replied, "That's what I'm going to do," making her upcoming vote apparent.

Donna scrunched up her face, indicating an opposing opinion.

Jenna said, "I haven't made a decision, but I'm leaning toward yes. I'm curious about Savannah, but I'm even more curious if there's another Byrd out there. What if it's someone who needs a family? Who would like to have us be part of his or her life?"

"What if it's someone who doesn't?" her sister countered. "If another other Byrd exists, he or she could want nothing to do with us. These types of things don't always turn out hunky-dory."

"I know, but after being around J.D and seeing how lost he is from not being able to remember his family, it's hard for me not to consider how important family is."

"Does that mean you're okay with what Dad did, too?"

Jenna scowled. "Hell, no. That's a whole other matter." Even if J.D. thought otherwise. "Dad created this mess."

Donna blew out her breath. "I'm glad you haven't gone completely over to the dark side."

Jenna found herself saying, "You know it's possible that Savannah isn't the hussy I've been assuming that she was. Dad could have seduced her into being with him. He could have taken advantage of her. You know how brazen he can be when he wants something."

Donna didn't disagree. But she didn't say that she was cutting Savannah any slack, either.

Jenna asked Tammy, "How do you think your brothers will vote?"

"I don't know. We'll just have to wait and see." Tammy's cell phone rang from her purse and she reached in and grabbed it. Obviously it was Doc. She all but glowed when she answered the summons. She got up and walked away to talk to him, waving goodbye to Donna and Jenna, and leaving them alone.

Neither said a word. The impending vote was only two days away, but the results, whatever they turned out to be, would last a lifetime.

Jenna arrived on J.D.'s doorstep with a slew of luggage and a worried expression, and he got worried, too.

"What's wrong?" he asked.

"I'm getting freaked out about the vote. Tammy's brothers will be here on Wednesday."

He took her luggage and brought it inside. "You already knew they were coming sometime this week."

She followed him inside. "I know. But now it seems so final."

"Are you sure you're not freaked out about *this?*" He motioned to the air between them. "About staying with me?"

"Why? Are you freaked out about it?"

"No." But he feared that he might have pushed the boundaries of their relationship, drawing her into something she couldn't handle.

"I want to stay with you. In fact, I think it's going to be a relief getting away from the main house for a while."

"So it's really the vote that's bothering you?"

She nodded. "If we search for Savannah, we'll know for sure if we have a brother or sister or cousin. And if we don't, I'll always be left wondering."

"So what are you going to do?"

"Vote yes."

He knew she'd been considering it, but she looked as if she'd just made up her mind for certain. "You'll be doing the right thing."

"Tammy is voting yes, too. But I think Donna is going to vote no."

"What about Tammy's brothers?"

"Tammy doesn't know."

They sat on the sofa together. "Does it have to be unanimous? Because if it does, it sounds like you're going to be deadlocked, regardless of how Tammy's brothers vote."

"We already agreed that the majority will rule."

"Then it still has a shot of going through."

"I hope so. Because I want to talk to Savannah and hear her side of what happened all those years ago."

"You're willing to hear her side, but not your dad's? He's the man who raised you. Who fed you and clothed you. Savannah is a stranger."

"Yes, he's the man who did all of that. But he's also the guy who turned Donna and me into the basket cases that we are."

He couldn't believe what he was hearing. "I barely know your sister, other than what you've told me about her, but from what I can tell, she isn't a basket case, and by God, neither are you. You're beautiful, hard-working, independent women. And if your dad helped shape you into those things, then he must have done something right."

She put her head on his shoulder. "Okay so maybe we're not basket cases. But we're not totally normal, either. Me with the husband checklist, and her with the inability to get close to people."

"Does this mean that you're giving up the list?"

She sat forward and laughed. "No."

He laughed, too. "Then why are you beating yourself up about it?"

"I guess I shouldn't be. Because someday the man from my list is going to appear, and I'll be living my dream life."

"As opposed to living with me in the dream cabin? You keep talking like that and you're going to make me jealous of this guy you're going to marry."

She searched his gaze. "Are you being serious?"

Was he? J.D. wasn't sure. But he said, "No. I was just goofing around."

"I should have known better than to think you would be jealous."

"I'm all for you marrying someone else."

"Stop rubbing it in."

"I'm not rubbing it in, I'm being supportive."

"If you say so."

Before it turned into an argument, he said, "Why don't we settle this with a kiss?"

"I'd rather settle it with some butterscotch pudding. Do you still have some of those?"

"Yes." But it stung that she'd avoided kissing him. "I'll get you one." He went into the kitchen and returned with the pudding and a spoon.

"Thanks." She peeled the top off the container and proceeded to eat her favorite treat.

J.D. watched her. "Can I kiss you after you're done?"

Her lips curved into a smile. "Only if you admit

that you're a little jealous of the prince who is going to marry me."

"The prince? Is that one of his requirements?"

"No. I was just being smart." She finished the pudding and set it aside. "You can kiss me if you want."

He put a hand on his heart, like a knight in a melodrama. "But I haven't sworn my jealousy yet."

"Now who's being smart?"

"Me. But I think maybe I am a little jealous. It's not that I want to be married." He sucked in his breath. "The idea of marriage still makes me panicky. But envisioning you with another man is a tough pill to swallow. Especially when I hear the way you talk about him."

"You've known from the beginning how important a husband is to me. But I'm glad you're jealous. It's better than you not caring."

"I do care. You're my lover and my friend. And I'm going to kiss you right proper. Naked and in bed."

He scooped her up and made her squeal. After carrying her to the bedroom, he plunked her down on the feather mattress, and she sank into it.

She grinned up at him. "Wow. This is comfy."

"I told you." He fell into bed with her. "I wonder if you're going to dream while you're here."

"My only dream is to be married someday, and I already know that's going to happen."

"Your list is your magic."

"I never thought of it that way before." She gazed into his eyes. "Thank you for saying that."

"What are friends for?" Immersed in her nearness, he peeled off her blouse and unhooked her bra. She in turn popped open the snaps on his shirt.

They removed the rest of their clothes and enjoyed

the luxury of bared bodies. He inhaled the fragrance of her skin, and she roamed her hands over his.

The foreplay continued until he couldn't take another minute of not having her. He opened the nightstand drawer. It was time for him to glove up, as the saying went. "I put all of the protection in here."

She peered inside. "Good thinking."

"I wanted to be prepared for you."

"You always are."

Yes, but someday he wouldn't be. Someday she would belong to someone else. Forcing his thoughts in a different direction, he said, "Tell me your most romantic fantasy."

"Besides flower petals in my honeymoon bed?"

"Yes, something besides that." He didn't want to think about her wedding night.

"Sometimes I imagine messing around in a barn."

He entered her, surrounding himself with her warmth. "You mean making love in an empty stall? We could sneak out one night and do that."

She arched her hips. "What if we got caught?"

"We'd be careful that no one else is around." He twined a finger around one of her wavy tendrils. "I'd like to see you with hay in your hair."

"I won't get hay in my hair if we bring a blanket with us."

"You will if we roll off the blanket." To show her how it might feel, he rolled over the bed, making the covers tangle. "So, what do you say, should we slip out to the barn one night?"

"And embark on my fantasy?"

"It's *our* fantasy now."

"Living with you is going to be fun."

"That's the idea." *Fun,* he thought. *Free.* But in spite of that, he kept a dangerously possessive hold on her.

After their lovemaking ended, they broke apart, but it wasn't long before they were locked in each other's arms once again.

For now, J.D. just couldn't seem to let go.

## *Chapter Ten*

On Wednesday afternoon, Jenna, Donna and Tammy gathered on the porch of the main house with Tammy's brothers.

The women were seated in scattered chairs, and the men stood against the railing. Aidan, the older of the two, frowned and turned away from the sun, adjusting the brim of his hat. Jenna didn't know him very well, but if she had to describe him, she'd say he was the strong, silent type. Nathan was just the opposite. Already he'd been cracking silly jokes, even in the midst of turmoil.

Jenna glanced at Tammy. She looked so tiny next to her brothers. But she was also the most genuinely relaxed of anyone here. Jenna could barely breathe. Donna wasn't in any better shape. She had her hands clasped tightly on her lap.

On a side table was a pitcher of iced tea and plastic tumblers that no one had touched. The lovely new porch swing was vacant, too, creaking softly from the wind and haunting the moment.

"Does anyone want to discuss this before we get started?" Tammy asked.

"Haven't we talked enough about it already?" Donna replied. "It's been consuming our lives."

*That was true,* Jenna thought. They were mired in it. She'd even skipped breakfast this morning, too anxious to eat. Soon it would be time for lunch, and her stomach would be growling like a junkyard dog.

Tammy replied, "We haven't discussed it at length with Aidan and Nathan."

Her brothers exchanged a glance. Was that good or bad? Jenna wondered.

"We talked amongst ourselves," Aidan said.

"You can share your thoughts with us," Tammy said.

"What for? This isn't a jury trial. We don't have to deliberate."

"I was just giving you a chance to speak your piece."

"We'll pass," Nathan said. "But thanks all the same, Tam-boy."

Tammy didn't flinch at the childhood nickname, but he'd said it affectionately. Besides, it was obvious that she wasn't a tomboy anymore. Then again, maybe she was. Maybe it would always be part of who she was—the old Tammy blending with the new.

Jenna glanced in the direction of the stables, where J.D. was working today. He'd wished her luck before she'd left the cabin, supporting her like the true friend he was. He was a prime example of an old/new person, except that he was still in the process of remembering his old self.

"Let's do this," Aidan said, cutting through the quiet.

Tammy volunteered to go first. "My vote is yes. I think we should hire the P.I."

No one reacted, but everyone already knew what her preference was.

"Who wants to be next?" she asked.

"I'll go." Jenna figured another yes was in order. "I'm in favor, too."

The men exchanged one of those private glances again. Had they been expecting Jenna to go the other way? Or had they guessed her right? It was obvious they'd tried to peg the women's votes ahead of time.

"How about you?" Nathan asked Donna.

"I'll wait until you boys have your say."

"All right. Then it's a no for me," Nathan said.

His brother concurred. "Also a no."

Jenna's heart sank. Donna was the tiebreaker, and that meant it was a lost cause. Clearly, she was going to side with the men.

"Come on, Donna," Nathan said. "Do us proud."

But instead of complying, she got up and poured herself a glass of tea. "I need to wet my whistle first."

Nathan chuffed. "And here I thought New Yorkers did everything fast."

Donna didn't falter. "A lady has the right to weigh her options."

Jenna's pulse pounded. Was her sister actually mulling it over at the last minute or just getting everyone's goat?

As she sipped her tea like a Southern belle, Nathan muttered, "Fiddle dee dee."

Tammy cracked a smile. Jenna thought it was funny, too, but she was too nervous to smile.

The wait continued.

Then Donna turned to Jenna. "I'm doing this for you, so remember that when Savannah hates us for invading her privacy or we end up butting heads with her disgruntled kid. If there is a kid," she concluded.

Jenna grinned. No matter what the future held, she adored her sister for thinking of her. "Okay."

The tiebreaker addressed the entire group. "Just to be clear, my vote is yes."

Aidan scowled. "You certainly had us fooled. We were sure that you were going to say no."

"I was. But women are notorious for changing their minds."

"Three to two," Tammy said. "The ayes have it."

Jenna's grin widened. "Who should we hire?"

Tammy had a ready answer. "How about Roland Walker? He's the P.I. Tex used to keep an eye on all of us, so he's already familiar with our family. I think it would be easier than bringing in someone new."

"Sure. Why not?" This from Donna. "Let's keep our scandals under one roof." She laughed a little. "And use the guy who knows how screwed up the Byrds are."

Everyone else laughed, too, even Aidan, which was saying a lot.

Soon the men went into the house, and Tammy followed them, giving the sisters a moment to themselves.

"Thank you," Jenna said. "What you did means everything to me."

"I knew how important it was to you. But I hope it doesn't come back to bite us in the butt."

"I don't think it will. But even if it does, I'll never forget that you sacrificed your vote for mine."

They got out of their chairs, and Jenna reached out to hug her selfless sibling. She couldn't remember the last time she hugged Donna.

But it felt incredible.

J.D. glanced up and saw Jenna rushing toward him with exuberance. He struggled to collect his wits, preparing to greet her.

His day had started off fine, but as it wore on, dark and disturbing feelings had begun coming over him. And now here he was, trapped in the ache of a family he couldn't remember. But it wasn't just a case of not remembering them; he'd been dealing with that all along. It was the foreboding sense that whatever had gone wrong in his family couldn't be fixed.

As Jenna approached him, he slapped a smile on his face. He wasn't about to drag her down with his discomfort.

"It went well, I take it?" he asked.

"You wouldn't believe how well."

While she chattered about the outcome, giving him the details, he stood beside the barn, wearing damp jeans and a pair of rubber boots. Aside from having troublesome thoughts for the last few hours, he'd been bathing horses.

"Can you believe it?" she said. "Donna voted yes for me."

He'd never seen her so energized. If he wasn't so dirty and sweaty, and if his emotions weren't teetering on a thread, he would've lifted her off the ground and given her a little twirl. "I'm glad it worked out for you."

"It more than worked out. This mess with Savannah brought Donna and me closer. And you should have seen how funny she made it all seem. She had everyone laughing by the time it was over, and Aidan doesn't laugh that easily."

It was obvious how proud she was of her sister, and how much love there really was between them.

Jenna kept chattering. "We agreed to use the P.I. Tex had used. He must be good or Tex wouldn't have hired him. I'll bet he locates Savannah in no time."

"You have hope."

"Yes, I do. Donna warned me that it could turn out badly, but I don't think it will. I told her that it didn't matter, though, because what's most important is what she did for me."

"Happiness looks good on you."

"Thank you." She took a moment to catch her breath. "So how's your day going?"

The question hit him like the recoil from a high-powered rifle, nearly knocking the truth out of him. But he said, "Fine," determined not to spoil her mood.

Her stomach growled, and she laughed. "I knew that was going to happen. I still haven't eaten today."

"Then go get something."

"I will. And then you know what I'm going to do? I'm going to ask Tammy if she'll give me a cooking lesson."

"So you can feed your future husband?"

"Yes, but so I can make dinner sometime for you, too. You've been offering to be my guinea pig. You're still willing, aren't you?"

He nodded. "You can cook for me anytime you want."

"What should I focus on? What type of meal?"

"It doesn't matter."

"Of course it does. I want to learn to make your favorite food." She cocked her head. "Do you have a favorite that you're aware of? Or something you recently acquired a taste for?"

He roamed his gaze over her, pushing his bad feelings aside. "The only recent taste I acquired is for you."

She blushed. "I'm being serious, J.D."

So was he.

"There must be something you favor."

"I'm partial to Japanese food." The information zoomed right out, without him expecting it. He even jerked in surprise.

So did Jenna. "Oh, wow. Did you just remember that?"

"Yes." But he didn't have a clue why it was his food of choice. All he knew was that it was.

"That's so cool." She smiled at his horse-washing attire. "A sushi cowboy. Who would have guessed?"

Certainly not him.

She said, "As much as I'd like to accommodate your selection, I think Japanese might be a bit too ambitious for me to try. I doubt Tammy cooks in that style, either. Anything else?"

He gave her the option of choosing. "What's your favorite food? Or better yet, what do you want to learn to make? What do you see yourself cooking?"

She concentrated on the question. "Mom used to make spaghetti and meatballs, and sometimes I used to sing that silly parody of 'Old Smoky.'"

"The one where the meatball rolls on to the ground when somebody sneezed?"

She grinned. "Yep."

He grinned, too. She was improving his day, minute by confusing minute. "Now that I'd like to see."

"Me singing the song or the meatball rolling on to the ground?"

He chuckled. "Both."

"Here's an idea. I can turn my lesson into a family dinner. Tammy and I can fix the food, and maybe Donna, too, and you, Doc, Aidan and Nathan can hang out with us. Then, when it's ready, everyone can eat."

"Sounds great."

"I'm going to give the household staff the night off. I want to keep this low-key, without anyone else around, except the Savannah voters and our significant others."

He didn't deny that he was her significant other. Temporary as their agreement was, he still fit the bill. "I'll be there." And hopefully without a dark cloud hovering over his head.

Hours later, J.D. assessed the flock in the kitchen. By definition, "flock" meant a number of birds feeding, resting or traveling together, and these Byrds intended to eat together this evening.

And eat hearty.

The upcoming menu consisted of the aforementioned spaghetti and meatballs, along with deep-fried zucchini, garlic bread and a big green salad. For dessert—ice cream and fresh berries.

Jenna's lesson was a time-consuming project. To keep the masses from going hungry, Tammy had prepared a relish tray, and her Texas-size brothers were stuffing cold meats and cheeses in their mouths.

Nathan, the more talkative of the two, asked J.D.,

"So, who are you, exactly? Besides the guy who lost his memory? What's your role around here?"

"I work on the Flying B. I'm dating Jenna, too. She's staying with me in the dream cabin."

"You mean Savannah's old cabin? Maybe it should be called the nightmare cabin, considering everything that went on."

"Hey," Doc interjected. "That cabin helped me win my girl."

Tammy sent her fiancé a loving look.

Nathan rolled his eyes and spoke to Jenna. "You're the slowest cook I've ever seen. Isn't that a device of some kind? A slow cooker? Maybe that should be your ranch nickname." He cocked a gunslinger stance. "Slow Cooker, the pokiest chef in the West."

"Shut up, you big brute." She threw a dish towel at her jokester cousin, but missed him by a mile.

*The Slow Cooker handle isn't half bad,* J.D. thought. Jenna had only made two or three meatballs compared to the dozens Tammy had made. But J.D. thought Jenna looked damned cute doing it.

"I hope you don't plan on marrying her," Nathan said. "You'll starve."

*Oh, cripes.* J.D. didn't know how to react or how to respond. He certainly couldn't tell the other man how many marriage discussions he and Jenna had engaged in, but with a different groom in mind. Clearly Jenna wasn't going to say it, either.

Tammy came to the rescue. "Nobody is getting married, except Mike and me."

Nathan went with the flow. "Yep, my baby sister nabbed a doctor, and a damned fine one."

"Thanks," Doc said.

"Remember I said that when you're choosing your best man." Nathan grinned, then gauged the activity, his gaze landing on Donna and Aidan, who'd been staying quiet. "You know what this party needs? Some vino from Tex's cellar."

Aidan finally spoke up. "We're having Chianti with dinner."

"I know, but it'll be forever before we eat. I think we need to get buzzed now. Allow me to do the honors."

After he left to pilfer the spirits, Aidan said to J.D., "Sometimes my brother is full of himself. I hope he isn't offending you."

"None taken. But thank you."

Nathan returned with two bottles. He read from the first label. "This lovely vintage is a Montepulciana." He did the same thing with the second one. "And this robust selection is a Barbera." He dropped the act and grinned. "Mix your reds, I always say."

"That's because you don't know anything about wine," his brother commented.

"I know enough to enjoy them." He popped open the corks and poured everyone a drink, whether they wanted one or not. "How about a little music?" He turned on the radio and scanned the dial until he found a song that amused him.

He extended a hand to Donna, trying to persuade her to dance to Billy Ray Cyrus's anthem with him.

She rebuffed his attempt to make a Buckshot Hills filly out of her, shooing him away to "Achy Breaky" with someone else.

Nathan waggled his eyebrows at his brother.

"Me?" Aidan shook his head. "Get real."

The carefree Byrd danced by himself, creating

an imaginary partner and swinging her around. Doc grinned and swept Tammy into his arms. When Jenna looked expectantly at J.D., he went for it, too. He led her into a two-step, and they laughed while they rocked to the rowdy beat.

The partnering didn't last long. Nathan started a line dance, and the rest of them followed. Even Aidan jumped in, kicking up his heels.

But not Donna. She darted over to the stove, as if she was saving the food from Billy Ray's old mullet.

"That one needs some country spirit," Nathan said. "Too bad there isn't a guy around to upset her Big City Apple cart."

Jenna and Tammy exchanged a behind-the-scenes glance, and J.D. assumed that they were thinking about Caleb Granger and his supposed attraction to Donna. But neither woman said anything to Nathan. Obviously they didn't trust him not to create a scene over it. Besides, Caleb was still out of town, and from what J.D. had heard about him from Manny, Caleb was a player with tons of women at his disposal. Donna didn't need her cart upset quite that far.

Soon the line dancers disbursed. Jenna and Tammy joined Donna at the stove, and the brothers went outside to grab some air.

Doc came over to J.D. and put his hand on his shoulder. "Tammy told me how your memory is starting to return. I'm glad you recalled some good things about yourself."

*Good things.* Doc was obviously referring to the Sam Houston/Cherokee information. J.D. wanted to tell him about the dark feelings he'd been dealing with today, but now wasn't the time. So he simply said, "Thanks."

"We'll miss you around here when you're gone."

"I'll miss this crazy clan, too." But mostly he would miss Jenna. As she bustled around the kitchen, barely getting anything done, he thought about the man she was going to marry. Whoever he was, he would be a lucky guy.

Overall, the dinner was a success. The meal was delicious, and Jenna seemed proud of her Slow Cooker accomplishments. The newly formed group ate in the formal dining room, with a linen tablecloth, polished silverware and a floral centerpiece. *The Byrds,* J.D. thought as he glanced around at their faces.

A wonderfully mixed-up flock learning to be a family.

## Chapter Eleven

The following morning at the cabin, J.D. and Jenna had breakfast—toaster waffles, doused in maple syrup.

She said, "I wonder if my next lesson should be waffles. Or do you like pancakes better?"

"I like either one." But mostly he liked her. She still had the same sunny disposition from yesterday. And he'd yet to tell her what was going on with him.

"Do you think it's the same batter?"

"What?"

"Pancakes and waffles?"

"I don't know."

"I'll have to talk to Tammy about it. She makes this really good chicken and waffles dish."

Barely hearing her, J.D. gazed at the clouds in his coffee.

"What's wrong? You seem preoccupied."

He glanced up. "I've been having bad feelings about my past."

She put down her fork. "What do you mean?"

He stopped eating, too. "I'm certain that whatever went wrong in my family can't be repaired."

"How can you be certain of something like that?"

"It's just what I feel, what I sense." Deep inside, where it counted.

"Do you have any memories to go along with those feelings?"

"No."

"Then I don't understand your certainty. You could be confused." She continued to evaluate the unknown situation. "What sort of thing could have happened that can't be repaired? Look at what's going on in my family and how we're coping with it."

"You haven't forgiven your dad."

"That's different."

"What makes your family different from mine?"

She clammed up.

"See," he said. "No difference."

"If I reached out to my dad, would you change your perspective about your family? Would you start to believe that whatever went wrong could be repaired?"

"I can't make a judgment call like that until I remember my past."

"We could hire Roland Walker to try to find out who you are. He would have a lot more time to devote to your case than the police."

He shook his head. "I appreciate the suggestion, but I'd rather let the sheriff's department handle it. Or better yet, to remember on my own."

"But you haven't remembered yet, and a P.I. would

delve deeper than the police. All they're doing is trying to find out your name and if you were carjacked."

"And that's exactly why I don't want Roland involved. I'm not comfortable with someone digging up bones."

"Does Doc know that you're having bad feelings?"

"I wanted to tell him last night, but it wasn't the right time."

"Would you mind if we talked to him together?"

"Not at all. In fact, I would prefer it." At this stage, he wanted to be as truthful as possible and for Jenna to know him as well as he knew himself, which wasn't saying much, he supposed. But it was the best he could do. "I'm not trying to hide anything from you. I think it's important to be honest. Otherwise our affair wouldn't seem right."

"Honesty is the very first quality on my list."

The vast blueness of her eyes nearly pulled him under, but her comment had packed an even bigger punch.

So much so, it became overly apparent.

"I'm sorry," she stammered. "I didn't mean to imply that you…"

He almost wished that she was, but it was wrong for him to feel that way, especially amid the murky waters in his mind. "I didn't think you were. We both know I'm not the guy from your list."

She went silent, and he studied her, intrigued by the way daylight zigzagged through the blinds and cast a glow on her hair. But there were always little things about her that fascinated him.

Interrupting the quiet, she picked up her fork. He resumed eating, as well.

She said, "I wonder if you're going to have any more dreams while you're here. Or if your memories will return while you're awake."

"If my memories are bad, I hope they don't come in dreams. Because if they did, then Nathan would be right. This would be the nightmare cabin."

"That would be awful."

He nodded, then asked, "Are you ever going to reach out to your dad?"

"I would if it would help you come to terms with your family and whatever is causing the darkness."

"You can't fix me, Jenna. You can only fix what's broken within yourself."

"I know. But I want to make you feel better."

"You are. Believe me. Just knowing that you care matters."

"Same goes for me."

Before it got too emotional, he said, "We better finish up and get to work."

"When should we talk to Doc?"

"Tonight, if he's around."

They cleared the table and left the cabin. They walked to the stables together, then went their separate ways. He rode fence with Hugh, and she went into the barn to tend to her horses. And although J.D. was swamped with work, he thought about Jenna throughout the day and suspected that she was thinking of him, too.

Doc stopped by the cabin that evening, and Jenna listened while he and J.D. talked.

"Do you think my mind is playing tricks on me?" J.D. asked.

"Do you think that's what is happening?" the other man asked in return.

"No, but Jenna mentioned it."

Doc didn't ask her to expound on her opinion, but there was no need. It was obvious that she was troubled by J.D having a past that couldn't be repaired. Or a past that he didn't *think* could be repaired. There was a difference. She knew that better than anyone, and it was starting to make her guilty for hanging on to her Daddy resentments.

J.D. spoke to Doc again. "Jenna suggested hiring Roland Walker to hunt down my identity, but I don't want to do that. It's too personal to bring a P.I. into it."

"I understand," came the professional reply. "Another option would be to talk to a psychologist. I can recommend someone, if you'd like."

"Why do I need to talk to someone else? I'm already talking to you."

"This isn't my field of expertise, J.D."

"But I'm comfortable with you."

"Then you can continue to confide in me. I want to help in any way I can."

"Give me your opinion. I want to know what you think, regardless of your field of expertise."

"All right." Doc's voice was strong and steady, like the man he was. "I think that you need to relax and not worry so much about it. It seems obvious, to me anyway, that you need more time to address your feelings. And I think your memories will become clear when your mind is able to process the past and accept it, whatever it entails."

It was good advice, Jenna thought, and made complete sense to her.

"That's pretty much what you told me in the beginning," J.D. said. "To relax and let things happen naturally."

"And it still applies."

"I've had uneasy feelings about myself from the start, but it's getting harder to handle now that they're progressing."

"But what about the positive things you've recalled? It's not all bad."

J.D. furrowed his brows. "Meaning what? That every cloud has a silver lining, even the stormy ones?"

"I'd certainly like to think so."

"Ditto," Jenna said.

J.D. shook his head. "There you go ganging up on me. You two did that at the hospital, convincing me to stay here."

"That didn't turn out so badly, did it?" Doc asked.

J.D.'s expression softened, and when he glanced at Jenna, her heart went sweet and gooey.

"It turned out really nice," he said, still looking at her.

Her heart went even gooier. She was working so incredibly hard *not* to fall in love with him, and at this point, all she could do was keep praying that she didn't melt at his feet.

J.D. continued to look at her. She wanted him to break eye contact, but at the same time, she wanted to freeze this moment and keep it forever.

*Forever.* A dangerous word. A dangerous wish.

On and on it went. The look. The emotional push-pull. The fear of falling in love with him.

Then, thankfully, Doc cleared his throat, snaring J.D.'s attention and making Jenna breathe easier.

J.D. said to Doc, "I'll keep your advice in mind."

"Just let me know any time you need to talk."

"Thanks. I appreciate it."

Both men stood up and shook hands. Jenna got to her feet, too. Doc smiled at her, and she suspected it was his way of trying to help her relax. No doubt he could tell that she was fighting her feelings for J.D.

After Tammy's fiancé left, Jenna went into the kitchen to heat a pan of milk, her way of dealing with her feelings.

"Are you making hot chocolate?" J.D. asked.

"No. Just the milk. I can make hot chocolate for you, though."

"That's okay. I don't want anything." He leaned against the counter. "Remember when I made tea for you at the motel?"

She nodded.

"I think it was because I used to know someone who drank tea. Someone I was close to."

She started. "A former lover?"

"I don't know. It was a random feeling." He motioned to the pan she'd put on the stove. "I prefer cold milk."

"I like it cold, too. But Mom used to warm it for me when I was a kid. It's a comfort thing."

"That's nice." He came forward and slipped his arms around her. "You know what gives me comfort? Being around you."

She returned his hug, breathing in his masculine beauty and keeping him close. "What am I going to do after you're gone?"

"Find the man of your dreams," he whispered.

*The man of my dreams,* she thought. The man she

loved. That was a lost cause. Because deep down, she knew that she'd already found him.

The week passed without incident. Roland Walker hadn't located Savannah yet or uncovered anything about her that indicated whether she'd had a child, J.D. hadn't remembered anything new about himself and Jenna was still struggling with the revelation that she loved him.

And now as she prepared to meet J.D. on their break, her pulse wouldn't stop pounding.

She removed their sack lunches from the fridge in the barn and headed to the spot they'd agreed upon, just east of the stables and beneath a shady tree.

Plunking down beneath the towering oak, she waited for him.

He arrived shortly, and as he walked toward her, he looked sinfully sexy, moving with a long, lean gait. He also had Tex's borrowed Stetson perched low on his head. Jenna was wearing a hat, too, with a red bandana tied around the outside of the crown.

"Afternoon," he said, and sat in the grass next to her.

She handed him his lunch, as nervous as a calf in the midst of being roped. Only it was her heart that was being lassoed.

"Are you okay?" he asked, obviously noticing that she seemed off. "Did something happen with Savannah?"

"No." Being honest about what was bothering her wasn't something she was capable of doing, not without admitting that she loved him. So she tried to wrangle in her emotions or at least not let them show. "There's no news. And I'm fine. Just hungry." She opened her sack and removed her sandwich, forcing a bite.

He didn't eat right away. Instead, he took a drink of his water. She watched him swallow, fascinated by the line of his neck and the way his Adam's apple bobbed with the effort.

"You were staring at me," he said afterward.

"Was I?"

"Uh-huh."

"Turnabout is fair play. You stare at me all the time, too."

"Guilty as charged. But neither of us should be doing it."

"Because it isn't polite to stare?"

"Yep." He leaned over and kissed her.

Heavens, he was the best kisser in the world. She wanted to crawl on to his lap and rub herself all over him, like a cat in heat. Or a woman in the throes of love.

"You taste like roast beef and avocado." He grinned. "Tastes good."

"I packed you the same lunch." She gestured to his sack. "Go for it."

"Don't mind if I do." He unwrapped his sandwich. "You're getting better at the kitchen stuff."

*Wife practice,* she thought, with a man who would never be her husband. "I'm trying."

He gazed at the bandana tied around her hat. Then blinked in an interested way.

"What?" she asked.

"The color just made me think of something. On the Native American medicine wheel, red symbolizes success and triumph."

"You just had another Cherokee memory."

"Apparently so." He sounded pleased. "And your hat-band was the trigger."

She wasn't feeling triumphant or successful. But she summoned a smile, for his sake. "That's nice, J.D."

"It's a lot better than those dark feelings."

"Are you still having those?"

"Yes." They sat quietly and ate, then he said, "I hope this isn't going to sound like a loaded question, but how do you feel about the Savannah situation now that you're interested in meeting her? Do you want there to be another Byrd? Or would you prefer that there is no child?"

It *was* a loaded question, and she considered it carefully. "If there is no child, it will be a relief not to have to worry about who that person is and how he or she will fit into our lives. But on the other hand, if there isn't, I might actually be disappointed. Like I lost someone in my family that I never even got to know."

"I would feel that way, too." He glanced away and frowned.

*Really, really* frowned, she noticed.

"Did you just remember something bad?" she asked, analyzing how quickly his mood had changed.

"The children." He stared straight ahead. "I remember them. Or sort of remember..."

She leaned toward him. "What children?"

He discarded his lunch, crinkling the bag in his distress. "There were kids in my family who got left behind. I don't know who they were or how many of them there were, but I can feel their existence."

"What do you mean? Left behind?"

"In foster care. Kids who were supposed to get adopted but never were. That's why I know about the foster-care system. That's why it's been so important to me."

Her heart dropped to her stomach. Was it possible that they were his kids? That he was their biological father? Or that he'd actually been married? Was that why the thought of having a wife and kids made him panic?

*No,* she thought. He was too kind, too decent to have given up on his children or let them be taken away from him. And with the recurring talk of marriage, with it being a constant topic, wouldn't he have remembered having a wife, especially now with the foster-children memory?

"Was it you?" she asked, just to see what he would say.

He blinked. "What?"

"Did you father them?"

"No. God, no. I wasn't their dad."

"Are you sure?"

"Yes. I'm absolutely certain that I've never been a parent."

She gladly accepted his response, grateful that his feelings were so strong in that regard. "I didn't think you were, but I thought I should mention it, in case it was possible."

He was still frowning, still visibly troubled. "I don't know whose kids they were, but losing them is part of the darkness. Of what went wrong in my family and why it can't be fixed." He paused. "Doc said that I would remember things when I can handle it. But I don't want to remember anything else. Not today."

"Then don't think about it anymore."

"I'm not going to. It makes my head hurt."

*It made his heart hurt, too,* she thought, feeling sad

for him. She wanted him to have a bright and happy future. She wanted that for herself, too.

And their families.

After work, Jenna thought long and hard about what she needed to do, and when she came to a decision, she told J.D. that she was going to go for a walk with her sister. But she didn't tell him why she'd summoned Donna. She didn't tell Donna, either.

So, as the women strolled along the ranch, a soft hush drifted between them.

"What's going on?" her sister finally asked.

"I have something important to talk to you about."

Donna stopped walking. Jenna did, too, and with the sun setting in the sky, she said, "I'm going to go see Dad on Saturday, and I'm going to ask him to tell me why he betrayed Uncle William and slept with Savannah. And no matter his excuse, I'm going to do my damnedest to forgive him."

Her sister took a step back, and a twig snapped beneath her shiny black boot. "Just like that? You're going to let him off the hook?"

"I'm in love with J.D."

Donna flinched in surprise or maybe it was confusion or both. "What does one have to do with the other?"

"J.D. has been saying that there are things in his family that can't be fixed, and now he's starting to remember some of those issues."

"So you're going to try to fix the way you feel about Dad? How is that going to help J.D.?"

"It isn't. But it's going to help me comes to terms with what Dad did. And hopefully it will help Dad in some way, too."

"Please don't ask me to go with you. I'm not ready to see him."

"I know you're not. I also know that this is more difficult for you than it is for me. I was always disappointed in him, but you used to idolize him."

The city girl set her jaw. "I did not."

"Say what you will, but I used to see the way you looked at him. You aspired to be like him. He was strong and tough, and he was your role model. I never expected much of him, but you did. And he let you down."

Donna took another step back, and Jenna thought her big sis looked like she was ready to bolt, to run straight back to New York as swiftly as her long, gorgeous legs would take her.

Then Donna said, "I don't want to have this conversation with you."

"Yes, I can see that." Hence, Jenna wasn't going to push it. "I just wanted you to know that I was driving to Houston on Saturday."

"Don't give Dad my regards."

"I won't."

Donna turned and walked away, but she didn't go far. She came back with a concerned expression. "Does J.D. know that you love him?"

"No."

"Are you going to tell him?"

Her heart clenched. "No."

"Why not?"

"Because it won't change anything. And because I wasn't supposed to get attached. He and I talked about it ahead of time, and I kept insisting that I wouldn't."

"I'm sorry if you're hurting."

"Thank you." She longed to hug Donna the way she'd

done on the day of the vote, but she feared that she might cry in her sister's arms. And that wouldn't do either of them any good.

They parted company, and Jenna continued to walk by herself, immersed in her surroundings. The Flying B was her home, the place that gave her hope, but would it be enough to sustain her after J.D. was gone?

She thought about Tammy and Doc and how lucky Tammy was. Her cousin had the ranch, but she had the man she loved, too. What if Jenna never found anyone to replace J.D.? What if she compared every man she met to him—to his qualities—instead of what was on her list?

Maybe she should throw that stupid list away.

She frowned at the path in front of her. She couldn't do it. She'd compiled it for a reason, and she was keeping it, especially since J.D had told her it was her magic.

Her magic. Her pain. Her confusion.

Before her emotions drove her straight into a ditch, she headed for the cabin, where she knew J.D. would be awaiting her return.

She went inside and came face-to-face with her lover, who was fresh from his evening shower and attired in a plain white T-shirt and crisply laundered jeans.

"How was your walk?" he asked.

She blew out the air in her lungs. "I told Donna what I needed to tell her." And now it was time to tell him, except for the part about loving him, of course. "I'm going to my dad's on Saturday."

"You are?" He widened his eyes. "To try to square things with him?"

She nodded. "What you recalled about your family

has made me think deeper about mine. I can't keep letting my wound fester. I have to find a way to heal it."

"I'm so proud of you and the progress you've made." He took her in his arms. "Knowing that you're going to be okay will make my leaving easier when the time comes."

She buried her cheek against his neck, her emotions going haywire again. "What if I'm not okay? What if I turn into a lonely old spinster, waiting for a man who never appears?"

"Are you kidding? Your future husband is out there and he's going to be everything you imagined."

She buried her face deeper into the warmth of his skin. "Are you still jealous of him?"

"Hell, yes. But I'm glad he exists, too. That he'll be there when you need him."

What she needed was for him to be J.D., not a nameless, faceless stranger.

He said, "Someday you're going to get married with your entire family in attendance, and it will be the best day of your life."

How could it be the best day of her life unless she was marrying him? "I don't want to think about my wedding right now." Unable to let go, she clung to him, like a love-fraught reed in the wind. "I just need to deal with going to Houston on Saturday."

And the reconciliation with her father.

## Chapter Twelve

As Jenna parked her truck and took in her surroundings, the familiar blue-and-white house stirred pangs of loneliness. But what did she expect, for this pristine suburban structure and its perfectly manicured lawn to give her a happy sense of home?

She would never forget the day she and Donna had moved in with their dad. They'd been two young girls raw from their mother's passing, and the ache was as vivid today as it had been then.

She exited her vehicle, her mind alive with deathly memories. The friends and neighbors who'd brought casseroles by had meant well, but their condolences hadn't helped. Dad, Donna and Jenna had made an awkward trio. The divorced father with his motherless children. The busy executive who'd been estranged from his own family. They'd been doomed from the start.

Jenna moved forward, taking the shrub-lined walk-way toward the front door. She'd called ahead and let Dad know that she was coming, only now that she was here, she wanted to turn tail and run. But she quickened her pace and approached the awning-covered stoop. She no longer had a key. She'd gotten her own apartment ages ago, and now, of course, she was living at the Flying B.

She rang the bell, and Dad opened the door, appearing like a cautious mirage. They gazed uncomfortably at each other. He was an attractive man for his age, with striking blue eyes and graying brown hair. He stayed in shape by hitting the gym. His only lazy indulgence was the TV game show that he plunked himself in front of each night.

She went inside. He kept the place tidy, especially for a bachelor, but it lacked warmth. It had been that way ever since she was a child. Something had always been missing.

"Do you want a cola?" he asked.

She shook her head. He kept pop around for guests, but he rarely entertained. She couldn't actually remember him dating anyone, either. If he had lovers, he never brought them home for her and Donna to see.

He spoke again. "Where do you want to sit?"

"The living room is fine."

He offered her the sofa. "I'm not much of a talker, Jenna."

"I know, Dad. But this is a discussion we need to have." She hadn't told him that she wanted to make amends. She'd just said that she wanted to discuss their family.

He sat in his easy chair, the one from which he normally watched TV, only the television was off.

She said, "I have a lot of questions about the past. But first I wanted to check to see if anyone informed you about the outcome of the vote."

"William called me and said it went through. His kids gave him the details. Tammy was in favor of hiring the P.I. and Aidan and Nathan weren't, but their votes were canceled out by yours and Donna's. So now Roland Walker is searching for Savannah."

That pretty much summed it up. "I didn't know that you and Uncle William were on speaking terms, other than snapping at each other."

"We're not. He called out of anger, to remind me of what a mess I made out of everyone's lives. How many times do I have to hear that?"

"As many times as it takes."

He heaved a heavy sigh. "So you're here to berate me, too?"

"No. Actually, I came here to forgive you, Dad."

"You could have fooled me."

She bristled. This was going to be harder than she'd thought. "Maybe I should just leave and forget it."

"No, please. Stay. I miss you and Donna." He shifted in his chair, looking big and tough and troubled. "How is your sister?"

"She's fine."

"Why didn't she come with you?"

"She isn't ready to make amends with you."

He didn't reply, but he seemed wounded. Did he know that Donna used to idolize him? Or had he been too consumed with himself all these years to notice?

Jenna hoped and prayed that forgiving him was truly

the right thing to do. Clearly he was hurting, but if it was self-indulgent pain, then it didn't count, not the way it should.

She asked, "How do you feel about us looking for Savannah and her possible child?"

He skirted the issue. "William is upset about it."

"I know. But how do *you* feel?"

He hesitated, obviously not keen about answering the question.

*"Dad."*

"I was in love with her, Jenna."

That was the last thing she'd expected to hear. And because it took her by complete surprise, she merely sat there, probably with a stupid look on her face.

He continued, "Out-of-my-head, out-of-my-young-heart in love. I even married your mother on the re-bound because I'd lost Savannah. Your mom reminded me a bit of her, but they weren't the same woman, and I never got over Savannah. She was always there, like a ghost who wouldn't stop torturing me."

Conflicted by his admission, Jenna tensed, feeling sorry for him and hating him at the same time. "Did Mom know about Savannah?"

"No. I didn't tell her that I was estranged from my family because of a girl. I didn't make up a story, either. I just said that it was too painful to talk about, and she accepted it. I think in the beginning, my rebel-boy pain made me more appealing to your mom."

Jenna's voice went sharp. "She wouldn't have found it appealing if she'd known you were pining over another woman."

"I tried to make the marriage work. Honestly, I did.

But I didn't love your mom the way I should have, and she began to lose feelings for me, too."

"I remember Mom being distraught over the divorce."

"You were six years old when we split up. How clear can your memories be?"

*Clear enough,* she thought. "I remember how often she cried. And how much time she started spending at her job. She didn't seem like the same Mommy anymore." But Jenna had stayed by her side, sticking like kindergarten paste, right up until the day she'd died.

He stared at the empty TV screen. "I never meant to hurt her."

"You hurt a lot of people."

"I didn't set out to do that."

She took an enormous breath, struggling to give him the benefit of the doubt. "Tell me more about Savannah and how your relationship with her unfolded."

"William and I were both home from school that summer. Me from Rice University and him from Texas A&M. It was our first year of college. William was majoring in animal husbandry so he could work beside Tex on the ranch, and I was majoring in business with a minor in economics, so I could get the hell off the Flying B someday."

She knew some of these details already, but she'd arranged this meeting to hear his version of the story, so she listened to the way he was telling it, concentrating on the emotional inflection in his voice.

He continued, "Right before summer break, William had gotten into a car accident and ended up with a fractured leg, a sprained wrist and some cuts and bruises on his face. So that's the condition he was in when he came home. He'd been dating Savannah for a while by then. She was a student at A&M, too. Since he was all banged up, she offered to drive him to the ranch and help nurse him back to health." He paused, then added, "I arrived a few days later, and from the moment I met Savannah, I was awestruck. But I kept telling myself that I was only attracted to her because she was William's girl. I'd always felt a raging sense of competition with my brother."

She interrupted. "Why, Dad?"

"Because Tex favored him. Tex never said so, but it was obvious to me from the time we were kids. William's love of the Flying B was a bond they shared, and it alienated me from them. I fought back by competing with William. But he was just as macho as I was, and he pushed back, competing with me, too. In retrospect, I probably created that holy-hell trait in him."

"Or maybe you both inherited it from Tex. Grandpa was an ornery old guy."

"That's for damn sure. Ornery when he was old. Ornery when he was young. Our father had always been a powerful force to be reckoned with." He glanced away.

She urged him on. "Finish telling me about Savannah."

He complied. "Since William was laid up, I spent a lot of time with her, entertaining her on the ranch. The Flying B was a heck of a lot more fun with her around. We took walks, we rode trail, we picnicked by the stream."

Jenna merely nodded. She'd been doing those same activities with J.D.

"She was charming and beautiful, and I started falling in love with her. Genuinely in love. I battled with my conscience every day, trying to make my feelings stop, but I couldn't. I wanted her so damned much. Finally, I reached the point of not caring that she was William's girl."

"How did she feel about you?"

"She went mad for me, too. In fact, she'd been awestruck over me from the moment we met, just the way I was over her. It wasn't the same between her and William. They had a nice easy relationship that she'd assumed was love. Only after she met me, she knew the difference. Of course she was terribly guilty over William, too. She kept saying that she needed to break the news to him. We even discussed coming clean and telling him together. One way or another, William had to be told."

"But neither of you followed through?"

He shook his head, frowned. "Actually, we did just the opposite. We kept sleeping together. But we'd never done it at the cabin until the night we got caught. Prior to that, we'd been having secret trysts, mostly in the hills, away from the Flying B."

Jenna went quiet. At this point she didn't know what to say. But her silence wasn't a problem, because her dad kept talking, as if he needed to get the whole sordid story off his chest.

He said, "Funny thing, too, when Savannah and William first arrived, Tex had insisted that she stay in the dream cabin because it was the farthest from the house. I think it was to stop her and William from getting frisky under his roof. He hadn't counted on me being tossed into the mix."

Once again, Jenna said nothing.

He spoke further. "After Savannah and I were together that night, I snuck out of there as fast I could, and ran smack dab into Tex, who'd gone for a walk to smoke one of his fancy-ass cigars. I was in the midst of tucking in my shirt and adjusting my belt. He knew instantly what I'd been doing with Savannah in the cabin. He lit into me, calling me every rotten name in the book. According to Tex, I was the biggest SOB that ever lived and Savannah was a trollop who'd cuckolded one twin for the other. He refused to listen to anything I had to say, so I didn't even bother trying to explain myself or tell him how much Savannah and I loved each other."

She went into question mode again. "So what did you do?"

"I blasted over to the main house to pack my things. But I was planning on going back to the cabin after Tex went to bed. To ask Savannah to run away with me." He gave a long drawn-out pause. "But later, when I returned to the cabin, she was gone. I figured that Tex had given her a piece of his mind and kicked her off the ranch. I left, too, and headed for A&M, where I thought she'd gone. But she didn't return to school. She just up and disappeared, and I never saw her again."

"And you had no idea that she'd taken a pregnancy test or that she suspected that she might be pregnant?"

"No. None."

"If there is a child, do you think it's yours? Or was she sleeping with William at the same time she was with you?"

"She wasn't with us at the same time. William will confirm that he hadn't slept with her after his accident. But he'd been with her before, so if there is a child, it could still be his. She could have been pregnant when she'd come to the ranch and not even known it."

"Tell me how you feel about the possibility of Savannah having a child, Dad."

"I'm hoping that there isn't one. I can't bear the thought of her and William having a son or daughter, for his sake as much as mine. But, by the same token, I can't handle being a father again. I'm already a lousy parent to you and Donna."

She extended her heart to him. After everything he'd told her, she empathized with him now. "You did the best you could."

"Do you still think I'm a monster for having an affair with my brother's girlfriend?"

"No, but I think she should have broken it off with William first. You and Savannah should have showed more restraint."

"Being in love messes people up."

"I know," she replied, suddenly trapped in her own life, her own feelings.

His gaze zoomed in on hers, his blue eyes filled with fatherly concern. "Is there a young man I should know about?"

Unable to hold back, she nodded. Then she proceeded to tell him about J.D.

Afterward, he said, "You need to tell him that you love him."

"But I promised him that I wouldn't get attached, and he's determined to leave the ranch after his memory returns."

He got up and sat beside her. "My affair with Savannah turned into a disaster, but at least we spoke about our feelings. In that regard, I don't have any regrets."

"You're right." So very right. "If J.D. leaves the ranch

without me telling him that I love him, I'll regret that for the rest of my life."

"It's possible that he loves you, too. But he's too mixed up with his amnesia to realize it. Once his memory comes back, it might work in your favor."

"Do you really think so?"

"Truthfully, I can't imagine him *not* loving you. You're a special girl, Jenna."

She put her head on his shoulder. "Thanks, Daddy."

"You haven't called me that since you were little."

They turned to look at each other, and she smiled. "I'm glad I came here. J.D. kept telling me that I should."

"I think I'd like that boy."

"I think so, too. There's a lot to like about him."

"There was a lot to like about Savannah, too. She was a foster child, and all she ever wanted was a family. I had a tough time understanding that since I was such an outsider in mine."

"J.D. has a connection to foster kids, too. Only he isn't quite sure who they are to him." She thought about his childhood dream, about his scattered memories. "Did Savannah dream while she was at the cabin?"

"I don't know. If she did, she never mentioned it."

"I haven't dreamed while I've been there."

"Not everyone does."

They sat quietly, then she asked, "Does Uncle William know that you loved Savannah? Have you ever told him?"

"No."

"You should tell him. You should apologize to him, too."

"After all of this time? Hell, we're practically old

men now." He made a face, aging himself even more—the lines around his eyes crinkling, his lips thinning.

"Yes, after all of this time." She reprimanded him. "Your apology is long overdue."

"Do you know how difficult that's going to be for me?"

"No more difficult than me telling J.D. that I love him."

He cursed beneath his breath.

She stared him down.

"Okay." He held out his hands in surrender. "I'll go out on a limb if you will." He lowered his hands and gentled his voice. "It would be nice if you tried to talk me up to your sister, too."

"I'll try." But first she was going to talk to J.D. If she waited, she feared her nerves would explode. She gathered her purse. "I'm going to go home now."

"Call me later and tell me how it went."

"You, too."

He walked her to her truck, and she climbed behind the wheel, anxious to get back to the Flying B.

But in the evening when she arrived, Jenna entered the cabin and found J.D. staring into space.

Worried, she asked, "What happened?" He looked as if someone had just died.

"I know who I am." He turned in her direction, like a zombie with its heart falling out of its chest. "I remember everything, including the murder of my wife."

## Chapter Thirteen

"Your *wife?* Her *murder?*"

J.D. nodded, Jenna's choppy questions echoing in his ears. His memories had come crashing back, shaking him to the core. He'd spent the last few hours holed up in the cabin remembering the most painful things imaginable.

She dropped onto the sofa as if her knees had just buckled.

"Kimie was gunned down at a convenience store," he said, wishing he'd caught Jenna before she'd fallen onto the furniture. She looked as white as death. But it was Kimie who was dead. "There was a robbery in progress when she walked into the store. The gunman panicked and shot her, killing her instantly. Then he turned and fired at the clerk, a young guy who was scared out of his wits and had only worked there for a few weeks." J.D. backed himself against the window, moving away from Jenna instead of toward her, with Kimie's lifeless body floating in his mind. "The clerk survived the injury and served as a witness in court."

"The gunman was apprehended?" Her voice vibrated.

He glanced out the window. The blinds were open, the darkness thick and vast. "He fled the scene, but he didn't get far. He was taken into custody the same night."

"I'm so sorry about your wife." She sounded tearful. "There was a moment, a couple of days ago, that I wondered if you'd been married. But it didn't seem possible. And I never would have thought…"

Was she misty-eyed? He didn't want to look at her to see. "There's nothing you can do. There isn't anything anyone can do."

"I wish there was."

He finally glanced at her. Her eyes *were* damp, and he suspected that she wanted to wrap him in her arms and to try to console him. But he couldn't bring himself to allow it, and she was obviously aware of how unapproachable he was. He stayed plastered against the window.

"When did you lose her?" she asked.

"Two years ago." But it seemed like yesterday, especially with the way his memories had come crashing back.

He glanced at Jenna again. By now she was sitting a little more forward on the sofa, and she looked as discomposed as he felt.

She spoke quietly. "What's your name?"

"Joel. Joel Daniel Newman."

"Do you want me to call you Joel?"

"No. I'm J.D. now. It still works as my initials." He didn't want to be Joel anymore. He'd been that to his wife. "Her full name was Kimie Ann Winters-Newman. We were married for six years. We were happy." His stomach went horribly tight. "I loved her, and she loved me. We were right together. So damned right. The only thing missing in our lives were children. We'd been trying to conceive, but couldn't. Kimie wasn't able to. So we decided to adopt. A whole passel of kids. That was our plan."

Jenna didn't reply, but she was riveted to his every word, gazing at him with her pretty blue eyes.

He went on. "We discovered how difficult it was to adopt an infant and learned how many foster kids were out there, needing homes."

"So the kids who'd been crowding your memories, who'd been left behind, are the ones you were hoping to adopt someday?"

He nodded. "The family that can never be repaired. Kimie and me and our nonexistent children." He paused to temper the quaver in his tone. He couldn't bear to break down in front of Jenna. "We were also looking into foreign adoption. With me being part Cherokee and her being part Japanese, we knew what it would take to raise kids from other cultures. We knew how important it would be to keep them connected to their roots and to teach them about ours." He considered the nickname Jenna had called him. "The sushi cowboy. Kimie would have liked that."

"Is she the tea drinker you were struggling to re-member?"

"Yes. She had a cup of herb tea almost every night

before we went to bed. Sometimes I fixed it for her. We had this easy rhythm, knowing each other's habits, catering to them."

She got teary again. "It makes sense now, the reason marriage and babies made you uncomfortable. It wasn't because you couldn't relate to that lifestyle. It's because you mourned it."

He didn't reply, and she went disturbingly quiet, too.

He shattered the silence. "Do you know why your hair fascinated me? Kimie said that some of our kids would be blond. Us with our dark hair, walking around with golden-haired children." Suddenly he wanted to touch Jenna's fair locks, to indulge in each wavy strand. But he stayed where he was. He was confused by his feelings. He shouldn't be thinking about Kimie while he was longing to touch Jenna. It only worsened the pain. "I should have never gotten you involved in my mixed-up life. I should have stayed at the homeless shelter."

"Don't talk like that."

"How else am I supposed to talk?" He could tell that she was confused, too, and that he'd dragged her into something neither of them could handle.

Jenna ached for J.D., but she also hurt for herself. His memories were like a boomerang flying between them.

Back and forth.

What a horrible twist of fate. At one time J.D. had been the ultimate family man, with the qualities from Jenna's list. Only he wasn't emotionally available anymore. His wife was gone, taken from him in a devastating way, and Jenna was sitting on the sidelines, wishing she could heal him, but knowing she couldn't. Telling him that she loved him was futile now.

"Where did you meet Kimie?" she asked, trying to envision him in happier times, trying to help him feel better.

"We went to the same high school. We saw each other around and flirted a little, but we didn't start dating until later."

"How old are you?" There was so much more she wanted to know about him—this man she loved, this man who would never belong to her.

"Thirty-three. I was twenty when Kimie and I first went out, twenty-five when we got married, and thirty-one when she died."

"I'm sorry," she said, not knowing what else to say yet realizing how meaningless those words were to him.

But even so, he moved forward, slowly, and joined her on the sofa. He still seemed dazed and distant, but he was coming out of his shell, at least a little.

"Have you talked to Doc?" she asked.

"Not yet." He exhaled an audible breath. "You're the first person I've told."

She wondered if he would flinch if she touched him. She didn't take the chance. They sat side by side, with no physical contact.

"How did your visit with your dad go?" he asked, as if suddenly becoming aware of where she had been when his memories surfaced.

"It went well. But we don't need to talk about that right now." There was still so much more she didn't know about him. "Why don't you tell me about your parents instead, and your brothers and sisters, if you have any?"

"I don't. But I had a happy childhood."

"Go on," she coaxed.

"My parents ran a horse farm in a small town in the Texas Panhandle, and that's where I grew up. I get my Cherokee blood from my mom. She taught me about our ancestors. She and Dad are good people, kind and loving." He paused. "When they retired, I purchased the farm from them, and they moved to Arizona. I loved that farm. So did Kimie." His voice cracked. "It's where we made our home together. After she died, my parents tried to talk me into going to Arizona and staying at their place, but I couldn't deal with being around anyone, not even them."

"So what did you do?"

"I sold the farm and started drifting. Sometimes I camped out in remote areas, for months at a time, where there wasn't another soul around. And sometimes I stayed at motels, staring at the walls and rarely leaving the room. I drifted all over Texas, going from town to town. Small towns, like the one I'd left behind."

*Like Buckshot Hills,* she thought. "Do you recall how you were injured?" The injury that had given him amnesia and had brought him to the Flying B. "Was it a carjacking?"

He nodded. "I stopped to help a man and a woman who appeared to be broken down by the side of the road. I was worried about the woman. That someone else might stop and something bad might happen to her. It never occurred to me that they were setting me up for a robbery."

Jenna understood why he'd been so quick to come to the couple's aid. He'd obviously been thinking about Kimie. "Your heart was in the right place."

He didn't comment on his heart. His broken heart, she thought.

He said, "They must have rigged their car so it wouldn't start. I think the woman struck me on the back of the head when I was leaning over the hood. I don't remember the blow itself, but I remember that the man was standing beside me, so he couldn't have been the one who hit me."

"Do you recall waking up?"

He nodded. "But I was too disoriented to think clearly, to contemplate where I was or why my head hurt so damned much."

"How long do you think you were like that before I found you?"

"The robbery took place about three miles from the Flying B Road. But how long I was wandering around is beyond me. They obviously stole my truck. They also got my cell phone, my I.D. and some cash and credit cards from my wallet, but my social-security card is in a safe-deposit box and the bulk of my money is in an investment account. There wasn't any evidence of the account in my belongings, so it's unlikely they know about it. And even if they discovered it existed, they wouldn't have been able to access it without drawing attention to themselves."

"Thank goodness for that. When are you going to call Deputy Tobbs and give him this information and tell him who you are?"

"Tomorrow. I'm too worn out to do it now. I've got too much going on inside me." He scrubbed a hand across his jaw. "How could I have forgotten her, Jenna?"

"Because it was too painful to remember." She stated the obvious, wishing, once again, that she could ease his sorrow, but knowing she couldn't. She'd never felt so helpless or so useless.

"It still seems wrong to have blocked her from my mind. Instead of remembering Kimie, I was falling for you."

Falling...

She'd been falling, too, only with the word *love* attached. J.D. wasn't making that claim. "You didn't do anything wrong. You have a right to keep living."

"I don't want that right. I want to disappear. I want to keep running."

"You can't drift forever."

"Yes, I can. I have enough money in my investment account to keep me going for a long time. And when it runs out, then I'll get ranch jobs, like this one. Temporary work so I don't have to put down roots. I don't ever want to put down roots again. It isn't worth it."

She looked into his eyes, trying to see the man he'd once been. But all she saw was emptiness. Still she said, "Maybe someday you'll feel differently."

He stood up and moved away from the sofa. "I'm going to pay you back for your hospitality, like I wanted to from the beginning."

"You know that doesn't matter to me."

"It matters to me, and now that I know I have money in the bank, I can give you what I owe you."

"If it makes you feel better, go ahead."

"I wonder if I should go to a motel tonight. I have enough cash from my wages for a few nights stay, and I—"

"What? Why?"

"I can't sleep in the same bed with you, Jenna. I wish I could, but after remembering Kimie..."

"Don't leave the ranch. Not this soon. Wait until you talk to Deputy Tobbs and get everything sorted out.

I'll go back to the main house, and you can stay here by yourself."

"Are you sure? I don't want to put you out."

"You aren't putting me out. I wouldn't be staying in the cabin if you weren't here, anyway. Besides, maybe you'll have a comforting dream tonight."

"About Kimie?" His voice jumped. "Do you think that's possible?"

"I don't know. But it's worth a shot."

"Then I'll stay here. Thank you."

Jenna got up, and they gazed awkwardly at each other.

"You've been such a good friend all along," he said. "And you still are."

"I want what's best for you." And sharing his bed wasn't in his best interest, not when he wanted to be alone. "I should pack my things now."

She went into the bedroom, trying to hold herself together, to keep from crying in earnest. Finally she was ready, everything shoved into her suitcases.

He loaded them into her truck. "You look like you're going on a major trip."

But she was only going to another house on the same property. *So close, yet so incredibly far,* she thought. She was going to miss snuggling in J.D.'s arms tonight. She was going to miss him for the rest of her life.

"I'll talk to you tomorrow," he said. "And if you see Doc, will you tell him what's going on and that I'll talk to him tomorrow, too?"

"Of course."

"Night, Jenna."

"Sleep well, J.D."

"I will if I dream. God, I hope I dream."

"I hope so, too." He needed Kimie more than he needed her. Jenna couldn't compete with that. Nor was she going to try.

After hauling her luggage into the house, Jenna confided in Doc and Tammy, who were in the kitchen, where Tammy was baking a boysenberry pie.

Both were genuinely concerned and felt badly that J.D.'s memories had triggered such tragic news. Doc said that he would visit J.D. in the morning, and Tammy gave Jenna a sweet hug.

Later, Jenna talked to Donna. They sat on Jenna's bed in their pajamas, with plates of the leftover pie between them.

"This must be the worst night of your life," Donna said.

"It was a good day until I got home and found out about J.D. I think it's nice that Dad loved Savannah."

"And married Mom on the rebound? What's nice about that?"

"That part upset me, too. But I could tell that Dad had never meant to hurt Mom. And now that I feel about J.D. the way I do, I understand how conflicted Dad was."

"Love isn't an excuse to behave badly."

"No it isn't, but when you're caught up in it, you do things you wouldn't normally do. Who knows? Maybe I'll end up marrying someone on the rebound, too. I mean, honestly, Donna, how am I ever going to love someone the way I love J.D.? It seems impossible to love another man with the same intensity that I feel for him."

"Why do you have to get married at all? What's wrong with staying single?"

Laden with loneliness, Jenna sighed. She'd never told Donna about her list, and now wasn't the time, especially since she couldn't imagine anyone except J.D. fitting the bill. "How am I going to have children if I don't get married?"

"You don't have to be married to have kids. Single women can adopt these days or use a surrogate or go to a sperm bank."

"I know, but I can't picture myself in the role of being a single mom. And none of those methods sounds appealing to me. I want a family the traditional way."

"Then I hope you get what you want someday. I hate seeing you hurt."

"At least I squared things with Dad. He wants you to forgive him, too."

Donna shook her head. "I can't deal with Dad's issues right now."

"He's going to make amends with Uncle William. He's going to call him and apologize."

"Really?" Donna arched a delicate brow. "And whose idea what that? Yours or his?"

"I suggested it, but he agreed fairly easily. We made a pact—I would tell J.D. that I loved him, and he would apologize to William."

"You're not keeping your end of the bargain."

"How can I, knowing what I know about his past?"

"You can't, I guess. But it seems sad for you to keep it a secret. It doesn't seem right for him to stop living, either."

"That's what I told him. Maybe if he has a dream about Kimie, he'll realize that."

"An angel dream?"

"I hadn't thought about it that way. But yes, I suppose so. Kimie would be his angel if she appears to him in a dream."

Donna reached for her hand. "I hope it happens the way you want it to."

The sisterly solace was much needed. Both of them went silent for a while, even after their fingers drifted apart and Jenna managed to stave off her tears, as she'd been doing for most of the night. Donna truly cared, and it truly mattered.

Jenna caught her breath and said, "What I want is for him to love me and want to be with me. Dad said that he couldn't imagine J.D. not being in love with me."

"Dad isn't the authority on love, but I agree, I can't imagine J.D not loving you."

"Thank you. But I actually think Dad is an authority. The way he talked about Savannah. About the way both of them felt about each other."

But it wasn't a comforting thought, considering how their father's life had turned out, and Jenna could only pray that she wasn't destined to follow in his shaky footsteps.

## Chapter Fourteen

In the morning, all Jenna could do was think about J.D. and how he was faring. But she wasn't going to go down to the cabin until Doc returned, and Doc was there now.

She looked across the breakfast table at Tammy. Her cousin had fixed the meal—pancakes—and they were waiting together.

Jenna took small bites, trying not to heighten the tightness in her stomach. Earlier she'd questioned Tammy about the preparation of the food. Not because this was the time to continue her cooking lessons, but because she was trying to keep her mind engaged. The batters for pancakes and waffles, she'd learned, were similar but not the same. Traditionally waffle batter was made with egg yolks and the whites were whipped separately and folded in just before cooking. It sounded complicated to her, but at the moment, everything was complicated.

"How are you holding up?" Tammy asked.

"Not well. I—"

The sound of footsteps interrupted their conversation. Doc entered the kitchen, and Jenna nearly knocked over her juice, catching the glass before it fell.

"Did J.D. dream last night?" she blurted, asking him the first thing that popped into her head.

"No, he didn't," Doc replied. "I suggested grief counseling, but he refuses. As you're aware, he was already struggling with this, drifting around aimlessly. But the amnesia has only made things worse."

Jenna understood. Now that J.D. was remembering the details of his wife's death, he was reliving the horror all over again. "I wish he would listen to you and see a grief counselor."

"Maybe you can talk him into it."

"I'll try." She left the table and her pancakes half eaten, but she knew that Tammy didn't mind.

When she arrived at the cabin, J.D. was sitting on one of the mismatched porch chairs, with shadows beneath his eyes. Obviously he'd had a restless night. She'd tossed and turned, too.

"Doc was just here," he said.

"I know. I spoke to him. Why don't you want to get grief counseling?"

"It won't do any good."

"How do you know it won't?"

"Counseling won't bring Kimie back." He frowned into the sun. "Why didn't I dream about her last night? Why didn't she appear to me? I wanted her to, so damned badly."

She wasn't able to answer his questions. "When I told Donna what you were hoping for, she called it an angel dream."

"That's nice. I like that."

"I think so, too." She sat beside him. "And there's still time to dream about her. You can stay at the cabin for as long as you need to."

"What if it doesn't happen?"

"Don't lose hope."

"My hope ended on the day she died. Besides, who am I trying to kid? How is a dream going to help? Even if she came to see me, she would only disappear again."

She didn't know what to say to comfort him. She wasn't able to comfort herself, either.

He left his chair, and the timeworn planks that made up the porch creaked beneath his feet. He stood beside the chipped wood rail, with the Flying B as his backdrop.

Jenna stayed seated and studied him. He was dressed in his original clothes, the jeans and shirt he'd been wearing on the afternoon she'd found him stumbling along the road. His hair was tousled, too, most likely from running his hands through it, also mirroring how he'd looked that day. She'd been attracted to him from the start, but she'd never imagined falling in love with him. Nor could she have predicted what his memories would unveil.

He said, "I called Deputy Tobbs earlier, before Doc came to see me. Now that the police know who I am, they're going to run a search on my stolen credit cards, my cell phone, my vehicle and everything else that might lead them to the carjackers. In the meantime, I need to apply for a temporary license and replacement credit cards. After I get my new ID, I can go to the bank and withdraw the money I owe you. I'm going to get a new cell, too, and buy a used truck."

"Did you contact your bank?"

He nodded. "My investment account is secure, like I assumed it would be."

She couldn't help but ask, "Did you tell Deputy Tobbs about your past? Did you tell him about Kimie?"

"Yes, and he said that he was sorry. That's what people always say."

"Because they are sorry."

"I know. But to me, they've become empty words. I've heard them more times than I could ever count." He changed the subject. "I'm still interested in hearing about your meeting with your dad. Will you tell me about it now?"

"Yes, of course." She relayed the details to him.

"Your Dad and Savannah were in love? None of us saw that coming."

"No, we didn't, and neither did they. Neither of them expected to feel that way about each other." She crossed her arms over her chest, hugging herself in a protective manner. Then she asked, "When did you know that you loved Kimie?"

"I don't recall the exact moment. But it happened easily." He frowned. "Everything came easily to me then. I lived a charmed life. Supportive parents, a thriving horse farm, a great girlfriend that I was looking forward to marrying."

Jenna kept questioning him, her curiosity too intense to ignore. "How did you propose?"

"The usual way, I guess. I bought a ring, took her out

to dinner and popped the question." He smiled a little. "I wasn't nervous because I knew she would say yes."

"Where was the wedding?"

"On the farm." He gazed out at the Flying B. "This would be a nice place for a wedding, too."

Her throat went dry. She could imagine marrying him here. "Donna is working on making it into a wedding location. She's designing a garden with a gazebo for those types of events."

He kept gazing at the ranch. "That sounds pretty."

"It will be."

He turned to look at her. "When I'm gone, I'm going to envision you in the gazebo with your groom by your side, taking the vows you've always wanted to take."

Tears banked her eyes. "And how should I envision you, J.D., drifting from town to town, lonely and filled with despair? You should stay here. You should live on the Flying B and make this your home."

"I can't."

"You could if you wanted to. Hugh would be glad to create a permanent position for you. You're an asset to the ranch."

"It would never work. Besides, it would be weird later when your husband is around."

Her husband? A stranger who no longer mattered? Her resolve snapped. "You're the man I want. *You.* Damn it, I love you, J.D.!" The crimson-hot admission flew out of her mouth so quickly, so violently, it could have been blood.

The image made her think of Kimie, and she flinched from the visual. His wife, dead on the convenience-store floor, soaked in red.

J.D. reacted just as badly. He gripped the railing behind him so tightly he was probably getting splinters from the wood. She waited for him to speak.

When he did, his expression was as taut as his hands. "Don't love me. Please, don't."

"I didn't mean for it to happen."

"Oh, Jenna." He returned to his seat. "You promised you wouldn't get attached." His tone was sad, not accusatory, but that only exaggerated her pain.

"I tried not to."

He leaned forward and put his forehead against hers. Her pulse jumped like a rocket. His skin was incredibly warm, and he was close enough to kiss. She envied Kimie for how desperately he'd loved her. That made Jenna's pain more pronounced, too. Envying a dead woman.

"You and I aren't meant to be," he told her, his breaths whispering across her face.

"I wish we were."

"So do I. But I can't be the man you need."

He pulled back, leaving her bereft. She merely sat there, aware of how broken she must look—glassy-eyed, unblinking.

"I'm sorry," he said, then scoffed at his own words. "Sorry. As if that helps, right?"

"Actually, it does. A little." Unlike him, she longed to be consoled. Regardless, she got to her feet. She couldn't remain on his porch, torturing herself with his presence. "We should probably keep our distance now."

"I'll try to get everything in order as soon as I can. Then I can leave, and you can try to forget that you were ever with me."

She shook her head. "I'll never forget, J.D."

"Nor will I," he replied as she walked away. "Never again."

J.D. followed through. He got his license, his new truck, a cell phone and everything else as quickly as possible. And now, on the day he was leaving, he made a point of saying goodbye to everyone on the ranch. He'd spent the morning with the ranch hands, portions of the afternoon with Doc and Tammy, and now, as dusk neared, he prepared to see Jenna.

He knew she was in the barn, avoiding him and working her tail off. That was mostly what she'd been doing since she'd told him that she loved him.

He never should've started the affair with her. He had no right to mess with her feelings when his had been so damned jumbled. A man with amnesia wasn't what Jenna needed. Of course a man with horrific memories wasn't what she needed, either. He was no good for her, either way.

J.D. entered the barn and headed for the section of the stables that housed the school horses. When he saw her, he released a rough breath. She was cleaning the hooves of one of the new geldings. She looked intent on her task, too intent, too focused. She was well aware that this was the day he was leaving, with no plan to ever come back.

He waited until she finished with the hooves, then he said her name, softer than he should have. "Jenna."

She glanced up, and their gazes met.

"J.D." She spoke his name just as softly.

He moved closer, and she exited the gelding's stall and met him in the breezeway.

"My truck is all packed," he said.

"So this is it?"

"Yes." The end. Their final farewell. "I don't know where I'm going. I'm just going to drive and see where the road takes me."

"It's supposed to rain later. A quick summer storm."

Somehow that seemed fitting. "I can handle the rain."

"Just be careful."

As their conversation faded, he looked around at the barn. They'd never crept out here on a moonlit night to make love. Heaven help him, he still had fantasies of Jenna with hay in her hair. He longed to kiss her goodbye, to feel her lips against his, but he refrained from suggesting it, knowing it would only make his departure more difficult.

Instead he said, "I never did have that dream. But it's probably my own fault for not believing that it would matter, anyway. Or maybe Kimie is just too far away to connect with me." He was beyond trying to figure anything out.

"Did you have any pictures of her in your truck? Did those get stolen, too?"

"I had a photograph in my wallet of the two of us together." So far the police had yet to solve his case, and he doubted that even if his vehicle was recovered, his belongings would still be in it. "But I have more pictures of her. The rest of them are in my safe-deposit box, back in the town where we lived."

She glanced at his hand. "Did you ever wear a wedding ring?"

"I did when she was alive."

"What did you do with it after she died?"

"I buried it with her."

"You buried everything with her—your heart, your soul, your life."

"I know, but I can't cope any other way."

"I think she would want a happier existence for you."

"I spent eleven years with Kimie, five as her boyfriend and six as her husband. Being happy without her isn't in my realm of thinking."

Yet, suddenly, he was worried about missing Jenna as badly as he'd been missing Kimie, and Jenna was still alive, standing right before him and willing to be his partner. But he wouldn't be good for her, he reiterated. She deserved someone new and fresh, not someone damaged from the past.

She said, "You should get going before the rain starts."

Yes, he should. But it wasn't the rain that concerned him. He needed to get away from Jenna before the thought of losing her worsened. He didn't have amnesia anymore, but he was as mixed-up as ever.

"Bye, Jenna."

"Goodbye, J.D. Joel Daniel," she added, using his birth name. "Strange, how I got your initials right."

"You got everything right. It's me that screwed things up."

"That isn't true. I'm the one who fell in love when I wasn't supposed to."

"People can't help falling in love." He took a chance and drew her into his arms, wrapping her in a hug that made him want to stay.

Jenna clutched his shoulders, holding him like a lifeline. Only he wasn't her salvation. Someday, the right man would come along and fill her with joy.

He ended the embrace, and they gazed at each other in a blaze of pain.

He walked away. She didn't follow him, and he didn't glance back to see what she was doing. But he suspected that her eyes were rimmed with tears.

He strode swiftly to his truck, got behind the wheel and steered it in the direction of nowhere, realizing that he was in love with Jenna, too.

Yes, by God, he *loved* her. Still, he didn't turn his vehicle around. He kept going.

Hours later, he drove straight into the rain. He drove and drove, the windshield wipers clapping, washing the water aside, only to have it return again.

As the night got darker and wetter, he squinted at the misty highway. Then, finally, he stopped at an average little motel, ready to rest his weary bones.

And when he crawled into bed, it was with Jenna Byrd on his mind.


Jenna went to bed that night in the dream cabin. She wanted to sleep where J.D. had been sleeping, to inhale his scent on the sheets, to hug a pillow to her body and imagine that he was holding her the way he used to.

As she closed her eyes, she wondered where he was. She missed him beyond reason. But she knew that she would.

She slept fitfully, dozing in and out of repose. But eventually she fell into uninterrupted slumber.

And dreamed.

She saw herself on the Flying B, walking barefoot through the grass, only there were clouds billowing near her feet, hovering just above the ground. She couldn't feel them, but they went on forever, stretching beyond the boundaries of her vision.

She kept walking toward something or someone, uncertain of her final destination.

Then the scene changed, and she was on another ranch. No, not a ranch. A horse-breeding farm. Outdoor pens shimmered with mares and foals, frolicking among the grass-level clouds, which looked more like spun sugar here.

Then she remembered J.D.'s youthful dream and the boy he'd once been, with sugar cubes in his pocket. This was his horse farm, she realized. His old place.

Jenna glanced across the farm and saw a dark-haired woman coming toward her. Kimie. J.D.'s murdered wife. There was no gunshot wound, no blood, nothing to indicate that she was dead, except the sweet heavenly groundcover.

Small and lean with exotic features, Kimie wore a simple ensemble—a denim shirt and blue jeans. Like Jenna, her feet were bare. Only she wasn't alone. She carried a child on her hip. A little girl, no more than two, with wavy blond hair, similar to Jenna's. Clearly, she represented one of the many foster kids Kimie and J.D. had hoped to adopt, and Kimie had chosen her because she was a delicate reminder of why J.D. had become fascinated with Jenna's sunny-colored hair.

Kimie stopped and put the child down, smoothed her pink dress and patted her on the bottom. The toddler smiled and started running toward Jenna, going as fast as her sturdy little legs would go. She tripped and disappeared in the cotton candy clouds. A millisecond later, she popped back up and continued to run.

Instinctively, Jenna got down on her knees and

opened her arms, welcoming the child into her embrace. Scooping her up, she hugged her close.

Kimie didn't come any closer. She watched from afar. Then she lifted her hand in a wave and vanished, an angel returning to her ethereal world and taking the clouds with her.

The little girl said, "Bye-bye," in a tiny voice, making tears come to Jenna's eyes.

The scene changed again, and she and the child were back on the Flying B. Jenna kissed the little girl's cheek, and more children appeared.

Hundreds of them.

They were everywhere, chattering and playing. All ages, all sizes, all nationalities. Every adoptable foster child in Texas was here, she thought, along with potential adoptees from other countries. Kimie had sent them, offering them to Jenna.

But what about J.D.? He was nowhere to be seen.

Still clutching the original girl, Jenna looked for him. The other children helped search, too, running all over the ranch, shouting his name. But no one found him.

Soon Jenna awakened, shrouded in darkness. She reached out to gather the children, but they were gone, even the little one she'd been carrying.

She turned on the light and burst into tears. She wanted to call J.D., but she couldn't. He hadn't given her his number. He was unreachable.

Just like in the dream.

# Chapter Fifteen

**J.D.** woke up with a start. He'd just had the most vivid dream, only he wasn't in it. But Jenna and Kimie were, along with scores of kids. They'd been calling his name at the end of the dream, but he wasn't able to answer because he wasn't there. He was here, alone in a pitch-black motel room.

He switched on the lamp and squinted at the invasion of the light. When he'd hoped for a dream, he'd never fathomed anything like this—Kimie and Jenna together, with depictions of the children he and Kimie had lost.

Jenna had looked so natural, holding the toddler in her arms. And his wife—clever, beautiful Kimie—making certain that the first child who appeared was blonde, like Jenna.

It didn't take a psychologist to figure out what it meant. Kimie was telling J.D. that she approved of

Jenna, as a woman and a future mother, but Kimie wasn't telling J.D. what to do. The choice was his. He could keep drifting or return to Jenna and create a family with her.

Really, it was a no-brainer and something he should have done without Kimie's intervention. But he'd been locked so deeply in his pain, he'd run off, even after he'd acknowledged to himself that he loved Jenna.

He glanced at the clock. It was four in the morning, or nearly four. 3:56 a.m.

He got out of bed. He wanted to call Jenna, but at this ungodly hour? It didn't seem right to rip her from sleep. Still, he wanted to hear her voice, to tell her that he'd made a mistake and that he loved her.

Would she appreciate his dream? Or would she feel slighted that he hadn't come to his senses until after Kimie had appeared?

There was only one way to know. He needed to call her. But he fixed a cup of coffee first, waiting for daylight.

And it was the longest wait of his life. He felt as if he might go mad with it. The numbers on the clock moved so slowly, he considering yelling at them to hurry.

To keep himself occupied, he opened the window and peered outside. The ground was damp with rain, but drops were no longer falling.

The wait continued.

Finally, *finally,* dawn broke through the gray-scattered sky, and he lifted his cell phone from the nightstand and dialed Jenna's cell. It rang and rang, until her voice mail came on. He didn't leave a message; he wanted to talk to her in person.

But he couldn't just sit around until she became available. He was already going stir-crazy. He took a shower and got dressed. Grabbing his bag, he made a beeline for his truck. He was hours away from the Flying B, but by damn, he was going there, as quickly as he could.

Then a terrible thought struck him. What if something deterred him? What if he was in an accident? He knew how quickly the unexpected could happen. Look at Kimie. After a hectic night of birthing foals, she'd dashed down to the corner store to buy a few things. Never in a million years could J.D. have imagined her not coming back.

Or coming back in a box.

His mind drifted to her funeral—the scrolled-wood coffin, the flickering candles, the wreaths of flowers, her family clutching each other and crying. J.D. hadn't cried, not in front of everyone. He'd kept his tears private. But he'd been inconsolable, nonetheless.

There were no guarantees that he was going to live happily-ever-after with Jenna. Something could happen to Jenna as easily as it could happen to him.

The thought of losing her someday nearly sent him into a panic. But he forced himself to breathe. He was sitting in the parking lot, obsessing about the darkness associated with death, even after he'd seen an angelic version of Kimie in a dream.

Doc had been right. J.D. needed grief counseling.

And he needed to leave Jenna a message, too, to tell her that he loved her, just in case he never made it back to the ranch. He dialed the number again, preparing for her voice mail. But Jenna answered.

"Hello?" she said in the customary way, and her voice was the most beautiful sound he'd ever heard.

"It's me," he replied. "J.D."

"Oh, my God." She gasped. "I'm so glad it's you. I slept in the dream cabin last night, and I had a dream where I was searching for you. Kimie was there in the beginning, and she…"

Jenna went on to describe the dream J.D. had experienced. Every detail was exact. Wonderfully astounded, he listened while she relayed every moment.

Afterward, he said, "Me, too."

"You, too, what?"

"I had the same dream."

The shock in her voice was evident. "You did?"

"Identical. I woke up with you and the kids calling my name." He told her his interpretation of it. Then he said, "I love you, Jenna, and I shouldn't have walked away. I knew that I loved you when I left. But I was scared. I'm still scared."

"Of what?"

"Losing each other."

"We aren't going to lose each other, J.D. We belong together."

"I belonged with Kimie, too, and look what happened to her." He paused to quell his shiver. "I'm going to get the grief counseling Doc recommended. I know I need it."

"Maybe that's the most important message Kimie was trying to convey."

That until he found himself, no one could find him, either? "I'm going to learn to tackle my fears, and I want to be with you while I'm working on it. I want to be with you for as long as God allows."

"Then come to me. Come home now."

"I will. I am." He started his engine, destined for the Flying B.

Jenna waited for J.D. at the dream cabin. In fact, she sat on the porch, wanting to see his truck as it rolled up.

Hours later, he was there, climbing out of his vehicle and coming toward her. She held out her arms, and he enfolded her in his. They held each other so tightly, air whooshed from her lungs, but she didn't care. All that mattered was that they were together.

He kissed her, and she melted from the feeling. It was the most powerful kiss they'd exchanged, the connection warm and soulful. When it ended, they caressed each other's faces, fingers gliding over familiar features.

"Will you marry me?" he asked. "Not right away. After I get the counseling I need."

Her heart soared. "You know I will."

He flashed his crooked grin. "And adopt hundreds of children with me?"

She laughed. She knew he was referring to the kids in the dream. "I don't think Kimie meant for us to take all of them. But we'll adopt as many as we can."

He lowered a hand to her stomach. "I'm going to plant some babes in your womb, too." He grinned again. "You're going to be one busy little mama."

"And you'll be a busy papa."

"Maybe we really will end up with hundreds of them."

"Goodness, can you imagine?"

"Not really, no." But he was still grinning. "We can

use my money to build a house. A big, kid-friendly house."

"On the Flying B," she added. "There's plenty of room for us to put down roots here."

"We should have the ceremony on the ranch, too. In the garden and gazebo Donna is designing. Ours will be the first Flying B wedding."

"Unless Doc and Tammy beat us to it."

He shrugged. "It's okay if they do. They already have a jump start on the engagement. But it's going to be fun to plan our wedding. 'Let's Make Love' is going to be our song."

"It already is." It was from the moment they'd danced to it at Lucy's. "I'll wear a long silky dress and those old-fashioned western boots. The kind that lace up the front."

"That works for me. I can already see you in my mind. The elegant country bride."

She thought about his other wife. The lovely young woman in the dream. The lady who'd blessed them with the gift of hope. "What did Kimie wear when you married her?"

"Her dress had a Japanese flair. Her mother made it for her. My mom got involved, too, and beaded a Native design on my jacket. I can show you the pictures from our wedding album when I go to my safe-deposit box and bring everything here."

"I'd love to see them." She was thrilled that he was able to talk about Kimie in a positive way. It was a good start and was only going to get better. "Do you think your parents are going to like me?"

"Are you kidding? They're going to adore you, and they're going to be grateful that I'm not drifting all over

Texas any more. I know they've been praying for me to make a new life."

"And now you are."

"Because of you." He looped her into his arms again. "I'm going to make sure that our bed is filled with rose petals on our wedding night. I want to make that fantasy happen for you."

"You still owe me a naughty night in the barn, too."

"I know. I thought about that when I left the ranch. How we hadn't done it. How I'd been missing out on seeing you with hay in your hair." He nuzzled her cheek. "We could do it tonight."

Sweet chills shimmied up and down her spine. She couldn't imagine a more romantic homecoming. She wanted to do luscious things with J.D.

Tonight, and every night thereafter.

They slipped into an empty stall at midnight, and J.D. spread a blanket on the ground. He'd brought a battery-operated lantern, too. He kept it on low, so it shone gently.

Jenna stood quietly, watching him with a loving expression, her hair tumbling over her shoulders and her dress flowing around booted ankles. She'd deliberately worn something that would be easy to remove, and he knew that she was naked underneath.

This was their moment. Their fantasy.

He extended his hand, and she came forward, joining him on the blanket. They kissed soft and slow, immersed in a bond only lovers could share.

He lifted her dress above her head. She'd become everything to him, everything good and pure. His future wife. The mother of his future children. The woman who loved him enough to help him heal.

J.D. didn't get undressed all the way. He merely opened his shirt and undid his pants.

"That's cheating," she said.

"Not if someone happens by. I can right myself real quick."

She lay there, all sweet and seductive, bare, except for her boots. Looking up at him, she asked, "What about me?"

"You, I'll wrap in the blanket."

"And ruin my good-girl reputation? That's not fair." But she was smiling as she said it.

"Your reputation won't be ruined." He smiled, too. "I'm going to marry you, remember? Right here on the ranch." He realized that he'd omitted a significant part of the wedding plans. "Do you want to shop for a ring tomorrow?" He held her hand up to the light. "A diamond we can pick out together."

"Of course I want to shop with you."

"We'll go bright and early. I want you to have a ring as soon as possible." To reflect their commitment and symbolize their unity. "God gave me a second chance to be with someone I love."

"And He gave me the man from my list." She pressed her lips to his ear. "I can't show it to you, not at the moment. But I can tell you what's on it."

Talk about sexy, whispering to him about her infamous list. "Yes, ma'am, you can. But I'm already familiar with some of it." Things she'd mentioned over the course of their affair. He recited what he knew. "You want an honest, marriage-minded, family oriented man who shares your love of horses and embraces the Flying B as his home."

"So far so good." She tugged him closer. "Chivalry is high on my priorities. Kindness, too. He must be giving and caring."

"That's understandable. Is there more?"

"Strong work ethic. Integrity. I also appreciate a man who has a sense of humor."

"Do you?" He circled her nipples, coaxing them into pearly pink nubs. "Because I seem to recall my sense of humor grating on you."

She made a breathy sound. "Yours is exceptionally wicked. It took some getting used to."

"Glad we cleared that up." He caressed her curves, up, down and all around. "What else?"

She leaned into him. "His physical attributes—tall, dark and handsome."

"That's a cliché."

"Not to me. I'm partial to dark hair and dark eyes."

He slipped his fingers between her legs and elicited a moan. "Anything else?"

"A man who knows how to make me..."

"Make you what?"

"Orgasm."

"You're a bad girl for including that." He sent her a dastardly smile. He'd always wondered if she'd put her sexual preferences on it. He'd even teased her in that regard, just as he couldn't help teasing her now, rubbing her most sensitive spot. "A very bad girl."

She arched under his ministrations. "If I'm going to spend the rest of my life with someone, he needs to know what's what."

He heightened the foreplay. "Like this?"

"Yes, just like that."

He continued to pleasure her, with his hands, his mouth. In response, she tunneled her fingers through his hair and lifted her hips, rife with sensual energy.

When he gave her the Big O, she muffled her excitement, biting down on her bottom lip to keep from crying out.

J.D. couldn't be more aroused. He snagged the condom from his pocket, shoved his jeans down, sheathed himself and entered her, full and deep. He made damned sure that they rolled off the blanket, too, and she got bits of hay in her hair.

They made love in a fever, each touch wild and thrilling. Heat pounded in his loins. Need shivered through his veins. She kissed him so hard, he dragged her on to his lap, encouraging her to ride him to completion.

Afterward, they collapsed in a heap of tangled limbs. Once they were able to move, she put her dress back on, and he fastened his clothes.

Quietly, they returned to the dream cabin. Not to dream, but to sleep. The new couple. In each other's arms.

Where they belonged.


A week later, Jenna, Tammy and Donna went into town, where they met with Roland Walker for an update. He told him exactly what he'd been doing to search Savannah, and even though he still didn't have any news of her, he was convinced that he would locate her. Roland was a confident man.

He was also a tad gruff, but Jenna liked him. She understood why Tex had hired him at one time, too. The P.I. was a good old boy, much like Tex had been.

Jenna considered Tex and his sons. By now, Dad had apologized to Uncle William, and they were working on making amends. They'd even planned a fishing trip.

She glanced over at Tammy. Her cousin was glad, of course, that their dads were trying to be brothers. Jenna was, too. But Donna hadn't said much about it.

After their meeting with Roland, they stopped by the local ice-cream parlor, shared a cafe table and ate dessert. Tammy got two scoops of vanilla, smothered in fruit toppings and colorful sprinkles, Jenna went for a banana split and Donna got frozen yogurt.

Donna, always the odd girl out.

Jenna and Tammy were both engaged and living at the Flying B, the future B and B, with their men. But Donna was busting her butt to get the heck out of Texas and return to New York, where she would continue to work day and night, trying to resume her city-girl career.

It made Jenna feel guilty for being so happy, so settled. The marquee-cut diamond on her finger was dazzling, and she was elated to have it. Tammy had a gorgeous engagement ring, too.

Again, Donna with nothing.

"I have something I want to show you," Jenna said to her sister. She reached into her purse and handed over her list.

Donna began reading. "What in the world is this?"

Jenna explained when she'd first written it, how she'd revised it to include the Flying B, how important it was to her, how J.D had called it her magic and finally, how J.D. turned out to have every single quality she'd imagined in a man.

"That's wonderful," her sister said, "but I don't see how this has anything to do with me."

"I wanted you to see it because I wanted you to be part of it somehow. But I was also hoping that it would inspire you. Not to find a husband, necessarily, but to find whatever it is you need to be joyful."

"Really? Oh." Donna hugged the list close to her heart. "No one has ever said anything like that to me before."

"I should have said it a long time ago. You're my sister, and I love you."

Was Donna holding back tears? She blinked her glamorous lashes, a bit too rapidly. "I love you, too."

Tammy smiled around her next bite. Then she said, "Can I get in on some of that love?"

Jenna grinned and leaned toward her cousin. "Of course you can. Tex knew exactly what he was doing when he brought us together. We're the best trio ever."

"We absolutely are." Tammy ate more ice cream to celebrate.

Jenna glanced at Donna. "You know, sis. It's okay if you secretly want a husband."

Donna shook her head. She laughed a little laugh. "Seriously, Jenna. Where do you come up with this stuff?"

"Most women want to get married someday."

"I'm not most women."

That was true, but still…

"Well, whatever it is you want, I hope you attain it."

"Thank you. That means a lot to me. But all I want is to get my career back on track."

Following Tammy's lead, Jenna attacked the ice cream in her dish. Then she said to Donna, "Since J.D.

and I aren't staying at the dream cabin anymore, you can sleep there now if you want."

"Whatever for?"

"To have a life-altering dream."

"I think I'll let nature take its course." Donna returned the list. "Why did you move out of the cabin?"

"It doesn't make sense for us to horde it." They were living in the main house while he was working on the plans for their custom home. In fact, he was going to hire Aidan and Nathan to build it. "We have everything we need."

"I'm happy for you," Donna told her. She turned to Tammy. "And you, too."

Jenna tucked the paper back into her purse. Donna might not want a husband, but that was what Jenna wanted for her.

Eventually.

For now, a hot fling with a sinful playboy would do. She smiled to herself. Maybe after Caleb returned from his leave of absence, he would take Donna for a sexy spin. Then later, she could marry the right man, a polished New Yorker or whatever.

"We better get back to the ranch soon," Donna said. "I've got a slew of work to do."

*Yep,* Jenna thought, *if anyone needed a little fun, it was my sister.*

A short while later Donna got her wish and they were back at the ranch, each going her own way.

Jenna met up with J.D., where he'd just turned some horses out into the arena, and he rewarded her with a tender kiss. Although he was making great strides on his own, he was scheduled to begin his grief counseling soon. Determined, Jenna thought, to keep his fears at bay and live life to the fullest. She couldn't be prouder.

Luckily, the robbery was behind him, too. The police had arrested the offenders, discovering that they were part of a carjacking ring that had been committing similar crimes all over the country. J.D. had already pressed charges, and Jenna was glad it was over.

In the quiet, they both turned toward the arena and watched the equine activity.

Then J.D. said, "How would you feel if I went back to breeding horses? Not a full-time operation, but just enough to bring some of my expertise to the Flying B. After the B and B is underway and after our house is built."

"I think that's a great idea." She remembered the precious foals she'd seen in the dream at his previous farm. "Mares and their babies."

"To go with Mama Jenna and our babies." He reached out and cradled her in his arms.

She put her head against his shoulder, and they stood in the sun, a wondrous future unfolding before them.

* * * * *

*A sneaky peek at next month...*

# Cherish™

**ROMANCE TO MELT THE HEART EVERY TIME**

## *My wish list for next month's titles...*

In stores from 21st June 2013:

☐ Falling for the Rebel Falcon – Lucy Gordon

& The Man Behind the Pinstripes – Melissa McClone

☐ Marriage for Her Baby – Raye Morgan

& The Making of a Princess – Teresa Carpenter

In stores from 5th July 2013:

☐ Marooned with the Maverick – Christine Rimmer

& Made in Texas! – Crystal Green

☐ Wish Upon a Matchmaker – Marie Ferrarella

& The Doctor and the Single Mum – Teresa Southwick

Available at WHSmith, Tesco, Asda, Eason, Amazon and Apple

## *Just can't wait?*

0613/23

# Special Offers

Every month we put together collections and longer reads written by your favourite authors.

Here are some of next month's highlights— and don't miss our fabulous discount online!

On sale 21st June

On sale 5th July

On sale 5th July

# MILLS & BOON
### Book Club

# *Join the Mills & Boon Book Club*

Want to read more **Cherish**™ books?
We're offering you **2 more** absolutely **FREE!**

We'll also treat you to these fabulous extras:

- Exclusive offers and much more!

- FREE home delivery

- FREE books and gifts with our special rewards scheme

*Get your free books now!*

**visit www.millsandboon.co.uk/bookclub**
**or call Customer Relations on 020 8288 2888**